The Highwayman's Daughter

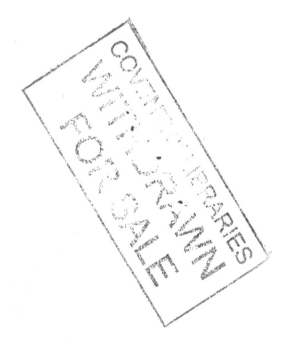

The Highwayman's Daughter

Henriette Gyland

Copyright © 2014 Henriette Gyland

Published 2014 by Choc Lit Limited
Penrose House, Crawley Drive, Camberley, Surrey GU15 2AB, UK
www.choc-lit.com

The right of Henriette Gyland to be identified as the Author of this Work
has been asserted by her in accordance with the Copyright, Designs and
Patents Act 1988

A CIP catalogue record for this book is available
from the British Library

ISBN 978-1-78189-071-4

Print
YY

Acknowledgements

A few years ago this manuscript was on the editor's desk at Choc Lit, but didn't quite meet with the approval of the Tasting Panel, so I put it to one side and concentrated on my contemporary novels instead. But I never forgot this story, which I had tremendous fun writing, and decided to rework it and send it to Choc Lit again. I would like to thank the Tasting Panel for passing it with flying colours this time! Also, a huge thank you to the Choc Lit team – working with you is a privilege.

My very special thanks to the dedicated team of librarians at Hounslow Reference Library for helping me create an image of what Hounslow Heath and the surrounding area would have looked like in 1768. When I close my eyes, I can almost see it, hear it and smell it.

No writer can write in an emotional vacuum, and this is where my wonderful family, friends and writing buddies come in. Thank you for your unwavering support and for always saying the right thing at the right time. I'm convinced you're all psychic!

Prologue

The wind howled mournfully across Hounslow Heath, and icy needles of rain stung the lone rider as he galloped across the desolate wilderness of prickly grasses and heather. The few twisted trees offered no shelter, but the man barely noticed. His gaze was fixed on a coach standing by the side of the road near the Old Heston Mill, abandoned and with no sign of horses, coachman or groom.

Jumping down from his horse, he rushed over to the door and flung it open, peering inside. The sight that met his eyes was not pretty and he recoiled momentarily.

'Damnation!'

He drew in a sharp breath, and the metallic tang of blood reached his nostrils, but nevertheless, he climbed inside and sat down on the velvet-covered seat to contemplate his grisly find. On the floor of the coach, half propped against the seat, sprawled a richly dressed lady, her face so pale it was almost grey. An enormous dark stain had spread across the skirts of her fine silk dress and although her eyes were closed, it was clear that she had gone to meet her maker.

In a wicker basket next to the woman lay what could have passed for a wax doll. As lifeless as its mother, the newborn infant looked like it was merely sleeping, but the small chest didn't rise and fall and the tiny hands would never grasp anything. The man swore again most foully.

'Stupid bitch,' he muttered, aiming a vicious kick at the woman's thigh. But he knew he was too late and the Grim Reaper had cheated him out of his revenge. The only thing he could deny her now was a decent burial. 'And by God, I will,' he hissed. 'Your brat as well.'

He quickly searched the interior of the coach, even shoving

his hands underneath the baby's bedding, but there was nothing left except the two bodies. Not even the rings that had once adorned the lady's fingers. Highwaymen? Most likely. And they'd be long gone now.

Frustrated and angry beyond measure, he left the coach and jumped onto his horse, heading back the way he'd come. There was nothing for him here except the bitter taste of defeat, a bilious lump at the back of his throat which threatened to choke him. Even in death she'd somehow managed to get the better of him. The only small mercy was that there was nothing connecting him to her death, or that of the infant.

A mercy indeed.

Chapter One

Silently cursing the lateness of the hour, Jack Blythe, Viscount Halliford, leaned back in the seat of his well-sprung carriage with a sigh as it rumbled along the Bath Road towards his father's estate at Lampton. With Jack was Rupert Blythe, his second cousin, although their relationship was more that of brothers. Rupert and his sister, Alethea, had been orphaned at an early age, and Jack's parents had taken them in and cared for them as if they were their own. As far as Jack was concerned, they were the siblings he'd never had.

As usual, Rupert was the reason they hadn't left London until after midnight. He'd insisted on visiting one of the gaming hells he frequented and had dragged a protesting Jack with him, even though he would have much preferred a quiet supper, followed by a brandy at Brooks's before returning home.

Jack was now nursing a sore head and the deflated sensation of a purse some fifty guineas lighter.

In hindsight, it had been a good decision to go with Rupert, though. He was in the habit of losing large sums, which he would then prevail upon Jack's father to settle for him. Because Jack's presence had curbed Rupert's recklessness, they had only stayed for a few hours, Even so, Rupert had managed to chance and lose a considerable amount of money. He did so with a certain flourish which Jack couldn't help but admire, although it also appalled him. Jack knew only too well how his father would react when Rupert appeared at the breakfast table in the morning; he would arrange to pay his ramshackle relative's debt, but the look of disapproval would be levied at Jack, not Rupert.

He glanced at his debonair cousin, taking in the opulence of his garments: the powdered wig, the patch beside his mouth, the exquisite French lace neck cloth and the expensive dove-grey silk coat with gold filigree embroidery on the pocket flaps, cuffs and front. With his eyes closed and his wig slightly askew, Rupert appeared to be asleep and quite likely drunk as well, but it could be pretence as Jack had learned to his detriment on several occasions. Rupert had an uncanny knack for reading his mind.

Wanting to keep his present thoughts to himself, Jack looked away and inspected his own more modest midnight-blue coat for any overt signs of their night on the town. It stank of tobacco smoke and the cheap perfume of the courtesans who had draped themselves over his arm the moment he entered the gaming den. He had been unable to shake them off, no matter how hard he'd tried.

Disgusted, he took off both his coat and his waistcoat; then loosened and flapped his shirt in order to dispel some of the odours. He would have to remember to tuck it back in when they arrived at the estate. If his father was still awake – and there was a good chance he might be, because the earl derived great pleasure from reading in his library till late – Jack wanted to look as presentable as possible.

Unlike his cousin, Jack wore no wig, preferring instead to tie his dark brown hair back with a ribbon of burgundy velvet. He undid it now, shook his hair loose, enjoying the freedom from any restraints, and was retying his hair when the coach lurched and stopped abruptly.

Rupert slid off his seat and landed in a heap on the floor.

'What? Why? Where?' he slurred incoherently.

A shot rang out, and one of the horses whinnied. The coach jerked momentarily until the driver had the horse under control again.

'Stand and deliver!' came the sharp command from outside the coach.

'It would appear we're being held up,' said Jack, trying not to sound perturbed even though he felt his stomach muscles clench.

'Damned brigands!' His slurring gone, Rupert was now fully awake. Jack suspected he might have been putting it on in the first place; Rupert had always been good at putting others at ease by playing the fob, but Jack knew better. 'There should be a law against bedevilling honest travellers.'

'Believe me, cousin, there are several.' Jack felt for the pistol he always had in the carriage when travelling and tucked it down the back of his waistband. If there was one thing he hated, it was highwaymen. He and his mother had had a nasty encounter with one when he was a small boy and he'd never forgotten the incident. The mere word made his skin prickle with icy needles as he recalled how the masked man had threatened Lady Lampton and cuffed Jack when he tried to protect her. He'd never felt so helpless and didn't want to feel that way ever again.

He opened the door of the passenger cabin and climbed out. 'What's the meaning of this?'

The coachman and his assistant were lying face down on the road with their hands behind their heads. Before Jack could make any further movement, the highwayman spurred his horse forward, and Jack had to jump back up on the coach step to avoid being trampled. A cocked pistol pointed to his face, and a savage pair of eyes stared at him through the slits of a black silk mask. The co-driver's blunderbuss was sticking up from the highwayman's saddlebag, but as it hadn't been fired, it would still be loaded. Jack swallowed involuntarily.

'You is bein' robbed, pretty boy, that's what!'

It was a young voice, the voice of a boy of no more than fifteen or sixteen perhaps, although Jack had no doubt he knew how to use a pistol.

Rupert appeared at the door. He had tidied himself from his inelegant landing; his wig was no longer askew and his embroidered tricorne hat completed the picture of a wealthy and powerful man demanding respect. It didn't have the effect on the highwayman which Rupert had presumably hoped for though. The lad curled his lips in a contemptuous sneer, and he backed up his horse a little, motioning with the pistol for both of them to step down from the coach. Jack wished Rupert had just stayed on the floor.

'If you'd be so kind, gen'lemen, to step away from the ve'cul, and then fill this here bag with yer valuerbels, I'd be much obliged.'

He tossed a sack at Rupert, who caught it against his chest with a grumbling protest. 'You'll hang for this,' he said coldly.

'A well-wisher, eh?' The boy grinned. 'Well, ain't I the lucky one. Now while I could stand 'ere all night baskin' in you wantin' the best for me an' all, I'd much rather you were quick about it so we can both get home to our beds.'

Muttering curses, Rupert put his purse and pocket watch in the bag, followed by his snuff box and cravat pin. Jack flung in his watch and purse while he kept his eyes on the highwayman's face.

'And your jewellery,' said the highwayman, pointing the pistol at Rupert's large gold and crystal ring.

With an oath Rupert yanked the ring off his well-groomed finger and tossed it in the bag.

'And you, sir.'

Jack eased his gold signet ring off and was just about to put it in the bag when the highwayman stopped him.

'Let me see that.'

Jack laid it in the palm of his hand and held it up for the boy to see, acutely aware that the pistol was aimed straight at his heart.

The boy pulled back. 'Keep it.'

Grateful, Jack returned it to his finger. The highwayman obviously wasn't stupid; Jack's ring was a family one and would be very difficult to sell. The gold could be melted down of course, but this would require the involvement of another person and thus expose the identity of the highwayman further.

Rupert stiffened beside him. 'Hell's teeth! Why are you favouring him? Give me back mine too, then.' He held out his hand peremptorily, but the highwayman just laughed.

'Not 'appy, are we, mister?' he mocked. 'Perhaps you'd like to contribute a little more to my charitable cause. Take off your coat.'

'Take off my ...?'

It was the first time Jack had ever seen his self-assured cousin struck dumb, and despite their predicament, he had to admit to deriving a certain perverse pleasure from it.

'And your waistcoat.'

'Now, look here, that's preposterous. What would you want with my clothing? The thought of the likes of you wearing my garments is positively indecent.' Rupert's tone was laced with sarcasm.

'Be thankful, sir, that I don't relieve you of yer breeches as well,' quipped the lad. It was clear from the way the corners of his mouth turned up that he was amused, but he was smart too. Quickly he inspected the distinctive coat, but then tossed it back at Rupert, keeping only the waistcoat.

The highwayman was tall, slim and lithe with an elegant mouth, Jack noticed, and a finely sculpted face. He was a good-looking boy, from what Jack could see, and would be a handsome man when fully grown. At this rate, however, he was more likely to end his days at Tyburn before his twentieth year, after which his body would be displayed in a gibbet on Hounslow Heath for the crows to pick over. And good riddance. One less menace on the roads, although if he was honest, Jack had to admit it seemed a terrible waste of a human life, especially one so young.

The boy's hair, an unruly mane of blue-black, was tied at the nape of his neck in a practical fashion, and he was clad entirely in black, including a silk mask covering his eyes. He had a marvellous command of his horse, steering it using only his knees and leaving his hands free. The animal was, as far as Jack could see, very fine.

As the boy watched Rupert undress, with a little wry smile, Jack studied him for other distinguishing marks, but found none – except perhaps his voice, which was clear and slightly high-pitched. From the youth's manner, Jack judged that this wasn't the first time he'd held up a coach, and he had to admire the confidence in one so young. Nevertheless someone was bound to finger him for his dastardly crimes one day.

Although taking great delight in vexing Rupert, the boy was being a perfect gentleman about the robbing. Jack wondered if this was due to the security afforded him by the pistol and whether the youngster had the nerve to use it. Recalling that the highwayman had already fired one, he decided to put it to the test.

'Young sir,' he said. 'Might we ask you to do us a favour? Our friends would laugh at us if we went home and told them we were robbed without so much as a token of resistance. Suppose you fire that pistol through the crown of my cousin's hat; it will at least look like we tried to foil you.'

Jack snatched the silk hat off Rupert's head, despite his cousin's protests, and held it up and away from himself.

The highwayman eyed him for a moment, his expression inscrutable in the half-light and under the cover of the mask. For a long tense moment Jack figured his bluff was called.

'Certainly, sir,' said the boy. He took aim and fired, and the bullet went clean through Rupert's hat.

Before the smoke had blown away, Jack dropped the hat and reached for the pistol he had hidden at the back of his waistband. He got no further. With lightning speed the boy had tossed aside his own pistol and drawn a rapier, and Jack felt the pressure of steel against his throat.

'Nice try, mister.' The highwayman chuckled. 'One more move, and I'll run you through.'

It wasn't the shock of cold steel against his skin which stilled Jack. It was what he saw. At that moment the full moon appeared from behind a cloud and bathed the heath in revealing light. Allowing his eyes to travel the length of the highwayman's sword arm to his profile, Jack spied beneath the now-parted cloak the unmistakable curve of a woman's breast.

'Your pistol, sir, if you please.'

Too shocked to do anything else, Jack hesitated and continued to stare at her. It shouldn't have come as a surprise that a woman had chosen to rob coaches for a living. Desperate people came in all guises. Nor did it astonish him that a woman could be good at it. After all, he had known a number of females who could shoot and ride as well as any man, his own mother, Lady Lampton, being one of them.

It was the coldness in the woman's eyes and the sharpness of her command which baffled him. The steady hand which pushed the point of the rapier against his windpipe hard enough for him to know she wouldn't hesitate for a moment to carry out her threat. She had a clear purpose in mind and executed it without hesitation. Up until now she had disguised her grit behind an insolent boyish exterior – she had even appeared to be amused by Rupert's complaining, as if she had every confidence that he would never succeed in catching her – but behind the façade was a person of infinite hardiness. Or foolhardiness, perhaps.

Jack had never met a woman like that before, and felt something stir inside him. Awareness. Attraction. *Desire*.

The woman, in turn, stared back at him, running her gaze down his face, neck and settling on his naked chest, which was clearly visible where his shirt was open at the neck. He thought he saw her eyes widen behind the mask, and she moistened her lips. And did her colour deepen, like the blush of an innocent young girl?

Interesting, he thought.

A small smile curved the corners of his mouth, and he

handed her the pistol. 'My mistake, young … sir.' His fingers brushed hers for an instant as she took the weapon from him and he could have sworn a charge sparked between them. He heard her draw in a hasty breath, so she must have felt it too. His heart thudded with sudden exhilaration.

Re-sheathing her rapier, the woman held Jack's loaded pistol trained at his heart and stared at him as if she sensed that his pause had been deliberate. Then she did something extraordinary. She shoved the pistol down her boot and drove her horse forward with a sudden blood-lust, effectively pinning him between the horse and the carriage. Quick as a falcon bringing down a hapless swallow, she produced a hidden knife, grabbed his hastily tied ponytail with one hand and cut it off. Quicker than she had charged, and before Jack had time to react, she retreated to a safe distance.

Jack was left in no doubt that she could just as easily have plunged the steel blade into his chest.

'Much obliged to you, gen'lemen,' she said and inclined her head. Within seconds she had disappeared into the night, and the sound of the horse's hooves was only a distant memory.

Jack bent to retrieve her discarded pistol as replacement for his own, while Rupert picked up his hat. As Jack restored the frightened coachmen to their seat on the box, he realised his own hands were shaking too, from alarm as well as anger. Clenching his fists, he returned to the coach, but it wasn't until they were well on their way again that he or Rupert felt like speaking again.

'Did you see what I saw?' Rupert whispered as if he feared the highwayman would still be around to overhear them.

'What would that be, cousin?'

'It was a woman. I'm telling you, I saw it as clear as day. No boy has curves like that.'

At the mention of curves Jack felt his blood fizzing, but tried to appear nonchalant. 'Yes, I noticed it too. It still doesn't change the fact that she nearly had you stripped of your breeches. In fact, if I'm not mistaken, she seemed to be enjoying your discomfiture.'

'Yes, indeed. Accursed female! That waistcoat was brand new. Cost me twenty guineas in Bond Street.'

Cost my father twenty guineas, Jack thought, but wisely kept that comment to himself. 'A great loss, to be sure,' he said.

'You didn't fare much better,' Rupert scoffed. 'Look at your hair.' He smirked at the sight of Jack's shortened tresses, which now reached no further than his jawbone. Then his expression darkened again. 'And you had her shoot a hole in my hat. Whatever for? It's no good to me now. I shall have to get a new one.' Sulking, Rupert worked his finger through the hole, fraying the delicate fabric further and rendering a salvageable hat completely useless.

'I was trying to save your dignity, cousin. It clearly didn't work.'

'Nothing would satisfy me except to see that strumpet hang,' grumbled Rupert. 'Say, what do you reckon we give the authorities a helping hand? There's bound to be a reward for catching this thief.'

'Naturally, we'll tell the magistrate what we know.'

'I have a better idea.' Rupert grinned. 'How about a wager?'

'A wager?' Jack's eyebrows rose.

'A hundred guineas. To the one who catches the girl first. She shouldn't be that difficult to find. What do you say?'

Jack hesitated. He hadn't forgotten the sword against his throat and the promptness with which she had reacted. She was armed to the teeth and would be dangerous. Nor did he agree with Rupert's assertion that she would be easy to find. He had an inkling that this woman knew how to cover her tracks expertly, and very likely she conducted her daily business in the obscurest and most humble of circumstances away from prying eyes.

There was another important consideration though – any

wager Rupert entered into would involve Jack's father's money. He could either stand by and let Rupert lose the money in anonymous gaming hells or he could try to ensure that it stayed in the family. Whatever he did, he would have to face his father's disapproval – a prospect he didn't particularly relish.

Thus torn, he recalled the flinty eyes behind the mask and the woman's pretty mouth, as well as his wounded pride that a female had bested him. The hunt would be a diverting challenge, and most importantly it would keep his cousin occupied in a more worthy pursuit than gambling away the Blythe family fortune.

He secretly acknowledged that it would also be a pleasure to steal a kiss from those luscious lips before handing the culprit over to the authorities. Although why he should want to do any such thing, he had no idea. He normally preferred his women small and biddable, nothing like the virago they'd encountered tonight. But he had no doubt that he would be the one to apprehend her, not Rupert. Certain elements were bound to give her away – it was clear, even when she was sitting on her horse, ramrod straight, that she was as tall as most men. And there was her voice too. He wondered if Rupert had noticed these things as well, but if he hadn't, it would give Jack an advantage.

'Very well, I'll take you up on it. A hundred guineas it is.'

They continued the rest of the journey in silence, lost in thought, and Jack ignored the calculating look which spread across his cousin's handsome features. This time he was determined to have the upper hand.

Chapter Two

Cora rode the horse hard until she reached the edge of the forest; then she slipped under the cover of the trees and waited to see if she was being followed. She didn't think it very likely: the coach horses would have to be unharnessed first, which would take time, and unless other riders had chanced upon the coach and volunteered to pursue the robber, she thought herself quite safe. Still, she waited behind the trunk of a large oak tree, her heart thumping in her chest as it always did when she had held up a coach.

There was no sound of pursuit, no hooves beating, no angry cries. In fact there were no sounds at all if you discounted the flapping wings and affronted squawking of a pheasant she had startled.

Forcing herself to breathe calmly, she untied the black mask from her face and slid it into her saddlebag. The blunderbuss too, as far as it would go; then she covered the handle with her cloak. The sack with the loot from the robbery hung from the pommel on her saddle, and she loosened it, and hid it safely away in her other saddlebag. Her father would know what she had been up to if he saw the mask and the blunderbuss, and she found it difficult to face his quiet disapproval, which stung far more than a thorough tongue-lashing might have done.

It was hard to explain to him that she did it for his sake. It was the only way she could make sure he ate properly; and the cough syrup she would buy to alleviate his cough was a luxury they could not afford otherwise. In truth, Ned had never asked for it, as he never asked for anything, and would instead take her to task for fussing, but it was the one thing she could do for him. Whatever lengths she had to go to, she was determined to do so as long as there was breath in her body.

There was another reason her heart was hammering in her

chest. The encounter with the men from the coach had rattled her or, more specifically, her encounter with one of them.

The quiet one. *The handsome one.* The one who had felt the steel of her blade without so much as batting an eyelid. He had nearly outwitted her. She recalled how he had reached for his pistol the moment she had made the mistake of putting a bullet through the other man's hat. There had been a calculating gleam in his eye, as if he had known all along she would fall for the trick and he was just waiting to shoot her in the belly. Not that he would be the sort of man who would do that. Only a cruel man would shoot a person in the belly instead of the head or heart so the victim would suffer a slow, agonising death. Somehow, she was sure he was not like that.

Definitely a gentleman. Unlike the other man. But then, who was she to criticise? It wasn't as if she behaved in a very gentlemanly fashion herself, in her guise as a youth. Robbing definitely wouldn't be considered good manners, that was for certain.

You've got to be more careful, she admonished herself with a shudder. Who would be there to look after Ned if something happened to her? It didn't bear thinking about.

Her eyes fell on the object she had stuffed into her coat pocket. The man's queue. It looked like an undulating hairy adder. Amusement pulled at the corners of her mouth. If only she could recapture the look on his face when she had sheared it off, his utter outrage and humiliation. Unlike most of his peers he wore no wig, and the hair was tied with a plush velvet ribbon. She was willing to wager that he had been mightily proud of it.

The thought made her smile, but then she sobered. It had been a stupid thing to do. Childish and unnecessary. What if it made him determined to hunt her down? She shuddered. She should have stuck with her original purpose. Everything else she had acquired tonight had monetary value. The waistcoat and trinkets she could sell, and the blunderbuss she would trade for a weapon which was more useful for hunting small animals in the forest. But the cut-off queue was of no use to her and she ought to get rid of it straight away. For some reason she found herself unable to part with it though. Instead, on impulse, she lifted it to her nose and breathed in his scent. The hair smelt of tobacco and sandalwood soap, inherently masculine, as well as a fragrance Cora had never encountered before, something intrinsically *him*.

Closing her eyes, she wondered briefly if the dark curls on his chest, which she had spied through his open shirt, were just as soft as the hair she held in her hand. Then she yanked it away from her face, horrified at the direction her thoughts were taking her. What was the matter with her?

She had grown up in a community of farm labourers. Talk was often coarse and of an explicit nature; she had seen horses and other farm animals mate and men work in nothing but their breeches when the weather was hot. She knew what happened between a man and a woman, but it was the thought that one day a man, someone as handsome and fine as the one she had encountered earlier, might do the same to her which sent her blood racing and made her catch her breath.

She checked herself when she suddenly remembered the way his searching eyes had run across her face. Would he be able to recognise her without her mask? The thought sent shivers down her spine, and the gelding stirred beneath her. But no, she was always careful to keep the heart-shaped birthmark on her cheek hidden and she didn't think anything else would give her away. He'd just unsettled her; that was all.

She ran her hand down the horse's neck. The gelding was of uncertain breed, and she'd had him from when he was a foal; he'd been a present from her father's close friend Gentleman George, who was currently in Newgate Prison waiting to be hanged for highway robbery. Sighing, she wished there was something she could do to repay George's kindness to her then, and ever since.

He hadn't wanted for well-wishers in prison, though. Probably something to do with the rumour that he had money stashed away from his robberies. The thought made her smile; she knew George better than almost anyone and wouldn't be surprised if he'd started the rumour himself, to inflate his own exploits. It would be just like him to do such a thing.

She turned and headed for home, as always amazed at the way the horse seemed to understand what she wanted before she had given a command. The horse reacted to even the slightest pressure from her knees and appeared to sense her mood as well. Right now he probably felt her confusion, and she patted him reassuringly.

'You did well back there, Samson.'

He neighed and tossed his head impatiently.

'Yes, you're right. It's time we were on our way.'

She told herself not to worry about being recognised. It was dark; she had been wearing a mask and a tricorne hat. There was no way the man could identify her. Besides there was no reason why it should even occur to him that the person behind the mask was a woman.

Resolutely she slung the severed queue over a branch of an oak tree and turned her horse to leave; then snatched it back almost immediately and tucked it inside her shirt, refusing to dwell on why she found it so difficult to let go. Perhaps it was best not to think about such matters too deeply.

What she did know was that the fine gentleman had damn well nearly shot her, and she had no doubt he wouldn't hesitate to try again should the opportunity present itself.

She was shaken awake at daybreak.

'Cora, it's time.'

Her father stood over her, already dressed and ready for the day's hay-making. When he saw she was awake, he nodded, satisfied, and left the room. If he had noticed that she had fallen asleep in her clothes yet again, he chose not to comment.

Swinging her legs out of bed, Cora went to the wash stand, where Ned had left the ewer filled with water, and washed herself carefully, cleaning off last night's dust. She hoped that Ned had been completely asleep when she returned and had not heard her scramble through the window into the small room at the back of the cottage, which she had to herself. Her father didn't hold with her nocturnal activities as a young highwayman.

The room was tiny and sparsely furnished with a narrow cot, the wash stand and an old chest, which contained Cora's meagre belongings. It smelt stuffy and of the musty hay in her mattress, and she opened the shutter to let in the fragrant July air.

Her family had moved to this part of England from the northern counties when Cora was nine. Within a year her mother had died, and Ned had vacated the only bedroom in their cramped labourer's cottage, insisting that she would soon be a young lady in need of privacy. He slept on the wooden bench in the main room of the cottage. Cora had objected, saying that she was happy on the bench, but Ned had remained firm.

In hindsight it had been a good decision, at least in winter time: Ned was closer to the fire, and, although it was banked down at night, Cora was confident that the warmth helped soothe her father's rheumatism and alleviate his cough a fraction.

It cut through her as she heard him hack and rasp through the thin wall, and she scrambled into an old dress visibly worn at the elbows and hem, and a grey smock. Grabbing her oversized linen bonnet, she entered the main room just as her father was overcome by another fit of coughing. His bony shoulders, protruding through his simple workman's shirt, shook violently as he tried to subdue the spasms in his chest.

'Father!' she said, startled by the violence of his coughing. 'Are you feeling worse this morning?' She rushed to his side, but he dismissed her concerns with an impatient wave of his hand.

'I'm well enough. Don't fuss so.'

Cora's heart wrenched. When did he get to be so thin? Her father's condition was worsening, and it seemed to be happening right before her eyes. She resolved to visit the apothecary's in town as soon as possible, now that she had enough coin.

'Here.' He placed a bowl of gruel in her hands. 'Eat up. We must be on our way soon. Hay-making waits for no man. We've got the whole of the western field to do today.'

Cora did as she was told and sat at the rough wooden table to eat her breakfast. Ned busied himself with preparing their lunch, hunks of cheese, bread and some dried meat, which he wrapped in a piece of cloth, and a canteen of water. All the while he regarded her intently, and Cora felt herself squirm under his stare.

'Where were you last night?' he asked.

Cora's head snapped up. So he had heard her climb in through the window after all. Or maybe he had heard Samson fretting impatiently for his reward. She had taken care to dismount away from the cottage and had led the horse by the bridle back to the rickety shelter that served as a stable, but Samson had refused to be quiet until he had been fed and rubbed down.

'Your saddle hung over the beam the other way around to yesterday,' he said in answer to her unvoiced question.

Cora chewed her lip and tried to think of a plausible story. She had used them all by now.

I couldn't sleep. Why take the horse?

I decided to go for a ride. In the night?

Old Faith was dying and the family asked me to sit with her. You should've told me, I'd have come with you.

Eliza thought her baby was coming and asked me to watch little Meg.

She was running out of ideas, and she had a sneaking suspicion that Ned wasn't fooled for a minute anyway.

Lowering her eyes in what she hoped was a suitably chaste manner, she said, 'I had a rendezvous.'

At that Ned threw his head back and laughed out loud. 'My daughter taking an interest in a lad ...? That'll be the day.' He turned serious again and fixed her with a penetrating stare. 'All right, have it your way. Just so you know, what you're doing is dangerous. Very dangerous. And if anything should happen to you ...' He left the sentence hanging, but Cora heard him loud and clear.

They spoke no further on the subject but hurried out of the door as soon as Cora had finished the breakfast. Hastily she pinned up her hair and donned her bonnet. Remembering Ned's warning, she debated whether to confess what had happened last night, but then thought better of it. It would only worry her father, and that was the last thing she wanted to do.

Lord Heston's estate lay two miles to the east of the forest, and about twenty men and women were already gathered on the edge of the field by the time Cora and Ned arrived. Lord Heston and his eldest son, Kit, a handsome lad of Cora's own age, were there to oversee the hay-making, as well as the estate foreman. The young man was looking at the group of high-spirited young women, fascinated it seemed, but when Cora went to join them, she felt his eyes on her, and her face grew hot under his scrutiny. She kept her eyes averted.

At the centre of the group was Mary Collins. 'Mark my words,' she was saying to the other girls, 'I intend to make him my husband.'

Her confident words made the others giggle. As the most beautiful girl in the village, with her peachy skin, cornflower-blue eyes and thick blonde hair, Mary was used to attracting the attention of men, and it was clear that the young master had noticed her.

'What makes you so sure he'll have you?' asked one of the other girls. 'Rich people marry their own kind.'

Mary ran her fingers through her hair and then tied her bonnet under her chin with studied care, the way a lady might do. 'Money isn't everything,' she said confidently. 'These fine families need fresh blood from time to time. They can't keep marrying simpering milksops all of them. And there's love too.'

Cora couldn't resist. 'Oh, is that the kind of love which lands you with a child in your belly and nothing for your trouble?'

Mary sent her a look of irritation. 'Well, if it isn't Miss High and Mighty, who thinks herself above marrying any man. Are you suggesting that I'm not good enough for the likes of him?'

'Not me.' Cora shook her head. 'It's the likes of him that are saying you're not good enough.'

'Well, we'll see about that. I don't intend to spend the rest of my life toiling in the fields all day with barely enough to live on.'

'You'd best keep your voice down, Mary,' said the other girl warningly, 'lest you want his lordship hearing you speak out of turn.'

'Pah,' Mary spat, but she said nothing further on the subject.

Despite Mary's arrogance Cora couldn't help agreeing with her. The labourers worked hard, and in the summer months they were provided for well enough, but in winter it was difficult to keep starvation at bay, especially for those with a large family to feed. She and Ned were luckier than most, living in the forest, where there were plenty of berries, herbs and wild onions to be found, and a rabbit from time to time, but others were not quite so fortunate.

And nothing Cora found in the forest could help pay for Ned's medicine.

Kit Heston kept eyeing Cora, much to Mary's chagrin. 'You

been makin' eyes at him behind my back, Cora Mardell? Of all the underhanded …'

'Calm down, Mary. I'm not interested in young Master Kit in the least.' Cora tried her best to sound soothing and sincere. It was the truth after all.

'Oh, yeah? Well, seein' as how you're blushing, you must have your eye on someone else then. Changed your tune, 'ave you?'

'I am *not* blushing.' Cora sent the other woman a furious look, but this only confirmed to the sharp-eyed Mary that she had hit the nail on the head. Which she had, but not in the way she imagined.

It wasn't the fine looks of Lord Heston's eldest son which danced in Cora's vision like a demon and made her breath catch in her throat, but a different face altogether. Chiselled features, an arrogant countenance and a naked chest through an open shirt. But a man like that would be even less likely to look twice at someone like Cora. He'd been an aristocrat through and through, no doubt about it, and Cora disliked them intensely. They all thought themselves above ordinary people, but by what right? None that Cora could see. She'd yet to meet one she could admire, young Master Kit included. Nothing would make her marry a man like that, no matter how handsome he was.

Ignoring the ribbing from the other women, Cora fought to calm herself. She hoped she never met the man from the coach again. At the same time, she couldn't deny that the thought of seeing him one more time, preferably unarmed, was a tantalising one.

It was also impossible and she'd do better to forget the whole thing.

The Earl of Lampton was an early riser. Although exceptionally privileged by birth, Jack's father did not believe in an idle aristocracy, and almost every day before breakfast he and the estate manager would take a morning tour of the stables and parts of the estate, discussing the day's work and what needed doing. Afterwards he would either be engaged in further conversation with the manager, in his study poring over the estate accounts, or corresponding with friends in the Lords.

He also attended parliament when it was in session. His spare time was spent with his horses, his dogs, and his wife – in that order.

Jack took a keen interest in matters relating to the estate as well and often accompanied his father on his morning tour. When he wasn't in town trying to keep an eye on his cousin, of course.

Sighing, he pushed open the door to the breakfast room. If Rupert continued to spend at this rate, he could ruin the estate's finances – and Jack and his father had worked too hard for him to allow that. Jack couldn't understand why his father turned a blind eye to Rupert's faults, but if Lord Lampton wouldn't try and control him, Jack would have to, for the sake of the estate and all those who relied on it. What irked him most was that the earl seemed unconcerned, almost as if he refused to see that his young cousin's conduct was becoming a genuine problem.

Jack wasn't surprised to find his hard-working father already seated in the breakfast room enjoying a plate of cold meats, freshly baked white bread and a jug of ale. What did surprise him, however, were his father's first words.

'I heard you and Rupert were robbed last night. I trust you have recovered from the ordeal?' Although the words were spoken languidly, with his habitual restraint, the earl couldn't hide his concern.

Jack smiled ironically. 'News travels fast,' he said while he helped himself to coffee from a silver urn on the sideboard and a plate of ham and eggs.

'I spoke with Josephs this morning. The man had a serious fright. After all, he was the first person to have a pistol pointed at him.'

Josephs, the coachman. Of course. Jack should have known his father would have heard of the episode almost before it had come to an end. In fact, he would hear of any episodes involving his son and Rupert for as long as his loyal servants were present.

'And I had a rapier at my throat,' said Jack, irritation prickling between his shoulder blades. Too late he realised how churlish he sounded. No doubt his father's informants had told him that too, and if he had chosen not to mention it, most likely it was because it was obvious that Jack had come to no harm.

'Yes, so I hear,' commented the earl drily. 'Why didn't you stay at the town house? You're welcome there any time; you know that. Or you could have stayed at your club.'

Jack sat down in front of him. 'I didn't want to open up the house just for one night, and as for staying at the club ...' He paused knowing that his next words would likely vex his father. 'I thought it best to get Rupert out of town for a spell. The gaming tables were proving to be too much of a temptation.'

'And since when have I appointed you to be his nursemaid?'

'Since you let him loose in London to squander away the family fortune,' Jack retorted and met his father's eyes.

The earl's eyebrows rose. 'Harsh words. Surely it hasn't come to that yet?'

'Perhaps not yet,' Jack conceded.

'So let me get this straight. Instead of letting your cousin lose a few harmless guineas in a den of iniquity, you both suffered losses because of a common thief?'

Hardly harmless, thought Jack, recalling the large sums changing hands. The highwaywoman had merely taken off with the dregs. Yet he felt himself flush at the rebuke. 'Yes, that about sums it up,' he snapped. 'Clearly I acted without proper forethought.'

'Steady on, son. I was merely concerned for your safety.

Most people are aware that travelling across the Heath at night is bad for your health, but perhaps that piece of information passed you by? Remember what happened to poor Lady Heston? Both you and Rupert need to take the threat of highwaymen seriously and not go travelling late in the night. I'll make sure I remind him of it too. You could have been killed.'

'Fortunately it didn't come to that.'

'Fortunately indeed.' This time the corners of the earl's eyes crinkled with amusement.

Jack returned the smile although inwardly he sighed. He was aware that his father made allowances for Rupert because he had lost his parents at a young age, but it still rankled that he was often taken to task for it and not Rupert. However, he had too much respect and affection for his father to let this develop into a full-scale argument.

The earl seemed to share this caution. 'Enough on the subject. After my cousin died, I swore I would see his children right, and I have no intention of going back on my promise. Rupert will soon settle down once he's sown a few wild oats.'

Jack nodded, although he didn't share his father's confidence. He sensed a recklessness in Rupert to which it seemed the earl was turning a blind eye. A wild streak bordering on ruthlessness, even, well-hidden behind the convivial exterior of an aloof and somewhat foppish man-about-town.

While he ate, he regarded his father surreptitiously. The epitome of a perfect nobleman, the earl was dressed in a white cambric shirt, pale yellow waistcoat and dark breeches. His coat of fine red wool had been slung carelessly over the back of a dining chair, and he was leaning back in his seat with one arm resting on top of the coat. His once jet-black hair was now a courtly pewter, cut short for the ease of wearing a wig when formalities required it, but his brilliant blue eyes had lost none of their lustre to age.

Not for the first time did Jack marvel at their different

looks; with his own brown hair and hazel eyes he knew he favoured his mother, Lady Lampton. Even Rupert's hair was black, as was Cousin Alethea's.

'Presumably you'll be speaking to the magistrate,' said the earl, interrupting Jack's train of thought.

'I'll ride into town later, although there's scarcely any point. The robber will be long gone by now.' Jack made no mention of the wager, knowing full well that his father would turn it against him and not Rupert, and he was certain that Rupert, when he finally resurfaced from the night's revels, would not mention it either.

'And you had a rapier at your throat, you said?' the earl continued. 'Quite an alarming experience, I should think.'

Jack finished his breakfast and wiped his mouth with a linen napkin. 'Not one I wish to repeat, although I think it may have been an idle threat.'

'How so?'

Jack hesitated. If he told his father the thief was a woman, the magistrate was likely to get wind of it too, even if Jack didn't tell him himself. And that would spoil the fun of tracking down the woman. He was aware that withholding information may not be the noble thing to do, but he was determined to win that wager with Rupert.

'The highwayman was a young boy,' he said instead. 'Something tells me he didn't have the nerve to run me through.'

'Perhaps you're right.' The earl sounded doubtful and studied Jack with a pensive look. 'I see you've lost your queue. Did this young robber have anything to do with that?'

Jack's hand flew to the nape of his neck and he muttered a curse. Having been so preoccupied with what he could remember about the highwaywoman, he had given scarce attention to his looks this morning, but his father's comment reminded him that the highwaywoman had shorn him like a spring lamb. *Devil take the wench!* Suddenly it became doubly important that he win the wager against Rupert; he was going to teach that girl a lesson she wouldn't soon forget.

The earl laughed. 'Looks like this young boy managed to best you.'

'For the time being.'

'I'll come with you,' the earl said.

'What? Where?' Jack was confused by the sudden change of subject.

'To the magistrate's. This is a serious matter.'

Jack was annoyed at the apparent lack of faith in his abilities, but how could he refuse without sounding churlish? He shrugged.

Just at that moment the countess appeared. As always Jack was awed by his mother's youthful looks. Her peaches and cream complexion was flawless, her waist still trim despite motherhood, her bearing straight. The only testament to her years was her grey hair, which she wore high and powdered in place of a wig. This morning she was dressed in an apple-green day gown with lace spilling from the sleeves, a white fichu at the neck, and she held a black straw hat with a matching ribbon in her hand. Her spaniel, Pepper, an elderly white and tan female, was trudging along beside her.

'Am I interrupting anything?' she enquired in a soft, throaty voice which spoke of her gentle breeding.

The earl kissed his wife on the cheek. 'Good morning, Lady Lampton. I trust you slept well?'

'I'm quite well,' she replied but her eyes were on Jack. 'You seem ... different. Oh, your hair! A drastic trim?'

Jack sent her a wry smile. 'Rupert and I were held up last night, on the Heath. For sport, the highwayman cut off my queue.'

'Goodness.' The countess paled and sat down beside him, her pretty hazel eyes deeply troubled. Jack hoped the shock didn't bring on another of her headaches; she had them often, and it worried him. 'But that's terrible; you could have been hurt. *Are* you hurt?'

'Only my dignity.'

The countess reached out to put a slender hand on his arm, but then, as if suddenly realising he was now a grown man and too old for such a show of motherly affection, she brought it to her throat instead. 'This cannot go on. Something must be done about this brigand. I hear such horrifying accounts.'

'Alice,' the earl entreated, 'you know better than to listen to idle chatter from the servants.'

'Not just the servants, husband. There's talk in the town. People are frightened.'

'Rest assured, something *will* be done. Jack and I are just on our way to see the magistrate. Would you be very much distressed, madam, if we postponed our morning walk?'

Seemingly recovered from her initial shock, the countess sent her husband a tight smile. 'Not at all. Seeing the magistrate is far more important. But how very kind of you to ask.'

Jack looked from one parent to the other. He'd always marvelled at their harmonious relationship. He had even modelled his own ideas of matrimony on theirs, but this was the first time he sensed that perhaps they were being *too* nice in their dealings with each other. Perhaps it had always been there and he'd only just noticed. But what to make of it?

'I'm sorry, Mother, if this causes you any inconvenience.'

'Nonsense,' said the countess. 'I shall walk with Alethea instead. No doubt she will make sure I get my exercise.' With that parting comment she glided back out of the breakfast room with the spaniel at her heels.

Raking was thirsty work, and before long Cora was reaching for her flask. Despite the sensible neckline and the long sleeves of her dress, small particles of dried grass had worked their way through her clothes, and she was itching everywhere. Finally, when the sun was high in the sky, the labourers retreated to the edge of the field to take their lunch in the shade of the trees. Sitting with Ned and the others on a large fallen tree trunk, Cora took off her bonnet and enjoyed for a moment the sensation of the light breeze caressing her sweaty neck.

Horses' hooves pounded on the lane, and she turned to see who was approaching. Lord Heston and his son seemed to have sprung to attention and hastened towards the newcomers. Cora hid a sneer – another nobleman and his offspring, these two even more hoity-toity by the look of it. The older man sat stiff in his saddle as if he'd had a poker rammed up his backside, and the younger one—

She stifled a gasp. *Dear God. No, it couldn't be!* She bent down and pretended to be looking for something on the ground while she quickly put her bonnet back on. Surreptitiously she glanced over her shoulder. It was him, she was sure of it. The man from last night, shorn hair blowing in the breeze. But how had he found her so quickly? She trembled violently and had to steady herself against their makeshift seat.

Stay calm, she thought. *He can't possibly know. He didn't see you, a woman, he saw a young lad.* She should get away from here. She had to—

But there was nowhere to go. If she ran, it would look strange and possibly rouse the man's suspicion. If she stayed, he might recognise her. She could only hope that by keeping her head lowered, he wouldn't think to notice her. Resolutely, she stayed close to her father and kept her eyes averted.

'It's a fine day, is it not?' said a voice nearby and, startled, Cora glanced up despite herself.

The man had ridden up to their small group and was addressing Ned and some of the other workmen kindly. Everyone rose, and she curtsied with the other women, but he waved his hand as if he didn't think the gesture necessary.

'Indeed, sir,' Ned answered politely. 'As fine as they come.'

'Looks like you'll be able to finish the wind cocks today.'

Although he was speaking to Ned, the man's eyes seem to roam over the little group, but when Cora looked up, and their eyes met very briefly, she could see nothing in his expression to indicate that he recognised her. Quickly, she lowered her head, making sure her bonnet shielded most of her face.

'Yes, sir, I reckon we will,' Ned replied.

The man and Ned spoke for a few more minutes, mainly about the weather and matters relating to this year's harvest. Emboldened by the fact he hadn't recognised her, Cora risked another glance at him. This time he looked directly at her, ignoring the others, and something in his eyes – a flirtatious twinkle and slow appraisal of her person – had her insides tied in a knot. Blushing furiously, she looked away.

The man regarded their group for a moment longer; then smiled and tilted his hat. 'Well, I wish you all a good day.' After one final long look at Cora, he rode away.

On shaky legs, Cora sat down on the tree trunk again, but not before she had caught the look in Mary's eyes and a ribald gesture from the girl next to her indicating a big belly. Annoyed, Cora moved closer to her father with gossip already ringing in her ears. There was no doubt the man, whoever he was, cut a dashing figure, but to come this close to someone she had recently robbed reminded her that what she was doing carried a real danger. If someone were to uncover her identity, she'd end her life on the gallows, no question about it. Swallowing hard, she glanced at her father.

What would happen to him if she died?

Chapter Three

Jack hadn't wanted to stop and talk to their neighbours, Lord Heston and his son, Kit, but the earl wanted to discuss the subject of selling one of his fields to Heston, so Jack quelled his impatience and greeted the neighbours cordially. Lord Heston, who was dressed in an exquisitely tailored riding coat, white silk stockings and black shoes with gold buckles, could easily have been described as a handsome man, if it hadn't been for a curiously unlined face completely devoid of any real emotion.

As always in his presence Jack experienced an involuntary shiver running down his back, and while his father and Lord Heston discussed estate matters, Jack turned to Kit to engage him in conversation. Kit was a handsome young man, tall with broad shoulders and the hallmark thick auburn hair of all the Heston boys, and negotiations were underway that he might one day marry Alethea.

Normally Kit was very affable but today he seemed subdued, cowed even. Even talking about hunting, shooting and fishing, which had always interested Kit, elicited no more than a few words, and – puzzled – Jack had soon given up. It would have been easier to converse with a stone.

Instead he'd allowed his gaze to roam, and it had landed on one of the haymakers, a beautiful girl, stretching out the kinks in her back by the looks of it. Fascinated, he'd ridden over to her group and spoken with one of the labourers, and eventually she had looked up and noticed him. Her reaction to him was most gratifying and he saw a flush stain her cheeks as she looked away again. On the ride home to Lampton Hall, he couldn't get her out of his mind. There had been something about her that captivated him, although for the life of him he couldn't say what. The sensuous way she'd moved? Her dark hair, shining in the sun? The fact she was taller than any woman of his acquaintance?

He shook his head. What was the matter with him? First the highwaywoman, now a common labourer. Was he going soft in the head? Perhaps he should have availed himself of the courtesan's services last night after all.

'Don't you agree?' The earl's voice startled him back to the present.

'I beg your pardon? I was wool-gathering I'm afraid.'

'I said'—as the earl repeated himself, Jack tried to clear his mind of images of lovely women. He had better things to do, such as catching himself a criminal. With a frown, his thoughts returned to their meeting with the magistrate.

They'd found the man at his home in Hounslow, finishing off his breakfast, and the frown on his face when the servant showed them in indicated his displeasure at being disturbed this early. His expression quickly turned to one of false delight at the sight of the earl.

'My lords, what a pleasant surprise,' he boomed and indicated for them to sit. 'To what do I owe this honour?'

A rotund, middle-aged man, Sir Christopher Blencowe wore an old-fashioned grey wig and severe suit of dark blue wool with silver buttons, and habitually carried a cane with a gilt metal handle. The cane was leaning against the sideboard, and Jack cast it a sideways glance; he had memories of a painful rap across the palm of his hand. As a boy he'd deliberately scared the magistrate's horse enough for it to bolt. His father's reaction at the time had been to laugh and thank the magistrate for sparing him the trouble of disciplining the boy himself.

But things had changed. Slowly Blencowe heaved his hulking frame out of the chair and bowed to them. If he noticed Jack's somewhat irregular haircut, he was too polite to comment on it, although his gaze rested on the loose tresses just a moment too long.

'I'd like to report a highway robbery,' replied Jack without preamble and accepted the offer of a seat, as did his father.

'Not that confounded youth again,' thundered the magistrate. 'Devil and all his cohorts take that young rascal!'

'You know about him?' Jack experienced a sense of relief that, apparently, only he and Rupert knew this to be a woman, and they were now free to carry out their bet without interference.

'Naturally. The varmint has been terrorising honest folk for months now, from Brentford to as far as Staines, and all the surrounding villages. No one is safe, except for those poor enough not to have anything worth robbing. I've been on his trail ever since, but every time he slips through the net.'

'How come we'd not been informed of this?' asked the earl.

The magistrate cleared his throat. 'With all due respect, my lord, you both seem to be spending rather a large proportion of your time up in London. A local matter such as this would hardly come to the attention of fashionable society.'

Jack heard the reproach and felt as though the words were mostly aimed at him. His father had the excuse of his parliamentary duties, but Jack? Was he really nothing but a wastrel in everyone's eyes? Silently he vowed to do something to rectify this impression and to show his genuine interest in local matters. Perhaps if he got Rupert interested in local matters too, Jack could keep him in line. He was well aware that one day he would inherit the estate and he couldn't just stand by and allow Rupert to ruin it.

He retrieved the highwaywoman's pistol from his pocket and placed it on Blencowe's desk. 'The culprit left this behind last night. Might it provide a clue to catching this thief?'

Blencowe examined the pistol, but then shook his head and handed it back to Jack. 'Sadly not. That model is common as muck and there are no distinguishing marks on it. You'd be better off selling it, my lord, as a small compensation for your losses.'

Jack nodded. He had suspected as much, but it was worth a try. He would keep it for next time he needed to travel at night.

'So what's being done to apprehend him?' the earl asked.

The magistrate scratched his head. 'I've had the constable scouring the outlying hamlets, but no one knows anything about him; or if they do, they're not telling. I'm quite sure this is a local person, and there must be someone out there who does know something.'

'How local, do you reckon?'

Again the elderly magistrate heaved himself out of his chair and crossed the room to a set of shelves lining one wall of his study. He pulled down a rolled-up map, spread it out on his desk and secured the four corners. Jack could see that several locations on the map had been marked with an ink dot.

'These are the sightings,' said Blencowe. 'Here and here' — he pointed to two dots, each with a circle around them — 'are definite confirmations that this was the same young man. At the other points the victims merely reported being robbed by a single individual, quite young, but the descriptions given were startlingly similar to those given by the boy's victims. It would seem the general consensus is that no one this young could be this bold.'

'It never crossed my own mind until yesterday,' admitted Jack, although he wasn't referring to a boy. In reality he only knew two kinds of women: ladies like his mother and cousin and members of their acquaintance, and the kind of female who hung around in gaming dens or Vauxhall Gardens, hoping to charm an unsuspecting young man with money to waste.

All he knew of labouring people was what he had learnt from his father as they discussed business matters for the estate. Judging by either her speech or her diction the highwaywoman probably came from the latter.

'No, and why should it?' said the magistrate dryly.

'Nevertheless we have a very resourceful mischief-maker on our hands leading us a merry dance. If word gets out and we don't catch him soon, I'll be a laughing stock. However'— he looked sideways at Jack, and there was a glint in his eyes that Jack recognised from the time Blencowe had caught him and Rupert stealing apples from his orchard—'I have, as you see, been compiling meticulous information. A pattern has emerged.'

Jack looked at the dots on the map, and suddenly he noticed it; there was a clear indication of an almost perfect oval shape stretching from Brentford to East Bedfont, concentrating on the Bath Road, where the highwaywoman had intercepted Jack's carriage last night, and the Staines Road.

'Do you permit, sir?' He took the pen from Blencowe's inkstand, dipped it in ink and marked the point where he and Rupert had been held up. The three confirmed identifications formed a triangle, and right in the centre was the forested area just south of Old Heston Mill.

Returning the pen to the inkstand, he said, 'Here is where my cousin and I were set upon; so perhaps this triangle is where we should be concentrating our efforts. I'm willing to bet that the highwayman has a hideout somewhere in that forest.'

'By Jove, Halliford, I believe you might be right!' said Blencowe. 'Still, it's a considerably large area and I haven't got the manpower to cover it. I suppose the most sensible course of action would be for me to call in the thief-takers.'

Jack raised his eyebrows. 'Is that really necessary, given their reputation?' Thief-takers were notoriously corrupt and would often extort protection money from the criminals they were supposed to catch instead of bringing them to justice.

'That is a concern, to be sure, but I'm at my wits' end.'

'I'm quite certain that between us and your men this fish will land itself in our net soon enough,' said Jack.

'And what about your losses, my lord?' The magistrate

sounded uncertain. 'Despite their reputation thief-takers have connections in the underworld, and tongues often wag.'

'Mere trinkets. It's the nerve of it. I'll be frank with you: it would give me the greatest pleasure to apprehend this thief myself.'

And that, Jack thought ruefully, *was nothing short of the truth.*

'Well, if you're sure,' said Blencowe. He carefully rolled up the map and returned it to its place on the shelf; then walked to the sideboard and placed his hand on a decanter. 'Care for a glass of brandy?' he said to his guests.

'No, thank you, Blencowe,' replied the earl. 'It's a little early for me.' Jack declined as well.

The magistrate scoffed and poured himself a generous measure. 'I don't know what you're up to, Halliford,' he said and eyed Jack sharply over his glass, 'and why you wouldn't want the thief-takers involved, but if you think you can catch this rapscallion yourself, you're welcome to try. In the meantime I'll continue with my own enquiries.'

'Of course,' said Jack. 'And naturally I'll share with you anything I manage to dig up.'

Awareness that he had already omitted to share one vital fact with Blencowe – that they were dealing with a woman – prickled uncomfortably at the back of his mind, and he knew the magistrate would have good reasons for thinking ill of him if he found out. However, he hoped to catch her before other travellers fell victim to her thieving.

And win the wager with Rupert in the bargain.

At sundown the labourers had finished raking the hay into wind cocks and began to disperse in different directions, some joking and laughing with relief that a long day of hard labour had finally come to an end, others in a more contemplative mood.

Walking a few yards behind Ned, Cora offered her arm to

Mrs Wilton, a widow who lived on the outskirts of the forest. She liked the older woman, on whose face years of deprivation, toil and grief had left their mark. A gentle soul, she had borne nine children and seen five of them, as well as two husbands, to the grave, but she remained as cheerful as ever and leaned gratefully on Cora's arm.

As the last rays of the sun bathed the treetops in a golden glow and warmed the back of her neck, Cora listened contentedly to the widow prattling on about this and that with no clear direction, as was her wont.

'And did you hear about the robbery on the Heath?' She squeezed Cora's arm. 'Frightful story and no mistake.'

Cora pricked up her ears and she sensed rather than saw Ned doing the same. 'Which robbery?' she said, keeping her voice level.

'Well, as I've heard tell, there's them two fine noblemen travelling along the road last night, when they're stopped by a gen'leman of the road, as it were, except he was no gen'leman at all, because after he's robbed them of all their worldly goods, he attacks one of them and shaves the poor man's head clean.'

'That's not tr—!' Cora checked herself and amended her tone. 'That's not true, surely? Who would do such a thing?'

'Aye,' said the widow, 'who indeed? If I hadn't seen him hang with my own two eyes, I'd say it was that brigand Blueskin come back to haunt us. Bears all the hallmarks of his dealings, nasty piece of work that he was.'

Horrified and bemused in equal measure at having her own modest exploits compared to those of the infamous cut-throat, who had even turned against his own partner, Cora allowed the widow to give her a full account of the hanging, which she had witnessed as a child.

The reminder that her actions were leading her closer and closer to the rope made her shudder, but she quickly suppressed it. Ned's illness gave her no other choice but to make money any way she could.

With the widow safely escorted back to her cottage, Ned and Cora returned home in silence. After their evening meal, rabbit stew with carrots, cabbage and coarse bread, Cora took herself off to her mother's grave, in a small clearing a little way from the cottage. It had been her mother's last wish to be buried here, close to those she loved. At first Ned had protested that she should be in consecrated ground, but in the end he had given in to her dying wish. Cora's mother had rarely left the cottage and the area surrounding it, and had insisted that neither should her mortal remains.

There was no headstone, but Ned had lovingly carved a wooden board, which was now weathered and grey with age. A smaller board next to it marked the grave of Cora's baby brother, Tom, whom had lived for no longer than his first day.

Her heart ached at the sight of both the graves. Her mother – once a lady's maid from a grand house – had not been cut out for the harsh living conditions in the forest, and the effects of several premature births and a difficult labour following her last pregnancy had been more than her frail body could cope with.

Worn out and grey with fatigue, her last breath had been a sigh of relief, but before she had died, she'd grabbed Cora's hand and squeezed it while her lips moved. Cora had had to bend very close to her mother to hear what she said.

'Remember, you're a lady,' she had whispered.

Sitting on the soft moss, Cora cleared away weeds and fallen leaves from the grave while she hummed a lullaby for her baby brother. Yet again she pondered her mother's last words, which might have been caused by fever, although she'd seemed lucid enough.

What could she possibly have meant?

Jack parted company from his father by the gates to Lampton Hall and rode home through the estate gardens rather than following the lane to the front of the house. Under a large oak tree he stopped and surveyed his father's mansion. The hall was perfectly situated among a wood of stately old oak trees but the sandstone house itself was set back, as if erected on an island of rolling green lawns.

The mansion was relatively new, having been designed in the previous century by a pupil of the great Inigo Jones. Influenced by Italian Palladian architecture, Lampton Hall was a smaller version of the Queen's House at Greenwich. The house was built over four storeys, and the main floor was accessed by a flight of external steps and south-facing portico. Tall windows ran right around the building like large dark eyes reflecting the sunlight.

However, for the moment Jack was oblivious to its splendour. Deep in thought, he stayed seated on his horse, pondering what his next move should be. It seemed prudent to begin his search in the forested area that he had identified on the map, but he was aware that it was a sizeable locality.

As his horse grew bored and started grazing, Jack saw movement out of the corner of his eye and shielded the sun with his hand to see better. In the distance Alethea was striding purposefully across the lawn, with Rupert in an embroidered coat and wig trailing twenty feet behind her.

Jack grinned to himself. Anyone accompanying Alethea on her morning walk only had himself to blame; she never strolled or sauntered but belted ahead as if her very life depended on it. Not even her polonaise gown of dove-grey taffeta seemed to hamper her forward movement.

He was just about to spur the lazy horse on and join them when Rupert caught up with Alethea and grabbed her arm, forcing her to turn around. Jack's grin became a frown; Rupert spoke urgently and Alethea wrested her arm away.

Another fight? Jack sighed. They seemed to have become more frequent of late. Most probably Rupert had made some minor quip which had set her off; Alethea was known for having a fiery temper.

He nudged the reluctant horse forward to meet them, dismounted when Alethea caught sight of him, and took the horse by the bit. She ran up and flung her arms around his neck, nearly toppling him over. The startled horse whinnied and shied away, the whites of its eyes stark against the chestnut coat. Jack reached out to put a steadying hand on its neck.

'Jack, are you all right?' she cried. 'I just heard what happened. I swear, if that brigand has injured you, I don't know what I'll do!'

'I'm absolutely fine.' He returned the embrace and her innocent affection, as always a little overwhelmed by Alethea's forcefulness, and then extricated himself gently from her stranglehold with a reassuring smile. 'We both are.'

He glanced in Rupert's direction, and Alethea followed his eyes with a look of loathing. She stepped back and crossed her arms.

'*He* has been following me all morning to make sure I don't meet anyone interesting,' she hissed. 'I swear he's nothing but a scarlet hypocrite. As if all his friends are suitable!' Scowling furiously, she sent her brother another glare.

Jack raised his eyebrows. 'He's your brother and he's devoted to you. As am I.'

'Hah!'

Rupert caught up with them, and once more Jack had to marvel at his cousin's effortless elegance. Not a single wig hair was out of place, nor did his face appear shiny from his exertions, in stark contrast to Alethea, who looked hot and cross, like a cat on a cauldron lid. 'Morning, cousin,' he said to Jack, 'I see you've already partaken of a bit of exercise.'

'I rode into Hounslow to speak with the magistrate about the robbery.'

'Ah. And did you tell him of our little discovery?'

Alethea looked from one to the other, her eyes suddenly alert. 'Which discovery?'

Jack hesitated. He hadn't mentioned to the magistrate nor

to his father that the culprit was a woman, and he doubted that Rupert had said anything about it either. It would spoil the enjoyment of the wager if the facts became known, and no doubt others would take it upon themselves to catch the daring wench. There was also a good chance that the thief would make a mistake if she was lured into thinking that her gender hadn't been discovered.

Yet now Alethea had the bit between her teeth, and Jack knew from experience that she wouldn't rest until she'd managed to wrestle further information out of them. He was confident he could withstand such onslaught, despite his affection for her, but whether Rupert could was another matter. What would she think of their less-than-honourable bet if she found out? The thought made him grimace.

He glanced at Rupert, a gesture which didn't pass her by, and then said, 'We discovered that the robber was a mere boy.'

'A boy?' said Alethea with a suspicious frown. 'How old was he?'

'Just a lad, really, and not much older than yourself.'

'Extraordinary.'

Rupert inclined his head with an indolent smile. 'Extraordinary indeed, especially since this boy was well-versed in the use of a pistol. He destroyed a perfectly good hat of mine, and now I shall have to make do with what the milliner in Hounslow can offer. Still, a gentleman needs a hat, especially if I'm to accompany you, dear Alethea.'

Giving her a mocking bow, Rupert grinned.

Alethea glowered back. 'I don't wish you to accompany me anywhere, thank you very much.' But it was clear her brother was intent on sticking to her like a limpet. Jack rolled his eyes, and found himself, as he had many times before in dealings with these two, caught between a rock and hard place.

Rupert left them at last, under the pretext that a ride might be just the tonic he needed, although Jack suspected it would take him the way of the magistrate's residence.

Alethea scowled at his retreating back and turned to Jack. 'I don't care what you say about my dear, charming brother, but he's becoming impossible and I don't like the way he draws you into his wicked ways.'

'He doesn't,' Jack said mildly.

'How can you defend him, Jack? How can you be so blind?'

'I'm not blind to Rupert's faults, Thea. I'm keeping him company in town in the hope that I may restrain him a little, not because I enjoy a life of wantonness. I'd rather be here; there's so much work to be done.'

'But your father is,' Alethea insisted. 'He refuses to see that Rupert is a spendthrift and a hanger-on who has no respect for how hard Uncle Geoffrey works to keep us all in comfortable circumstances. If he doesn't stop him, soon the estate will be mortgaged to the hilt. I can't bear it, after all the kindness your parents have shown to us. I wish I could repay them somehow.'

'You're exaggerating, Alethea. I've tried speaking to Father about Rupert's behaviour; but Father thinks I'm overreacting. Anyway, no one is expecting anything back – you're family. Besides, it won't come to that, I promise. It is my hope that Rupert will see sense eventually and go into a profession.'

'He won't; he's too indolent.' Alethea shook her head. 'Damn it, Jack, can't you see what sort of game he's playing?'

Jack was well aware what Rupert got up to in town but hadn't realised Alethea knew too. Instead he said, 'Language, Alethea. Remember you're a lady.'

Alethea tossed her black curls and stomped her foot. 'And what of it? Should only men and low-born women be allowed to express their true feelings?'

'All right, all right,' said Jack. He held up his hands soothingly, bemused and bewildered at the same time, wondering where Alethea's hot-headedness came from. She'd been brought up by his mother, and although the countess enjoyed hunting with an abandon rarely seen in ladies, she was otherwise mild-mannered and graceful, and the earl was very restrained. 'Just make sure Father doesn't hear you. Or Mother.'

'You won't tell?' Alethea's lips formed a perfect pout, and – giving in – Jack threw his head back and laughed.

'Never,' he said and tousled her hair.

As they walked back to the stables, arm in arm, with the horse ambling after them, he couldn't help wondering if Blencowe would be as forthcoming with Rupert as he had been with Jack this morning.

Chapter Four

Having left his cousin and sister on the lawn, Rupert headed for the stables. The head groom wasn't there, nor were any of the other grooms. The only person around was a young boy, the eldest son of the head groom. Rupert tapped him on the shoulder with his cane and the lad jumped.

'Where's your father, boy?'

The boy straightened up, leaned on his shovel and regarded Rupert with barely disguised derision. ''E's with the earl and Mr Southey in the south field, sir, helpin' a filly with her young 'un.'

'Well, go and get him, then. I need to ride into town.'

'I can't, sir. They was not to be disturbed. The foal's took everyone by surprise, and the filly's havin' difficulties, like.'

Rupert felt his blood boil, and it took all the restraint he possessed not to clip the urchin round the ears. He was sure no one treated Cousin Jack like this. If *Rupert* were the heir to Lampton ... 'Well, you saddle my horse, then, and make it fast,' he barked.

'Yes, Master Rupert.' The boy went about his business with deliberate slowness, or so it seemed to Rupert. He fumed quietly. His run-in with Alethea this morning had left him feeling very cross already and the accidental meeting with Jack had, once again, confirmed to Rupert that he was merely tolerated within the family. On top of that it irritated him that Jack had been the quicker of the two of them to see the magistrate. They had undoubtedly shared valuable information, thus putting Rupert at a disadvantage in winning the wager.

And win the bet he must. He'd always enjoyed gambling, horse racing and betting on other sports. He had confidence in his abilities, although he had noticed that recently the cards had not been in his favour. But this bet was for more than sport and entertainment. All his life he'd been treated as inferior to Jack – damn it he'd *felt* inferior! – and sometimes ... just sometimes he'd wished his sainted cousin dead. Perhaps by catching this thief, he could show them all what he was really made of.

He must see the magistrate immediately – the damned hat could wait.

The stable boy brought him his horse at last, and Rupert mounted it, only to slide precariously in the saddle. He jumped down and caught the boy by the hair. 'My saddle is loose. You did that deliberately, didn't you?'

The boy's eyes were huge with fright as Rupert shook him by the hair. 'No, sir. I swear I never. The stallion, he must-a blown up his belly, like.'

'You're supposed to wait and then re-tighten the girth, you dullard.'

'But you wanted 'im done fast, sir,' protested the boy.

Overcome by a sudden rage, white-hot and coursing through his veins, Rupert felt himself snap. 'Are you gainsaying me, you little rascal?'

'No, sir, I ...'

The boy didn't have time to finish. Rupert tossed him to the ground as if he were a sack of potatoes, and brought his cane down on his hamstrings. The boy cried out in pain and tried to crawl away. This only served to incense Rupert further. He raised the cane and swung it again, as hard as he could, this time landing a blow on the boy's back. The boy howled, and Rupert scooped him up by the scruff of the neck and shook him hard.

'Now see to my horse properly,' he growled, 'or you'll know what real pain is.'

'Yes, s-sir.' Snivelling, the boy wiped his nose on his sleeve and tightened the girth, pulling as hard as his small hands could manage.

Pushing him aside, Rupert mounted. He looked down at the boy and then raised his cane. The boy flinched away and Rupert laughed. 'Just so you know what's in store for you should you decide to tell anyone about this little interlude.'

'I-I won't breathe a word, sir.'

'Very good.' His good mood restored, Rupert tossed the boy a farthing; it landed on the ground. 'Here you go, then. For your trouble.'

He set off at a brisk canter, and didn't notice the boy glaring after him, a look of utter contempt on his face. The coin lay untouched in the dirty straw.

The following day was market day, and since there was no more work to be done in the fields for the moment, Cora decided to go to town. She put on her only good gown, a dark grey skirt and a faded blue cotton bodice, a second-hand purchase which she usually kept for Sunday best. Over it she donned a clean white apron, tied back her black curls with a piece of string and chose an old straw bonnet as protection against the sun.

Ned had left early that morning to check his traps for rabbits, and as always this activity gave her a twinge in the stomach. If he should be caught by his lordship's gamekeeper, there was a risk they would hang him; but Ned was careful, he said.

She collected the eggs from the hen coop, and carefully placed them in a basket on top of a piece of cloth, under which lay the rich man's waistcoat as well as the ring and the watches she had stolen. Her contact in town would know what to do with them.

Touching the items again was an uncomfortable reminder of how she'd obtained them, but only a few days ago she'd noticed that Ned's medicine bottle was nearly empty, and she had to find a way to pay for it to be replenished.

She picked up the bottle and slipped it in the basket with

the other things. It was completely empty now. This morning he had taken the last dose under her watchful eye, because she had a sneaking suspicion her father would pour the foul-tasting liquid away if she didn't keep a close watch. Her father didn't seem quite as concerned about his illness as she did. Sometimes she suspected he would welcome death just so he could be reunited with his wife, but Cora couldn't bear for that to happen. He was all the family she had left.

With her basket over her arm she walked through the forest and across the Heath. It was a cumbersome walk in the scraggy heather and prickly gorse, and when she arrived at Hospital Bridge she already felt hot and sticky. Squinting up at the sun, she realised it was going to be even warmer, and she sat down on a log by the roadside in the hope that someone would offer her a ride. Soon enough a farmer turned up in a hay wagon pulled by two oxen.

'Going to town?' he asked kindly. When Cora nodded, he said, 'It's a long way to be carrying them eggs. Hop on.'

Cora thanked him and walked to the back of the wagon. There were already two other passengers, an elderly woman carrying a basket of strawberries and a young man about Cora's age with four chickens in a cage. The chickens squawked nervously as Cora climbed up, and the man moved them further up the wagon to give her room.

'Thank you.' Cora smiled at him.

The young man went red as a beetroot and turned away. 'You're welcome.'

Cora tended to have that effect on the young men of her acquaintance, and although she was used to it, it bothered her slightly. It was almost as if every young man she encountered was in awe or afraid of her, and because of it she had never had the pleasure of walking out with one. She was almost as tall as her father and had often wondered if that frightened them off, but didn't know for certain. Sighing, she watched as the bridge slowly disappeared from view. It would be nice if just once a man could look her in the eye without blushing and turning away.

Then she recalled the men she had robbed and felt a peculiar flutter in her chest. One of them had done just that. In fact, he hadn't even flinched when she'd held Ned's old sword to his throat, threatening to run him through. Now there was a man she'd like to have met under different circumstances. Instead, she'd have to run in the opposite direction if she ever encountered him again. It was a lowering thought.

'Nice day for it, ain't it?' said the woman beside her. 'Got myself some lovely strawberries in 'ere. Should sell in no time.'

Cora agreed, and they passed a pleasant journey into town chatting about all manner of things. Even the young man joined in eventually and offered an opinion or two, although he was still careful not to look directly at Cora.

When she had sold her eggs, she went to see her father's contact, an old Jew who had moved out from London's east in the seventeen-thirties, when his shop had been burnt down. Cora had known Mr Isaacs and his now deceased wife, Ruth, since she was a little girl. Ned would bring Mr Isaacs some business – what sort of business Cora didn't know – and they would have a drink together, and in the kitchen the childless Mrs Isaacs would fuss over Cora and feed her hot white bread until Cora was so full she thought she would never eat another thing.

Although the couple were tolerated in Hounslow, they were also viewed with some suspicion, and had never really been accepted by the other tradesmen. Ned had befriended them years ago, though, and Cora knew Mr Isaacs would never betray her.

With her worry for Ned on her mind, she pushed open the door to the pawnshop and stepped inside a dusty world that had been wondrous when she'd been a child. She still remembered the many strange things people would pawn, and, looking about her now, it seemed nothing much had changed. There was everything from watches and jewellery to silk hats and shoes on display. Someone had even pawned a set of false teeth, two rows of carved ivory set in a wooden frame.

Mr Isaacs emerged from behind a curtain at the back of the shop and rushed forward to embrace her. 'Cora, Cora, Cora!' he exclaimed and kissed her on both cheeks, as was his custom, tickling her with his grey ringlets. 'How are you, my wayward *Fraulein*?'

He stepped back, still with his hands on her shoulders, shaking his head and tutting while he muttered something in Yiddish. 'And beautiful as always. Hasn't a young squire had the good sense to snap you up yet?'

'No such luck, Mr Isaacs. I expect I'll die an old maid.'

'Nonsense!' he cackled. 'When you're not looking, they will come.'

'I'm not looking and they're not coming,' said Cora and laughed at this strange logic.

Mr Isaacs was pensive. 'If you're willing, I can arrange for a nice Jewish lad to take you to wife. You'll have to convert, of course ...'

'That's very solicitous of you, Mr Isaacs, but the God I have is good enough for me.' Having said that, God had not spared her pain. Cora felt a sharp pang as she thought of her mother and the baby brother who didn't live beyond his first day, but she knew they'd be reunited in the next world.

'Well said, my dear. Well said.' Mr Isaacs spread his hands out. 'Anyway, what can I help you with, now that you're here?'

'I have some items to sell.'

Mr Isaacs sent her a long look; then he said, 'Mm, like that, is it? You had better come around the back, I think.'

He held open the curtain for her, and they retreated to a small office heaving with large leather-bound account ledgers. Apart from the pawnshop activities, Mr Isaacs also lent money to those who could not obtain a loan by other means. This required careful accounting, and Mr Isaacs was a meticulous businessman. Although people loathed having to use his services, they came back to him again and again, because he had a reputation for not squeezing his customers. Instead he allowed them ample time to pay off their debt, unlike some of the other local moneylenders, who were known for resorting to violent methods should the money not be forthcoming on the due date.

Less well-known was Isaacs' sideline as purveyor of stolen goods. With his numerous contacts in London an item bought by Mr Isaacs would disappear within a day. Still, it was a risky enterprise, and he closed the curtain firmly behind them before offering Cora a seat. He sat down on the opposite side of a narrow desk, which carried a blackened burn mark in one corner, and draped a square of protective felt over it.

Cora lifted the cloth in her basket aside and placed the two fob watches, the ring and the luxurious silk waistcoat on the desk before him.

Mr Isaacs raised his eyebrows. 'I've heard tales of a young rascally fellow stripping one victim naked and scalping another. Of course, I took them to be exaggerations, although I thought they carried the hallmarks of your, er – shall we say – handiwork. Does your father know?'

'He suspects.'

Mr Isaacs sucked his teeth. 'How *is* your father, by the way?'

'His cough is plaguing him, and the medicine is costly.'

'May God watch over him.'

'Let's hope so.' *Please don't take Ned away,* she thought. *He's all I have.*

Mr Isaacs reached across the desk and patted Cora's hand. 'You're a good girl. Now, let's take a look at what you've brought.'

He examined the fob watches carefully, turning them this way and that in the light from a high window behind him.

Then he studied the ring with the help of an optical device which made his eye appear enormous. 'Lovely, lovely,' he said. 'This should be easy enough to sell on. An exquisite piece of jewellery but not too distinct. The same goes for one of the fob watches, but the other is engraved, which makes it more difficult. Here, see for yourself.'

He passed the watch to Cora. She turned it over and read the inscription on the back. 'To dearest Jack. Your loving Alethea'. She knew which of the two men this watch had belonged to – the handsome one whose queue she had sheared off – but who was Alethea? His betrothed? His wife? She felt a warm flush spread across her cheeks and returned the watch to the table; it suddenly felt too hot in her hand. Irrational though it was, she was beset by an absurd feeling of jealousy that raged and curdled in her chest until she was able to calm herself.

Mr Isaacs was watching her closely, as if he could read her mind. It was an uncomfortable thought and briskly she returned to the business in hand.

'What about the waistcoat?'

Mr Isaacs shrugged. 'As for the waistcoat, although it's a very fine garment indeed, it isn't the sort of thing my associates in London deal in. Selling it around here could prove difficult as it's too recognisable, but I do know a seamstress who can fashion it into a set of ladies' reticules.'

Cora ran her hand over the fine fabric. It seemed a shame to cut it up. Also, it would mean the involvement of yet another person, and however trustworthy this seamstress might be, Cora decided to err on the side of caution.

'I'll hold on to it for the time being, then,' she said. 'As well as the engraved watch.'

Mr Isaacs shook his head lightly and muttered something that sounded suspiciously like an oath. 'Have a care, Cora. If you're caught with these items, you'll be transported. Or worse. And who will then visit an old man like me, eh?'

'I'm very careful,' she said, but her own words of reassurance couldn't prevent a cold feeling from stealing over her. 'And I'll always visit you.'

Besides, she had just had an idea for a completely different use for the waistcoat, one which might cause some speculation, but it was the least she could do for a man who treated her as a daughter.

She'd promised Gentleman George that she would be with him until the very end, and now George could meet his maker dressed like a true gentleman.

After her visit to Mr Isaacs, Cora made her way to the apothecary. In contrast to Mr Isaacs' dusty premises, hidden away in a narrow side street, the apothecary's shop on the High Street was a paragon of respectability. The bay-fronted window contained a three-tiered display of labelled brown jars, each with a description of the contents, and the pestle and mortar sign above the shop was newly painted.

Mr Byrd, the proprietor, greeted her with the time-honoured friendliness of a Hounslow trader. Because the town was the last major coaching stop en route to the west of England, trade was booming, and the shopkeepers were good-natured and content.

The apothecary was a rotund man in his fifties with a short grey horsehair wig befitting his profession and a pair of *pince-nez* glasses permanently perched on the end of a colossal nose.

'What'll it be today, Miss Mardell?' he asked. 'Some more of that tincture for your father's chest ague?'

'Yes, please. If you could prepare the same for him, I'd be much obliged, Mr Byrd.'

'Certainly. If you'd be good enough to wait.' He indicated that Cora should take a seat and began mixing the ingredients.

Cora sat down gingerly and looked about her. The counter, shelves and cupboards had all been painted a mossy green, and the oak floor had been polished to a high shine. As always when she entered Mr Byrd's establishment, she was filled with a sense of awe at all the cures that existed.

On one wall hung a copy of Mr Byrd's apothecary's license and a certificate in minor surgery, and a large collection of delft drug jars and slender-necked bottles for storing medications lined the wall behind the counter together with several heavy tomes of pharmacy books. Implements for compounding, weighing and dispensing drugs stood on the counter where Mr Byrd was in the process of selecting the ingredients for Ned's medicine.

In addition to prescribing remedies, Mr Byrd also made house calls to treat patients, acted as a surgeon and trained apprentices. His services were expensive and the only way Cora could afford them was through her clandestine activities. Today, however, with the money from the robbery and what Mr Isaacs had paid her for the ring and the watch, she was confident that she would be able to pay for the tincture without suffering the embarrassment of having to ask Mr Byrd for credit, *and* have money to spare at the same time.

Feeling optimistic about the future, she turned towards the door as the next customer walked in. The blood drained from her face with the shock of recognition. The man she had robbed – the handsome one, again – had just entered the shop, and he was staring right at her.

Her heart raced uncontrollably with fear and she rose from the chair. She didn't have such a large bonnet to hide behind this time – would he recognise her? If he did, all he had to do was to point the finger and insist that she be searched and she would be caught red-handed, unable to offer a plausible explanation for why his engraved fob watch was nestling on the bottom of her basket. And then it would be prison and the gallows. Her gaze darted, looking for an escape route, but as her dupe was blocking the doorway, there was only one alternative: jumping over the apothecary counter and scarpering out the back.

Acknowledging her by raising his hat, he approached the counter and stood right next to her. Cora's breath caught in her throat, and her hands moved as if on their own accord to hoist up her skirt in order to run.

But just as she was about to flee, the man was distracted by the apothecary. 'Lord Halliford, it's a pleasure to see you as always,' he said obsequiously. 'All's well at Lampton Hall, I hope. Pray, how may I be of assistance?'

'Some of your vinegar of roses, if you would be so kind, Mr Byrd. The countess is complaining of a headache.'

Rational thinking returned. The man, Lord Halliford, it seemed, had thought her male; there was no reason why he should suspect a plainly dressed country girl. If anything, he might remember her from the hayfield, but that was not so bad. Just to be safe though, she averted her eyes and kept them firmly fixed on the floor. But even though she couldn't see his face, the sense that his eyes were roaming over her stayed with her. The sooner she could leave, the better.

Chapter Five

The crossroads, where those who had taken their own lives were buried, was said to be haunted. Country-folk told stories of ghostly sightings, of drunken farmers on horseback being chased across the fields and timid plough-boys having to make a run for it, but as far as Rupert was concerned, those who chose to destroy themselves deserved nothing. Life was for the taking, and he wanted to make damned sure he got his due. Winning the wager with his cousin was just one step in that direction. He rode past the crossroads, along the Lampton Road towards Hounslow, passing orchards heavy with unripened apples, pears and plums; he breathed in the scent of the flowers on the fruit trees and praised himself lucky he wasn't given to such fancies as ghost stories.

Hounslow, where several busy coaching routes crossed, was a town hard at work at all times, but by midday, when Rupert arrived, it was simply bustling. The Bath Road was narrow and in addition to the farmers' carts there were people on horseback, pedlars, pedestrians, mongrels and other stray animals. Coaches clattered up the High Street, between the buildings on each side, destined for the countless coaching inns. Because of the town's position – at the end of the first stage out of London and the last place where coaches from the West Country changed horses – there were usually more horses than people on the streets.

The hustle and bustle made Rupert sit up straighter in the saddle, in readiness for any snide comments about what had happened the night before. The local rumour mill worked overtime and there was a good chance the folk of Hounslow had heard of Rupert's humiliation at the hands of the highwayman. He could well imagine the knowing looks and the sniggers behind his back. Jealousy curdled inside him at the awareness that he didn't enjoy the same popularity as his cousin, and he had no particular wish to draw attention today.

The milliner in Hounslow smiled as Rupert entered his shop. 'Mr Blythe, to what do I owe this unexpected pleasure?' He bowed slightly, enough to show deference to one of his betters, but not enough to show the kind of respect Rupert knew was his due. He clenched his fists. When he had improved his station in life the townsfolk would change their attitude, he'd make sure of it.

'I need a new hat,' he said sharply. 'This one has a hole in it.' Bristling, he lay the torn tricorne on the counter and looked about him. Rolls of felt and dark-coloured material were spread everywhere on shelves and counters and were even displayed in the bay-fronted window, but it was unlikely this man would be able to equip him with a hat of the same modishness as his ruined one. It would have to do. He was loath to travel to fashionable Bond Street for fear of being accosted by disgruntled tradesmen whose bills he had neglected to pay. Surely they must know his uncle was good for the money.

'Ah,' said the milliner. 'Moth problems, sir?'

'No. A bullet.'

'A bullet?' The hat maker raised his eyebrows. 'Was it a hunting incident, sir?'

'Well, of course not!' snapped Rupert and speared his hat through the hole with his finger. 'If I'd acquired a hole like that in my hat during a hunting accident, I'd be dead. No, it was a most audacious robbery, and not two miles from my uncle, Lord Lampton's, estate.'

'That is outrageous indeed, sir,' said the milliner, obsequiousness replaced by genuine horror. 'It would seem this town is beleaguered by marauders and footpads roaming the Heath. Something ought to be done about it.'

'Oh, believe me, something will,' muttered Rupert.

He perused the rolls of fabric in the shop, which as well as supplying hats sold fashionable materials for clothing. His gaze fell on a roll of luxurious brocade silk and he was reminded that the highwaywoman had more than just ruined his hat; the wench had also stolen his new waistcoat.

Clenching his fists, he said, 'Just give me a hat. Dark felt. Anything you have in store.'

The man bowed and returned with a small number of ready-made hats. Rupert took one and inspected himself in a mirror. The burgundy tricorne was passable enough and sat well on his powdered wig, which he had tied with a black ribbon. It was better than he had expected.

'Very well, I'll take it.' He made arrangements for the bill to be sent to Lampton Hall and then made his way to the nearest tailor. There he ordered a cream cotton waistcoat tamboured with silk and silver thread, and while he was at it a new formal day coat of felted wool and silver-gilt buttons.

Reasonably pleased with his purchases, he was about to leave the shop when a thought occurred to him. The highwaywoman would very likely have no use for a silk brocade waistcoat. She could turn a pretty penny if she sold it to a fence, and in a town the size of Hounslow there was bound to be a market for second-hand clothing, whether stolen or not.

He turned back to the tailor. 'Where would I find second-hand clothing in this town?'

The man sent him a curious look: he had, after all, just spent a small fortune on a brand new coat and waistcoat.

'Well, sir, sometimes old clothes find their ways to the market, but that's a bit sporadic. If you're after a more permanent outlet, there's York's establishment down beyond the smithy, although I must add this would be an unlikely place for a fine gentleman such as yourself to be visiting.'

'Just give me the address, man, and let me be the judge of that,' Rupert snapped.

The man rattled off an address which was indeed in the less salubrious part of town, and Rupert left the shop.

He found the place easily enough, tucked away from the main road. Barefoot children were playing in the dirt, two drunks were engaged in a slurred debate and a shifty-looking character followed Rupert's entry to the alleyway from under hooded eyelids. Rupert squared his shoulders and pushed the door open.

A bell clanged discordantly as he entered the shop, and immediately he was assailed by the odours of what seemed like mountains of unwashed clothing. He resisted the temptation to cover his nose with his handkerchief; he had come here for information, and causing offence to the proprietor from the start would obviously not be advisable.

Proprietress, as it turned out.

From behind a ragged curtain at the back of the shop appeared the strangest woman he had ever seen. She may have been pretty in her heyday, perhaps even a fêted beauty, or the mistress of a gentleman, but years of hard living and debauchery had ravaged her face and caused her body to sag in the most unattractive of places. The woman was wearing an unfashionable raspberry-red mantua gown, which had once been exquisitely embroidered with silver thread, but was now distinctly tatty. Rupert judged her to be no older than his aunt, the Countess of Lampton, or possibly even a little younger.

This hardly mattered. He hadn't come here seeking female company, but was in search of information. A little carefully applied charm would never go amiss.

'Mistress,' he said and bowed deeply, 'how fare you on this fine morning?'

'I fare well enough, kind sir, and even more so now due to your esteemed visit. How may I be of assistance to you?'

Rupert smiled. He had been right in his initial assessment; the woman had once moved in the higher echelons of society. Her manners were impeccable, although studied, as if they hadn't come naturally to her. She had been born to a different life, he guessed, and had used the only assets she possessed to make her way in life: her beauty and her body. Rupert had known many women like her, had bedded a fair number too. He could spot them a mile off.

'I would like to enquire with you, mistress, how a person may go about selling a silk waistcoat in a town such as this.'

The proprietress's irregularly shaved eyebrows rose, and she batted her eyelashes in a manner she obviously thought beguiling. 'Sell, my lord? Pardon my presumption but you don't look like the sort of man who's in need of selling anything.'

'Not me,' he replied curtly. 'Recently, an item of clothing was ... purloined from me, and I'm anxious to purchase it back.' He didn't mention that he had no intention of ever wearing the waistcoat again after the highwaywoman had had her dirty hands on it. However, it could provide a clue to catching the thief – if she decided to sell it locally, she might try her luck here.

'Pray, what sort of item?' she asked.

Rupert gave a description of the waistcoat, and the woman had trouble hiding a smirk. 'I know of it, sir. There are rumours in town that a fine gentleman was robbed of his clothes two nights ago on the Heath. Even his breeches. One of the items stolen fits the description you just gave me.'

'That's a damned lie! The brigand ruined my hat and robbed me of my waistcoat, but I'm telling you this, madam, I would just as soon have shot him before allowing him to humiliate me further!'

'Of course, sir, I'm merely reporting what I've heard,' the woman said with a little smile, which Rupert had a sudden urge to wipe off her mealy-mouthed face. Permanently.

Was the whole town grinning behind his back, even this good-for-nothing ex-courtesan? How dare she? He couldn't think what he might have done to deserve such censure.

Of course, there was the business with the maid who got herself into trouble. His uncle had forced him to see the wench right, and out of his own allowance too, but her father, a local man, had grumbled about her being ruined and nonsense like that. And there was the innkeeper who had insisted Rupert settle his bill immediately and not run an account. A fight had developed in which Rupert had sustained a black eye, and because he made such a fuss about it the innkeeper landed in gaol for a fortnight and lost his business. The ridiculous little man had actually sworn revenge.

But his indiscretions had been a couple of years ago, when he had not been well-versed in the ways of the world. Surely the whole town couldn't have been harbouring ill feelings towards him all this time? Especially since lately he had been spending most of his time in London, with Cousin Jack tagging along as the censorious chaperone. It seemed he couldn't get rid of the fellow, no matter how hard he tried.

He was brought up short as an idea occurred to him. He knew that his uncle's title and estate had never been his to inherit, and it was resentment over the fact that Jack would get everything and he himself only a paltry sum that made him freely spend of his uncle's money for as long he could. However, if Jack was out of the picture, Rupert, as the son of Lord Lampton's cousin, would be next in line. In fact, there was no one else, all other lines of the family having died out. Perhaps there was a way of ridding himself of his annoying cousin? For good.

If Jack should meet with an accident while they were chasing the intrepid highwaywoman ... If Rupert could lead him into a trap ...

It was certainly worth losing a hundred guineas over.

A lot of 'ifs', he thought, *but it might just work.* And if it didn't, Jack would be none the wiser.

'Everything all right, sir?' asked the proprietress, seemingly startled by his silence.

'More than all right.' He smiled affably. 'I say, mistress, if a person should come into your shop wanting to sell a waistcoat of said description, would you be gracious enough to send word so I can see this person for myself?'

'That depends, sir.'

'Naturally.' He fished a calling card out of his pocket

and handed it to her with a flourish. 'You will of course be generously rewarded.'

'Yeah, 'ow generously?' she asked, betraying her roots.

'Five guineas.'

'Ain't no person's conscience worth less than ten,' she countered.

Rupert felt the familiar rush of blood in his ears at her insolence, but he controlled himself. 'Eight, madam. A guinea now, the rest upon delivery. Will that suffice?'

She gave a gap-toothed smile. 'Aye, sir, that's very generous an' all. You can rely on me. But don't get your 'opes up, mind. Could be your thief has a fence and you won't see your pretty waistcoat ever again.'

Rupert was willing to take that risk.

Jack had sensed the woman's eyes upon him the moment he entered the apothecary's shop. He was used to attracting the attention of young women, and he would have thought nothing of it if she hadn't been so intent on hiding her face as soon as he acknowledged her presence and raised his hat politely.

As he'd stated his business with Mr Byrd, he'd tried to catch her eye, intrigued, but she'd kept her gaze lowered.

'I'll get right to it, m'lord.' Mr Byrd abandoned what he had been doing and turned to retrieve a delft jar from the shelf behind him.

Jack cleared his throat and indicated the woman with the straw hat. 'Do serve your other customer first. I'm happy to wait.'

'Her errand is of minor importance, sir,' said Mr Byrd over his shoulder.

'No, I insist.' Jack tried hard to keep the steel out of his voice. He had been born into privilege but was acutely aware that for the majority this was not so, and he was damned if he was going to get a reputation for abusing that privilege. Besides, his mother's headache was hardly life-threatening.

'Of course, m'lord. If that is your wish.' Mr Byrd returned to his former task, mixing ingredients for a draught, by the looks of it, and Jack spent the time studying the woman. Something about her was familiar, but he couldn't quite place her.

Annoyingly she kept her face turned away so he only got a glimpse of a very pretty profile, and any attempts at engaging her in polite conversation about the weather and suchlike were similarly thwarted, apart from a mumbled, 'Thank you kindly, sir,' when he insisted she was to be served before him.

The apothecary handed the woman a small glass bottle and named his price. She paid without demur. The whole transaction was conducted briskly; the apothecary because he was anxious not to offend his other, higher-ranked customer, and the girl because she seemed keen to be on her way. She put the bottle in her basket gently, as if it was a prized item.

She walked quickly to the door, but Jack intercepted her and opened it for her. 'Allow me.'

For the first time she looked up, almost as if drawn to against her will, and Jack recognised her as the girl he'd had seen at the hay-making. It was her height which stood out – she barely had to lift her face to meet his gaze. He found himself being openly assessed by a pair of intelligent eyes of startling colour – so light they appeared almost luminous. He blinked in surprise; the air left his lungs with a whoosh and he struggled to speak. Her face was a perfect oval framed by masses of dark hair, which she had made a brave attempt at taming with a piece of twine, and her pert nose was sprinkled with a dusting of freckles. Such exceptional yet unsophisticated beauty was unexpected, but he hardly registered it because he was still reeling from the impact of those dazzling eyes. To calm his suddenly racing heart, he cleared his throat for a second time and found his voice.

'Madam, I …' he croaked, but she didn't stay to hear him out.

Instead she jumped like a startled animal and scuttled out through the open door and into the High Street. Before Jack had had a chance to fully recover his wits, she had disappeared into the throng.

Stupefied, he returned to the apothecary. Those eyes … he had seen their like before, he was certain, but where? Frowning, he shook his head.

'Who was that young lady?' he asked curtly.

'Hardly a lady, m'lord.' The apothecary shook his head. 'She's a labourer. Common as muck, if you ask me. I trust she didn't discomfit you, sir?'

'She was perfectly well mannered, thank you. What's her name?'

'Oh, you don't want to be bothering with the likes of that one, m'lord. As the saying goes, appearances can be deceptive.'

'Let me be the judge of that, if you please,' Jack replied. Mr Byrd's presumption that he couldn't be interested in a woman just because she wasn't a lady annoyed him. He needed to know who she was and he wasn't going to let their different stations in life stand in his way. 'What is the woman's name, if you please?'

'Sir, I'm not sure—'

'The name, Mr Byrd.' This time he injected a measure of steel in his voice; he hated to take advantage of his rank, but if the alternative was never finding the young woman again, he'd do whatever he had to.

'Why, sir, that's Miss Mardell. She lives with her father in the wo—'

The woods.

The apothecary didn't get a chance to finish the sentence as Jack turned on his heel and flew out the door. On the High Street he stopped and craned his neck in the direction he had seen her go only a moment ago, but there was no sign of her. He set off at full speed after her, oblivious to the cries from the apothecary.

Chapter Six

Rupert left the shop in a pensive mood. It had been a long shot, and he knew it, but he had to try every avenue. What to do now though? He had already seen the magistrate and had no further excuse for seeking out the man. Besides, Blencowe didn't like him much.

Deep in thought, he completed a couple more purchases before retiring to the Old Bell Inn for a hearty repast of eel pie and a jug of ale. As he ate, he kept his eyes and ears open for any information which might come in handy, but the main topics among the patrons were the hopes for this year's harvest, the falling price of sugar and how the villagers at nearby Stanwell had averted the threat of enclosures by petitioning parliament. It was all so desperately tedious, and Rupert stifled a yawn.

Feeling thoroughly disheartened, he was about to leave when he spied an old man sitting alone in the corner of the inn sucking on a clay pipe. Old men had a habit of knowing what goes on in the local area, he thought as he approached the man and offered him a drink.

'That's mighty kind of you, young sir,' said the old man and indicated for Rupert to sit down. 'Don't mind if I do.'

Having ordered a tankard of ale from a passing serving wench, he set about questioning the man. They talked for a bit about various subjects, and Rupert learned that the old man was the grandfather to the landlord, and that he'd been a coachman for hire until aching joints put a stop to that. As carefully as possible Rupert tried to steer the conversation onto highwaymen and robbery and was rewarded with a knowing look.

'And what might your interest be in such like?' asked the old man. 'You wouldn't by any chance be that young fella that were stripped of his breeches, would you?'

Rupert scowled. No bloody secrets in this town. 'Waistcoat,' he corrected automatically.

The old man cackled. 'Wish I coulda been there. Would've given me eye teeth to see a fine fellow like you taken down a peg or two.'

'Yes, well, I'm sorry to have deprived you of your entertainment, but all in all it was a damned unpleasant experience, and I'm rather keen to apprehend the brigand, as you can imagine.' He forced himself to smile, although it irritated him that he had to play the other man's game. 'I figured that a person like yourself, of advanced years, might know where would be the best place for me to look.'

The old man sucked his pipe with a thoughtful expression. 'That ain't gonna be easy, not by a long stretch, but by my reckoning thieves and highwaymen are likely to know of each other's business, especially in a town this size. If you can get one o' them to talk, you might learn something o' another, so to speak.'

Exasperated, Rupert clenched his fists under the table. 'And where might I meet such a fellow? They don't exactly call attention to their existence in daylight.'

'Well,' the old man said slowly, bopping his head up and down, as if he enjoyed vexing his drinking companion, 'there's one up at Newgate waiting to have his neck stretched.'

Rupert pricked up his ears. 'And what, pray, is the name of this gaol bird?'

'The name's Gentleman George. About three weeks ago the constable and his men caught him in the The Black Dog while he was in his cups. He wasn't content with robbing from those that could afford it, such as yourself, if you will forgive me for speaking so freely, sir, and he's been a thorn in the side of ordinary folk in these parts. There are many around here, meself being one of them, who won't be sorry to see the back of him. People are wary of coming into town and selling their goods if they've no safe way of returning home with their proceeds, and that's bad for business, my grandson's included.' He grinned. 'Although I dare say there are some among the fairer sex who'll miss him. I hear he's been getting regular visits from veiled ladies.'

At the word 'ladies' Rupert's interest was further piqued. One couldn't by any stretch of the imagination call the woman who had held up the carriage a 'lady', but she definitely belonged to the fairer sex, as the man put it. If this Gentleman George was known to her, it was possible she may have visited him. Perhaps the imprisoned highwayman could provide some clue to the woman's identity.

'Newgate, you said?'

'Yes, sir. The trial was held last week, and his execution will be next time they put up the Tyburn Tree. I hear he's partial to brandy and a pipe of woodbine,' the old man added with a mischievous wink.

After that he entered into a long-winded speech about highwaymen, and how his coach was once held up when he was conveying a lady and her maid. Rupert listened with only half an ear. Normally he would have had no compunction about telling a prattling old geezer to hold his tongue but for the moment he was content to let the man's words wash over him.

'... and the robber scared me and my grandson off well and good. Next thing I hear, the lady is dead, as well as her newborn babe. Murdered, no doubt. A dreadful business and no mistake.'

'You left the passengers unprotected? An infant too?' Rupert arched his eyebrows. He had not heard any story of ladies murdered by highwaymen, nor their children, not of recent years at any rate, but the man was old and was probably embellishing an ancient tale, the kind that became more elaborate with each telling. Then a thought occurred to him.

'Are you by any chance referring to Lady Heston?' he said.

But the old man's eyes had taken on a faraway expression, and he'd begun to mutter to himself. Rupert could hardly make out what he was saying but it sounded like 'curse that Duval chit.'

'So it wasn't Lady Heston?' he pressed.

Coming out of his reverie, the old man sent him a startled look. 'I never knew the identity of the passengers.'

'You mentioned the name Duval.'

'It means nothing. Nothing!' The old man brought his tankard to his lips, and Rupert noticed that the man's hands were trembling. It perplexed him. He'd never heard the name before, but it clearly meant something to this fellow.

'Don't listen to him. He's always rambling when he's had a bit.' The innkeeper was suddenly looming over their table, startling Rupert. 'Come on, Grandpa, it's time you went and had a bit of a nap.'

'All right, all right, Jem, my boy, if you say so. Always nagging, he is,' he said to Rupert with another wink. 'Nag, nag, nag, all day long. 'Tis like having a missus and a 'alf.'

Rupert watched the innkeeper lead the old drunkard away. As if sensing Rupert's eyes on his back, the innkeeper turned and gave him a hard stare. Bemused, Rupert watched the pair until they were out of sight, and then he rose, putting on his new hat. There was no reason why he should take the ramblings on an old man seriously, but the innkeeper's interruption had piqued his interest. Why should the man care if his grandfather prattled to all and sundry about his past life? Unless there was something he didn't want him to talk about …

Rupert went over the conversation in his mind. It had started with highwaymen, and then turned to what he thought might be a reference to Lady Heston. The old geezer had seemed startled when Rupert mentioned her for the second time, and then clammed up. Had the man been there the night she died?

Highwaymen had a way of knowing each other, the old man had said. Could there be a connection to this particular highway robber? Probably not, but Rupert had to explore every avenue if he were to catch the thief, and surely there was no harm in looking into it.

Leaning against a vegetable cart, Cora breathed a sigh of relief. When Lord Halliford had entered the shop, she had feared she was going to have an apoplexy from the way her heart hammered in her chest. It had taken all the nerve she possessed to stay calm while she waited, but what on earth had possessed her to stare at him when he opened the door for her? The sensible thing would have been to keep eyes to the ground, but his mere presence had compelled her to look up. She must have been mad.

She was uncertain how much of her face the two men had seen on the night of the robbery, but she was certain her mask had covered the distinctive birthmark on her cheek. And she was also sure that neither of the men had guessed the thief was a woman; but what if she was wrong? Perhaps it was only a matter of time before someone saw through her disguise. If she got caught, Ned would be left to fend for himself, and he was far too frail to survive another winter on his own. What then? For his sake, as well as her own, she had to stop taking so many chances.

But the tincture is so costly. The argument she'd had with herself many times echoed in her head. Ned needed it, and there was no other way they could afford it.

'What'll it be today, dearie?'

Forcing herself to breathe slowly after her brisk trot down the street, Cora plastered on a smile and turned to the farmer's wife. 'I'll have some of your onions, mistress, and a couple of carrots, please.' With the few swedes she had left at home, she could make a stew out of the root vegetables and some leftover bacon, and with any luck Ned might have found some herbs. If she cooked it all up and left it warming over the fire, it would easily serve as two hearty meals and be far better than anything they had eaten in a while.

'And a head of cabbage, if you'd be so good,' she added, feeling flush.

'Right you are, my love.' Under Cora's watchful eye the woman selected three onions, two large, succulent-looking carrots and a cabbage, and placed the vegetables in Cora's basket.

When Cora reached for her money, she brushed against something soft and furry in her pocket and with a little squeak realised that the man's pigtail was in there, yet another piece of evidence. She brought her hand to her throat and rubbed it to dispel the sensation of an imagined noose tightening around her neck. Then she calmed herself. She hadn't been caught and her identity was still protected.

She paid the woman, who eyed her warily, as if she wondered whether Cora had escaped from Bedlam, and turned away only to collide with a broad chest in a fine royal-blue wool coat.

Lord Halliford stared down at her, and it was clear from his expression that he would not be letting her escape this time. His face was a grim mask, his hazel eyes cold, and before she had time to react, he caught her wrist in an iron grip.

'A word, madam, if you please.'

Cora looked around her desperately but who could help? The stall-holder's eyes were nearly popping out of her head with the prospect of gossip and intrigue. Who would believe a poor girl over a gentleman such as him? She had no choice but to comply.

'Not here,' he said. 'In private.' He dragged her away and Cora almost tripped over her own feet in order to keep up with him.

'I don't understand, sir,' she protested in her most innocent voice. 'Have I caused offence in any way? If so, you have my sincere apologies.'

He stopped abruptly, and Cora all but fell into his arms. 'You know perfectly well what you've done,' he snarled. A slender, manicured finger reached out and caressed her eyebrow; then ran down the side of her face to her cheekbone and birthmark. His touch was light and cool, like the brush of a feather, yet Cora's skin burned as though he had seared her with a branding iron. She jerked back in surprise, but he kept a crushing grip on her arm.

'I've never met another woman as tall as you. And I'd never forget your voice. Don't try to deny it. You and I have an appointment with the magistrate.' He proceeded to drag her further away from curious onlookers and the safety of the market. 'He's most anxious to meet you.'

Cora was sure the blood must have left her face. As she had feared, the net was tightening around her. She had to get away from him, but how?

Instead of pulling her in the direction of the magistrate's residence, to her great surprise he dragged her into the cobbled yard of The George Inn. It was quiet, enclosed on all four sides, except the alley they had walked through. Wisteria vines hung from deserted balconies, the leaves offering plenty of shelter from prying eyes. There was no one nearby, and this terrified Cora. What did he want from her? Was he planning to violate her before handing her over to the authorities? It wouldn't be the first time this had happened to a young woman on the wrong side of the law.

But it wasn't her own fate which worried her the most. It was the uncertain fate of her father. Who would care for him? The thought of him sick and abandoned made her heart ache.

Lord Halliford stopped abruptly and glanced around him as if to check that they were alone; then he swung her around to face him.

Cora swallowed hard. 'Please, sir,' she begged. 'I implore you, please do not turn me over to the authorities. I know I did wrong, but it was out of desperation. My father is ill and—'

'Spare me your sad tales,' he scoffed. 'I'm not as lame-brained as that.'

'But it's the truth, m'lord,' Cora protested. 'He suffers from an illness of the chest, and the medicine is expensive.' Was it her imagination or did he loosen the grip on her wrist a little? Encouraged she went on, 'I'll do anything, sir. Anything. I'll be your mistress if it pleases you. Anything, as long as you'll let me care for my father.'

Be his *mistress*? Jack stared at the wench, unsure whether to castigate her or simply laugh. Was there no end to her presumption?

Yet he couldn't deny his attraction to her. His fingers tingled where they gripped her wrist, and her nearness was making his blood sing, leaving him curiously light-headed. The connection he'd felt between them on the night of the robbery was still there, even more so now that she was within his grasp. His eyes slid over her figure appraisingly and settled on her bosom, which had given the game away on that moonlit night. Although it was modestly covered by a plain bodice now, and she was of slender build, close up no amount of binding would lead her to be mistaken for a boy.

Coupled with her height, her hair and the sound of her voice, there was no doubt in his mind that he was face to face with the infamous female who had robbed him.

What luck, he thought. Could it really be this easy? Only two days after this woman had robbed him at gun point – not to mention the point of her no doubt very sharp rapier – one of his mother's headaches had taken him into town, and he'd stumbled across the highwaywoman without her disguise. And now she wanted to deceive him into letting her go.

Except he wanted to know her better. That was why he had dragged her here and not to magistrate's, he realised now. He held on to her tighter to stop her from running away, pulling her close so their bodies met, and although she gasped, he had to give her credit for not flinching away. Instead she met his insulting scrutiny with her head held high and a look of defiance in her strangely coloured eyes. Jack felt something primal stir in his belly. He hadn't bedded a woman in over a year. He had begun to find courtesans boring, and gently brought up girls would expect to be wed first – so far he hadn't met any he could imagine sharing his life with. And now an incredibly beautiful woman was offering herself to him, not willingly perhaps, but as payment for his silence. All he had to do was to drag her upstairs to one of the bedchambers and have her.

Disgusted by his own train of thought, he loosened his grip on her wrist. He never *had* and never *would* treat a young woman like that, be she a lady or a serving girl. But what was he supposed to do with her? He wanted justice, didn't he? Except somehow, with her standing there looking both defiant and vulnerable, he couldn't just simply hand her over to the authorities.

Perhaps her story was true. He'd seen her in the apothecary's buying a cough tincture, which tied in with what she'd said about her father. Could he really condemn her for trying to save someone she loved – and thereby condemn her father for something he had no part in? He looked into her eyes and saw honesty, not guile, behind her defiance, and slowly he released her and pushed her away from him.

'Be assured your honour is safe with me, madam. I have no use for a mistress. I—'

He'd got no further when she cut him off with a curt, 'Good!' and took off, sprinting down the alley faster than he'd thought possible.

'Damn it all to hell!'

He set off in pursuit, but a stagecoach drawn by four sweaty horses came clattering towards him and blocked his way. He tried to get round it, but the alley was narrow and as soon as the vehicle stopped exhausted passengers began to climb down from the top seat and spill out of the coach, and he found himself in a sea of arms and legs, petticoats and carpet bags.

'Excuse me, but ...'

'Ruffian!' huffed a blowzy matron in black bombazine and an oversized mob cap. She lashed out at him with her parasol as he tried to squeeze past her, and he had no choice but to clamber through the coach and out the other side, much to the consternation of those passengers who had yet to alight.

'I say!' exclaimed one.

'Bounder!' cried another.

'Oi, you!' yelled the coachman. 'Watch where yer bleedin' goin'!'

Jack shouted a few apologies and ran out of the yard. He had lost his hat somewhere, probably inside the coach, but he had no time to stop. He *had* to catch up with the girl. He knew her name, but that was no guarantee he would find her again.

When he came out into the High Street, she had a clear head start, but Jack could still see her. He was fit and he quickly gained on her. She shrieked as he made a grab for her and dodged sideways down a narrow alley. Jack followed her but his leather shoes with their fashionable heels had nothing on his quarry's sturdy boots, and he skidded on something foul and slippery, banging his elbow against the wall as he tried to keep his balance.

Cursing, he hung on to the wall for support while he fought to combat the dizzy feeling from the knock to his elbow; then he picked up the pursuit with grim determination. If she thought she could get the better of him, she could think again. He would *make* her think again.

Suddenly he laughed. He had been on her trail ever since she'd robbed him; then chased her through town, and had, he realised now to his chagrin, enjoyed every moment of it. Miss Mardell's presence shook him alive, but it was the chase which made him see the funny side. He'd begun to take himself far too seriously. When that had started, he couldn't say –

probably when he'd decided to try and curb Rupert's excesses. His attraction to the highwaywoman had shown him that there was more to life than following his wayward younger cousin around, and for that reason he had to find her again.

Cora's heart raced wildly and her lungs felt as if they were going to explode. When she'd dashed down the alley, her pursuer had stopped, and she'd felt herself safe from him. Now he was behind her again, so close that she could hear his ragged breathing, and gaining fast. Hampered by her heavy shopping basket, which she was reluctant to let go of, it was only a matter of time before she was caught.

And then what?

In a split second she made a decision and dodged sideways again, this time hurtling through the backyard of a blacksmith. The blacksmith was using his bellows, and sparks flew as Cora tore through his workshop, with Jack hot on her heels.

'What the blazes …?'

She thought she heard her pursuer shouting an apology, but couldn't be sure. Nor did she care – her only intent was to get away. His nearness when he'd held her fast had caused her pulse to race and her breath to shorten, but despite his effect on her, she couldn't afford to trust him, or anyone else for that matter. When the opportunity to give him the slip had presented itself, she hadn't hesitated. If he thought she would walk blindly to the gallows, he was sorely mistaken.

Spurred on by fear, Cora ran as fast as her legs would carry her, out on to the High Street and didn't see the coach thundering towards her, horses springing.

Cora screamed as the horse reared, whinnying and with hooves thrashing, and she held up her arm to ward off the inevitable blow. A hoof caught her on the shoulder, and she fell to the ground with the horse kicking wildly over her.

Swearing, the coachman struggled to rein in the terrified animal, but the rattling of the pole chains seemed to antagonise it further. The eyes of the enormous beast rolled back in its head, its ears flattened and it bucked and reared, agitating the other horses. The coach jerked forward bit by bit despite the coachman's attempts at restraining the animals. Cora scrambled to get up but her arms and legs were strangely uncoordinated, and she could only crawl on her belly in the dirt.

She lost her sense of time; everything around her seemed distorted and happened with preternatural slowness. A man attempted to pull her to safety but was forced back by the thrashing hooves; a woman screamed; a crying child tugged at his mother's apron. Cora wanted to plead for help but her throat was full of dust and no sound came. Her life, for what it was worth, flashed before her eyes. Ned, Uncle George, Mr Isaacs. Her mother. Baby Tom. Choked, she mourned those she had lost and those she was about to lose.

Then a hand caught the horse's bridle. A strong, decisive hand.

'Whoa!' Lord Halliford held on tight as the horse whinnied and reared, and with his other hand he stroked it on the muzzle. 'Easy girl,' he said. 'Easy now.'

The mare tossed her head and scraped her hooves, but slowly she began to respond to Lord Halliford's calming influence. As the onlookers helped Cora to her feet, picking up the things which had spilled out of her shopping basket – mercifully only the vegetables and not her stolen goods – his lordship whispered soothing words to the horse as if they were the only souls in the world. The mare snorted and pushed against his hand in a last show of defiance, but finally accepted his mastery. Only then did he let go of the bridle.

Lord Halliford had saved her from being run over. He could have let the horses trample her to death and saved himself the trouble of bringing her to justice, yet he hadn't. Why?

'You crazy mare!' grumbled the coachman. 'You wanna kill us all?' But he was glaring at Cora as he said so and she wasn't sure whether he was referring to her or the horse.

He saved me.

The thought went over and over in her head. He didn't have to, but he did. She'd sensed his attraction to her, and couldn't deny her own attraction to him, but that still didn't change the fact that she'd robbed him, tricked him, and run from him. Gratitude mixed with shame spread in her chest that he'd still thought her life worth saving.

'You all right, dear?' The woman with the little boy, who was now bouncing on her hip with a dirty thumb in his mouth, looked at Cora with concern. ''Twas a close one, and all. Best be more careful next time you're thinking of crossing the road.'

'Y-yes, I'm all right. Thank you.' She wasn't though. Her recklessness had nearly got her killed, and then Ned would have been alone. The thought made her shake uncontrollably.

'Well, if you're sure, luvvie.' It seemed Cora's trembling hadn't escaped the woman, and she sounded uncertain.

Cora nodded. 'I'm sure.'

'Well, mind how you go, eh.' With a final glance at Cora, the woman left. The little boy stared at Cora with large frightened eyes, and it struck her just how dreadful it would have been for the child if he had witnessed a person being trampled to death by horses. Not to mention seeing a woman being dragged kicking and screaming to the magistrate's house and later hanged. It was a sobering thought.

Without turning, Cora sensed Lord Halliford's presence right behind her. Her entire body tingled with awareness of him, from the base of her scalp to the small of her back where his hand had rested when he had pulled her close. Her breath came in short bursts, both from the effect he had on her and the certain knowledge that he would likely want her severely punished for her crimes.

Slowly, she turned to face him. There was no way out now; she was too exhausted to run.

She almost laughed at the sight of him. His shorn hair stood out in all directions, like the prickles on a hedgehog; black coal dust from the smithy graced the front of his elegant blue coat, and his white silk stockings were frayed and besmirched. He looked like a scarecrow.

The finest scarecrow Cora had ever laid eyes on.

'M'lord, I …'

'Madam.'

Suddenly his hazel eyes were full of humour, and he surprised her by bowing deeply. With practised flourish, he swung, not a hat, for she saw now that he must have lost it earlier, but something round and green.

'Your cabbage, I believe.'

Cora stared at the head of cabbage in his hand, and then back at him. This was a different person to the one who had chased her with such fervour, and suspiciously she snatched it out of his hand and returned it to her basket. It must have rolled out when she'd fallen, but a quick feel in her basket, while she kept a close eye on her nemesis, told her that nothing else was missing, not even the waistcoat, which still lay tucked securely underneath the rough cloth.

He kept his eyes on her face and, mesmerised, she found herself returning the gaze despite the hotness which flared in her cheeks. The amusement was still there in his eyes, but something deeper too, a part of him which was deadly serious. Desire, passion, need. He took a step closer, bringing his face only inches from hers. Cora's breath caught in her throat, and for a long, delicious, *dreadful* moment she thought, feared – no, *hoped*, devil take it! – that he might kiss her.

Instead he took her free hand, the one not clutching the basket for dear life, and lifted it to his lips.

The pressure of his warm lips against her skin lasted only a moment, but it scorched her soul and woke a longing in her which no man had ever done before. Heat seared through her from deep in her belly, spreading, teasing and tingling in her veins until she feared she could no longer stand it. Her lips parted, and involuntarily she took a step closer.

She wanted him. Now.

Chapter Seven

The naked lust he glimpsed in her eyes slammed into Jack with the force of a river bursting a dam. He had met women intent on bedding him before, to which he had experienced merely an instinctive, tepid response from his own body.

But Miss Mardell was no saucy and skilled seductress. She was, as far as he could tell, quite the beginner in such matters, and that she should long for him in this way touched him deeply. What puzzled him was that he'd given her no reason to trust him, yet she did not run this time.

All he had to do was to reach out and do with her what he wanted. His head swam with potential scenarios, some so rude they would make even a courtesan blush, while others almost made his heart stop. His breathing became laboured, and the stirring in his groin built to an unbearable ache, straining against his breeches and begging for release.

Sometimes, in the dead of night, he lay awake and thought of the woman he would one day love, but she'd always been faceless, a shadow on the periphery of his consciousness. Now here she stood, real flesh and blood and no longer an invention, and had almost been killed in front of his eyes. His heart squeezed with fear and longing, his earlier joviality with the cabbage forgotten. He didn't want her punished or harmed in any way, but what was to be done? Perhaps he should take her back to the inn, where they could discuss it without an audience. Or better still, force her to take him to her home so she could hand back what she had stolen.

Then he saw himself as she would: commanding her one way or the other, and he did something which surprised even himself.

Dropping her hand gently, he whispered, 'Go!'

He didn't have to say it twice. With an unfathomable look she turned on her heel and left, limping a little from her fall, and Jack watched her go with a singular pang in his chest. It was fitting, he thought wryly, that her birthmark – he'd noticed it earlier when he'd traced the soft curve from her eyebrow to her cheek – should be shaped as the symbol of love.

She was frightened of him, and he understood why, but he had let her go to show her that he meant her no harm, to gain her trust. Undoubtedly she would go into hiding now, but he intended to find her again – by God he would! – and when he did, he wasn't going to let her go again.

Ever.

Rupert was on his way home when a commotion caught his attention. He told his valet, Hodges, to stay put and rode down the High Street to see what it was all about and was met by a common enough spectacle. A village girl had got herself entangled with a coach and lay on the ground in front of it with the horses threatening to bolt.

A fool of a man was trying to reach the unfortunate girl; around him people were screaming or looking horror-struck or both; dirty children were howling and wiping their runny noses on their mothers' garments. Rupert sniffed. It was all very disagreeable.

Uninterested, he stayed on his horse and treated himself to a pinch of snuff, the finest he had been able to procure while he was in London. After all, there was nothing he could do except keep well out of the way, unless he fancied getting hurt in the process of saving some low-born wench, and he most decidedly did not.

He was turning his horse around to ride back the way he'd come when he caught sight of movement from the corner of his eye. A man ran out from a yard and seemingly without thought to his own safety rushed towards the rearing horse and grabbed the bridle. The horse almost kicked the brainless buffoon in the chest, but the man managed to hold on and calm the animal down.

Grudgingly Rupert had to admit that here was a person – although clearly an imbecile for attempting such dangerous tactics – who knew almost as much about horses as he himself did.

Then his mouth fell open in surprise when he saw that the crazy hero was none other than his cousin Jack.

He urged his horse forward and opened his mouth to speak, but something held him back. Instead he retreated behind a hay wagon, from where he could watch the spectacle unfold. There was something altogether curious about Jack's appearance; he looked as if he had taken part in a bout of fisticuffs.

Saintly Cousin Jack, he snorted to himself, in a fight? Over what? A winsome country girl? Surely not!

'This I must see,' he muttered and stayed where he was.

A couple of people helped the girl to her feet while Jack pacified the horse. Then he handed the woman a head of cabbage. Rupert chuckled to himself. This was getting more and more curious, and although he was too far away to overhear any conversation, it was clear that something was going on between them.

Jack kissed the woman's hand. It was not an affectation as dictated by society, but a personal, intimate gesture, as if they were lovers. For a moment Rupert's good humour vanished and was replaced by sorrow: he had often imagined that his father must have kissed his mother like that, but his father had died when Rupert was very young, and he had no real recollection of his parents' relationship.

If his parents had lived, life would have been different. Basking in their pride, he would have gone into a profession, married a well-bred girl, and never have hankered after something he knew he couldn't have. Rupert wouldn't have been the poor relation.

If they had lived. But they hadn't.

Instead he resided in Jack's shadow as an inferior

comparison. Although his uncle, the earl, was generous enough and would no doubt settle a large allowance on him once he married, the knowledge ate away at him that Jack stood to gain everything Rupert coveted. Status, title and respect. His face a grim mask, he clenched his fists so hard at the unfairness that his fingernails dug into the palms of his hands.

If only ... He allowed himself to follow the thought to its natural conclusion. *If only Jack were dead.*

If this was the case, Rupert would inherit more than just debts, which was all his father had left him. Then no one could question either his legal rights to the estate or his moral rights.

He shook his head at where his thoughts had taken him again. Causing his cousin to be discredited elicited no qualms, but murder ...

And Jack was well on his way to ruining his own name; he really didn't need Rupert's help. Just look at the way he was simpering over the country girl. A man in his position was expected to marry well – even a mistress should be of some breeding too.

With wry amusement Rupert watched his cousin and the girl seemingly lost in each other's eyes. There was no doubt the girl was pretty, if you liked that sort of thing, but there was something else about her, a certain bearing perhaps, that intrigued him.

He narrowed his eyes and paid more attention to Jack's paramour, or whatever she was. She was wearing an ugly, plain dress and a tattered old straw hat, which was now dangling on one shoulder, attached to her neck by only a ribbon, but it was her hair, masses of dark curls, which caught Rupert's eye. It was the same colour as that of the highwaywoman, and her height and stature were similar too.

'I wonder,' he muttered to himself. Could it be that his cousin had outwitted him and already tracked down the thieving wench? *Devil take the man!*

But Jack was letting the woman go. Rupert frowned. If she really was the one who had robbed them, Jack would not have done that. So what exactly was his cousin's interest in this woman?

Intrigued, he decided to follow her.

Hidden behind the hay wagon, he turned his horse quietly and followed the woman at a safe distance down the High Street and past the tailor's, where Hodges had emerged from the shop with a large parcel under his arm and a surprised expression on his bovine face.

'Sir?'

'Not now, man, damn it!' he snarled. 'I'm on a mission. Take the parcel back to Lampton. I'll be along later.'

The valet's eyes fell on the girl, who was now about twenty yards ahead of his master; then he nodded grimly. 'Right you are, sir.'

Rupert grinned to himself. He was known for being a dandy and a bit of a ladies' man and had made no attempts at refuting this image, though if he was entirely honest with himself, it had been a while since he had encountered a female who really excited him. There was something unique about this one though.

He told himself that this had absolutely nothing to do with the fact his cousin seemed rather smitten by her.

He followed her slowly out of town, where a farmer offered her a lift on the seat of his wagon alongside a large number of children. Rupert kept even further back as the brats at the back of the wagon started to pull faces at him. He was tempted to ride up beside them and teach the little varmints a lesson, but the need to employ subterfuge stayed his whip hand.

Instead he ground his teeth and bided his time.

At Hospital Bridge the woman got down from the wagon, thanked the farmer and dove into the copse at the side of the road. When the wagon was out of sight, Rupert did the same. There was no sign of her, but Rupert wasn't concerned. If she lived in the forest, there was bound to be smoke rising from a chimney somewhere.

Sure enough, he soon spotted a thin grey column rising in the distance and headed in that direction. It wasn't easy; the forest was at its densest here, and there was no real path, only narrow tracks that could have been made by human or animal alike. He ripped his new stockings on a hostile bramble, and his wig snagged on the branch of a tree, forcing him to go back and retrieve it. Angrily, he snapped the branch in half. He was beginning to doubt the wisdom of his venture.

Just then he caught the smell of wood smoke and came upon a small clearing. He stopped and surveyed the surroundings. In the middle of the clearing sat a tumbledown labourer's cottage with a small shack a little distance away. There was no one in sight, but the door was open, so Rupert assumed that the inhabitants were inside.

He returned to the cover of the forest and under the canopy of the trees he worked his way around to the side of building, where there were no windows. Then he tied his horse to a tree, stroked the animal reassuringly, and crept towards the cottage. It seemed a good bet that this was where the woman had gone, but in order to be sure he needed to get closer. When he was halfway across the clearing, he heard voices. Agitated voices, one female, another of a lower timbre, unmistakeably male.

A husband perhaps. Or an accomplice.

'... has happened?'

'I've been ...'

'... followed?'

'... don't think ...'

Rupert stopped, overcome by indecision. It was one thing to overpower a female, however spirited she might be, but another to take on a burly male accomplice. Or *accomplices*. Just because he had only heard one man didn't mean there weren't others inside the cottage or nearby. Damn it all, why hadn't he thought to bring a pistol?

A rustle and a soft nickering startled him. From the shack a horse had stuck its nose out over a makeshift stable door and was eyeing him expectantly. He approached the beast and stroked it on its soft muzzle. The horse, a handsome gelding with a white star below the forelock, pushed gently against his hand and snorted appreciatively.

'What is it, boy?' Rupert whispered. He had always had an affinity with animals. 'Don't they feed you enough? Is that it, hm?'

The horse gave another low snort and stomped softly in the hay as if in agreement. It made Rupert wonder why he should come upon such a fine specimen by a labourer's cottage in the forest. Horses were expensive creatures; they required proper feed, not just grass and hay, plenty of exercise and expert care that a labourer couldn't afford, nor have the time for.

The animal could be stolen, of course, and if this place was indeed a thief's hideout, that fitted well enough, but he hadn't heard of any horses going missing in the area. The theft of a fine horse such as this would cause enough of a stir for the word to go around.

Another mystery.

After checking that the inhabitants of the cottage hadn't discovered his presence, Rupert opened the gate and slid inside the small stable shack. The horse welcomed him with a little nicker and allowed him to run a hand appreciatively over its back and down his flanks. Although the animal was perhaps a little on the thin side, it appeared strong and in good health otherwise.

Something else caught Rupert's attention.

He hadn't been as close to the highwaywoman as Jack had, and, given his cousin had a rapier at his throat at the time, Rupert certainly hadn't envied him the position. But whereas Jack might have got a very good look at the woman, Rupert had had his eyes on something else.

He may not pay much attention to women: courtesans were much like each other, and simpering debutantes bored him rigid. But he knew his horses.

Like the highwaywoman's horse, this beast had white markings on its front legs extending from the edge of the hoof halfway up the middle of the leg, a so-called half-stocking. Along with the star and stripe on the nose, the horse's markings were as unique as Rupert was himself.

There was no mistaking it; he had found the thieving harlot and her accomplices. But there was no way he could take them down single-handedly, and he didn't much care to try. He caressed the fine animal one more time, slipped out of the stable, and crept back to his own horse. He would have to come back with reinforcements, and soon, but as no one had attempted to flee the cottage, he suspected the criminals thought themselves safe for the time being.

They were in for a surprise.

Cora and Ned packed as many of their belongings as they could carry, leaving behind anything which wasn't necessary to their survival. Cora collected their few cooking implements in her basket, together with what food they had. The strong, salty smell of the bacon suddenly made her stomach churn, and, swallowing back her revulsion, she quickly wrapped it in a cloth and then hid the two pistols, the blunderbuss and the rapier at the bottom of her trunk.

What they owned didn't amount to much, and barely any time had passed before they were ready to leave. Cora saddled Samson, and they bundled as much as they could into the saddle bags, leaving the rest of their belongings to dangle from the pommel.

They needed to get as far away from the area as possible, and fast. Unfortunately, travelling required money, and although Cora still had a few guineas left she knew it wouldn't be enough. Holding up another coach might bring some much needed funds, but dared she do it? If she did, she'd be taking an enormous risk with her own life, as well as Ned's.

Fear settled like a hard lump in the pit of her stomach, coupled with wretchedness – because she couldn't see any other way. Then she looked at Ned, saw his slumped shoulders and how his chest heaved from the exertions of packing, and made a difficult decision.

She thought of Lord Halliford. When he'd told her to go, she'd not hesitated for a moment, but her own reaction surprised her. Even though she was still shaken after her brush with the horse, she found herself examining her feelings for *him* more than the fact that she'd nearly died. The strength of his arm as he'd held back the horse, the heat from his lips when he kissed her hand, the humour in his eyes. Each fragmented scene repeated itself over and over in her mind.

She must have lost her mind. Lord Halliford had revealed that he knew her identity – knowledge that could mean the death of herself and her father. She knew that Ned would never survive seeing his only child hanged for robbery; if that happened, she'd have his demise on her conscience as well as all her other crimes.

It was an impossible situation.

And yet, when she'd looked into Lord Halliford's eyes, she'd forgotten everything except the mad desire that swept through her. What was the matter with her? Was her brain addled? She could find no other reason for acting like such a fool. Well, no more.

A coughing fit from Ned brought her back to reality, and his frail, thin body was painful to behold. Cora helped him sit down, but – respectful of his dignity – she averted her eyes until he had the cough under control. It was some time before he was able to speak.

Ned turned a blind eye to her nightly excursions, pretending that he knew nothing of them, but the silent reproach in his eyes when she endangered herself said more than enough.

'We'll stay with Mrs Wilton,' said Ned. 'Her cottage is closer to the Bath Road, and we can travel as far as Longford tonight. I expect we'll get passage from there to the West Country on the early coach.'

Cora nodded, although her mind wasn't really on their travel plans. Fear still gripped her as she considered her scheme for another nightly excursion. It was too soon after her last hold-up, and the magistrate and his men were bound to be on high alert. Coach drivers would be armed, and passengers very likely too, but for Ned she would risk anything.

Rupert returned to the clearing in the woods with two loaded pistols and his rapier. The magistrate had proved to be immovable when Rupert had tried to persuade him, bellowing than he couldn't arrest all and sundry based on a mere hunch and accusing Rupert of wasting his time. In the end Rupert had decided that a gentleman like himself, well-versed in the use of a pistol and a blade, would be enough of a match for a woman and a couple of ruffians.

However, the place was deserted.

Hell and damnation! Frustrated, Rupert slammed the door to the cottage so hard one of the rusty hinges came loose from the door jamb. He should have cornered the woman while he had the chance. Now he didn't even have a name and not a clue as to where she'd gone.

He could stake out the cottage again in case they returned, or he could take himself off to Newgate to see the condemned highwayman in the hope that he might provide a clue to where the woman and her accomplices might go. It would require a certain amount of finesse, but he already had an idea.

Chapter Eight

Jack couldn't sleep. His mind stayed focused on what had happened earlier – the chase through town, the near-fatal accident with the coach, but most of all his own reaction to the highwaywoman. After tossing and turning for hours, trying unsuccessfully to relax, he finally gave up and pushed the covers aside. He put on a robe and retreated to the window seat, where he stared out into the night.

But he wasn't taking in the beauty of the starry sky or the perfect full moon, which shone like a pale silver disc. Before his eyes was the face of Miss Mardell. He ran his hands through his hair, and then cursed loudly when they reached where his queue had been. *Confounded hoyden!* But he had to smile at her audacity: she was magnificent.

Frowning again, he channelled his thoughts back to the woman's face, and her eyes in particular. The colour of her irises was unusual, a light grey-blue, like the moon above him. But it was something more than just her eye colour that was fascinating him: it was the combination of those eyes, her hair, and her build too. He was sure he'd seen that combination somewhere before, but where? Why did it tug at his memory so?

He jolted upright and nearly tumbled off the window seat when the answer came to him. After dressing quickly, he lit a candle and left the room. The two springer spaniels, Lady and Duke, who slept outside his bedroom door, stretched, yawned and then followed him eagerly, tails wagging. Jack bent down and fondled the ears of one of them, a tan and white female with deep brown eyes and a chocolate-coloured nose.

Lady had been with him from when she was a puppy, and she was an excellent hunting dog. She had borne him two litters, of which he had kept only Duke. In contrast to his mother, Duke had a lot to learn; he moved hither and thither on the carpeted stairwell as if pretending to be on the scent of something – hell, anything! – to please his master.

Jack gave a sharp command. 'Here, Duke, heel!'

The spaniel slunk back to his side with a sheepish expression, and with a friendly nudge Lady put her offspring in his place.

With purposeful strides Jack made his way to the family portrait gallery with the dogs trotting at his heels. When he got there, he ignored the paintings on the walls, depicting illustrious ancestors of both sexes, and traversed the length of the elegant room to a narrow door hidden in the panelling. It had no handle, but as the son and heir of the Earl of Lampton, he knew the secret of the opening mechanism. All he had to do was insert one finger into what looked like a fault in the wood and the door opened.

As a mark of the housekeeper's efficiency the well-oiled lock sprang open without a sound and, ordering the dogs to lie down in the gallery, Jack stepped inside the small storage room. It smelled faintly musty, and he resolved to do something about the dampness in the room at the first opportunity.

The room housed the china and silver service the Blythe family used only for special occasions, together with a couple of large vases, a dining chair in need of reupholstering, and extra candle-holders.

There was also a large painting facing the wall which had been placed here around the time Rupert and Alethea came to live with them. The only reason he knew about its existence was because he used to hide from his governess in the store cupboard when she wanted to test him on his Latin verbs. Jack turned it around and put it on the dining chair, then held up his candle to study it more closely. The gilded pinewood frame had been attacked by woodworm, the paint was peeling, and in places it looked as if mice had been feasting on the canvas, but the face of person in the portrait was discernible enough.

Captain Cecil Francis Blythe: the earl's first cousin, the black sheep of the family – and Rupert and Alethea's father.

And there, at last, was the answer to Jack's conundrum – the captain had luminous grey-blue eyes, so dazzling it was as if the painting had its own source of light. Just like Miss Mardell. In his mind's eye he recalled their intensity when she had met his gaze, demurely at the apothecary's, flashing with defiance in the yard of the coaching inn, and alight with longing matching his own after he'd rescued her from being trampled by the horses.

From their first encounter he had sensed a special bond between them, and here was the evidence that his mind hadn't been playing tricks on him – as well as the answer to why the memory of her eyes had kept him awake. Not only did they hold a special beauty for him because they belonged to her, but it would also seem that she might be distantly related to him, albeit on the wrong side of the blanket. The colour was surely too unusual for it to be a coincidence, and thinking about it, Miss Mardell bore a certain resemblance to Alethea as well – the black curly hair; the tall, slender frame and the magnolia skin.

Jack frowned as wonder at his discovery turned to shock and anger on Miss Mardell's behalf. Who was her mother, and how exactly did she know the captain?

I can guess, he thought with a contemptuous snort. Miss Mardell was clearly poor: if they were related, then someone in his family must have done wrong by her. His father had taken Rupert and Alethea under his wing on the death of their parents so perhaps if there was a family connection he could be persuaded to show Miss Mardell some generosity too, that way she wouldn't have to risk her life trying to provide for her family.

But if they were related, would this get in the way of his budding friendship with Miss Mardell? If her mother had been wronged by the captain, Miss Mardell would likely resent his family, and rightly so. For her sake he needed to get to the bottom of this and prise some information out of his father. A secret like this was bound to be known to the head of the family.

Unfortunately the earl was called away on business to London, and it wasn't until late the following evening that Jack finally had a chance to speak to his father alone. The earl had retired to the library and looked up when Jack entered this sacred space. Bookcases of carved mahogany with glass doors lined the room, a large roll-top desk stood against the wall between two large windows, and a colourful Turkish rug lay in the centre of the floor. Jack breathed in the scent of leather from the many bound volumes on the shelves, and was immediately transported back to his childhood, when, on a rare occasion, he had been allowed to sit with his father in the study, reverently turning the pages of one of the precious books.

This evening, however, he noticed the piles of paper on the earl's normally tidy desk, and for the first time it struck him perhaps his father might be finding it difficult to keep on top of the paperwork. The earl was getting old.

His father sat in a wing chair in front of the marble chimney piece. A decanter and two glasses stood on a side table of gilded pinewood between the chairs.

'What's on your mind, Jack?' he asked. He dropped the book of poetry he was reading into his lap and regarded his son expectantly.

Having had the possible connection between his father's cousin and the highwaywoman on his mind all day, Jack was momentarily at a loss how to begin. He poured himself a brandy from the decanter and dropped down in a chair opposite the earl. Swirling the brandy in his glass, he took a sip and looked at the fire. Flames were licking an oak log, and the only sound in the room was the faint hissing of the tree sap.

This was his father's world; a genteel existence, a place to retire after having diligently performed his daily duties and safe-guarded the family inheritance. A fire in the summer months was the earl's only real extravagance; he enjoyed his books and the quietude of the library, as well the congenial company of his family and the challenges of running a busy estate; he was not a dissolute man.

Jack had a terrible feeling that bringing up the subject of a family by-blow, and what was morally owed to her, would upset the apple cart.

'Tell me about your cousin, the captain, Rupert and Alethea's father,' he said at last.

The earl looked startled. 'My cousin? What makes you ask that?'

'I would like to know everything you'd care to tell me about him. I know he did something unforgivable, and you don't like him mentioned, but as your heir I think I have a right to know what that was.'

The earl sighed. 'Well, I suppose questions were bound to be raised one day, although I had expected it to be Rupert or Alethea asking them, not you.'

He paused and took a hearty swig from his glass; then he stared into the fire for a long time, as if painful memories made talking difficult. Finally, he said, 'Since you're the first to ask, I will answer you, but you must promise me that you won't share what I say with your cousins. I think it's only fair they hear the story from me.'

'You have my word,' said Jack.

'Well, as you know, before you were born Cecil was first in line to inherit from me – he was my first cousin and the only other Blythe male alive. I must say, your birth came as a great relief; I'm afraid Cecil was the last person I would've wanted to hand the earldom to.'

Jack leaned forward and rested his elbows on his knees. 'Why? What happened?'

'I didn't take you for a dimwit, son,' said the earl. 'There was a scandal.'

'What sort of scandal? A woman?' Jack's face reddened a little from his father's gentle rebuke.

The earl swirled the brandy in his glass and stared into the fire again. 'Affairs of the heart,' he mused, 'can have disastrous consequences. And yes, a woman was partly to blame, the catalyst, perhaps. It's a terrible thing, being in love with the wrong person.'

Jack shrugged to hide his embarrassment at the turn the conversation had taken. 'I wouldn't know, sir.'

'Never been in love?' The earl eyed his son quizzically, but Jack thought he detected an element of concern too.

'In lust, perhaps. Not love.' He was not yet decided about his feelings for Miss Mardell, but whether it was love or lust, his father would no doubt judge her to be the *wrong person*.

'Lust, yes.' His father grinned, but then his smile faded. 'That's very different to love. Love can make even the sanest person *non compos mentis*. Anyway, the lady married her betrothed and Cecil went abroad, in the hope that he would forget her. Sadly, it had the opposite effect. "Absence makes the heart grow fonder." I'm sure you've heard that expression.'

Jack nodded. 'Of course.'

'At first I thought all would be well. Cecil later married Elizabeth, and ... er, Rupert was born. Cecil's wife was a little beauty and I foolishly thought he'd chosen her because she made him forget his former love. I was mistaken.'

'How so?'

'Rupert's mother may have been lovely, but she was a biddable little thing who never questioned anything he did; she was the perfect wife for him. And while she sat at home with the newborn Rupert, Cecil was planning to elope with the married woman whom he desired above all.' The earl sighed and stared into the fire. 'It was a damnable business.'

'What happened next? Did he father an illegitimate child by this woman?'

Lord Lampton frowned. 'What makes you ask that?'

'Oh, just a guess.'

'Well, I think he might have. The woman he loved was locked in her room until the birth of the baby, at which point she seems to have escaped, but she died from complications of the birth, and the child with her. A tragic outcome.'

Jack was listening intently, but the story wasn't developing quite the way he'd envisaged. If the captain's child had died, he was still no nearer to finding out how Cora fitted in the picture. 'Could he have fathered more than one?'

'If so, I have no knowledge of it.'

'And what then?'

'Cecil had been embezzling funds to finance their elopement; when this was discovered, he was arrested. He made Elizabeth, pregnant with Alethea, bring him a pistol, and shot himself in gaol before he could be punished. Best thing for him, really, but it created quite a scandal, as you can imagine. For Rupert and Thea's sake, we never speak of it.'

Jack sat back in his chair. From the little information he'd had, he'd only known his father's cousin had died suddenly. Hearing that it was suicide, and in prison too, shook him more than he'd thought possible, and it took a moment before he could speak again. 'And who was the woman your cousin loved? The one who died?'

'It's better you don't know. It's all in the past and forgotten now.'

'Maybe not.' Jack clenched his fists in his lap as he recalled Miss Mardell's eyes.

'What do you mean?'

'The highw— a young woman, a local woman, who I, eh, have become acquainted with recently, has the same eyes as your cousin Cecil – very light grey-blue, almost translucent. Surely that can't be a coincidence?'

'The devil you say!' The earl turned to his son, visibly startled.

Taken aback by this sudden change in his father's countenance, Jack asked, 'Do you know her, sir?'

'No, not at all. How could I?' The earl swirled the brandy in his glass and then took a hefty swig. 'But it is undeniably curious. Perhaps Cecil sowed a few other wild oats in his time.'

'Yes, perhaps.' Jack decided to let the subject drop. He'd learned all he could for now and he sensed there was no point pressing his father for more answers. Perhaps he'd try again another day. He was still curious as to who Cecil's lover might have been, and his father's reaction when he'd mentioned Miss Mardell's eyes had also intrigued him. When he tracked her down again, he had a few questions for her too.

Rupert had never been to the notorious Newgate Prison, although he had driven past it a few times. The smell was legendary. It was said that shopkeepers never stood in the doorways nor displayed wares outside due to the unsavoury atmosphere in the vicinity of the prison, and Rupert certainly saw no evidence to challenge this account.

The prison was situated on the corner of Newgate Street and Old Bailey, just inside the City of London, so the traffic was heavy when they arrived. Rupert left his man-servant, Hodges, to find them a suitable inn and asked him to return and wait for him when he had done so.

He pulled a scented handkerchief out of his pocket and held it up to cover his nose, although it did little to hold the incredible stench of human filth at bay. He walked through the old city gate, with its fabled portcullis rising four storeys high between two crenellated towers, and continued on to the keeper's house, where, for a few coins, his wish to see the condemned prisoner known as Gentleman George was granted.

'Popular one, ain't he, sir?' said the prison keeper and sent him a sly look. 'Though 'is 'igh and mightiness's other visitors 'appen to be ladies, if you get my drift.' He rattled a set of keys set on a large ring and opened a hatch in the floor to the condemned prisoners' area.

Rupert had heard stories about Newgate Prison, but nothing could have prepared him for the sight which met him when he followed the prison keeper down into this subterranean dungeon, a dark room constructed entirely of stone. What appeared to be an open sewer running through the centre sent out an unearthly stench which permeated every corner.

The noise of the place was hellish, an intolerable cacophony of roaring, swearing and the ghoulish cries of those the rest of society had washed their hands of. He followed the keeper across the floor, which was strewn with all manner of filth and vermin and crunched under his feet like seaside shells strewn over a garden walk.

Some of the prisoners were manacled to the floor with hooks and chains. They lay like swine on the ground, yelling incoherently, and as he walked past some of them stretched their hands out to touch his legs and the hem of his coat. Stepping aside to avoid being grabbed, he felt as if a black cloud had descended upon him, and he could scarcely breathe, both because of the smell and the inhumanity of the place.

He knew he ought to feel pity for these poor creatures, but the only feeling he could muster was contempt for how base they had allowed themselves to become, how low they had sunk, as if they had fallen through the gate into Purgatory itself and were nothing but beasts. And what the dirt would do to his new silk shoes he hardly dared contemplate. They had cost him a pretty penny and all for nothing now.

The man he'd come to see was more fortunate than some of the other prisoners. He occupied a solitary cell at the far end of the dungeon and had been furnished with a mattress stuffed with straw and a small table with two stools, which had likely cost him an extortionate sum. How a cut-throat like

Gentleman George had come upon a large enough sum to pay for such relative luxuries was anyone's guess, but Rupert was willing to wager that one or two of the prisoner's lady visitors had something to do with this. Right now he was sitting on one of the stools, intent upon a game of solitaire with a crumpled deck of cards, and didn't acknowledge them.

'Gen'leman, someone to see you,' said the keeper, rattling his keys.

The condemned highwayman slowly peeled his gaze away from the cards and looked up at Rupert with an insolent expression. 'What for? Do I owe you money, sir? In that case, you're too late for I'll be dancing the Tyburn jig in a few days, and I haven't got a shilling to my name and no way of acquiring any either.'

'Leave us,' said Rupert to the keeper. 'I wish to speak with this gentleman alone.'

The keeper sent him an uncertain look. 'Are you sure, sir? This one's dangerous.'

'I'll be fine.' Rupert had noticed that although the condemned man lived in reasonable comfort compared to some of the other prisoners, his ankles were shackled to the floor. Dangerous the robber might be, but Rupert reckoned he stood a fair chance against a man thus restrained. And he didn't want the keeper to eavesdrop on the conversation.

'Well, it'll be on your head, sir,' said the keeper. 'I won't be held responsible if he wrings your noble neck. When you're finished, rap on the door, and I'll let you out.'

'Yes, fine,' Rupert snapped. 'Now be off.'

The keeper left them. Through the window grille Rupert watched how he kicked a couple of prisoners on his way back across the maggoty floor.

'Blood-sucking whoreson,' muttered Gentleman George. He rose and with a bow indicated that Rupert should sit down on the stool opposite him. 'Why don't you take the weight off your feet, sir, and tell me what I can do for you?'

Rupert accepted the offer of a seat but wiped it with his handkerchief before sitting down. 'It's more what I can do for you, I think,' he said. 'I've heard of your exploits, which, may I add, I have much admired, and have come to pay my respects in your hour of need.'

Gentleman George threw his head back and laughed. 'Pull the other one! I may be locked up, but I'm nobody's fool. You've come here because you want something from me, and as I haven't got anything other than the clothes on my back, I reckon it's information you're after.'

'Quite right. So it is.' Rupert placed a bottle of brandy on the table between them, along with two small glasses, a clay pipe and a pouch of the finest woodbine he had been able to procure in Hounslow. 'But first I think we need a drink. I find that a conversation is always more enjoyable with a bit of brandy inside to warm a person up.' *And it loosens the tongue*, he thought to himself.

Gentleman George's eyes lit up. 'Very generous. Very generous indeed, sir. Can't fault you, and it is, as you say, my hour of need. Haven't had a drop since the day they caught me. Ironic, one might say, that enjoying a drink, which is what gave me the greatest pleasure in life, will be the death of me,' he added with a wink.

'That certainly is ironic,' said Rupert, 'but here, let me pour you some brandy while you stuff your pipe.' He popped the cork and poured them both a generous measure. 'To you – may your dance at Tyburn be a short one.'

'Amen to that, sir.' George emptied his glass in one; then licked his lips and held it out for a refill.

Rupert obliged him, and, raising his own glass, took a small sip.

'Ahh, that's better.' Gentleman George knocked back his second drink. 'Makes me feel like a man again. You seek information, you say. What kind of information?' He held out his glass.

'I seek a highwayman.'

'Well, seems like you've found him.'

'I seek a different highwayman,' Rupert said and gripped his glass tightly so as not to wipe the smug grin off the other man's face with his fist. 'A young man, a lad really, who has been putting the fear of God into the people of Hounslow and surrounds for a good few months, holding up coaches and riders.'

'A young man, you say?' Narrowing his eyes, Gentleman George emptied his glass again. 'I've not heard of any young lads robbing coaches, and it's only been a few weeks since I was outside of this place. Of course I don't know everything that goes on, but I do know a fair bit. You wish to apprehend this young rascal?'

Rupert shook his head. 'Not apprehend. I wish to talk to him.'

'And why do you want to talk to this young man?' Gentleman George reached for the bottle and poured himself another glass. His hand trembled slightly, and he sloshed brandy beside the glass. Having filled it to the brim, he lifted it to his lips, but drank only a little.

The highwayman was suspicious now, Rupert could see that. He would have to proceed very carefully. He assumed that the robber in question was known to Gentleman George, and, if so, he would be well aware this was no boy, but a woman. The question was, were they on friendly terms, or were they enemies? Gentleman George was caught because someone had betrayed him – or so the story went – and it wasn't impossible that that someone was the highwaywoman, or perhaps an associate of hers. If they were deadly enemies, Gentleman George would have no scruples about selling her out.

If, on the other hand, they were allies, or even companions, Rupert sensed that this man, however low he had sunk and however soon he would feel the rope around his neck, wouldn't give her away, not for all the brandy in the world.

'The thing is,' he said, proceeding cautiously, 'I want to talk to this young highwayman because I need to warn him. You see, he made the mistake of holding up a cousin of mine the other night, and I'm afraid my cousin is very observant. He noticed one or two things about this young rascal which, shall we say, made him determined to meet up with ... him ... again.'

Gentleman George scowled at him, suspicion still lurking in his eyes. 'What sort of things would that be?'

'Something that made him feel rather amorous, I'm sorry to say. In short, my cousin believes the young scoundrel to be a woman.'

'Never.' George's voice wobbled ever so slightly, giving away the fact that he was getting nervous. Rupert decided to continue prodding.

'Oh, yes, no doubt about it. And my cousin is a great one for the ladies, I have to say. Once he sets his sights on a particular wench, there's no stopping him. Now he reckons that the young lady wouldn't be holding up coaches off her own bat. She must have been taught by someone, or forced even, and who better than a master highwayman?' It had to be someone close to her and presumably occupations like that ran in the family like any other. 'Perhaps a relative of hers?' he finished, and was pleased to see George's knuckles turn white because he was gripping his glass so hard.

'A likely tale,' the man spat, but he wouldn't look Rupert in the eye.

'No? Well, let me tell you, my cousin has been making enquiries, and the net is beginning to tighten around the lady and her accomplice. Soon they might find themselves in the same position as you, unless the lady is handed over to my cousin. Trust me, my cousin's ruthless enough to use every means at his disposal and I just want to warn her. I'm all for law and order, but it pains me to see a woman's virtue threatened in this manner and it would pain me even more to see her hang for something she'd been made to do by unscrupulous relatives. I'm quite sure it's not her fault.'

'The devil you do! I don't believe a word of it.'

'But you do know the name of this highwayman? Don't bother denying it; I can see it in your eyes.' Rupert leaned forward, making his gaze as threatening as he possibly could. 'You'd better tell me, or I'll make damned sure you'll suffer a lingering death. Imagine that hempen rope squeezing your windpipe, your legs kicking out for purchase, your bowels loosening. You're looking at a long, slow, painful death.'

Gentleman George blanched, but spluttered, 'Never!'

Rupert pressed home his advantage – he could see the highwayman's hands trembling now. 'Trust me, there are ways of prolonging your Tyburn dance. I know the beadle and he's an expert. A tidy sum and ...' He let the threat hang in the air.

After a lengthy silence, George whispered, 'It could be Mardell, but then again maybe not.' The word came out as if slowly torn from his body, his eyes seemed sunken and hollow, his shoulders hunched. *A broken man,* Rupert thought and almost felt pity for him. Almost, but not quite.

'Mardell, is it? Well, thank you for that very useful piece of information.' With a smirk Rupert rose. 'And now I must bid you goodb—'

He never finished the sentence. Gentleman George jumped up from his seat with a roar, knocking over the rickety table. The brandy bottle and the glasses toppled to the floor and smashed into a thousand pieces. Before Rupert had time to think, the man's hands were around his neck. 'You mangy cur! You son of an ill-gotten whore! A pox on you!'

He tried to wrench free, but the highwayman had him in an iron grip and was shaking him like a rag doll. Rupert felt his lungs burn and his eyes pop. The room swam around him and grew darker, until he was on the very edge of consciousness. He saw his life before him and then darkness began to take over completely ...

Suddenly he was pulled free and thrown roughly to the ground, coughing and spluttering. When he became aware of his surroundings again, he realised he was lying face down in the dirty straw with his hand on something soft and foul. Horrified, he sat and scrambled away from the lumpy bundle next to him.

'I told you he was dangerous,' said the keeper, 'but you didn't believe me, did you?' A hand came down and yanked Rupert to his feet. It was then he noticed that the bundle on the ground was Gentleman George, and that the keeper was holding a truncheon in his hand.

'Trust me, 'e won't be getting up for the rest of the day.' The keeper hawked up a gob of spit and aimed it at the condemned man, who lay on the ground moaning faintly. 'Scum o' the earth, the lot o' them!'

Rupert wiped his hands on his handkerchief, tossed it to the ground and straightened his clothes and his wig as best he could. He hesitated for a moment, and then aimed a kick at the man on the floor, which caught him in a tender place judging by the growl he emitted. He had got what he came for, he hoped, but his best riding jacket was ruined, and someone had to pay.

The keeper laughed. 'Let's get you out of here, sir. Leave the vermin to 'is miserable life. Ain't much of it left anyhow.'

When Rupert was halfway across the vaulted dungeon, Gentleman George shouted at him; after the beating he was only just loud enough for Rupert to hear.

'You leave Ned's girl alone! If you as much as touch one hair on her head, I swear, as God is my witness, I'll come back and haunt you! You'll never know sleep again!'

Rupert paid him no attention. It was an empty threat if ever he'd heard one – he didn't believe in ghosts. This world was for the living.

Chapter Nine

After the conversation with his father, Jack was even more determined to see Miss Mardell again, and he set off early next morning with Lady and Duke gambolling at his heels to track her down. The apothecary had said she lived in the woods, and if he concentrated on the triangle he'd marked on the magistrate's map, he was confident he would find her.

Saddling the horse with only the help of a bleary-eyed stable lad, he dismissed the boy's offer to accompany him and followed the road out towards Heston Mill. It had rained in the night, and the muddy, pot-holed road glistened silvery-brown in the pale morning light. Passing the gibbets on the Heath, where they had been erected to strike fear into the hearts of anyone contemplating breaking the law, he averted his eyes and held a handkerchief to his face against the stink of decay.

Crows circled the caged skeletons, and Jack felt a shiver run down his back. Although he had no doubt these criminals deserved a harsh punishment for their crimes, there was something ungodly about the sight of a man's bones being picked clean by birds. Could the souls of these unfortunates ever be at rest, he wondered?

When he reached the mill, he turned off the road and made his way south, with the magistrate's map and the ink dot sightings firmly imprinted on his mind. Dense heather glimmering with moisture made riding difficult and cumbersome, but here and there tussocks of blue-green grass provided a safer footing for Jack's horse. Soon low bushes and heather gave way to woodland, and as he followed a path of worn grass and compacted mud, the trees grew denser.

Duke took the opportunity to explore, running from tree to tree on the trail of a scent only perceptible to dogs, and Jack brought him back with a sharp command. The spaniel slunk back to his master, tongue lolling, and didn't seem penitent at all.

'Stay!' Jack grumbled.

He stopped and listened, but all he could hear were the squabbling crows in the distance and raindrops dripping from leaf to leaf. Pulling his cloak tighter around him, he urged his horse into the thicket. He was acting purely on a hunch, but the pattern of the robberies and the need for the perpetrator to get off the road and out of sight as quickly as possible told him that the highwaywoman had to have a hideout somewhere in the centre of that pattern.

'That's what I would do,' he muttered, partly to convince himself that this wasn't a complete fool's errand and partly to quell the uncanny feeling that he wasn't welcome here, that he was being watched.

The sun had come out and cast a dappled light among the trees. Jack attempted to keep heading south, although on several occasions he was hindered by thorny brambles or trees with low branches threatening to unhorse him.

A fallow deer burst out of the thicket. The horse whinnied and reared, taking off in fright, and before Jack could get it under control, a low-lying branch knocked him out of his seat. He landed in an uncomfortable and undignified heap in the wet undergrowth. The dogs came running as if to make sure he was unharmed, their guarding instincts to the fore.

'Hell's teeth!'

Momentarily winded, he lay on the ground; then he got up and brushed dirt and wet leaves off his clothing. He looked around for his horse, but it had disappeared, and he swore long and fluently. It probably hadn't gone very far, he thought, and felt encouraged by that. With the forest as dense as it was, it wouldn't take long before the reins got caught on a branch.

He glanced around him again and saw that there was a clearing just ahead of him in the woods. Cautiously, he sneaked towards a tree and peered into the open space, still sheltered by the dense bushes and undergrowth. At the other end of the clearing he spied a dilapidated labourer's cottage, almost hidden by a row of thick brambles. Jack eased closer while he tried to think of a suitable excuse as to why he was here in the forest, by what was clearly someone's home. If it turned out to be the home of the highwaywoman herself – and he was quietly confident it might be – he could only hope that she wouldn't bolt at the sight of him. He felt for his rapier, which he had buckled on when he left; if she felt herself backed into a corner, he had no doubt that she would defend herself, but he hoped it wouldn't come to that.

He could have saved himself the worry. A surreptitious glance through a window told him the cottage was empty. The fire had been put out and all was quiet. It seemed probable that the occupant wouldn't be back for some time. *Damnation!* Jack considered searching the cottage for evidence of a highwaywoman's activities, but thought it best to leave the place undisturbed. If this really was her hideout he did not want to alert her to the fact that someone was on her trail.

Behind the cottage he found his horse inside a lean-to munching away at a remnant of hay. Following him obediently, Lady and Duke sniffed around.

'I might have known,' he muttered. 'Always filling your belly, aren't you?'

The lean-to appeared to be some sort of makeshift stable. So whoever lived in this cottage owned a horse; not something most farm labourers could afford. He made a mental note of that. He also wondered where the horse was; if the occupants of the cottage were helping with the harvest, they wouldn't bring their horse, and it was far too valuable to leave on its own. Then he looked around him and thought he had the answer. Grass grew sporadically among the trees; probably the owners had led the horse further into the woods, where it could graze undisturbed. It could be anywhere.

Taking his horse by the bit, Jack began to drag it outside, but having found warm, dry hay, the animal wasn't prepared to come willingly. It tossed its head and tried to nip him.

'If you don't come this instant, I'm going to sell you to the bloody pie-maker.' Jack cursed and pulled hard at the reins, and the horse reluctantly accepted his authority.

Leading the recalcitrant beast, he walked around to the other side of the cottage to investigate further. To his surprise he found what looked like a well-tended grave, or rather two graves, with weather-beaten boards serving as headstones. One carved board was smaller than the other; a child, he thought, and was overcome by a sudden sadness. He remembered well his anguish when his little brother, a boy of two and a half, had died from congestion of the lungs.

Henry had been a mischievous little cherub with dark curls and cornflower-blue eyes, very like his cousin Alethea. His loss had left a gap in the family, dulled his mother's smile, and cast a splinter in his heart.

Although he felt as if he was intruding upon this poor family's private grief, he tethered his capricious horse, knelt by the larger of the two graves and brushed the vegetation aside to read the faint inscription.

Sarah Mardell (nee Duval)
b. 1730 d. 1759
Beloved wife and mother
Reunited with her mistress

Jack frowned at the woman's family name. Having learned his nation's and county's history, he was familiar with the name of Duval. A gallant and courteous rogue, Claude Duval was probably the most dashing highwayman ever to haunt the roads of England.

Some of his exploits had taken place on Hounslow Heath, where one version of a famous story recounted that he had held up a coach and danced with a lady who played the flageolet, after which he had robbed her of only one hundred pounds of a four-hundred-pound booty, allowing 'the fair owner to ransom the rest by dancing a coranto with him on the Heath'. Like so many others of his ilk Duval had ended his days at Tyburn almost a hundred years ago, but the romance prevailed.

And there was something else. A story closer to home, more recent than the exploits of the legendary highwayman.

Lady Heston, the wife of his neighbour Lord Heston, had – sick with childbed fever and grief after the birth of a stillborn daughter – taken off in the middle of the night with only a young, inexperienced maid for company. The coach had later been found abandoned, with Lady Heston dead inside, clutching the stillborn baby, and her valuables and the maid gone.

A manhunt had ensued, but no one had managed to track down the elusive maid, who at best deserved to be punished for thieving, or worse, for luring the sick woman into a vulnerable situation and hastening her demise. He couldn't remember the name of the maid, but the word "mistress" on the gravestone caught his attention. Who else had a mistress but for a servant? Perhaps the chit's name had been Duval.

Only one person might be able to answer his questions. As he returned to his horse, he was deep in thought. The barking of his dogs brought him back to the present; he looked up and saw them jumping around a familiar figure.

Miss Mardell.

He raised his eyes and pinned her with a stare. So she hadn't left yet. Why, he wondered. Could the torrential rain the previous night have prevented her from travelling, or was there another reason, something to do with him? No, that was just hope. But why had she come back here? She must have known he was likely to track her down.

Then he glanced back at the grave and realised this place must have a special meaning to her.

'Well, if it isn't Miss Mardell,' he said, noting her disquiet at the way his dogs had her trapped. Lady and Duke wouldn't harm her, but he would let her believe it if it meant he could talk to her.

'M-my lord,' she stammered and backed away from the dogs a little. 'How do you know my name?'

'The apothecary.'

'I see.' She raised her chin. 'What are you doing here?'

'That's obvious, isn't it? I'm looking for you. I feared you might have left for good, but here you are.' He smiled at her and felt his insides curl when she smiled back briefly. Then she turned wary again.

'I had left, but ...' She glanced at the grave behind him; then asked curtly, 'Why were you looking for me? You let me go, if you recall.'

'Well, for one thing I wanted to see you again and, for another, I wanted to ask you some questions. But first I'd like you to do something for me.'

'What can you possibly want from me, unless it is to serve you in one capacity or other?' Backing further way from the dogs, she sent him a haughty look.

Jack marvelled at her self-possession even as the double-meaning of her words shamed him a little. With one hand placed on her hip and her strange eyes blazing defiance, she was challenging him despite being at a total disadvantage. Again, he found himself amazed and even more determined to help her whether she was a distant relation or not – to risk her life holding up coaches she must be desperate.

The thought had formed in his mind when he'd seen the captain's painting, and he had been contemplating it since then. He had never resented that the earl had taken his orphaned relatives under his wing – it was only natural – but it did irk him a little that his father refused to see Rupert for what he was, a spendthrift and a gambler. His father paid for

Rupert's excesses without complaint; if Miss Mardell was a relation too, she deserved the same generosity.

But first he had to convince her.

'I'd like to introduce you to my family,' he replied.

'I beg your pardon?' She cast him a suspicious glance; then spread her hands wide. 'But I have no lady's clothes, m'lord. This is my finest gown. It serves me well enough for church' — she tossed her head at that — 'but it wouldn't be fitting in Society.'

'No need to worry about that. I'll provide you with something. The clothes themselves are unimportant. What matters are your eyes. I have reason to believe that you're the daughter – illegitimate child, if I may be so bold – of my father's cousin, Captain Cecil Francis Blythe. He had eyes the same as yours.'

To his surprise the girl threw her head back and laughed. The sound, soft and musical, echoed in the empty forest and, entranced, Jack stared at the movement of her slender neck and the way her full lips stretched over a set of strong, white teeth. Blood thrummed in his ears, and a familiar warmth spread in his belly.

Those lips ...

'M'lord, you're jesting. How could I possibly be related to you, even distantly? I see no resemblance at all. Anyway, what makes you the authority on a person's eyes? I'm sure they cannot be that unusual.'

'It's not just the eyes. You look a bit like my Cousin Alethea too, Cecil's daughter.'

The girl sobered and pierced him with a look. 'You flatter me, sir, to liken me to a high-born lady, but I'm afraid you're mistaken. My father's name is Ned, and my mother was Sarah, and never was a couple more devoted to each other. Besides I fancy I take after my father in looks.'

'If you would only come with me to Lampton to see the captain's portrait for yourself, perhaps you might change your mind.'

'And dolling me up like a lady? What's the purpose of that?'

'On the night of the robbery, you spoke in a very common manner – to hide your identity I assume. But I've had the pleasure of speaking with you since, and your diction reveals a certain level of education.'

'My mother taught me to read and write,' she said and stuck out her chin. 'She was a lady's maid, and her mistress saw to her education.'

'Just so. If you were to wear a lady's dress, it would make the resemblance more noticeable. Without the distraction of your – pardon me – simple clothes, we're more likely to convince my father that he must do right by you,' said Jack. 'If you're family, he should help you.'

The girl scoffed at that. 'Do right by me! I'm not saying I believe you, but if what you claim is true, that I am the illegitimate child of this captain of yours, an earl will have no reason to believe he needs to see me right.'

'We'll see about that,' said Jack.

The girl muttered a most unladylike oath, and it was Jack's turn to laugh. She really was quite delightful. 'What is your name?' he asked, although he already knew her surname.

'Cora,' she replied almost reluctantly. 'Cora Mardell.'

'And I'm Jack. Well, Cora Mardell, do we have a deal?'

Jack sensed her indecision. She was clearly not convinced by what he had told her, but if she carried on robbing coaches, whatever her reasons, she would get caught eventually and no doubt hang for it. He couldn't let that happen.

He suspected from the way she was chewing her lip that she was intrigued by his claims. That she was itching to get away from him was evident too, but his dogs sat either side of her and she probably knew he could make them trip her up if he commanded it. Besides, he would catch her soon enough if she tried to make a run for it – he had a horse right here, and she didn't.

All in all, he had her pretty well cornered. Along the line

the wager with Rupert had lost its importance; helping Miss Mardell, whether she appreciated it or not, had become far more important, not to mention the prospect of spending time in her company. She fascinated him and made him want to be a better man. And he could not deny the chemistry between them.

'Well?' he said, one eyebrow raised. 'I'm waiting for an answer.'

She looked to be on the verge of replying when a rabbit bolted out of a nearby hole and both dogs took off in pursuit, barking with excitement. It happened so fast Jack didn't have a chance to call them back, and Cora must have seen him hesitate. She didn't.

'The answer is no!' she shouted and dove off into the undergrowth, disappearing faster than the rabbit and its pursuers.

Jack was about to follow, but then shook his head and stayed put. What was the point? She probably knew these woods better than anyone and she'd lead him a merry dance before getting him lost.

'Bloody hell,' he muttered. He'd thought her convinced, but she was obviously still wary of him. Could he blame her? Not really. He had the power to unmask her as a notorious highwayman and criminal, and not doing so would be a dereliction of duty for any honourable man. She would be well aware of that and he hadn't exactly given her proper reassurances that he wasn't going to take her to the magistrate. If he'd been in her shoes, he wouldn't have trusted him either.

He whistled for the dogs, who trotted back and looked shamefaced as he scolded them. 'You are a daft pair,' he told them, but he knew they found rabbits irresistible.

As for Miss Mardell – Cora – he'd have to find some other way of convincing her.

Chapter Ten

Before he did anything else, Jack wanted to find out more about the name he'd seen on the grave marker: Duval – perhaps it would help him discover whether Cora really was related to Captain Blythe. He needed to talk to Mrs Bartlett, Lord Heston's cook.

Lord Heston was their nearest neighbour, and although the two families were not close, they maintained neighbourly relations. It was too early to call on his lordship when Jack arrived, so he rode around to the servants' entrance. Bartlett was in the kitchen kneading dough in a bowl while a maid was scrubbing the floor and another tending a large oven beside the open kitchen hearth. When the cook saw Jack, she left her work and hugged him in a cloud of flour.

'Well now, and if it ain't my favourite young'un!' she exclaimed and pinched his cheek.

This was a blatant lie; anyone who took the trouble to visit Mrs Bartlett in her domain and sample her cooking was a favourite, except perhaps Lord Heston himself. She commanded Jack to step inside and made him sit down at the scrubbed kitchen table, where she poured him a tankard of ale. Then she proceeded to ply him with home-made biscuits and sweetmeats.

'Just the ale, please, Bartlett,' Jack said, holding up his hands. He added with a grin, 'Or a glass of brandy if you have it.'

Pretending to cuff him over the head, to the consternation of the maids who were watching, goggle-eyed, Mrs Bartlett harrumphed. 'You horrid boy! Brandy? At this hour? And what would your father think? I bet the earl'd have a thing or two to say about that, you wastrel.'

Coming from Mrs Bartlett, the words stung. As a boy Jack

had often visited Bartlett, mainly because the irascible French chef in his father's kitchens hated the sight of children. He had come to regard the Hestons' cook as a friend. She was more astute than many others, and though she had always been pleased to see Jack, she was less welcoming to Rupert. Now, as she mock-scolded him, he had to remind himself that it was his own fault she thought the worst of his London exploits, but he had learned that Rupert seemed more able to control his excesses when Jack was around so it was a price he had to pay. He sincerely hoped Bartlett didn't mean it.

'It would be the cane for me, I'm afraid,' he joked.

Mrs Bartlett put her floury hands on her wide hips. 'Oh, you *are* the devil!' Then she turned serious. 'I heard as how your carriage was held up. Are you all right, my lad?'

'Was it a highwayman, sir?' The scullery maid had stopped scrubbing the floor and was staring at Jack with large, round eyes. 'Did 'e fire a pistol an' all?'

'Oh, hold your tongue, girl!' Mrs Bartlett snapped but her gaze was on Jack.

'He did indeed.'

Both women gasped.

'We came to no harm,' Jack went on, reassuring them all. 'This was a true gentleman of the road, so to speak, and he was kind enough to relieve us only of our valuables.' He didn't mention the rapier and the cold glint in Cora's eyes. No need to upset Mrs Bartlett any further.

Mrs Bartlett crossed her arms over her ample bosom and regarded him with small, piggy eyes in her broad face. Jack met her steely gaze, but was the first to look away.

'Don't you try pulling the wool over my eyes, young fellow,' she said. 'I've known you since you were a babe in arms. I also heard tell that the brigand cut off all your hair, although I can see with my own two eyes that it ain't quite true. Still, you seem to be missing a fair bit.'

Jack ran his hand through his hair to the nape of his neck,

in a gesture which had almost become second nature. He'd tried tidying the hair up, but it still insisted on sticking out in all directions. 'The scoundrel's idea of a joke, I suspect.'

The kitchen maid suppressed a giggle, and Mrs Bartlett glared at her. 'Not very funny, was it, with him getting a knife out and all?' She returned to her dough, kneading it angrily, as if she imagined pounding the robber's face with her beefy fists. 'Anyway, as long as you're all right is what matters. The Lord willing, they'll catch the miscreant soon, and the good folk around here can sleep soundly in their beds again.'

'Let's hope they do,' Jack said, and hoped they didn't.

Bartlett would be horrified if she knew he was aware of the robber's identity and wasn't planning to hand her over to the authorities. He longed to explain, but realised that in this instance, and whatever desperation had driven Cora to her crimes, he didn't think he and Bartlett would see eye to eye. And why should she, he conceded. As far as the cook was aware, this highway robber was dangerous, as most of them undoubtedly were. Therefore the fewer people who knew, the better, for Cora's safety.

The subject brought to a suitable close, for the time being at least, Jack considered broaching the other matter. It was after all the reason he was here. He would have to tread very carefully though if he was to avoid arousing Mrs Bartlett's suspicions: he was willing to swear Lord Heston's cook could read minds.

He sipped some of his ale and stared out the window, putting on a pensive expression. 'All this talk of highwaymen has put me in mind of that old story about the first Lady Heston. Her coach was found near the road, was it not? I wonder if she was held up by a gentleman of the road too.'

Mrs Bartlett shook her head. 'Now why would you be going and reminding me of that? What a tragic business, and no mistake.'

'I was merely curious and thought it a possibility.'

'Aye, it's possible, and I've thought so myself many a time.'

'Do you have any idea why the lady would put herself at risk in such a way? Was she not herself perhaps?'

The cook eyed him sharply, and Jack schooled his features into a neutral expression. Then she shrugged. 'Oh, well, I suppose there's no harm in telling you. It's so long ago now, and at any rate most of it is already known in the neighbourhood. There was trouble in his lordship's marriage, with the master occasionally insisting Lady Sophia weren't allowed out of her room. He were away when Lady Sophia was confined. It was a difficult birth, but then they often are with the first one, or so I've heard. Lasted thirty-six hours and counting, with the babe being the wrong way around. There were fears both and mother and child would die. None of us were getting a wink of sleep, and I was called in the night to bring some chicken broth. Had to feed Lady Sophia like a child: God rest her soul, but she didn't have the life left in her to hold the spoon.'

She paused, and a shadow crossed her face. 'I remember her whispering to me as I fed her, so I leaned closer, like, to hear. "Bartlett," she said to me, "is my daughter very beautiful?" "Aye," I said, "as beautiful as yourself and more, m'lady, with masses of dark hair and a right lustful pair of lungs on her." I thought that would please her, you see, but she went even paler than before, although I'd never thought it possible. She was like a ghost already.'

'So the baby was doing well?' asked Jack. He experienced the familiar pang when he thought of little Henry as well as the tiny grave in the woods.

Bartlett nodded. 'Oh, I remember it as if it were yesterday. Not something you forget in a hurry, the way my lady screamed. Aye, the wee thing seemed to me like she was going to pull through all right, but never having had a babe meself who am I to say? I remember thinking that his lordship weren't going to be pleased about it being a girl and would probably rather the babe died. Of course, he got his wish, didn't he?'

Mrs Bartlett lifted the dough of out the bowl, sprinkled some flour on the kitchen table, and pummelled it into the shape of a large loaf. Watching her knuckles making deep indentations in the dough, Jack could guess who the cook imagined she was clobbering now.

'What happened then?' he prodded gently, although he knew the gist of the story. Everyone around here did.

'She took off, that's what happened,' came the terse reply, 'but where she found the strength only God knows. Crazy as a coot, although it pains me to say it.' Mrs Bartlett shook her head in disbelief and muttered something unintelligible. 'She and the babe were found a couple of days later. His lordship said at first it couldn't be his wife and refused to have the body in the house. But some of us, meself included, were asked to identify her on oath and he had to accept it. I always said he was too shocked to believe it, the poor man. Crazed with grief.'

This was the opening Jack had been waiting for. 'Didn't she have help though? A maid went with her?'

'Oh, yes. Sarah, her name was. Sarah Duval.' Mrs Bartlett nodded, and then sent Jack a sharp look. 'Terrible things they accused her of, but I said it back then and I'm saying it again now: 'tis all lies. That one wouldn't hurt a fly. She was as gentle as they come, a slip of a girl, not much older than your cousin Alethea is now, and delicate with it. Almost like a lady herself, but with no airs and graces, mind. Not like the hoity-toity madam what's looking after my Lady Heston now.'

She launched into a tirade over the uppity maid. '… thinks herself better than the rest of us, with her going on about how working in a fine house will throw her into the path of a gentleman who'll marry her and buy her fine clothes. I've never heard such foolishness in my life, when everyone knows there's them and there's us, and, begging your pardon, Master Jack, but the two don't mix and that's all there is to it.'

Mrs Bartlett placed the dough on a bread paddle and

pushed it in the oven; then she wiped her hands on her apron and sat down opposite Jack with a mug of ale.

'Only this morning she said something to Jane here' — she nodded in the direction of the kitchen maid — 'about her having similar prospects, and I said to her she had no business filling Jane's head with silly ideas, and that nothing will come of it except trouble.'

'Quite right, Bartlett,' Jack said non-committally. He let her words wash over him. He wasn't interested in the maid and her misguided opinions. Instead he wondered how he was going to get Mrs Bartlett back on the subject of Sarah Duval. Then he remembered the last line on the makeshift headstone out in the woods: *Reunited with her mistress.*

'Was the first Lady Heston's maid very fond of her mistress?'

Mrs Bartlett nodded. 'What? Oh, her. Yes. Loved her with a passion, did Sarah. It was always, "Lady Heston says this, Lady Heston did that," like there was no one else on earth whose good opinion mattered to her. I always thought ...' The cook paused and looked over Jack's shoulder with a wistful expression in her eyes. 'I always thought if I'd ever had a daughter of me own that she'd be a lovely one such as sweet little Sarah, but it's more likely any children of mine would have been like me sister's brood. Brazen hussies the lot of them, leaving her to fend for herself in her old age. Sarah wouldn't have abandoned anyone. I'm sure of it.'

'So can you explain why she wasn't with Lady Heston when the carriage was found?'

Mrs Bartlett shook her head. 'Never made much sense to me. She wouldn't have left her ladyship's side unless she had a very good reason. Perhaps someone scared the poor girl away. Or abducted her.' She shuddered. 'You hear such horrible things. Shouldn't wonder at it if she was raped and murdered even.'

'Perhaps Sarah feared that she would be blamed for Lady Heston's death,' Jack suggested.

'Perhaps.' Mrs Bartlett's face was grim. 'Though I dare say she'd have stayed to look after the babe. I've always thought, with that little 'un seemingly in such good health, that she must have succumbed because Sarah weren't there to look after her. When they found the carriage, it was plain to see the wee scrap had been dead for some time.'

Jack sat up straighter as a thought struck him. Maybe the maid wasn't the clue to the mystery after all, but the baby. 'Did you see the infant yourself when they brought Lady Heston back?'

'Aye, all cold and purple-skinned she was, and sort of faded at the same time, if that makes any sense.'

Jack felt a shiver run down his back and he raised his eyebrows. 'Faded?'

'The baby's hair had sort of lost its colour, if you like, but with the death hue on her skin it was hard to tell. One dead baby looks much like another, I suppose, and it were dark, weren't it, when mother and child were laid out the next evening. I remember having to send out for extra candles.'

Frowning, Jack stared at Mrs Bartlett, not quite willing to believe where his thoughts were taking him. Was it possible that the maid had switched Lord Heston's baby girl for another? And if so, why?

Mrs Bartlett cleared the cups away, but her gaze never left Jack's face. Narrowing her eyes suspiciously, she said, 'I don't see you often, my boy, and today you only see fit to plague me with burdensome questions. Why? Have you any news?'

'I have reason to believe that Sarah Duval is dead.'

'Well, and haven't we thought so for a long time?' Mrs Bartlett wiped away a tear with her apron. 'Still, 'tis sad to have it confirmed. The poor, misguided girl. How came you by this news?'

'She died a wife and mother,' Jack said in the hope of easing Mrs Bartlett's distress. 'I've seen her grave and it seems she was well loved.'

Mrs Bartlett found a cotton handkerchief in the pocket of her apron and blew her nose with a spectacular trumpeting sound. 'A small blessing, I suppose. The girl made something of her life, then. A lesson for you two feckless girls,' she said to the maids, but there was no venom in her sting.

'It still pains me that people said such terrible things about her,' she continued. 'Especially his lordship. It were like he blamed her for everything, and, like it or not, I've never quite forgiven 'im for that.'

The kitchen maid patted the cook on the back awkwardly, and Jack said, 'Now, now, Bartlett, I'm sure you have. Why else would you still be here? And you know that if you should ever tire of the Heston household, Lampton would welcome you with open arms.'

Having dried her eyes, Mrs Bartlett shook her head. 'Oh, aye, and I'd be fighting over me own kitchen with that Frenchie cook of your father's. No, thank you kindly. His lordship may not be the kindest of masters, but I'm perfectly content here and that's not likely to change.'

He left Mrs Bartlett before lunch. Retrieving his horse from the stable lad, Jack tossed the boy a coin, and then left the way he had come, avoiding the main thoroughfare to the house. It wasn't exactly befitting his station in life to go visiting the servants and not their masters, and as he had learned what he needed from Mrs Bartlett, he saw no reason to speak to Lord Heston about the matter. If there was a connection between Cora and Lady Heston's baby, however unlikely that was, he didn't want to discuss it with Lord Heston until he knew more. It was an old family tragedy of which he was certain his neighbour didn't need reminding, and besides, it had been difficult enough to find a pretext for raising the subject with Mrs Bartlett.

Lord Heston was nobody's fool either. Quite the contrary.

Unfortunately, skirting the edges of the estate wheat fields, he chanced upon Lord Heston and Kit. Jack swore inwardly.

'Halliford? What brings you here?' asked Lord Heston as he reigned in his horse and raised his hat in greeting. 'Has the earl given proper thought to my proposal about the north field?'

Clearing his throat to reply, Jack nodded a greeting at Kit, but the boy kept his face lowered. Jack frowned, and then noticed the purplish bruise extending from Kit's temple to his cheekbone, covering the eye, which looked fused shut from the swelling. He opened his mouth to make a joke about youthful fisticuffs, but then shut it again immediately. Kit was trying to hide his injury, and Jack suddenly understood. Lord Heston was known for his tyrannical nature, but Jack had always taken the rumours that the man was brutish towards his own family with a pinch of salt. Perhaps the rumours were true.

Overcome by sudden outrage, Jack wondered how he could help Kit without souring his family's relationship with their closest neighbour. He couldn't just stand aside while this young man was beaten by his own father. He'd have to think of something. He tightened his grip on the reins and replied carefully, 'I believe my father is still considering the matter.'

'Really?' Lord Heston gave him an indolent smile. 'I'm surprised he can afford to hold on to it.'

'I'm sure my father knows what he's doing.'

'Very well,' said Lord Heston. 'I shall wait until he comes to a decision. Pray, Halliford, to what do I owe the honour of your visit, then?'

The question was delivered lazily, as though the answer was of minor importance, but there was no mistaking the command behind it. Irritation prickled between Jack's shoulder blades at Lord Heston's presumption. The man had a way of getting under his skin.

'I sought you out, Lord Heston,' he replied coolly, 'on account of a private matter which I thought would be of some interest to you. Finding you away from home, I decided to call upon Mrs Bartlett, with whom, as you know, I have been acquainted for a number of years.' The words sounded stilted even to his own ears, but Jack couldn't help it. He always had trouble being polite when speaking to Lord Heston.

'And did you find her as expected?' enquired Lord Heston.

'I found Mrs Bartlett in excellent health, thank you.'

'My staff have no cause for complaint.' Lord Heston gave a bloodless smile. 'A private matter, you said?'

'Yes.' Jack found himself backed into a corner – there was no way of retreating now. If he did, Lord Heston would very likely question Mrs Bartlett and she would regale him with their entire conversation, word for word, no doubt.

'Leave us, Kit,' said Lord Heston.

Bidding Jack goodbye, Kit rode ahead with the look of a prisoner who had been granted an unexpected pardon. Jack glanced after him. He would have to find some way to help the young man – perhaps invite him to Lampton more often. It would also give Kit and Alethea a chance to get to know each other better, which would stand them in good stead if the betrothal went ahead in accordance with the earl's and Lord Heston's wishes.

He turned back to face Lord Heston, who was regarding him with an impenetrable expression.

'Well?'

'The matter I wished to speak to you about concerns a young maid by the name of Sarah Duval, who was in your employ at the time of your first wife's, well …'

'Our family tragedy. Yes, thank you, Halliford, I don't need reminding, but if you have any news of that thieving wench, I'd be much obliged if you'd be good enough to share it with me.'

Jack cleared his throat. 'I have it on good authority that the maid is dead.'

'Whose authority?'

'I saw her grave, in the woods south of the mill, with my own eyes,' said Jack.

'In the woods?' Lord Heston arched his eyebrows, then he laughed, and it wasn't a pleasant sound. 'My, my. The search went far and wide for that strumpet, all that time she was right under our noses. So she's truly dead?'

'Yes.'

'Good. Now if you'll excuse me, Halliford, I have important estate matters to attend to.'

Jack watched Lord Heston ride away, but stayed for a moment staring out over the fields in contemplation. His hunt for Cora had turned into a need to help her, as well as a curiosity about her history, and so far his findings were intriguing.

Chapter Eleven

Cora ran until her lungs were bursting, and when she stopped at last she heard no sounds of pursuit. It would seem that Jack had decided not to follow her this time, thank goodness. He'd called himself Jack, which suited him somehow. She allowed herself a little smile, but then returned to reality. She should never have gone out there in the first place, but she missed her mother and baby brother and had wanted to say goodbye to them one last time. From now on she'd stay at Mrs Wilton's cottage until it was time to leave the area. Fear and shame needled her stomach at the thought of holding up another carriage, but it was the only way for her to find the money she needed to get Ned to safety.

She made her way back to the cottage, deep in thought. Lord Halliford's claim that she was the illegitimate child of a noble captain was extraordinary. She didn't take Jack for a stupid man; he'd managed to find her and Ned's home in the forest, and not many people knew precisely where it was. That was why she couldn't dismiss his words outright. Her mother had been a maid once, and a nobleman taking advantage of a woman belonging to the lower orders was, however despicable, quite commonplace.

The more she thought of it, the more her mother's last words began to make sense.

Remember, you're a lady.

Strictly speaking, being the illegitimate child of a nobleman made her nothing of the sort, but to her mother, at the point of death it probably made a sort of sense.

But why would Jack tell her this at all? What did he stand to gain by introducing an illegitimate relative to the family, unless it was for the purposes of vexing his father. If, and it was undoubtedly a big 'if', Cora had any claim at all on an inheritance from the late captain, helping her would only deplete the funds of the estate, and, from rumours abounding in town, the earl could ill afford it.

She didn't trust him; didn't believe he wouldn't give her to the authorities when he had finished whatever game he was playing. And he clearly had designs on her – his eyes had told her that as surely as if he'd said the words. Tempting as she found it to spend more time with him and get to know him better, who was to say he wouldn't just use her and then hand her over to the magistrate?

And she had to consider the safety of her heart. Much to her dismay, she'd already discovered that she couldn't trust herself around him, and what if the worst happened, and she succumbed to her desires only to find it was then too late for herself and Ned to get away? She shuddered at the thought. She had come very close already and felt the danger as if it burned her.

When she arrived at Mrs Wilton's cottage, her head was swimming with the possibility that she might not be who she thought she was. She plucked up the courage to ask her father something she'd never for a moment thought was in doubt. She had to know.

'Where have you been, girl?' Ned's hand clamped down hard on her wrist as soon as she entered the cottage, his strength unmistakable despite his illness. 'I've been worried sick about you, wandering about like that.'

As if to punctuate his words, his body was suddenly beset by a hacking cough.

'Sorry, Father. Here, let me get you something to drink.'

'Just … answer the … question.'

Her father waved her away, but she ignored him and poured him a tankard of ale, which he accepted with a querulous expression. He watched Cora in silence as she sat down on a stool beside him.

'First of all, I need to tell you something,' she said. 'The man who rumbled me was Lord Halliford.'

Ned frowned. 'I know who he is, but I don't see what difference it makes. He spends most of his time up in London carousing, but he's nobody's fool. If he's uncovered your identity, the sooner we can be out of the county the better. I wouldn't trust the likes of him further than I can spit.'

'Actually, he let me go,' said Cora. She decided not to mention her second run-in with him just now in the woods.

'He let you go? Why?'

'He made an extraordinary claim about my parentage.'

'Did he, now? And, pray, what's it to him?'

Cora looked at her father. From the wary expression in his eyes she wondered if he knew what she was going to ask him. The realisation cut through her. 'It's true, then?' she said, more to herself than to him.

'What's true, my heart?'

'Lord Halliford claims I'm the illegitimate daughter of his father's cousin, Captain Blythe. Apparently the resemblance is striking; we have the same eyes.'

'Pah! Resemblances mean nothing. We're all created in His image after all.' Ned dismissed Cora with a wave of his hand, but failed to meet her eyes. Cora's stomach tightened.

'Please, tell me the truth. He says my eyes are unusual, and perhaps he's right. I didn't get them by accident, did I? Are you my ...' She hesitated, unable to finish the question. 'Did the captain get my mother into trouble?'

Ned set the tankard on the table and put his hands on her shoulders, reassuring her with his infinitely gentle eyes and an expression which spoke only of a father's true love for his daughter.

'Whatever your blood line, Cora, you'll always be my child.'

'So it *is* true,' she whispered.

'Aye, it is. But there's more.'

Ned let go of her and Cora waited to hear what else he had to say, this man whom she had always thought to be her father. Her mind was in turmoil.

'The good captain,' Ned began, 'did not beget you by your mother, Sarah. If the resemblance is as striking as Halliford claims, the captain probably fathered you, but by a different woman altogether.'

Cora blanched. This she had not anticipated. She had expected to hear the age-old tale of a maid seduced by the master of the house. She had even been prepared for the possibility that she was the result of a rape, but the notion that Sarah might not have been her mother at all had never entered her mind.

Tears stung her eyes. Her beautiful mother, so gentle and frail, whose only ambition in life was to have a family, had carried one child to term in her womb, and that child wasn't Cora. It shouldn't matter, but it did. Not wanting to give vent to her hurt and anger, she clenched her fists in her lap.

Ned waited in silence while she battled with her rage and frustration, then he said, 'Your natural mother was Lady Heston.'

'Lady Heston?' Cora looked up. 'The woman who ran away and was found dead in a coach?' The story was well-known.

'The very same.'

Ned dug inside his shirt and pulled out a small bundle. 'Here. This is the only proof I have of your identity. It has preyed on my conscience for many years, and I have often debated whether I should give it to you, but I was afraid that I might lose you if I did. Whenever I tried to tell you, it never seemed to be quite the right moment. Forgive me.'

Cora stared at the bundle in her hand, and then back at her father. Well, he was her father, wasn't he? He had fed her, clothed her, taught her to walk, talk, picked her up when she fell over, scolded her, comforted her and gone without when there was little to eat. Only a real father did those things.

'Oh, Father,' she said and sent him an affectionate look, 'of course I forgive you. It must have been a dreadful burden for you. I never knew how troubled you were.'

Ned smiled. 'Open it,' he said.

She pulled back the corners of the cloth to reveal a pendant and a ring. The pendant was a miniature painting depicting an elegant lady in watercolour on ivory, and the ring was a plain band of gold with an inscription inside it. Cora held it up in the sunlight to read: 'To My Lady Heart. C'.

'C?' she said, raising her eyebrows.

Ned shrugged. 'I can't be certain, but I think it must have been a gift from her husband. Lord Heston's Christian name is Charles.'

'I see,' Cora said. This was hardly proof, though; one could argue that Ned might have come by these items at any time. 'And how did these items end up in your possession?' she asked.

'Sarah, your … mother, gave them to me after Lady Heston died.'

'Did she steal them?'

'No.' Ned had a fierce look in his eyes. 'She took them to give to Lady Heston's child one day.'

Cora shook her head. 'I still don't understand. Lady Heston died with her child in her arms. How can these things be proof of *my* identity?'

Ned rose and paced the room, but then stopped and looked at her as if there was something important on his mind. He shook his head and turned away.

'Father?'

Cora got up and stood behind him, her hand on his shoulder, beseeching him to look at her. Finally he turned and sent her a wry smile.

'I once made my living as a highwayman,' Ned said. 'Just as you support us now, much to my horror. Although it has to be said, George taught you well. Anyhow, I was the one who held up the lady's coach.'

Cora stared at him, unable to comprehend what he'd just told her. Her law-abiding father, a highwayman?

'Not only that,' he said, 'but I switched the babies.'

'You switched ... in God's name, why?'

'Because Lady Heston implored me to. She feared for your life, feared what her husband would do to you when he discovered that you couldn't possibly be his daughter.' Smiling wistfully, Ned gave her arm a squeeze. 'I always suspected that she must have been unfaithful to her husband. Why else would she have launched herself so desperately into the night? I just never knew who her lover was. Now I do. And so do you.'

'Tell me everything from the beginning, please. I need to understand,' Cora begged.

Cora listened in amazement as Ned told her exactly what had happened that night. Desperate for a few shillings so he could feed himself, he had held up a coach amid a dreadful storm. But a pitiful sight had greeted him when he opened the door, a woman close to death, her newborn baby tucked into a basket beside her. He hadn't been able to deny the woman's dying wishes to save her baby from her husband.

Cora smiled when he described her mother, Sarah, sitting in his horse's saddle with as much dignity as a queen, making Ned almost dizzy from her presence.

'And so it was I found myself with an infant in my arms and a hoity-toity lady's maid straddling my horse. I had a curious feeling that I'd been hood-winked,' he told her.

They'd travelled through the woods to the Ewers' place, where just that morning Ben Ewer's wife had given birth to stillborn girl. After switching the babies, Ned and Sarah had taken Cora home.

'Of all the possessions I have acquired robbing from the rich,' Ned said, 'I have never held anything quite so precious in my arms.'

Chapter Twelve

'And then what happened? You and Mo— I mean Sarah, fell in love?' Cora stared at Ned, still shaken by all these revelations.

Ned smiled and shook his head. 'Not right away, no, although I won't deny I was smitten. She'd had a shock, so I gave her time and ...' He shrugged. 'Yes, we fell in love. We moved away from this area, so no one ever knew you weren't really our child.'

'And Lady Heston's ... remains? Who discovered them?'

'I've no idea. Before we left, I unleashed the horses and shooed them off across the heath. I'm guessing the coach was found in the morning or soon after, but I didn't stay to find out. I had to get you and Sarah away from there, and fast.'

'So where did you go?' Cora needed to know every last detail.

'Well, back to my humble cottage first.' Ned smiled. 'That was when you stole my heart too.'

'Me?' Cora laughed. 'But I was just a baby.'

'Aye, but when we got there, you were wide awake. You seemed to be studying me as if I were the strangest thing you'd ever laid eyes on. I was probably just being fanciful; I've heard newborn babies can't see that well. But your tiny fists were waving furiously and when I slipped my little finger inside your hand, your tiny perfect fingers closed around it, and that was it. You had me.'

Cora smiled. 'You're too soft-hearted for your own good,' she murmured. 'Was it your idea to call me Cora or did I already have a name?'

'No, Lady Heston never said. But you had that birthmark on your cheek and very distinctive it was too, shaped like a heart. It gave me an idea – I said to myself, I'll call you Cora, short for *corazon*, the Spanish word for "heart". I'd learned a handful of words, probably none fit for a lady's ears, from a travelling Spaniard I'd once shared a jug of ale with. It seemed fitting, and Sarah agreed.' He sighed and sent her a tired smile. 'You're my heart and always will be, child.'

Cora stared at him, not quite able to take in what she'd just heard. When the impact of Ned's words finally hit home, she felt as if her innards had been ripped out. 'So ... so ...' she said, struggling against the hard lump in her throat, 'all this time, we've been living a lie?'

'I assure you, my heart, Sarah and I were your mother and father in every sense of the word except through blood. No one loved you as she did. You were the first thing on her mind when she woke in the mornings, and her last thought before bed. Just as you occupy my thoughts now.'

And you mine, Cora wanted to add, but her tongue seemed stuck. She knew one thing, though: she had to get the money they needed to leave this place. She had to protect him as he had once protected her. Get him away from Jack so he couldn't threaten them anymore. It was too dangerous to stay.

'Are we done, m'lord?' The groom called down from the box.

He and Jack had driven from the outskirts of Hounslow to The Black Dog and back three times now. The groom could hardly disguise the impatience in his voice and Jack heartily agreed with the man. The constant dips in the bumpy road were beginning to grate on his nerves, and every time they passed the gibbets he felt the small hairs rise on the back of his neck.

Instead of his own carriage, Jack had chosen one without the family crest; it had been taken out of commission a while back and mice had chewed and nested in the leather seats till practically all the stuffing spilled out.

'Another turn, if you please, Benning,' he called back, and then cursed as the wretched carriage dipped into a hole in the road, and he knocked his head against the carriage window.

And after that another turn, he added to himself. *I intend to do this all damn night if that's what it takes to find her.*

For a moment, assailed by doubt that he would ever see Cora again, he regretted his decision not to pursue her, but he knew it would have been futile. This was better. It had to be. He suspected she would leave the county altogether and settle somewhere else, now he knew her identity. He would if he were her, and for that she would need travel money, he'd bet his last penny on it. For an experienced highwaywoman there was an easy solution to that problem. And she didn't seem like the type of woman who would wait once she'd decided on a course of action. She would do it tonight. He was even making it easy for her, travelling along the most deserted part of the Heath in a carriage with lanterns blazing and only one unarmed man on the box.

When they reached the ten-mile stone, Benning turned the carriage around, and with much cussing of the horses, they were heading back to The Black Dog.

A shot rang out, and the carriage came to an abrupt stop. *At last!* Tensing, Jack cocked the pistol in his right hand and peeked out of the window. In the glare from the many lanterns he and Benning had strapped on he could see a dark figure on horseback pointing a pistol, but he couldn't be sure it was Cora.

Through the walls of the carriage he heard the muffled order for Benning to step down and lie by the side of the road. It was a young voice – not unlike a woman's – and his confidence was restored. It seemed Cora had walked right into his trap.

'You in there! Step out of the carriage!' Cora yelled at the closed door.

Jack had to hand it to her; she was good and took no chances. Cora knew the dangers, that if she pulled open the door, there was a good chance she would find herself staring down the barrel of a pistol. Jack needed to lure her closer.

'I can't!' he called back, making his voice high-pitched, like a hysterical old crone's. 'You have me frightened out of my wits, and my old limbs won't move.'

'Step out of the vehicle, now,' shouted Cora, 'or your driver's a dead man! You want that on your conscience, you old bag?'

Benning whimpered pathetically on the ground, and Jack cried theatrically, 'Lord, have mercy on us all.'

'Oh, for the love of God!' Jack heard Cora groan impatiently. She yanked the door open and pointed her pistol into the dark.

Jack was faster. He caught her pistol arm, pulled her inside the carriage, pushed her flat on her stomach and sat on her, pinning her with his weight.

'What the ...?'

'Hello,' he said pleasantly, 'we meet again.'

'You!' Cora hissed.

She kicked out and fought to get up, but Jack was too heavy for her. 'No, no, no,' he said, 'we don't play like that, my dear.' Grabbing her wrist, he wrenched the pistol out of her hand and uncocked it, placing it out of reach on the vermin-chewed seat. 'There, now we're all safe and sound. Or, on second thoughts, maybe not.'

He put his hand under her black cloak and felt for her second pistol; it was tucked halfway down the front of her breeches. His hand brushed against her naked skin, and for a moment he kept it there, enjoying the sensation of her soft, warm belly against his fingertips. Cora gasped.

Chuckling, Jack pulled out the pistol; then he unclipped her rapier and slung it on top of the pistols. Only then did he turn her over, although he kept her trapped between his legs and her wrists pinned down with his hands.

Cora snarled in frustration and glared at him. 'What do you want from me? Are you going to violate me, is that it? How very noble of you.'

'You're very appealing, but no, not today. As for being noble, well, taking a woman against her will is hardly less noble than robbing honest, hard-working folk at pistol point, don't you think? No,' he said, 'I want to talk with you.'

'Is that what they call it now?' Cora muttered defiantly. He wondered whether under different circumstances she would have liked to get intimate with him, but he would never do so against her will. He let go of her wrists and eased off her; then lifted her and sat her down, none too gently, opposite her weapons.

'Yes, just talk,' he said and removed her mask.

Flopping back against the seat, Cora rubbed her wrists and eyed him belligerently. With his pistol trained on her, Jack stared back, excited and disturbed by her presence. Her eyes blazed in challenge, but he recalled the softer look he'd seen in them on another occasion and knew she wasn't as indifferent to him as she pretended to be right now. The thought pleased him, absurdly so, and there were a thousand things he would have wanted to say to her, if he hadn't found himself strangely tongue-tied.

Unwittingly, Benning came to the rescue. 'M'lord?' he called tentatively from outside the carriage. 'I heard a commotion, and I thought ...'

'Everything is in order, Benning. I've caught the miscreant.'

Benning stuck a dishevelled head inside the carriage, grinning from ear to ear. 'Capital, m'lord, capital! I suppose we'll be off to the magistrate's now?'

Cora's eyes widened and her whole body tensed, like that of a cat ready to spring. Her gaze fell on her weapons, and Jack placed his hand over them – he knew what she was contemplating, and it would do her no good.

'Not so fast, Benning. This young person and I have some business to discuss. If you'd be so good as to tie his horse to the back of the carriage we can continue along as before. Oh, and, Benning,' he added, with a hint of steel in his voice, 'anything you see and hear tonight is strictly between us. Do I make myself clear?'

'Yes, m'lord. I ain't gonna breathe a word.'

He handed him Cora's weapons. 'You'd better take these, just to be on the safe side.' He winked at Cora, who glowered at him.

'Right you are.' With a meaningful look in Cora's direction Benning dusted down his coat, took the pistols and the rapier, and retreated from the carriage, muttering something about lords and their hare-brained schemes.

Jack closed the door and rapped on the roof, and soon they were rattling along the Bath Road again. In her corner Cora sulked, but she seemed more at ease now it was apparent Jack wasn't planning on turning her over to the authorities. He didn't doubt for a moment that she would bolt at the first opportunity, and he resolved to make sure such an opportunity wouldn't arise.

Eventually, curiosity must have got the better of her. 'Is that my pistol you're holding?' she asked with a bad-tempered toss of the head.

He shrugged. 'I have yours, you had mine. Let's not quibble about pistols. Let's talk.'

'What do you want to talk about?'

'I wanted to pick up our conversation from where we left off earlier,' Jack replied. 'I'm quite certain you're the daughter of my father's late cousin, and as I've said before I believe my father should do right by you.'

Cora was silent for a moment; then she laughed and for Jack it was as if someone had let the sun in. 'I must admit, m'lord, you're not like other noblemen I've met. Most lords would wish to forget their illegitimate relatives, if that is indeed what I am.'

'You don't believe me?'

Cora regarded him warily, and from what he could see of the changing expressions on her face, she seemed to be engaged in some kind of internal debate. 'Whether I'm the daughter of your captain, I do not know, sir, but I have good reason to believe that I am the child of Lady Heston. When I was hardly a day old, my father held up the coach in which the lady was travelling. She was feverish and dying and in her addled state she implored him to take me away and keep me safe from her husband. Although what I should have to fear from Lord Heston I can't imagine. I have no wish to lay any claims to his property. Nor would I be able to.'

Jack nodded; he had already guessed as much from his investigation. 'And so you were brought up as the child of a highwayman and a maid.'

'What do you know of my mother ... I mean ... of Sarah Duval?' Cora asked.

'I've been making enquiries.'

Sitting up abruptly, she sent him a startled look. 'Enquiries?'

'Oh, Cora, you must know I have no intention of handing you over to the magistrate. If I wanted to, we would be heading there right now, not chatting amiably in a carriage. And I have no wish to harm your father either. You must trust me in this. You do trust me, don't you?'

She was quiet for a while, but then she nodded.

'Good,' he said. 'Now, I've not shared my findings with anyone. I'm aware that Sarah Duval was accused of having robbed Lady Heston and that there was a reward for her capture when she disappeared. I'm also aware that she's been beyond reach these past nine years,' he added gently.

Cora smiled sadly. 'It ... it broke my heart to see her suffer as she did. One miscarriage after the next. She was so tired and weak, and yet she never complained. Of course, I was only a child, I didn't understand as much then. Being a family was all she ever wanted, and when her wish was finally granted, we thought ...' She lowered her eyes, and it was some time before she was able to speak again. When she did, it was with a rebellious glare and a toss of her head. 'I will never think of her as anything other than my mother, regardless of what anyone says.'

'I understand that,' said Jack. 'Truly, I do. The bonds we form are not governed merely by blood. But there's also such a thing as duty.'

'Duty?' Cora's tone was enquiring, but he detected a note of disappointment.

'I feel it's my duty to make sure you're looked after, as a member of my family. Robbing coaches will only lead you to the end of a rope.'

'Provided you're correct,' she countered.

'I'll admit that first I was working from the assumption that the good captain had got a young girl in trouble, in this case your ... mother, but what you've told me about Lady Heston makes more sense. My father mentioned that there had been some scandal and his cousin was in love with a married woman.'

He had given her a lot to think about, and so had her father by the sounds of it. It was only reasonable that he gave her a moment to absorb these facts. Then he continued. 'It seems clear to me that Cecil Blythe and Lady Heston had an affair, and that she fled her husband's wrath when she saw that her child had the same distinctive eyes as her lover as well as his colouring.'

Cora shook her head and smiled. 'A tall tale, indeed.'

'At least humour me and let me show you his portrait,' said Jack. 'It will become apparent to you that there are other similarities.'

'Is that what this abduction is about? You want to show me the family gallery? At this hour?'

A smile tugged the corners of her mouth and Jack had a sudden urge to lean over and kiss it, but he resisted the temptation. Cora was listening, not running down the alleyways of Hounslow or through the woods, and he didn't want to lose her. Nor did he wish to see her in danger again, as she had been when she tripped in front of the coach. The mere thought of it still gave him nightmares.

'There's no time like the present,' he said with a shrug.

'Have you taken leave of your senses? Are we to sneak in the back door like thieves?' Cora gave a snort of laughter.

'Well, we may have to do a little sneaking,' Jack conceded with a grin. 'I expect everyone will be asleep by now, but I'm very happy to take you through the front door if using a more convenient side door offends your sensibilities.' He lifted his eyebrow.

'My sensibilities are just fine,' Cora harrumphed, 'but thank you all the same for that consideration. It matters not to me which door we use. I still think this it quite ridiculous.'

'Not so.' Jack smiled and tossed her a bundle from the seat beside him. 'Which brings me to this. I figured you'd be in breeches tonight, so I brought you a dress. On the outside chance that someone should come upon us while we are *sneaking*, I'd rather not be mistaken for a sodomite. You will admit I think of everything.'

She smiled saucily. 'Why anyone should think you were engaged in any kind of intimate pursuit, I can't imagine.'

'I'm very glad to hear it,' he replied and held her gaze until she looked away with an unmistakable blush in her cheeks. He was going to enjoy this night, he was sure of it.

Chapter Thirteen

Cora unfolded the bundle without further protest. She had to go along with whatever he suggested if she was to have a chance of saving her life and being able to provide for Ned, but so far Lord Halliford had stuck by what he'd said, and she saw no reason to mistrust him. Inside was a sumptuous gown of sunflower-yellow taffeta. Although it was plain, the torso was tightly fitted with a low décolletage and a finely pleated back. The sleeves were elbow length with ruched frills of matching silk, and the bundle also included a set of stays with narrow blue ribbons to cover the seams. She ran her hand over the exquisite material. Never had she held anything quite so fine, except for the stolen waistcoat, and she tried not to think about that right now. Then for the second time her cheeks heated with embarrassment.

'Not everything,' she said in a low voice.

'What?' Jack leaned over and examined the bundle of clothes. 'I must apologise if I have forgotten some intimate garments, but you can wear the dress over your breeches, can you not?'

'No, it's all here, sir. But if I dress like this and we sneak into your home, I could be mistaken for your mistress.'

'You've used that word before, when you offered yourself to me at the coaching inn, and I declined politely. You do not have to offer yourself again.'

'I did not offer myself to you!' Cora argued.

'Well, you could've fooled me.' Jack shrugged.

'I'd rather be taken for a thief than a whore.'

'A whore?' Jack said archly. 'This dress belonged to my mother.'

'I'm sorry, I meant no offence, but will she not miss it?' With regret Cora put the dress on the seat beside her.

Jack reached over and handed it back to her. 'Trust me, she never wears it, and the cut is too grown-up for my cousin Alethea.'

Alethea. That was the inscription on the fob watch, and she felt absurdly delighted by the revelation that Alethea was his cousin, not his betrothed.

'Please, put the dress on for me,' Jack said. 'I would like to see you wear it.'

'Why?'

'Because I believe it will suit you.'

Cora eyed him suspiciously, but his gaze was nothing but frank and she relaxed a little. 'I can't get changed in the carriage. It lurches too much and I'd like a little privacy.'

She tossed her hair, hoping to come across as dignified, although she suspected she sounded rather churlish. What girl would say no to the joy of wearing a garment like that?

'You're not planning to run off again, are you?'

'On foot? Without my pistols?'

'No, I suppose not,' Jack conceded. He knocked on the roof and gave Benning orders to stop the carriage at the first convenient place. Soon, they came to a halt and Jack stepped outside, followed by Cora. Jack told Benning to wait, and then led the way under the cover of the large oak trees to a secluded spot.

'Where are we?' Cora asked.

'On the outskirts of my father's estate. I felt it was best to approach the house from the east. This way we'll come upon the house from the side, away from the view from the main windows.'

'That's fine with me,' said Cora, although inside she felt a heavy lump settle in her chest. Jack had said that they would have to do some sneaking. It made sense: she was wanted as a highwaywoman, and even if he wasn't going to hand her over to the authorities, someone else might. But what if it was also because he was ashamed of her? The thought vexed her, but she couldn't change the reality of their situation: he was a nobleman and she was a labourer, despite all his presumptions about her blood line.

When they stopped, she got out to change under the cover of a particularly large oak tree. She could have changed in the carriage, but donning garments like these required space. Quickly she shrugged out of her coat.

'Turn around,' she said. 'I won't have you peeking.'

Jack lifted his hat and bowed low. 'But you may require assistance, my lady. Besides, I won't be able to see anything in the dark.'

She aimed a kick at him and snorted when her stockinged foot connected with his shin.

'Ow! You little minx! That hurt.'

'Good. Now turn around.'

Grumbling, he did as she asked, and Cora quickly took off her breeches, shirt and stockings. Jack had indeed thought of everything, including a fine cotton shift, but Cora didn't bother with it, preferring instead to keep her linen shift on. She didn't trust him not to look – had it been Jack changing in front of her, she would have given in to temptation and sneaked a peek.

She had no trouble donning the petticoat and the silk stockings, but when it came to fastening the stays, she ran into problems. They were designed to be done up at the back with the assistance of a maid – it was not a garment a person could manage single-handedly.

'Jack,' she called. In the forest he'd introduced himself thus, and she'd looked at the inscribed watch so many times since that she had come to think of him as Jack in her mind. Even so, she couldn't suppress a sense of awkwardness from using his given name for the first time.

Startled, he turned around. 'How do you know my name?'

'You volunteered it when you chanced upon me in the forest. And from your watch,' she added. Her cheeks flamed.

'Mm, yes, so I did. As for the watch, I wouldn't mind it back some time.'

Cora tossed her head. 'I'll think about it. In the meantime, could you lace me up?'

'It'll be my pleasure, madam,' he replied, a little too eagerly, she thought.

She felt his hands on her back, brushing gently against the skin on her neck as he began tightening the laces from the top, and with each gentle tug at the ribbons her breathing became increasingly laboured.

Every time Jack pulled and pushed, she felt his soft breath on the back of her neck, a warm, feather-light caress in the cool evening air. She closed her eyes and gave in to the exquisite sensation. Something stirred in her belly and her groin, and her cheeks flamed hotter than ever before. Just as well he couldn't see her expression in the dark.

'There, you're done,' he said.

He reached out and touched one of her black curls, which had broken free of her ribbon, tying it back up. A delicious and excruciating shiver ran down her back. She felt his hands on her hips without him touching her, felt the length of his body pressing against hers although there was a hands-breadth of air between them. A stifled moan escaped her lips. She wanted him so much.

'Oh, Cora,' he sighed, and she felt his breath on her neck. 'I want you too, but this isn't the time.'

She rounded on him, furious with herself that her thoughts had been so obvious. 'I don't know what you're talking about, sir. Don't you go taking liberties, else I'll injure your other leg!'

Holding up his hands, he laughed. '*Sir* is it, now? What happened to *Jack*? Peace. Just put on the gown, if you please.'

She crossed her arms hoping that her belligerence would hide how she truly felt. 'I don't want to play this game anymore.'

'All I'm asking is that you put on the dress,' he said and held it out to her. 'I would dearly like to see you wear it.'

'Oh, if I must!' She snatched it off him and put it on.

She'd never worn a dress like this before, and despite the layers of fabric, she felt suddenly exposed.

But it wasn't just this vulnerability that gave her a thrill of anticipation. Perhaps if she could look like a lady, that would be one less obstacle between them.

Slivers of moonlight spilled through the foliage of the oak tree, but not enough to see properly, and Jack pulled her out from under the branches and back towards the coach. She felt his eyes on her and she lifted her head to brazen it out. Many times she'd held up a coach at gun point, and she would not let herself be cowed by Jack.

His gaze was on her face, not running lewdly over her body as she had expected, and she found it impossible to look away. Her heart thudded audibly in her chest, or so it seemed; her lips parted as if of their own accord, and she was compelled to take a step towards him.

Jack took her hands in his. 'My God, you are beautiful,' he said with a catch in his throat.

Cora felt as if the world slid away and there was only Jack, with his sparkling eyes, his lips against her fingertips. Their bodies were nearly touching – had she taken that final step, or had he? His hand caressed her cheek, and he whispered unintelligible words that made perfect sense, and she knew at that moment that if she lived to be a hundred no other man could ever produce such longing in her.

She slipped her arms around his neck and stepped into his embrace, but the sound of the groom clearing his throat reminded her of where they were, and they flew apart. Jack's expression darkened, and for a moment Cora thought he might rebuke the man, but then he shrugged and smiled.

'Benning has quite rightly reminded us of our purpose and the lateness of the hour,' he said, in a slightly exasperated tone at the interruption. 'Would that we had more time, Cora, but perhaps another day.' He held out his arm to her. 'Your carriage awaits, my lady.'

Cora forced herself to smile. It had been nothing but a fantasy and now the spell was broken. Jack was a lord and she was a lowly labourer on the wrong side of the law.

The drive didn't last long. Benning stopped the carriage under cover of a large red beech tree and Jack helped Cora down. She had lived in the area for a decade and had seen Lampton Hall a couple of times, but never in moonlight. The four-storey sandstone mansion sat in a clearing of the woods with a circular gravelled drive, a marble fountain in the centre and wide stone steps leading up to the door. It was a modest residence for an earl, or so she'd heard, but the grandeur of the place made Cora feel small and insignificant.

Jack held out his hand. Cora hesitated a little, but then took it, unable to stop herself from touching him, if only their hands. It was warm and dry, and his strong fingers gripped hers reassuringly. Following Jack round to the side of the house, Cora understood why they had stopped the carriage at a distance; taking the carriage up the gravelled drive would make too much noise and render secrecy impossible. Despite her curiosity, she was concerned that their venture was nothing but a game for Jack. It was the prerogative of the rich to indulge in such jocularity, but Cora was acutely aware that if were they caught, it would be her reputation that would be ruined, not Jack's. But after all the revelations about her parenthood, especially from her father, she just wanted to understand, and it gave her an opportunity to spend more time with Jack. She tried not to think about what Ned would have to say about it.

As she followed Jack down a few steps at the side of the house and in through a servants' door, excitement stole over her and a shiver ran up her spine. They entered a long wide passage and doorways revealed the purpose of the rooms they passed: kitchen, scullery, laundry room, a dining area, boot room and pantry.

A corridor ran down either side of the main passage and Jack held a finger to his lips. It wasn't until they reached a curving staircase that he whispered, 'Cook's and the housekeeper's private quarters. On the other side, the butler's.'

'Where do the other servants sleep?' Cora asked quietly.

'Upstairs in the attics. Come.' Jack put his hand on the small of her back and led her up the gloomy stairwell.

Heat snaked through her despite her layers of clothing, and she imagined Jack's hand caressing her naked skin. Then she reminded herself of everything that stood between them – men like Jack might bed women like her, but they never married them. Although he was acting the perfect gentleman with her now, this was their reality. Disappointment washed over her. Even so, she was glad of the support. The steps were precipitous with her unaccustomed skirts and she clung on to him.

They emerged through a concealed door and found themselves at the end of a large gallery with bare floorboards. Jack let go of her hand and lit a three-armed candelabra. Cora started as something growled nearby, but when her eyes became accustomed to the light, she noticed two large spaniels staring at her, the smaller of the two with its fangs bared. Jack's dogs again.

'Lady, Duke, come and say hello to Cora.' Jack clapped on the side of his leg and the dogs ran up to him, tails wagging. He took Cora's hand again but this time held it out for the dogs to sniff. The larger of the two dogs accepted her immediately as a friend, but the smaller dog eyed her warily.

'It's all right, Lady. Cora's my friend.' Jack sat down on his haunches and ruffled Lady's ears. 'They're good hunting dogs,' he said, 'although I think Lady fancies herself more as a guard dog.'

'I'm gathering that.' Cora smiled. He had taken her hand

again, as if it was natural for him to do so, and had called her a friend. The consideration touched her, but it still didn't change the fact that men like Jack did not marry women like her. 'Just as well they didn't alert the whole house to our presence.'

Jack shrugged. 'Why should they? I live here.'

So he did; another reminder of their different circumstances. Any intimacy between them would be as far away from the marital bed as you could possibly get, should Jack feel inclined to take her up on the offer she had made at the coaching inn.

Oh, what had possessed her to make it in the first place? Desperation, was the answer. She wanted the same kind of love and equality she'd witnessed between Ned and Sarah, not to be someone's mistress and always at a disadvantage.

And because of her crimes there was the threat of the gallows hanging over her head. When he had yanked her inside the carriage, she had thought it the beginning of the end. Even though he'd reassured her he had no intention of handing her to the magistrate it wouldn't stop anyone else, should her secret become known. She shivered and rubbed her arms with her hands.

'Are you cold?' asked Jack.

'I'm well enough. No need to concern yourself.'

Jack placed the candelabra on the floor, took off his coat and draped it over her shoulders. 'Forgive me,' he said. 'The gallery never really warms up, even in summer. I'm so used to it that it didn't occur to me how cold it must feel to a lady without a shawl.'

A *lady*. He had called her a lady.

Cora felt a tremendous heat suffuse her cheeks. What was the matter with her? It was this damned dress, surely, for making her feel so ... so different. 'Thank you. Are you going to show me this painting or not?' she said, more sharply than she had intended. His solicitousness confused her.

'Naturally, that's why we're here. This way.'

Jack picked up the candles again, signalled for the dogs to

follow, and made his way across the gallery. The heels of his shoes clacked against the wooden floor and Cora feared that he would rouse the whole household, but they reached the other side without being challenged by either servant or lord. Perhaps the occupants of the house were used to wanderings about in the night.

Cora felt the eyes of the portraits staring at them, disapprovingly, she was certain, and she was only too happy when Jack stopped by a partially concealed door.

'It's a storeroom,' Jack explained. 'The captain is a bit of a black sheep, I'm afraid. There was a scandal,' he added.

'It's probably nothing compared to the scandal that will follow when people get wind of your madcap idea. Whoever heard of restoring the illegitimate child of a black sheep to the bosom of a respectable family?'

Jack laughed. 'I suppose, when put like that, it does sound rather witless.'

'It certainly does.'

The room was small, airless and seemed to be full of all manner of things in need of repair. Not quite what Cora had expected to find, but then again, she had no knowledge of how people like Jack lived. Beckoning her closer, Jack held the candles aloft to allow her to view the portrait, which was propped up on a chair with a broken seat. She bent forward to examine the painting more closely, but then stepped back with a gasp.

'Dear Lord!'

She was looking into her own eyes.

Chapter Fourteen

'The likeness is startling, is it not?' said Jack.

Untamed black curls, very light grey-blue eyes – just like her own. And the other features were remarkably similar too. Swallowing hard, Cora merely nodded. How could this be? When Jack had first mentioned it she had been incredulous, then intrigued, although she never fully believed that it could be true. But after what Ned had told her, she couldn't deny the truth of it. Now, looking at the portrait, she saw there could be no mistake, and the small similarity in looks she had always felt existed between herself and Ned became mere coincidence. There was no doubt the sitter in the portrait was closely related to her.

The notorious Captain Blythe, cousin to the Earl of Lampton and a member of one of the finest families in England, had begotten a common thief. How strange the world was.

'Well?' Jack insisted. 'It does put a new perspective on things, doesn't it?'

Cora nodded again but still found herself unable to speak. So much had happened in the last few days, and her world, as she had always perceived it to be, had changed dramatically. Not only were her parents not who she thought they were, there was the added complication of her attraction to Jack. Except attraction was one thing, but the kind of love she'd witnessed in her parents' marriage was a privilege afforded very few, she knew.

Was it love she felt for Jack or was it merely lust? Either way, there could be no proper association between them, whether she was the captain's illegitimate daughter or not. First and foremost she was the result of her upbringing, not her blood. Jack didn't seem to realise that. Or perhaps he was so used to having his way that he merely ignored what was obvious to Cora.

Someone had to knock some sense into his woolly head.

'I agree that your theory must be right,' she began, but then she paused, unsure how to proceed. 'It won't change anything, though. I may carry blue blood in my veins, but I still feel like Cora, plain and simple.'

'It'll change everything! We are without a doubt second cousins. You carry the blood of this family in your veins, and even if the captain's behaviour was scandalous, that can be no fault of yours.' Jack ran his hand through his shorn hair. 'Even my father would agree with that,' he added with a frown. 'I'm sure he would, although there was the small matter of embezzlement as well … but that's neither here nor there. It was done out of love, pure and simple.'

'But you don't *know*?' said Cora.

'I know my father well enough to *believe* that he would agree with me,' he conceded. 'He would regard it as his duty to settle some money on you. An annual allowance which would allow you to live in comfort, if not luxury. You'd be able to marry and—'

'And what about Ned?' Cora interrupted. 'The man who brought me up and is my father in almost every sense of the word? Is he to be the hired help while I'm lording it in the fine salons, selling myself to the highest bidder?'

'No. Ned can … well, he'll be there with you, won't he? And as for you selling yourself, I know what kind of cattle market the marriage business is, but surely that wouldn't apply to you.'

'What's that supposed to mean?' said Cora.

He led them out of the storeroom and locked the door behind them. 'You'd be able to marry for love, not convenience,' he went on. 'You'd have enough money to live on should you choose not to marry, but not enough to be the object of fortune hunters. And you'd be safe.' Briefly, he brushed her cheek with his finger.

'You're quite mad, you know,' Cora said, her cheek burning

where he'd touched it. But he was right. If her future was secured, so was Ned's.

She was aware of the terrible risk every time she held up a coach, but the sound of his coughing made her insides clench and she had to do something. The costly tincture from the apothecary alleviated his symptoms a little, although it didn't cure him altogether. It was only a matter of time before her father's ravaged body couldn't take the strain any more, but if she agreed to Jack's plan, at least Ned could live out his days in comfort without having to worry about money.

It didn't matter that Ned hadn't fathered her. She loved him and would do anything for him. Even if it meant swallowing her pride and going hat in hand to the earl.

As if sensing that her resistance was waning, Jack said, 'So will you go with me to see my father on the subject?'

'I will. Although he'll probably send me packing.'

Jack put the candelabra on a shelf and placed his hands on her shoulders. 'Thank you, Cora,' he said. 'It means a lot to me.'

'How can it?' she whispered, her whole body tingling from his touch. 'How can it mean anything to you?'

'Because I want you to be safe. I couldn't bear it if anything happened to you.'

'I robbed you. You should hate me.'

'But I don't. You … you have bewitched me, Cora. I can think of nothing but you. Day and night. I want us to …'

He didn't finish the sentence. Instead he pulled her close and before she knew it, his mouth was on hers. Flames of lust shot through her and she clung to him, returning his kiss with inexperienced vigour. This was a proper kiss, a man's kiss, and she never wanted it to end.

He laughed softly against her mouth. 'Come, let me show you,' he whispered. 'Take my lead.'

Cupping her chin with one hand, he stroked her neck and shoulder with the other until her head fell back and her lips parted. Slowly, he covered her mouth with his, teased it open with his tongue and then took possession of it with a sudden urgency which had her gasping. Cora wanted to pull back, aware what this possession was mimicking, but her body seemed disconnected from her will, and instead she ran her hands down his back, pressing him closer to her, enjoying the way he ravaged her mouth, his hot breath, the sweet taste of him, his hard body and the evidence of his lust pressed against her pelvis. Her tongue met his thrust for thrust and her sense of triumph was complete when she felt him quiver with barely suppressed need.

I'm having that effect on him, she thought. The realisation was both frightening and delicious at the same time.

'I want you, Cora.' Jack's breath came in hot staccato bursts against her swollen lips and he held her gaze, hard and fiercely. 'I want you so much.'

'I know.' Drunk with her own power, she wriggled her pelvis against his. 'I want you too, but this will only lead to grief. Our circumstances ... are so different.'

'Never mind our circumstances. But you're right, we must wait until—'

'Jack?'

A shaft of light spilled into the darkened gallery and Cora and Jack leapt apart. A figure entered at the far end of the room and the dogs got up to greet the newcomer, their tails wagging.

'Jack, is that you?'

'Alethea!' Jack said in a strangled voice. 'You surprised me.'

Cora watched as Jack's cousin came further into the room, and she wished herself anywhere but here.

Alethea's eyes went from Jack to Cora, then back again. 'So I see,' she said. 'I worried when you didn't come home this evening, and when I saw the carriage from the window, I ...' She paused, biting her lip.

'This isn't what you think, Alethea.'

'Oh? And what am I thinking, dear cousin? That you're making illicit love to your paramour in our home or that you've merely chosen an unconventional time to show a young lady our family gallery?' Cora felt a prickle at the back of her neck at her words.

'Alethea!' Jack hissed.

'Dear me,' said Alethea with mock sincerity, 'am I not supposed to know of such matters? What am I? A young ninny? Come on, Jack, is she a lady friend whom I can greet politely or am I required to faint dead away?'

Cora bit her lip to stop herself from laughing. She could not have imagined this: Jack lost for words.

'A friend, then,' said Alethea. 'Aren't you going to introduce us?'

'Of course.' Jack cleared his throat. 'Alethea, this is Cora, who'—Cora sent him a sharp look—'is indeed a friend of mine. Cora, this is Alethea, my cousin, who, well, let's just say you don't want to enter into a battle of wits with her.'

Cora lowered her eyes and bobbed a curtsey, as convention dictated when in the company of her betters. 'Very pleased to meet you, miss.'

'And I you.' Alethea came closer and extended her hand. Looking up, Cora marvelled at how many rules of convention this girl was capable of breaking in one go. Then something made her step back in alarm.

'What?' asked Alethea. 'What did I say? Oh, my Lord, you look like …' She didn't finish the sentence. Instead she brought a hand to her chest and her eyes widened until it seemed they could get no bigger.

Cora covered her mouth with her hand to stop herself from crying out as she stared at Jack's young cousin. There was a likeness again, although not as strong, to the captain. Her ebony hair fell in unruly curls about her face and in the light from the candles Cora could see that Alethea was tall, like her. She was the captain's daughter and, Cora realised, her half-sister.

A thousand thoughts scrambled through her mind. *A sister!* How wonderful, and yet terrifying. What could they possibly have in common?

Cora's eyes flew from Jack to his cousin, and then back again. Had he brought her here, not just to see the painting, but also to meet Alethea? If so, why?

Or maybe … maybe it had been meant as a reminder that despite their obvious attraction to each other Cora inhabited a completely different world to Jack and Alethea, and could never hope to be like them or even fit in. Jack would have his sport with her, and then marry within his own social sphere. Well, if he thought he could treat Cora Mardell like that, he could think again.

Humiliation and anger burned in her cheeks, and her distrust of him returned. She pulled away as he reached out to her and ran out of the gallery, ignoring Jack's plea and Alethea's confusion.

'Cora! Wait!'

She hurtled down the stone staircase as fast as she could in the darkness. Halfway down her ankle twisted as she trod on the hem of her dress, and her foot was yanked beneath her as it tangled in the fabric. She fell the rest of the way down and landed with a bump in the servants' passage.

Sobbing and cursing, she pulled herself up but cried out in pain she tried to put her right foot down. She grabbed a broom which leaned against the wall nearby and used it for support as she hobbled down the passage.

She had to get out of there. Now. Whatever their explanations, she didn't trust Jack anymore and certainly wouldn't let him ensnare her into playing any more foolish and irresponsible games, or allow him to toy with her feelings further. It was all right for the likes him to indulge in such idle pursuits, but it was people like her who ended up paying the price. For a short while he had beguiled her with the prospect of a better life for herself and Ned, but it had been nothing but a false hope. Lord Halliford was like everyone else belonging to his class, in pursuit of his own entertainment regardless of who got hurt in the process. Well, she was having none of it.

Gritting her teeth against the pain in her ankle, Cora hobbled down the corridor, brushing past the startled butler, who had come to investigate the noise.

Lord Halliford might be an aristocratic pleasure-seeker, but there was no escaping the deplorable fact that Cora had well and truly lost her heart to him.

Jack was just in time to see Cora hurl herself onto her horse and disappear into the night, a yellow dot in the distance. He could pursue her, of course, but by the time he had saddled his own horse, she would be long gone and he doubted she was heading for the cottage in the woods anyway.

A low moan interrupted his thoughts. Just a few feet away from him lay a broken flower pot and a crumpled heap of a man. Jack rushed over to help Benning up.

'Are you hurt?' he asked, the concern in his voice carrying in the still night air.

Groaning, the groom rubbed his head. 'Aye, my lord, I reckon I am.'

'Well, you'd better have that knock tended to. Cook will put a cold compress on it.'

'I'm made of sterner stuff than that,' Benning protested, 'even if that young scallywag packs quite a punch.'

'Glad to hear it, but I'd feel happier knowing you've been seen to. And remember our agreement: you saw and heard nothing.'

'Right you are, my lord. I've not seen nor heard nothin'. That being that, if I hadn't known this were a lad in a dress, I'd have taken 'im for a female, punch or no punch,' Benning added with a sly look.

'Not even my father must know about this.'

'You have my word, my lord,' the groom reassured him.

'Not even his lordship.' Benning had always been loyal to Jack and trusted his judgement, but they both knew that the earl would probably hear of it one way or another.

Clutching his sore head, Benning stumbled indoors, and Jack became aware of Alethea standing behind him.

'I'm sorry I interrupted you,' she said.

'No matter. You weren't to know.' Jack ran his hands through his unruly hair and stared out into the night. He hadn't meant to be gruff with his cousin, but Cora frustrated him.

'Are you serious about this woman?' Alethea put her hand on his arm. 'If so, I wish you every happiness. From the bottom of my heart.'

Jack didn't reply; it wasn't that simple. He had to find Cora first, and then persuade her to trust him again, and then ... Then what?

He cursed himself for having let her go, for having kissed her, although she'd kissed him back readily enough. Perhaps it had been too soon, and he'd only succeeded in making her question his motives. He couldn't blame her for that; they had been about as clear as mud. One thing he did know – when he found her, he would make sure she didn't get away again. He knew she wasn't indifferent to him and he was eager to pick up from where they'd been when Alethea had interrupted them. There was still much he wanted to say to her. His feelings for her had stolen over him so gradually he hadn't realised exactly when, but he knew now that he wanted her by his side, in his life, if she was willing.

At the bottom of the servants' stairs he retrieved his coat, which Cora had dropped when she fell.

'Damnation!' he muttered under his breath as he checked the pockets: his purse was missing. Oh, yes, he certainly had things to say to her.

Cora rode for a good mile, until she was certain she wasn't being followed. She hadn't meant to hit the groom on the head with a flower pot, but when he'd refused to hand over her weapons, desperation had seized her. She regretted it and hoped the man hadn't suffered a grievous injury. He might not have even chased her anyway; Jack, however, was another matter.

She remembered the look in his eyes when he'd kissed her. He was a man who knew what he wanted and how to get it. He appeared to have full confidence in his plans to help her situation; but it seemed that he also wanted ... her.

That was the worst part.

Catching her breath after her breakneck ride across the Heath, Cora dismounted and leaned against Samson with her arms wrapped around his neck.

Something both wonderful and terrible had happened between her and Jack tonight. She couldn't deny it, nor did she wish to. The memory of his strong arms around her made her go almost giddy with longing and she sighed against the horse's mane, aware of the futility in imagining herself and Jack together. She was the illegitimate by-blow of the earl's scandalous cousin, and even in the unlikely event society chose to turn a blind eye to that, there was no way she and Ned could ever fit into Jack's world – whatever Jack said. She couldn't bear the thought of trying to force Ned to be something other than he was – he would insist on trying out of love for Cora – but they had no place here. She had to find a different way to secure his comfort – maybe the air in another country would do him good.

There could be no marriage between her and Jack. Perhaps she could be with him as his mistress, but that could lead to only lust and dishonour and abandonment – one day, he'd have to marry. Cora could live with the lust and the dishonour, but the thought that Jack might one day abandon her made her heart ache. Best not to allow herself such thoughts in the first place.

The kiss had been magical, but it had been ruined by her

return to reality. Sniffing loudly, she pulled herself together and patted Samson on the neck.

'It's all right, my friend, it's all right. I haven't lost my wits altogether.'

Samson snorted as if in agreement and nudged her gently with his glossy head.

'Let's get you home, shall we?' Stroking his nose, she guided the horse to a tree and tied the reins to it. 'I just need to get out of these clothes before Father sees me.'

Cora grabbed the bundle of clothes and weapons she'd swiped when fleeing Jack's home and quickly changed out of the yellow dress, though the stays were impossible to unfasten so she kept them on under her jacket and shirt. For some reason getting back into her old clothes broke the spell and she was able to laugh at herself over how Jack had so nearly managed to persuade her that she could be part of his world when it was clear she never would. Samson stomped his hoof as if he too was relieved to be free of the curious enchantment.

She placed the yellow dress carefully in one of her saddle bags. Although it pained her to part with such an exquisite garment, she knew she couldn't keep it – it would only serve as a reminder of her humiliation, even if Jack hadn't intended it as such. She would ensure that it found its way back to Lady Lampton again.

Pulling herself back up in the saddle, Cora looked behind her one more time. She could no longer see the house, of course, but there was still that strange tug, the pull of adventure, of emotion, and if she had been a fanciful sort, she could easily have imagined hearing the echo of Jack calling her name.

But she wasn't given to fancies. She was a no-nonsense, sensible young woman with a sick father to care for.

And she was on the run.

With renewed determination she picked up the reins and steered Samson in the direction of Mrs Wilton's cottage. She and Ned were leaving for good, and she doubted that she would ever see Jack again.

She should have felt relief at her narrow escape, so why did it feel as if there was a huge, gaping hole in her chest where her heart should have been?

'Where've you been? Your father has been worrying himself sick.'

Cora turned at the sound of Mrs Wilton's throaty voice. She had rubbed Samson down and seen to it that he had fresh water and a couple of turnips when Mrs Wilton appeared at the lean-to where she stored her firewood, and which served as a temporary shelter for the horse.

'I had an errand to run,' Cora replied, guilt gnawing at her insides for leaving Ned so soon after they had abandoned their cottage. 'Is my father all right?'

Mrs Wilton eyed Cora's breeches and jacket and looked as if she was about to comment, but then she merely shrugged. 'As well as can be expected with the ague. I gave 'im some of that fancy tincture. Lord knows it won't cure 'im, but he's resting now, so I suppose it must've done 'im some good.'

'Thank you, Mrs Wilton,' said Cora. 'I appreciate all you've done for us. If there's anything we can do to repay—'

Mrs Wilton gave a dismissive wave. 'Pah! At my age there ain't much excitement in life, so you've done me a favour just by visitin'. Now, go and see to your father, you wayward girl. He's been asking for you all evening.'

Cora ducked inside Mrs Wilton's cramped cottage and went straight to her father, who lay on the only bed in the dwelling. She and Ned were poor, but nothing compared to Mrs Wilton, who lived in what could only be called a hovel. Cora was thankful that the older woman, who was as thin and scrawny as they came, had had the foresight to push the bed closer to the fire. It was banked down for the night now but gave off enough heat to keep Ned comfortable. He always suffered more when he was cold, and the evening was chilly despite it being high summer.

Her father opened his eyes as she knelt down beside the bed. In the sparse light from the fire and a candle on the table she noticed that his eyes had taken on a feverish shine and his hand was clammy to the touch. A hard lump formed in her stomach.

'Where have you been?' Ned asked and sat up. He waved her hand away with an impatient gesture when she tried to prop up the straw-filled cushion behind him, and Cora moved back, allowing him his pride.

'I'm not in my dotage yet, girl,' he growled as he rose from the bed and moved to sit in a wooden chair closer to the fire, 'and I'm not an invalid either.'

'No, Father.'

He sent her a suspicious look. 'And you don't fool me with your simpering. Where have you been, and in those clothes?'

It seemed a little late in the day for feeble explanations. Ned had known what she got up to for a while anyway. 'We needed travel money,' she said simply. 'I held up a carriage.'

Behind her Mrs Wilton gasped, but Ned regarded her steadily, with a twinkle in his eye and an almost imperceptible smile tugging the corners of his lips. 'I see,' he said slowly. 'And were you in luck?'

Cora dug into one of her saddle bags and handed him the purse she had lifted out of Jack's pocket when she lay at the bottom of the stairs. Holding it brought back memories of their kiss and sent the blood rushing to her cheeks, as well as a feeling of shame that she had stolen from him so coldly. Her hand shook, but she controlled herself and handed the purse to Ned, in the hope that her father hadn't noticed her agitation. Without a word he took it and poured the coins out into his hand, counted them and handed half to Mrs Wilton together with the purse. 'For your trouble, Martha.'

A look of understanding passed between them. 'You don't owe me anything, Ned.'

'I know,' he replied in a rasping voice, 'but I'd be a damn sight happier knowing that you're well looked after. Keep the money in a safe place and burn the purse.'

'I ain't in my dotage either,' protested Mrs Wilton, and they exchanged another look. 'I know how to take care of meself.'

Ned and Martha, was it? Cora raised her eyebrows. She didn't blame her father for his generosity towards Mrs Wilton; after all it was what she would have done if the widow had allowed her to, but it worried her that they had so little money left. When they travelled, they would need to buy food, and the tincture for Ned's cough would need replenishing eventually. What then? Would they find work and lodgings, or would they be doomed to stay on the road forever? There was no way her father would survive such an ordeal.

'You're a foolhardy girl,' Ned said, turning to Cora again, 'but a brave one. No father could be prouder of his daughter than I am.'

Cora took his hand. 'And no daughter could have a more attentive father than you. But I must beg your permission to let me do one last thing before we leave. I need to say goodbye to Uncle George before ... before they hang him tomorrow.'

Ned clasped her hand in his with what seemed like the last of his strength. 'Cora, it's too dangerous.'

'Why should it be dangerous?'

'The thought of you walking into Newgate fills me with dread.'

'I can look after myself,' Cora insisted. 'Please, Father, say you'll let me. I have no desire to go against your wishes, but ... I believe I must go.'

'I know you can. That's not what worries me.'

'What is it, then?'

Shaking his head, Ned stared into the embers of the fire, and it seemed like an age before he spoke again, this time in a voice so low that Cora had to strain to hear what he was saying. 'As you know there are those who believe that George left behind a secret stash, a treasure if you like, before he was arrested.'

'Yes, I've heard the story,' Cora scoffed. 'It gets better each time it's told.' When Ned said nothing, she asked, 'It is just a story, isn't it? It's not true?' She'd always thought so, but perhaps Ned knew differently.

'Of course it's not true. George likes his drink a little too much to have put anything aside.' Ned shrugged. 'But it's a popular myth and there are some who believe it. You can be certain that someone will be watching the prison for any of George's cronies going in. If you're recognised, there's a good chance these characters will think George has revealed his secret to you.'

'Why should he reveal it to me?' Cora asked. 'If, indeed, there is anything to reveal?'

Ned patted her hand and gave her a tired smile. 'Because, dear heart, everyone knows that he saw you as the child he never had. If he reveals anything to anyone, it'd be to you and no other.'

Defeated, Cora sat back on her haunches and stared into the fire. The tale of George's secret loot was legendary; had been even when he was a free man. The threat Ned referred to was real.

But she had an idea. 'I won't go as me. I'll go as a fine lady, in a veil, and I doubt if anyone will recognise me.' She rose and pulled the yellow dress out of the saddle bag, then held it up in front of her.

Mrs Wilton clasped her hands together. 'Lord in Heaven! That is a handsome gown. I never saw one quite so fine.' She stretched out her hand and ran an arthritic finger over the fabric gently, almost reverently, as if she feared that the material would snag on her rough labourer's hands.

'Are you robbing the clothes off people's backs now?' Ned grumbled. 'Or are you risking your life riffling through their luggage?'

'No, I found this inside the carriage itself,' Cora lied. 'Perhaps someone changed clothes during the journey.' Carefully, without meeting Ned's eyes, she lay the dress over the back of the rickety chair.

'Perhaps.'

Cora's skin prickled under her father's penetrating stare, but she set her mouth in a firm line. *If only you knew,* she thought. *If only you knew that your beloved daughter was nearly ensnared into ...*

Into what exactly? She had assumed that Jack had been manipulating her because the arrival of his cousin in the gallery, at such a late hour and at a moment when Cora had felt entirely vulnerable, had seemed too deliberate, almost as if Jack had engineered it. Except that didn't quite tally with the way he'd acted with her, the kindness he'd shown her and his gentle humour. Their attraction was mutual, she was sure of that. Maybe she had been a little hasty. After all, she hadn't given him much chance to explain.

Either way, there was little doubt that she had acted like a fool, and she pushed the thought aside, not wanting to be reminded of it. She had a hanging to go to.

Mrs Wilton was still admiring the dress and didn't seem to have noticed the looks which passed between father and daughter. 'You're quite right, Cora, my love, I don't think anyone will recognise you in that. But you'll be needing a chaperone.'

'A chaperone?' Cora laughed. 'I'm not some pasty-faced little miss who can't go to the outhouse without an escort. I can take—'

'Take care of yourself?' said Ned. 'Aye, we know that, but Martha's right. A young lady wouldn't go anywhere without either her maid or a relative to accompany her. It wouldn't be considered proper, and improper behaviour is likely to rouse suspicion. That's what we want to avoid.' He coughed suddenly, for a long time, as if the effort of scolding her had been too much.

Cora watched his shoulders heave with the effort of catching his breath. Realisation hit her that Ned would soon be taken from her and she swore she would bring him somewhere safe, somewhere warm. Spain, perhaps, the country that had inspired her name. Ned was all she had in the world and she was determined that his last few months should be as comfortable as possible.

She'd never believed the stories of Gentleman George's treasure, but it wouldn't hurt to find out if the story held some truth, would it?

'All right,' she said, 'tell me what you think I should do.'

Chapter Fifteen

After his visit to Newgate, Rupert had begun making enquiries about the man named Mardell, whom Gentleman George had inadvertently fingered, but no one was talking. He was met with blank stares bordering on the hostile, from men and women alike, and he cursed the fact that the townsfolk of Hounslow had such long memories when it came to his exploits.

Eventually he managed to corner a lad, and a combination of threatening to shake the poor youth until his teeth fell out and the promise of a coin yielded information he had partly surmised anyway – that Mardell lived with his daughter in a cottage in the woods near Hospital Bridge. This information left him exactly nowhere – he had seen for himself that Mardell's cottage was deserted and knew that the man and his daughter must be long gone.

Frustrated, he took himself back to the magistrate.

Blencowe received him in less than good humour.

'What brings you here at this late hour, Blythe?' he bellowed from behind his desk. 'If it's to do with that thieving lad who's terrorising us all, I'm afraid I have no intelligence which I haven't already shared with you.'

'I may have some information for you.'

'Indeed?' Blencowe raised his eyebrows.

'Are you familiar with a man named Mardell?' Rupert said.

'Mardell?' Blencowe frowned and appeared to be thinking hard. 'The name is familiar. Yes, I recollect now. The man is a common labourer, but if you believe him to be our highwayman, you're grossly mistaken. The sightings all report a lad, not a man Mardell's age. Besides, it's common knowledge that Mardell suffers from an ague of the chest and has a rasping cough likely to give him away.'

Rupert hesitated. Blencowe had already refused to help him once; if he wanted him to change his mind, now was the time to own up to the fact that the 'lad' in question was, in fact, a woman. Except he was certain Jack must have kept this piece of information from the magistrate, for reasons of his own, and Rupert would do the same. Otherwise his chances of winning that wager against his saintly cousin were very slim.

'Not Mardell,' Rupert said. 'A relative of his.'

'Relative, pah! The only relative Mardell has is a daughter, and I seriously doubt a mere female has enough mettle to put the fear of God into our hapless travellers. No, it has to be a young man we're looking for.'

'So ... Mardell has no nephews or any other known young associates?'

'None whatsoever,' Blencowe replied. 'So, if you have nothing else to add, I should like to attend to my dinner.'

Blencowe rose to signal that the meeting was at an end, and Rupert had no choice but to thank the magistrate for his time and bid him goodnight, which he did smiling affably yet gritting his teeth. Outside he gave vent to his frustration and threw his cane to the ground. To Blencowe he was nothing but a time-waster, and always had been, that much was clear.

Muttering curses, he forced himself to apply some logic. What would he do if he were in the highwaywoman's position? They had already left their cottage, but may be planning to leave the area for good. If this was the case, they would need travel money, quickly, which probably meant robbing another coach. But he'd not heard of any attacks since the one directed at himself and Jack, so he could either patrol the Bath Road and wait for the highwaywoman to strike or he could follow Jack to see what he got up to. Except Jack had proved rather adept at giving him the slip lately. Or he could go back to the Mardells' cottage in the hope of finding some clue to where they might be headed, something which he may have missed the first time.

Picking up his cane again, he resolved to go back there at first light, which was far earlier than he was accustomed to rising. However, desperate measures were called for under the circumstances.

Cora and Mrs Wilton set off at daybreak the next morning. Mrs Wilton, carrying a covered basket over her arm, wore a white cotton cap and a long shawl, which hid the fact that her dress had seen better days, and Cora had opted for the breeches and jacket. She tied her hair back in a queue and pulled her tricorne hat over her eyes to hide her face from curious looks.

But nobody took any notice of them, an old woman and her son going to London. Soon they struck lucky and hitched a ride on the back of a wagon transporting kegs of ale from Isleworth Brewery to an inn near Drury Lane.

Cora hadn't been to London since before her mother died, but she remembered some of the landmarks they passed from her last journey: Kew Bridge and the town of Kew on the other side of the Thames, the villages of Hammersmith and Kensington. By the church in Kensington the road widened, and the traffic grew heavier. In addition to the slow-moving wagons and market carts, stagecoaches, horsemen and travelling carriages all bustled towards London, and the smell of the road and the rumbling of wheels over granite stones filled the morning air.

Between Kensington and Hyde Park stood the Halfway House Inn, reputed to be a meeting place for highwaymen's touts, who gathered here, ready to send word to Hounslow Heath and other places on the western roads when wealthy families or merchants were setting out. Situated on the road side of the park, the inn stood all alone with its sinister reputation, and Cora felt a slight shiver as they passed it. She may have broken the law on occasion, and hit Jack's groom out of desperation, but she would never intentionally harm any of her victims.

Others were far more brutal.

As they drew nearer to London, the din rose. Street vendors touted their wares and the crowds grew denser and more vociferous.

But nothing could have prepared her for the narrow streets between Drury Lane and Oxford Street. What before had seemed crowded and busy, rich and poor, colourful and drab, all rolled into one, was replaced by the most unimaginable filth and squalid misery. Wretched houses with broken windows patched with rags and paper, gutters in the street, clothes drying and slops emptying from the windows, children with matted hair walking barefoot. And everywhere men and women, of all ages and in every variety of scanty and dirty clothing, were lounging, drinking, smoking, fighting and swearing.

Horrified, Cora tried not to stare, but found it difficult. There was poverty in and around the town of Hounslow, people living in far more woeful circumstances than herself and Ned, but nothing like this. It was a different world.

The wagon stopped in front of The Black Lion, a disreputable-looking ale house, and Cora and Martha climbed down and thanked the drayman.

'Mind how you go, fella me lad,' he said to Cora and nodded his head for emphasis. 'This ain't no place to bring yer ma.'

He began unloading the kegs with the help of the taproom boy, and soon forgot about his passengers, who slipped in the back through an enclosed yard. A group of men engaged in a game of dice paid little attention to the young man who slipped into a back room, and no one batted an eyelid when the same young man emerged dressed as a woman. Perhaps such sights were commonplace in the vicinity of a theatre, Cora thought with amusement.

In her yellow dress and a slightly tattered black veil Martha had lent her, Cora followed her companion, who had been to

London a few times before, along the Strand and Fleet Street to Newgate. The streets were a beehive of activity, but even in a crowd such as this, Jack's mother's yellow dress was eye-catching. Already she was attracting a number of stares, a few leering, some courteous, despite her wearing a veil. Or perhaps because of the veil. Either way it made her feel uncomfortable, as if she was being watched.

The smell greeted them first as they turned into Old Bailey. It was as if the gates of Hell had opened and spilled forth all its misery and malodour. Martha covered her nose with her shawl, but Cora didn't. This was where Gentleman George was forced to spend the last few hours of his life; he had no choice but to accept it, so Cora would do the same.

Still, it struck her as deviant, inhuman even, that shopkeepers, innkeepers and delivery men would go about their business as if their neighbour was just another building, and not the most notorious prison in the whole of England.

The hustle and bustle here was the same as elsewhere in this sprawling city, completely heedless of what misery lay beyond these walls producing the near-unbearable stench. Passers-by were within a few yards of men and women whose days were numbered, who had lost all hope and whose lives would soon end in violent and shameful death.

Cora stopped in front of the portcullis gate and looked up at the four-storeyed front looming over her. There was no hope for George. Last-minute reprieves from the king were rare, and why should Uncle George get one anyway? He had no one to plead his cause and had committed all the crimes with which he had been charged. Probably more. There was no doubt about his guilt. The only thing Cora could do for her father's friend was to return his dignity to him.

She breathed in and almost gagged from the noxious air. 'Soap,' she said to Martha. 'I need soap.'

'Soap?' Martha squawked. 'What'll you be needing that for? Old George can't eat that for 'is last meal!'

'For washing,' said Cora, still staring up at the imposing prison façade.

'You look clean enough to me.'

'Not for me. For Uncle George.'

Finally Martha understood. She squeezed Cora's arm with her claw-like hand. 'You're a good girl, Cora. Your father's right to be proud of you. He probably don't say it much, but I know 'e is.'

Cora put her hand over Martha's. For a brief moment she wanted to laugh at the absurdity of it all. Here she was, a country girl by day, highwaywoman by night and possibly a fine lady by blood, in stolen finery, walking into a prison, a veritable lion's den, with only soap and a silk waistcoat for the condemned man. Her father might be proud of her, but he was right about her actions: this was utter madness.

It was also the right thing to do.

On the bustling Newgate Street they found a shop selling household goods; Cora purchased a pound of lye soap and dropped it in the basket Martha was carrying; then, holding their breath, they walked in through the prison gate.

At the gatekeeper's house Martha's basket and pockets were searched, but when the guard turned to Cora, she held her head high.

'My good man, do I look like the sort of personage who would bring a weapon to a condemned criminal?'

The guard eyed her expensive dress and her veil and Cora hoped he wouldn't notice that the veil was a bit threadbare in places and the dress a little too short – or the pistol concealed in her pocket.

'I'm sorry, m'lady, just doin' me job.'

If he noticed that Martha was far too old to be a lady's maid, he omitted to mention it, and Cora drew a sigh of relief. 'I apologise for inconveniencing you, but may I trouble you for a pail of water?'

The gatekeeper narrowed his eyes and Cora had a nasty

feeling that he saw right through her disguise and was toying with her. Maybe the man had listened to the rumours of Gentleman George's alleged treasure and was waiting to pounce on anyone who may have further information. A drop of perspiration ran down her back and she suppressed a shiver.

'Certainly, m'lady,' he said at last. 'Although, begging your pardon, but what'll you be needing the water for?'

'I believe it to be Gentleman George's last wish to meet his maker with a clean shirt and well-combed hair.' *And you could do with a proper wash yourself.*

The gatekeeper cackled at that. 'I dare say you'll need more than a pail of water for that. Scum, they all are in 'ere. Just scum. Ain't no one here clean enough to go anywhere other than straight to Hell. It'll cost you.'

Cora jutted out her chin. She hated to have to part with some of the little travel money they had but if she kicked up a fuss, she might draw unwelcome attention to herself and Martha. 'Of course. Will a shilling suffice?'

'That's most generous, m'lady. Most generous indeed.' While Cora dug out a shilling from her purse, the gatekeeper signalled to the other guard, who left the room, then he grabbed the coin Cora handed him and slipped it into the pocket of his waistcoat. A moment later the other guard returned with a pail of murky water.

'Here you are, m'lady. Although I fear it'll take more than water to make this prisoner presentable.' He winked at the gatekeeper, who chuckled menacingly, and it was with some trepidation that Cora and Martha followed him through a labyrinth of stairs and corridors to a cell on the third floor.

'These cells are for those who only have hours left before their execution,' the guard explained. 'It gives them a chance to spruce up before the 'anging so they can put on a proper show, like. Not disappoint the specta'ors.'

Cora stiffened. She was aware that crowds at a hanging expected a performance from the condemned, but hearing the guard talking about it so matter-of-factly, as if it was no different from an ordinary theatre production, brought it home to her that people were actually looking forward to seeing men die today.

And one of those men was a dear friend.

The guard unlocked a thick wooden door with a metal grille at the top. 'Someone paid us handsomely to give him a private cell. A fine lady, like yerself.'

He sent Cora a sly look as if to gauge her reaction to the news that the prisoner had other female admirers – which was what he assumed Cora to be – but she ignored him. When the door swung open with a clang, all she had eyes for was the disconsolate figure sitting on a high-backed chair staring up at the blue sky beyond the barred window. Chains attached to a ring in the wall kept his ankles shackled, but the prisoner wasn't otherwise restrained. He did not turn around when Cora entered.

'That'll be all,' she heard Martha say to the guard. 'We'll give you a holler when we're finished.'

'I'll be right outside. This cove's dangerous.'

'Looks more like 'alf-dead already,' Martha muttered when the guard had left them with a cheerful whistle and a jangle of keys as he locked the door behind him.

Half-dead? Ripping off her veil, Cora crossed to where George sat, but he didn't turn around, almost as if the fight had gone out of him a long time ago. Panic gripped Cora's heart. Uncle George loved the freedom of the Heath, the sun and wind on his face when he rode and, of course, spending his evenings at a convivial inn. Had prison taken away his soul already? She would never forgive herself if Uncle George died without ever really knowing that she had come to say goodbye.

She put her hand on his shoulder, and only then did he turn, with empty eyes and a distant smile on his lips. 'My lady,' he said and inclined his head regally although he did not get up, 'to what do I owe this unexpected pleasure?'

Cora bit her lip. It was worse than she feared; prison had indeed robbed her friend of his sanity. 'Uncle George? It's Cora.' She whispered in case the guard was still listening.

'Cora …' He nodded slowly as if tasting her words. 'But of course you are. A beautiful name for a beautiful lady.'

'Cora Mardell. Ned's daughter.'

A shadow passed across his face and reality returned to his eyes. He gripped her hand and squeezed it. 'Cora? Little Cora? Can it be?' His gaze ran over her, searchingly, until it seemed he had drunk in all her features and was satisfied with what he saw. Then his face lit up. 'It is you! And in a fine lady's clothes. How can that be? And why have you come to see an old man die? This is no place for you.'

'You're not old, Uncle George,' she replied and squeezed his hand in return, then quickly stopped as he winced in pain. He looked terrible. One of his eyes was badly swollen, his bottom lip had split, and underneath his torn shirt he was covered in cuts and bruises, some of them oozing yellow pus. And he stank. Gently Cora peeled aside the shirt to reveal a large bruise on his side with a peculiar protrusion under the skin.

A broken rib, she thought. *Perhaps several.* Uncle George had taken a severe beating.

'Who did this to you?' she asked, seething with rage. 'The guards?'

George groaned unintelligibly.

'Who?' Cora insisted.

It was a while before he answered. 'There was a man … can't remember his name.' George exhaled. 'Maybe he didn't give it. I … I don't remember things so well these days. The mind … is not what it was. But he was a nobleman.'

Cora's thoughts flew to Jack. If he possessed the intelligence she credited him with, he would have surmised that highwaymen were likely to be known to each other. Who better to question than a man who had no means of escape?

She looked down at her old friend, at his beaten-up face,

once so kind and gentlemanly, and clenched her fists. Jack couldn't have done this, not the Jack she knew, but if she ever found who had reduced a beloved friend to this pathetic state, she would … well, she would rip him to shreds.

'Whoa,' croaked George and looked at Cora with a twinkle in his good eye. 'I know that face. Doesn't bode well.'

'Can you describe this man to me?' Cora asked and moved aside so he could get comfortable. *Please, God, let it not be Jack. I couldn't bear the thought.*

'It seemed like an age ago, though I don't suppose it is. You lose all sense of time in a place like this.' He was quiet for a moment. 'A young man, a dandy. Your own age or thereabouts. Fine clothes, exquisitely crafted wig, a patch here.' He indicated a point beside his mouth. 'Or maybe it was real, I dunno. You can never tell with these types.'

'A gentleman,' George continued, 'but only skin deep.'

'I don't understand.'

'There was something nasty about him, lurking beneath the surface.' George narrowed his eyes. 'And he wanted to know about you specifically. Have you crossed this man?'

Cora shook her head. 'I don't think so. He sounds wholly unfamiliar.' But as soon as she said it, the image of a gentleman with a patch beside his mouth came to mind; Jack's companion on the night of the robbery. But who was he and what did he want from her? She had robbed him, certainly, but was that enough to induce a man such as he to enter a notorious prison to visit a highwayman? And how had he made the connection between herself and Gentleman George?

Cora stilled as dread rose in her chest. 'What did you tell him, Uncle George?' she asked, articulating her words with care.

'Nothing!' he said, drawing himself up in indignation. 'Absolutely nothing. Although—' He stopped, and his face drained of colour so suddenly that Cora feared he might collapse.

'Although?'

'I might have said something – inadvertently, mind – about your father's cottage in the forest. I don't exactly recall. I'd had a few, you see. He'd brought a bottle of fine brandy, and, well, with one thing after another ...' He trailed off, imploring her wide-eyed to forgive his indiscretion.

Dread turned to abject horror and Cora glanced at Martha, who shook her head imperceptibly as if to say Ned would be safe for the time being. Her father had been right in urging them to flee immediately, and since they hadn't left any trace of where they'd gone, it was very unlikely that anyone would suspect them of being but a mile away.

Still, the sooner she and Ned were on their way, the better. There must be no delays. Today the authorities would be concerned with keeping order at the hanging; tomorrow was a different matter.

She patted George's hand. 'It's all right, Uncle George. My father and I left yesterday. You needn't concern yourself. We'll be fine.'

Gentleman George nodded, then sent her a curiously detached smile. 'Did you know that Jack Sheppard was held in this very cell before he was hanged?' The effort of sitting up had given his skin a waxy sheen and his eyes shone feverishly.

Naturally, Cora had heard of Sheppard, an infamous pickpocket and highwayman – what person hadn't? But she worried about George's sudden and seemingly random reference to the man; was he close to losing his mind? Perhaps the suppurating sores had brought on a real fever. Even if he was contemplating breaking out of prison, like the illustrious Sheppard had, she doubted he would make it in his condition.

'No, I didn't know that,' she replied. 'Is that what you're planning to do?'

Smiling sadly, George shook his head. 'Nay, my girl, I have no such plans. What a man has done will catch up with him in the end. That's the way of the world. I'd rather it was here, on

God's green Earth, than in the afterlife, if you get my meaning. It's just that …' He trailed off, and his shoulders sank.

'What, Uncle George?' Cora prodded gently.

'I wonder if it'll take a long time to die.'

Cora's stomach clenched with sudden horror. She had been so determined to help him go to the gallows with dignity that she'd forgotten hanging could be an agonisingly slow death, and that even the bravest person would struggle when dangling from a rope by his neck.

'You're a big man, Uncle George. I'm sure your passing will be quick.' She swallowed hard, and then said, 'But if it'll help, I promise I'll pull down on your legs when you … when you …' Unable to finish the sentence, she looked away.

'Bless you, Cora, but I've already paid the hangman handsomely to do that for me. As long your lovely face is the last thing I see, it'll be enough. Then I'll know what an angel looks like when I meet one.'

'I can promise you that,' she said and fought hard against her tears. It wouldn't do to show weakness; for Uncle George's sake she needed to be courageous. 'Can you stand?' she asked. 'I have a present for you.'

'Aye, I reckon I can.' George gripped the arms of his chair and with what seemed like superhuman effort forced himself upright. 'A drop of brandy would be darned welcome right now. For medicinal purposes, you understand. To ease the pain a little. I don't suppose you have any on you?'

In response to his imploring look Cora shook her head. She hadn't thought of that, much to her chagrin; she knew that when a man drank to excess the way Uncle George had done, depriving him of liquor would do more harm than good.

'I might be able to help you,' Martha said and stepped forward. For the first time George seemed to realise that there was someone else in the cell with them. 'Mind you, it'll be gin – that's all the likes of me can afford.'

Martha reached inside a deep pocket in her dress and

produced a small silver hip flask. Cora raised her eyes questioningly, but the older woman shrugged. 'Belonged to my dear departed, that one, though Lud knows what poor soul 'e robbed to acquire it. Never could bring meself to part with it, not even when there weren't enough to eat.'

Gentleman George took the proffered bottle and drank the contents greedily, like a babe at the breast. 'Ah, that's better,' he said, although his prison pallor didn't improve. 'Clears the cobwebs. Now, where were we?'

'I brought this for you,' Cora said. She handed him the soap and pail of water and produced one of Ned's shirts from under her petticoats.

'And this.'

She handed the waistcoat to George. Admiring the exquisite embroidery, he remained silent, but when he finally spoke, there was a catch in his voice.

'Thank you, Cora Mardell. Thank you for restoring a man's dignity. You don't just look like an angel, you are one, bless you.'

At ten o'clock, shortly after Cora and Martha had said goodbye to Gentleman George, the ox-carts conveying the condemned prisoners left Newgate Prison. Six men were to be hung, two to each ox-cart, and each of them travelled the route with a noose about the neck and their elbows pinned back. Only Gentleman George was handcuffed, being considered a particular security risk, although he sat in the first row in the cart, a place of honour reserved for highwaymen and those who robbed the mail.

Cora and Martha followed the carts, together with countless other people, some of them relatives and acquaintances of the condemned, others merely spectators. With each step taking them closer to Tyburn, Cora felt an agonising ache in her chest.

The procession stopped at St Sepulchre's, where the condemned men heard the bellman's final proclamation and received a floral wreath. Then they journeyed along Holborn, St Giles and Oxford Road, stopping at various alehouses, where the prisoners were offered wine.

London was always *en fête* on hanging day, and the huge crowds lining the route bombarded the popular prisoners with flowers and nosegays, but hurled mud, stones, excrement and dead cats and dogs at those whose crimes they disapproved of. Cora was relieved to see that her father's old friend received only flowers.

All too soon they had travelled the three miles to the Tyburn Tree, and Cora's insides revolted in earnest. This was the end; after today she would never see George again, never hear his raucous laughter or look upon his friendly face. Squeezing her eyes shut and clenching her fists to get a grip on herself, she felt Martha's hand on her arm.

'It'll soon be over, dear. Then we can say a prayer and hope for a safe passing.'

Unable to speak, Cora merely nodded.

By the gallows outside Tyburn village a carnival atmosphere existed. There were all manner of street vendors hawking their wares: food, drink, trinkets. Entertainers, doomsday preachers, pick-pockets and beggars mingled with the spectators, and the noise from the crowd, the shrillness of the cries and the howls, was a feverish jangling sound. Cora witnessed no emotion suitable to the occasion. No sorrow or seriousness, only ribaldry, debauchery and drunkenness.

Hanging days were public holidays, and the enterprising villagers had wasted no time in erecting spectator stands around the hanging tree and extracting an extortionate fee for a seat. On a rare occasion the spectators stands collapsed, killing and maiming hundreds of people, but today they looked quite sturdy.

Cora squeezed through the crowds to get as close to George as she could. She had promised him that she would be the last person he would see, and she intended to keep that promise even if it meant attracting stares and sneering comments about pushing in and not keeping her place.

Finally she managed to get close to George's ox-cart.

'There you are!' he said and his face lit up. 'I couldn't see you. Thought I'd lost you.'

'I said I'd be here, and so I am.' Cora lifted her veil so he could see her face.

'My dear. This is no place for you.'

'It's exactly the place for me,' she replied firmly despite her unsettled stomach, 'and this is where I'm staying.'

The Ordinary was reading a prayer, and despite the noise from the crowd his voice carried loud and clear on the summer breeze.

'I am the resurrection and the life,' he recited. 'He that believeth in me, though he were dead, yet shall he live.'

Cora wasn't listening; her eyes were on the hangman, who was fastening the nooses to the Triple Tree: three wooden posts set out in a triangle, with crossbars running between them. All the prisoners would be hanged at the same time, and the hangman was moving steadily closer to George. Cora's chest ached so hard she could only gasp.

'Uncle George ...'

'You'd think today was your hanging, not mine.' Chuckling, he beckoned her closer and Cora clambered up on the cart. 'I pray you won't share the same fate as me. But just to be on the safe side, I'll put in a good word for you with Him upstairs, shall I?'

Smiling through tears, Cora hugged him. It was so like George to jest in the last moments of his life.

'Wish me luck,' he said as the hangman fastened the rope above him. 'Pray that I go to the right place and not to eternal Hell and damnation.'

'You won't,' she whispered. 'You're a good man. I'll always remember you.'

Testing that the noose was sound, the hangman glanced at

Cora. 'You'd best get yourself down, little lady, lest you get tangled with the cart.' Of George he asked, not unkindly, 'Are you ready?'

'As ready as I'll ever be.' George's eyes bore into Cora's. 'Goodbye, my dear.'

After that it seemed as if time had somehow slowed down. The ox-carts were driven away, and the six men suddenly dangled from their necks. Instinct took over, and each of them kicked out and bucked against their restraints, groaning and gagging. Even George, who had been so stoic only a moment before, looked to be panicking.

Surrounded by the jeering crowds Cora watched the horrifying spectacle, unable to do anything, wishing it would stop. But she knew it could take a person as long as fifteen minutes to die. She had become separated from Martha, and without the older woman's reassuring presence she stumbled towards George's jerking body, not knowing if she had it in her to do what must be done.

The hangman pre-empted her. ''Ere, let me.' He stopped her with a strong arm, hoisted himself up George's body and kneeled on the dangling man's shoulders while holding on to the rope. With a gruesome, final rattle in his throat, George was gone, and Cora covered her face with her hands.

How long she stood there, shaking with grief and terror, she couldn't tell, but her misery was interrupted by a coarse voice.

'That's her! The Mardell girl. Get her!'

Chapter Sixteen

Cora swung around and saw three burly men bearing down on her.

'Get her!' one of them shouted again.

Wasting no time, Cora hoisted up her skirts and pushed through the throng. The three men dived into the crowd and did the same, but it was easier for one person to push through than for three, and this gave her a head start. She was under no illusion that she could outrun them and it seemed her only chance was to outwit them. If only she could reach Tyburn village, there would be plenty of places for her to hide.

When she was clear of the other spectators, she ran as fast as she could. She had no idea who these men were, but they clearly knew who she was. But why were they after her? Because of Uncle George's fabled treasure? Just as well she'd thought to arm herself. She felt for her pistol in the pocket of her dress. Her heart was beating so fast, she thought it might leave her ribcage altogether, and she felt nausea rise in her throat.

Glancing over her shoulder, she checked to see if the men had caught up with her, and when she spied nothing, she dived into an alleyway. As she did so, her veil caught on a nail and was ripped off. She bolted down the alley, searching for a way out. There had to be a door, or a gate. Or at least a window she could climb through. Nothing.

With frantic hands she searched the brickwork in case she'd overlooked something, a hole or a gap to squeeze through, but the walls were solid and unyielding. At the end of the alley stood an old beer barrel. Hoisting up her skirts, Cora climbed onto the barrel and try to pull herself up on to the roof of one of the houses, but the roof tiles were slippery with moss, and she fell back down.

She heard a scuffing noise behind her and turned slowly, her heart hammering wildly in her chest. She was trapped, and the only way out was blocked by the three men. One of them, a bow-legged, swarthy man, was holding the black veil in his hand.

'No way out, li'l lady,' he said, as they advanced slowly, menacingly. 'You'll have to talk to us.'

'What do you want?' She pulled her pistol out of her pocket and tossed her head in challenge. The men stopped, uncertain. Then one of them produced a knife. Grinning from ear to ear and showing off a set of blackened teeth, he tossed it from one hand to the other and caught it deftly. 'Ho, the lady's armed. What d'you say, lads – reckon she'll fire?'

'I will,' said Cora. She pointed the pistol at each of the men in turn, willing her hand not to tremble. She'd never fired on another person before.

'We only want to talk to you about Gen'leman George's treasure,' Blacktooth said.

'I don't know anything about that.' Cora took a step backwards as they advanced on her again. What was the matter with them? *I'm pointing a pistol at them, for Heaven's sake!*

'Aye, and William Pitt's the king o' England,' Blacktooth said and spat a slimy string of tobacco juice on the ground. 'We think you do.'

Cora shuddered with revulsion. 'I don't know where you get your information, but you're wrong. There is no treasure, and if you come any closer, I'll shoot.'

The men exchanged a quick look; then Bow-Legs laughed and pulled open his shirt, baring his chest. 'Go on, then. Let's see what yer made of.'

Cora swallowed. This time her hand trembled visibly

'No treasure?' Bow-Legs smiled, but his eyes remained firmly on her pistol hand. ''Ear that, Jimbo? Reckon the lass is telling the truth?'

Jim shook his head. He was a little younger than the other two, with greasy red hair and pimples on his cheeks. 'I reckon not. George told me so hisself not long ago, and I reckon 'e'd know whether 'e had treasure or no.'

'That was just the drink talking,' said Cora. Panic mounted as she took another few steps backwards. 'He liked his drink, and he liked telling stories.'

'Don't get clever with me, li'l lady,' snarled Bow-Legs. 'If Jim 'ere heard tell of treasure, I'll take 'is word for it any day over the word of some harlot.'

'Even if there was treasure, why would he tell me?' asked Cora.

'Because you're Ned Mardell's girl, and everyone knows 'e doted on you. We saw you kissing him and all. Lost him to the gallows? Poor lass, eh, but I reckon the three of us can make up for that.'

Suddenly, fast as a snake Bow-Legs knocked the pistol out of her hand and pinned her against the wall, his foul breath so hot on her face she had to cover her nose with her hand. She knew very well what he had in mind, and the thought of the likes of him touching her was nauseating.

'No, please, I beg you! George told me nothing. You must believe me.' And even if he had, she would never betray his trust to these men.

'Well, maybe you do, maybe you don't, but we're gonna have a whole lot of fun finding out, aren't we, fellas?'

Jim and Blacktooth grinned.

'And it starts right now,' said Bow-Legs. Twisting the black veil in his hand, he flung it over her neck like a makeshift noose and pulled her close, as if to kiss her.

Gagging, Cora acted on instinct and kneed him in the groin. He dropped to the ground like a felled tree, groaning. Before the others had time to react, Cora elbowed Blacktooth in the eye. Howling, he clutched his face, and Cora kicked him on the shin, then swung to face Jim.

Jim was faster. He caught her by the wrist, twisted her arm up behind her, and slammed her head against the brick wall of the alleyway.

Cora screamed with shock and pain. Then everything went black.

Jack galloped through Tyburn village, his horse's hooves kicking up a cloud of dust behind him. Frantically he looked for any sign of Cora, but saw no one except a boy loitering by a horse trough.

'You there! Did you see a lady in a yellow dress come this way?'

The boy pointed to an ale house across the street. 'Yes, m'lord. She went down that way. Chased by three men, she were. Didn't look too friendly.'

He surged forward with only one thought. Cora was in danger. He'd come to the hanging hoping that she might be there, showing support for another member of her highwayman fraternity. But no sooner as he'd spotted her in the crowd, she'd turned on her heels and run, followed by three burly men.

Jack spurred his horse in the direction the boy was pointing, and unsheathed his rapier. His blood ran cold when he saw Cora lying on the ground in a heap of yellow silk with her black curls spilling out over the dirt. Three men were standing over her; they must have been debating amongst themselves what to do next and didn't notice him at first.

Raising his rapier, Jack spurred his horse forward and bore down on them. At the sound of the horse's hooves, they turned and Jack saw their eyes widen as they recoiled. Unkempt and unwashed, these men were mere ruffians, and whilst it was easy enough attacking a woman, an armed man on a horse was quite a different matter.

Halfway down the alley he reined in the horse and allowed it to dance a little, its flailing hooves presenting as much danger as his rapier. 'Leave the lady alone, or it'll be the worse for you,' he shouted. His words echoed off the walls of the narrow passage, making them sound louder than they actually were. The men jumped.

'What the ...?' One of the men picked up a pistol lying on the ground, but Jack saw him and pulled out his own.

'Don't even think about it,' he growled. 'I bet I'm a much better shot than you'll ever be, even left-handed.'

The man hesitated and Jack nudged his horse into motion. 'Go on, get out of here!' he bellowed. Two of the men did as they were told without further thought, fleeing past him in fright. The third, who was still clutching the pistol, stood his ground for a moment, bolder than the others.

'This 'ere ain't no lady, *sir*.' He hawked a large gob of spit, which landed on the ground beside Cora.

Jack felt his temper flare with unexpected force, but he managed to control himself. 'When I want your opinion, I'll ask for it,' he said coldly and whipped the pistol out of the man's hand with a few deft moves of his rapier. Then he pointed the weapon at the man's throat and saw him swallow nervously. 'Now get yourself out of here before I decide to see just how much pressure the skin on your filthy neck can withstand.' To emphasise his words he swiped the tip of the blade sideways, and the man gasped, touching the wound instinctively and then staring in horror at the smear of blood on his fingers.

'It's a scratch,' said Jack. 'You'll live. Now, get you gone!'

The man bolted, staying close to the wall, and as he passed he shot Jack a look of pure hatred.

When he was certain that the men were gone, Jack knelt beside Cora. She was as still and pale as death, and his insides twisted in agony.

Don't be dead. Please don't be dead.

In just a few short days she'd become the single most important person in his life, and he hadn't even noticed it happening. Lusting after her had turned into wanting her respect, her affection, and a need to protect her. If she'd have him, he would commit himself to her, and devil take convention.

His lips moving in a silent prayer, he felt her neck for signs of life and relief washed over him when he detected a faint pulse. A dark contusion was forming on her temple, her hands were cut and bruised, her dress torn and she had lost one of her shoes, but she appeared otherwise unharmed.

Recalling the murderous expression on the ruffian's face, Jack had a nasty feeling that the three men would soon return with reinforcements. He needed to get Cora away from here, but although his quick examination had revealed only superficial wounds, he had no idea just how hard a blow she had taken to the head. Taking her home to Lampton was out of the question, at least until she had been seen by a physician.

Gently he lifted her up in his arms, and a small moan escaped her.

'Cora, my sweet,' he whispered, 'what have they done to you?' *And why?*

Her eyelids fluttered briefly; then she opened her eyes. 'Jack?'

He felt her body stiffen, her hands bracing against his chest. 'Don't fight me, Cora. Now is not the time for sparring.'

He read the wariness in her eyes, and something else too, something deeper. He couldn't quite decipher it, but it had his nerve endings tingling with awareness. 'I'm not going to hurt you,' he said. 'You can trust me, Cora. You do trust me, don't you?'

A pause, then her wariness subsided, and she relaxed against his chest. 'Yes, Jack. Forgive me,' she added in a whisper.

'Forgive *you*?' He pressed a kiss to her brow. 'It is I who must beg your forgiveness.'

As he lifted her onto his horse, picked up the pistol, and

then climbed up behind her, he cursed himself. Cursed himself all the way to Hell and back again.

The blame was his, and his alone. He had tried to persuade her that she could be a lady, as if her years of living in poverty had never happened. He had revelled in catching her and dressing her up but he had not thought about the possible consequences for her. In a wool dress and a plain bonnet she could blend in with the crowd, in her breeches and coat she could defend herself – as he'd learned to his cost – but wearing the silk dress of a countess she'd been fair game.

And he hadn't been there to offer his protection when the inevitable attack occurred.

Shame stole over him as he realised what a fool he had been. *What were you thinking, Halliford? You great big lumbering idiot.*

Even if they could persuade his father to give her an allowance, it wouldn't change the differences between them. She'd understood it of course, had tried to tell him she could never fit into his world. And he didn't want her to change. If he tried to change her, she wouldn't be the Cora he had come to respect and admire. The woman he had come to love.

He had loved Cora from the moment she had pointed her rapier at his throat and stared at him with a ferocity which belied her beauty. He had tried to persuade himself that he had been driven by duty. And all the while he had been blind to the simple fact that his heart would beat faster in her presence, his breath shallow, his stomach tight.

Love, he thought again and glanced down at Cora, who slumped against him with her eyes closed. He tightened his grip and pulled her closer. A lock of black hair fell across her face and fluttered as she exhaled.

Slowly she opened her eyes and looked up at him with a faint smile on her lips. Jack could only guess at what she saw, but if his expression matched what was in his heart, she couldn't fail to guess his feelings. Her strange, pale eyes widened and her lips parted. Desire shot through him. He wanted to bend his head and kiss her till he had no breath left in his body, to never let her go.

But first he wanted her somewhere safe. The three ruffians might return and take another stab at him, and what they wanted from Cora didn't bear thinking about. He tightened his arm around her and checked his pistol was within easy reach.

'Jack, I … I …' she began, but then trailed off, chewing her bottom lip.

'Yes, my l— Cora?' he said. Now was not the time for declarations.

'I, er … I don't feel well.'

'What?' Jack's bubble burst abruptly. 'Oh, dear God!'

Just in time, he swung her sideways and held her over the horse's flank as she emptied the contents of her stomach. Again and again she heaved until it seemed there could be nothing left inside her, drawing the unwelcome attention of a few passers-by who were returning from the hanging. Finally she sat up, pasty-faced yet determined, and wiped her mouth with the back of her hand.

'Apologies, I would have passed you my handkerchief if I'd been fast enough,' he said.

Cora smiled sheepishly. 'I think I could still do with it.'

Laughing, Jack dug inside his breast pocket. 'I'll say this, Cora – life's anything but dull around you.'

She glared at him and wiped her hand and her mouth one more time; then held the handkerchief out to him. 'Keep it,' he said, rolling his eyes. 'You might need it again.'

'I'm all right,' she protested.

'Cora, you've taken a blow to the head. How serious, I don't know, but judging from the violence of your sickness just now, it might have caused some damage in your brain. You need to be checked by a physician.'

'I don't have time for physicians,' Cora said. 'I need to get home.'

'You'll get home soon enough, but not until I'm reassured that you're well.' Jack steered the horse towards the outskirts of the village.

Cora stiffened. 'Where are you taking me?'

'Somewhere you can be examined in some privacy.'

He didn't mention his worry that the men might be looking for them, and the sooner he got her to safety, the better. The inn would be crowded, and even if the men managed to track them down, they would be safe enough inside. When Cora had been examined, he would send word to Lampton Hall for his carriage to be brought.

'Let me go,' Cora said and tried to wriggle away from his grasp, but she was either too weak or her struggling was half-hearted. Reassured that she wasn't going anywhere soon, Jack kept a firm grip on her and pressed a kiss to her hair.

'Are you always this querulous, even when a person has your best interests at heart?'

Cora didn't answer. Instead her breathing became laboured as if she struggled not to vomit again. Jack sincerely hoped she wasn't going to.

He stopped at an inn on Tyburn Lane and cast a quick look over his shoulder to see if they were being followed. There was no evidence that they were and he dismounted quickly to help Cora down. Stumbling, she held on to him for support, and Jack tossed the reins to a barefoot boy who was sweeping the yard with a broom that was too big for him.

'See to my horse, and you will be generously rewarded,' he said using his most authoritative voice.

'Yes, m'lord.' The boy jumped at the chance of earning a few coins and led the horse away.

'They'll be full,' Cora scoffed weakly. 'It's hanging day.'

'I'm a viscount. It might not be fair that my title gets me special treatment, but when your well-being's at stake, I'm prepared to pull rank.' He sent her a look of concern. 'Can you walk unaided?'

'You're an ass, Jack. Did anyone ever tell you that?'

'Frequently.'

'Of course I can walk. I wish you'd stop fussing. They didn't strike me that hard. I … Oh!'

Jack caught her just in time, as, with a stifled moan, she went limp in his arms. His heart thudding violently against his ribcage, he lifted her and pushed open the door to the inn with his foot.

'A bed for the lady,' he demanded loudly.

The rotund innkeeper greeted them, wiping his hands nervously on a cloth which hung from his belt. 'Beggin' your pardon, sir, but we're quite booked up. It's hanging day today and …'

Jack sent him a furious look. 'Are you blind? The lady is ill. She needs a physician, a bed, with fresh linen, hot water and towels. And I need someone to send word to Lord Lampton at Lampton Hall. And be quick about it, man!'

'Yes, m'lord. Right away, m'lord.' The innkeeper turned away and yelled for someone in the back room. 'Lizzie! See to their needs! I'll go fetch Mrs Garrett.'

'A female physician?' Jack raised his eyebrows, but then reconsidered; since he'd met Cora he'd started to realise that women could do anything a man could do.

The innkeeper shook his head. 'We have no physician in the village. There's the apothecary, but he'll be at the hanging or in his cups, or both. Mrs Garrett has much experience of illness and will be of more use.'

'That'll have to do,' Jack said and followed the innkeeper's wife up to a small, airless room. Gently he lay Cora down on the bed, which looked clean, thankfully, and smoothed back her hair. Her face was deathly pale, and her chest rose and fell almost imperceptibly with short, erratic breaths. Jack's insides clenched. What worried him most was that Cora had seemed fine before she suddenly lost consciousness. He only hoped that Mrs Garrett lived up to her reputation.

Cora still appeared to have difficulties breathing so he threw open the windows of the room and went to loosen her gown and stays.

Ridiculous garments, he thought savagely. Why had he made her wear it? But he knew the answer to that: because he'd been trying to make her fit into his life, instead of accepting her as she was. He vowed that would change.

Cora moaned, but she seemed more comfortable now, and, holding her hand, Jack waited anxiously for the wise woman to arrive.

The innkeeper's wife, a buxom woman with beefy arms, returned with water and towels. Jack thanked her, then dipped a corner of a towel in the hot water and began to bathe Cora's wounds. As he'd suspected, they were only skin-deep, and he breathed a sigh of relief.

'Oh, the poor lady,' said the innkeeper's wife. 'Whatever caused her to be in such a state?'

'She was attacked,' Jack replied, 'by three men, no less.'

'Dear me, such times we live in. And did they ... did they violate her?'

Jack caught her eye, and saw a barely suppressed excitement at the prospect of being in possession of some juicy gossip, but he saw sympathy too. 'No, I arrived just in time,' he said, 'although I strongly suspect we haven't heard the last of them. Is there a chance we could post a guard outside the room, please?'

'Oh, don't you fret, my lord. Between Will and myself and the taproom boy we'll make sure no one comes up them stairs that 'aven't booked for the night. Your lady friend will be quite safe here.'

'I'll be staying here myself,' said Jack.

'Right you are, my lord.' If the innkeeper's wife thought it unseemly that a gentleman chose to stay in a lady's bedroom, she was too wise to comment. 'Just give us a holler if you need anything, but I must warn you it'll get mighty busy today.'

'Thank you.'

The woman left the room, closing the door firmly behind her, and Jack returned to his vigil, watching Cora sleep.

His mind strayed to the two courtesans who had failed to impress him during his last visit to the gaming den – was it really only a few days ago? It felt like an age.

He was a different man now. Overcome by shame he remembered how unprincipled he had allowed himself to become in order to keep his spendthrift cousin in check. He had obviously failed at this task in spectacular fashion, to such an extent that he had thought nothing of entering into a wager for a woman's life. Cora's life. Rupert was no doubt still trying to track her down, and when he did, he would have no reason not to hand her over to the authorities. But this was no game for Cora; it was a matter of life and death, as the hanging had illustrated.

She belonged to the underbelly of society, to a world populated by the sort of men who had died on the scaffold today, and, like the courtesans in the gaming den, she was on the outside of respectability, with neither name nor money to protect herself and her loved ones.

Jack clenched her hand, receiving a twitch in response, and swore to himself for the umpteenth time that despite her obvious ability to take care of herself he would help her, if she would let him, and see her right somehow.

A knock on the door and a scuffling noise made him turn just as an old woman entered followed by the anxious innkeeper. The man was wringing his hands, no doubt worried what it would do to the reputation of his inn should a well-bred lady die while under his roof. In contrast the old woman was as calm as Jack's own mother might have been in similar circumstances.

'That'll be the patient, then,' she said matter-of-factly. 'Let's 'ave a look at you.'

There was something about her weather-beaten face, small

bird-like eyes and long, tanned fingers which made Jack relax, and he moved aside to give the woman room to examine Cora. She lifted one of Cora's eyelids and peered at the eye; then inspected the contusion and gently moved Cora's head from side to side. Her efficient hands moved down the bodice of the gown prodding Cora's ribs one by one; then squeezed her arms through the dress. Cora moaned faintly but didn't wake.

Moving back, the woman said, 'There's certainly been some shaking of the brain, and a few cuts and bruises. This other injury seems a little older.' She pushed down one of Cora's sleeves to reveal a large, purple half-moon shaped bruise the length of a hand.

He remembered her fall in front of the stage coach. 'I suppose it must be. Perhaps she was kicked by a horse.'

Mrs Garrett nodded. 'Could well be. She'll need complete bed rest for a week. Is there anywhere more suitable? Not that I doubt the efficiency of your establishment, Will,' she said to the innkeeper, 'but it ain't suitable as a sick room.'

'I'm sending for my carriage to have her brought to my father's estate,' said Jack.

'Aye, that's good, my lord, but you can't move her today. You'll need to wait to see how she is in the morning before travelling anywhere.'

'I'm not sure she's safe here.'

'My lord,' the old woman admonished him sternly, 'commotions of the brain shouldn't be taken lightly. Putting 'er in a carriage now will just shake the brain further and cause more damage. You must wait till the mornin'.'

'Very well,' said Jack, 'but I'll need a guard outside the door at all times.'

'I'll see to it, my lord,' the innkeeper said. 'The taproom boy is stationed outside the door, and there's me brother-in-law down the smithy's. He'll help out too.'

'Thank you, I appreciate it,' said Jack. 'You'll be well paid for your trouble.'

The innkeeper bowed and left the room. Jack returned to Cora's bedside, taking her cold hand in his and cradling it against his cheek. She looked so broken as she lay there, and he feared she might die.

Mrs Garrett put her hand on his shoulder. 'She's strong, this one, my lord. I reckon she'll be fit as a fiddle soon enough.'

'I hope so. She's … I'm very, eh …'

'Fond of her?'

'Yes,' Jack said simply. No point in denying it.

'Then you must stop her gallivanting around gettin' herself hurt.'

Meeting the old woman's eyes, Jack grimaced. 'Trust me, that's easier said than done.'

'I bet this one leads you a merry dance, m'lord,' Mrs Garrett cackled. 'I only hope it's worth the kind of heartache which is store for you.' She made as if to leave, and Jack paid her for her services. When her fingers had closed around the half crown, she said, 'That's most generous, sir. Good luck to you. Cos you're going to need it.'

Chuckling to herself, she left the room, and Jack returned to Cora's bedside, where he took off his jacket and loosened his neck cloth, settling down to a long vigil.

Chapter Seventeen

He was startled awake by Cora's cries. The room was dark apart from a sliver of moonlight spilling in through the open window.

Disorientated, it took him a moment to realise where he was, and why. Had he really slept all this time? No, he had a vague recollection of eating a bowl of mutton stew and drinking a jug of ale.

Cora was sitting up in bed her eyes glistening with unshed tears. 'He's gone! He's gone!' she repeated as if she wasn't fully awake.

Jack reached out and put a reassuring hand on her arm as more images from the evening before returned to him. The innkeeper's wife had made Cora comfortable for the night, undressing her down to her shift, briskly and efficiently as if she undressed ladies on a daily basis, and Jack had found himself averting his eyes to preserve Cora's dignity.

'Who's gone?'

Startled, she turned to face him, and then blinked as if she didn't quite believe her eyes. 'George. George is gone. What are you doing here? I need to go home!'

'You can't go home,' he said. 'Not yet anyway. You received a blow to the head and fainted from it. I took you to an inn to have you checked over. The wise woman said you need to rest before you can go anywhere. You don't remember what happened?'

She was quiet for a moment. 'Yes. I remember now. Those men … they were after George's treasure.'

'Treasure, eh?' Jack smiled. 'And why would they come after you? Do you know where this treasure is?'

'No. I don't think there is any. They were mistaken, but … Oh, Jack!' Cora sent him a forlorn look. 'His last thoughts were for me. He was about to die, and all he could think of was for me to stay safe. And then I get in trouble the minute he's gone!' Cora turned away to cover up her grief.

Moving to sit on the edge of the bed, Jack ran his hand up and down her naked shoulder. Her skin was warm and peachy-smooth, and his fingers tingled with the awareness. 'Hey, hey, hey,' he whispered, 'it's fine if you wish to cry.'

'I'm not crying!' she snapped.

Cora heaved a sigh, and although he couldn't see her tears, Jack felt her shoulders shudder. He edged closer and put his arm around her until she stopped shaking. Brushing back a wayward curl from her face, he asked her the question that had been on his mind since he'd seen her kiss the condemned man. 'Were you very close to this highwayman?' He would not allow himself to be jealous if her answer was yes; he didn't own her, and if she chose to tell him of her own accord, it meant she trusted him enough to do so. It would be enough.

Cora turned suddenly, bringing her beautiful face only inches from his. 'Uncle George was a dear friend, an old friend. I've known him since I was a child. He gave me Samson.' She smiled.

'Samson?'

'My horse.'

'Ah. A magnificent beast.'

'Great company too,' said Cora. 'Like George himself.' She smiled as if recalling a fond memory and leaned her head against Jack's chest. She ran her hand across to where his shirt was open, almost absently, and Jack shifted, hoping she wouldn't notice the effect her caress had on him. This was hardly the time.

'When my family returned from the northern counties,' she said, 'George took us under his wing, especially me. He was always giving me things. And Ned too. Once, after my mother died, and Ned was ill with grief, George brought us a pheasant and showed me how to prepare it.'

'Poached from my father's land, perhaps?'

Cora grinned. 'Naturally. Us thieves don't pay for anything if we can avoid it.'

'Naturally.'

Her breath came hot against his chest, and Jack felt a beast stir in his belly. Gently he placed a finger under her chin, and she looked up, meeting his eyes and moistening her lips. Jack inched a little closer, until his lips almost touched hers.

But he pulled back. What was he thinking? Cora had been seriously hurt, and he was feeling amorous …? What sort of a gentleman was he? *Not a gentleman at all,* he thought, answering his own question.

Cora caressed his cheek with the back of her hand. 'Jack?'

'Yes?' he replied, his voice thick with emotion.

'I …' Her fingers came to rest on his jaw bone, and she kept them there as if she was measuring his face. 'You've come to mean a lot to me. You're nothing like I thought you would be. How a person of the nobility would be. Perhaps you are … unique.' She smiled softly, her grey-blue eyes warm and alluring.

'Perhaps I am,' he replied, and immediately thought how glib that sounded.

'I thought I was going to die,' she whispered, 'and then you were there. You saved my life. It would make me very happy if—'

'Cora, don't …'

'If you were to make love to me.'

Jack swallowed hard. 'But your injuries … You're not well.'

'I'm well enough.'

'We mustn't,' he insisted.

Something flashed in her eyes, disappointment mixed with anger, and something else, a longing matching his own. It took his breath away. 'I thought you wanted me. Would it be so wrong of us to enjoy this moment? Neither of us know what the future will bring.'

'Cora, I desire you more than anything in the world, but I will *not* dishonour you.' Jack pulled back, but she gripped his arm firmly.

'If you were to make love to me, it would be the greatest honour of all.'

'You don't mean that,' he said. 'Love-making out of wedlock is a sin.'

'And I suppose Saint Jack has never sinned before?' A mischievous smile tugged the corners of her mouth.

'Well, maybe I have,' he admitted.

He recalled his earlier vow that he'd commit himself to her if she'd have him, and was searching for words suitable for a proposal when Cora laughed, took his face between her hands and kissed him. Desire shot through him like an arrow. His ears thrummed as her scent and her warmth teased his senses, and her very nearness filled his mind till nothing else mattered.

Greedily possessing her mouth, he traced her collarbone with his fingertips, then down to her breast, undoing the fastenings of her shift and then lifting it over her head. Cora's slender fingers did the same with his shirt. Her eyes locked with his, full of trust.

'You make me feel alive,' she whispered against his lips.

'And you have my heart,' he whispered back as he pushed the covers aside. 'I want to see all of you.'

Pausing, he gave himself a moment to appreciate her beauty. In the light from the moon her skin shimmered with life, and her black hair spread across the pillow like a sable halo. As he caressed her with his eyes, he ran a finger down the length of her body, from the dip in her throat to her navel; then he cupped her breast and brought his tongue to the nipple. To his intense delight, Cora gasped from shock and pleasure. He knew then that he would be her first lover. The realisation hit him that she was giving him the greatest gift she had, herself, and he wanted to hug her close and thank her, but the words stayed unformed in his throat.

By God, he was such a dolt. He really didn't deserve her.

'You like that?' he whispered against her hardened nipple.

'Mm.'

'You might like this even more.'

Slowly he moved his hand down her belly and found her silken black curls. Cora's eyes widened, but she made no move to stop him, and gently he caressed her soft folds before sliding his finger inside her. Cora moaned with pleasure and spread her legs further, and he dipped his head to kiss her belly button, then traced a finger to the throbbing pulse in her neck. His erection pushed hard against her thigh, the pressure within him building to almost unbearable heights. It was too much.

'Cora,' he whispered against her mouth, 'my beautiful Cora. You drive me insane.'

Sliding her arms around his neck, Cora pulled Jack on top of her. Raising himself up on his elbows, Jack sent her a questioning look, but Cora stopped his unvoiced doubts with a finger against his lips. She guided the tip of him inside her, but then her courage seemed to fail her and she placed her hands against his chest, eyeing him warily.

'Will it hurt?' she asked.

'A little perhaps, but I'll be as gentle as I can. Unless you want me to stop ...?'

She shook her head. 'I want you, Jack,' she whispered. 'All of you.'

Slowly he pushed further inside her, felt her tense and go tighter. Hating the thought of hurting her, he tried hard to hold back, but the sensation of filling her, of being encased by her warmth, and the way she moved around him, tipped him over the edge, and he let go of his control just as she arched up to meet him. Bringing her hands around his buttocks, she took him all the way inside her.

Eyes locked, they fell into a rhythm. Jack stroked her body, her hair, cheeks, and she met him thrust for thrust as the intensity built, responding to his every touch with a sigh, a kiss, a whisper. He gave himself to her with passion and love, and read in her eyes as their bodies came together that there could be no other for her, just as it was for him.

When she climaxed, he covered her mouth with his and lost himself in her.

When he woke she was gone.

Cursing softly, he remained in bed for a moment while he got his bearings. He had no recollection of when they had fallen asleep. After their first love-making, they had lain for a while caressing and whispering, and then made love again. Afterwards, cradling her head against his shoulder and basking in her trust of him, he'd revelled in her scent and the warmth of her body curled up to his. He had never known a sweeter moment.

The rest was a blur.

A quick search of the room proved that she had stolen his breeches and jacket and left him the torn yellow dress. Stomping around the room, he swore long and hard; then he sat down on the edge of the bed and laughed until tears were running down his cheeks.

Cora had given him the slip, again, but if she thought she'd seen the last of Jack Blythe, she could think again. He'd track her down even if it meant travelling to the ends of the earth.

Chapter Eighteen

Rupert ventured back to the woods to inspect the Mardells' cottage, but his search yielded nothing. A clump of dried mud on the floor indicated that no one had been back there since before the last time it had rained. And that was days ago.

Disappointed, he scoured the area around the cottage for signs of hoof prints, which might at least have indicated the direction in which they had gone, but all the prints petered out in the long grass between the trees. He was about to give up when he spotted a weathered board sticking up from the ground near a large tree, and when he moved closer he saw that it was a grave.

Curious, he cleared away a few fallen twigs and leaves to read the inscription.

'Hell's bells!' he muttered and sat back on his haunches while he contemplated the significance of his find.

The grave was evidently that of Mardell's wife, but it was her maiden name which set his mind churning.

Duval.

Not only did she share the name of a notorious highwayman, he had heard that name recently. Rupert recalled his conversation with the old man at The Bell Inn; hadn't the fellow muttered that very name before clamming up? He thought of the old Heston scandal – a wife leaving in the middle of the night, with her newborn child and a maid in tow, and perishing alone on a deserted road. When she had been found there was no sign of the maid or the lady's jewellery, nor of the coachmen.

The old man had denied any knowledge of his passengers on the night his coach was held up, but what if he knew exactly who he had been carrying, or had worked it out later? What if "that Duval chit" he had cursed was none other than Lady Heston's maid?

But how had she met Mardell? And why was she lying here, in a grave, as plain as day, when she had clean disappeared from the area nearly twenty years ago?

A shiver ran down his spine when he began to see what might have happened. Mardell had held up the coach, and the strumpet of a maid had run off with him, as well as Lady Heston's belongings. The couple had likely left for another part of the country, only to return later when the fuss had died down. With a daughter.

'Well, well, well,' he said to himself. 'It would seem thievery runs in the family.'

And the old man from the inn was the nearest thing he had to a witness.

Rupert smiled. The link was tenuous, but there might be another way to track down the highwaywoman, or her father, or even both, and without Blencowe's help.

He got back on his horse and headed towards town, his hands gripping the reins tightly from excitement.

The Bell Inn wasn't open yet, but the door was ajar, and a serving girl was sweeping yesterday's filth off the thick oak floor.

His excitement having put him in a good mood, Rupert tilted his hat to her. 'Morning. Kindly fetch the landlord, if you please. I'd like a private word with him.'

Startled, the girl dropped the broom; then she curtsied awkwardly before scrambling towards a room at the back.

'Mr Tyrrell, Mr Tyrrell, a gen'leman to see you. Personally!'

Rupert acknowledged this with a condescending nod.

The landlord appeared from the back room wiping his hands on a cloth. Recognising Rupert from his recent visit, he narrowed his eyes. 'To what do I owe this honour, sir? I'm afraid we're not open for business yet.'

'I'm not here for ale,' Rupert replied, 'only a quiet word on a delicate matter.'

Tyrrell sent him a suspicious look, and then glanced at the

serving girl. 'Leave us, Betsy,' he commanded, firmly but not unkindly.

'Yes, Mr Tyrrell.' The girl leaned the broom against the wall and then stared back at both of them, goggle-eyed, before disappearing through the open door.

'My latest recruit,' Tyrrell explained.

'A comely lass,' Rupert said, although he thought nothing of the sort.

'Indeed. This way.' Tyrrell led them to a table at the back, away from the door and prying eyes. 'I'm curious, sir,' he said when they were both seated, 'as to what you could possibly have to say to me which may be of a delicate nature. When people approach me thus, I find it is usually a delicate matter to themselves.' A knowing smile tugged at the corner of his mouth as he spoke.

'It pertains to something your grandfather recounted to me during my last visit.' Rupert remained polite, but longed to wipe the smirk off the landlord's face.

'My grandfather is an old fool and in his cups more often than not.'

'Your grandfather spoke of the time he was a coachman for hire, and the coach was held up by a highwayman. He mentioned that the passengers were later found dead. Would you care to elaborate?'

The landlord crossed his arms. 'I know nothing of that. As I said, my grandfather is prone to rambling.'

'You were there that evening, and I'm not leaving your establishment until you tell me about it!' Rupert suddenly snapped and raised his voice, but his threat was an empty one, and they both knew it.

The landlord stared, then he shouted over his shoulder. 'Betsy, the peace-keeper!'

The serving girl must have been hovering outside the open door because before Rupert had time to react she ran back in and handed the landlord a wooden club, then dashed out again. The landlord rose and banged the club down onto the table.

'Get out,' he growled, 'or it'll be your head I'm hitting next, gentleman or no gentleman!'

Rupert jumped up from his seat and raised his cane to strike the other man, but then thought better of it. The cane was made for leisurely strolls in the park, not for duelling, and it would be no match against the landlord's heavy club. Outmanoeuvred, but with his dignity intact, he picked up his hat and made to leave.

'Rest assured, I will be back. You *will* tell me what I want to know.'

'Rest assured, I will be ready for you, *sir*,' the landlord spat.

As Rupert reached the door, a hunched figure appeared in the doorway.

'Jem, my boy, what's the rumpus all about? A body can't go out without yer getting yerself into all sorts o' trouble.'

Quick as lightning Rupert kicked the door shut, grabbed the old man by the arm and twisted it high behind his back.

Old Man Tyrrell cried out in shock and pain, and Rupert had the satisfaction of seeing the cocky landlord pale.

'Let him go. He's an old man, and he knows nothing.'

'I beg to differ,' Rupert said. 'He knows a fair bit, and I have just the right idea of how to extract the information. I reckon these old bones will snap like twigs. What say you, shall we put it to the test?' To prove his point he twisted the arm higher, and the old man yelled again.

The landlord dropped his club on the floor. 'All right, all right! Don't hurt him.'

'Then tell me what I need to know,' Rupert said and loosened his grip on the old man, but only a fraction.

'What do you know of a woman named Duval?'

'Duval?' asked the landlord. 'Never heard of her.'

'She was married to a man named Mardell. I take it you've heard of him?'

'Well, yes, everyone knows Mardell. What does he have to do with anything?'

'Never you mind. Just tell me where I might find him. His cottage seems to have been abandoned.'

The landlord scratched his head. 'Never knew him too well. A strange cove, keeps himself to himself, although his daughter is well known about town. And a welcome sight too.'

'Yes, yes,' Rupert said, 'but someone must know him.'

'Well, there's the widow, Mrs Wilton. She seems to know him better than most. She might know where to find him.'

The landlord gave him directions to the widow's cottage; it was at the outskirts of the forest, not so far from where he and Jack had been held up.

'Excellent. See, that wasn't so difficult, was it?' He smirked and let go of the old man, shoving him towards the landlord for good measure. 'Good day to you both.'

Arriving at the widow's cottage, Rupert saw smoke rising from the chimney. And better still he recognised the horse grazing nearby. Quietly he slipped away before the occupants were alerted to his presence. He hoped Blencowe would believe him this time – especially when he mentioned the Duval connection, but if not he'd do his damnedest to persuade the man this wasn't a wild goose chase.

Under no circumstances would he try to apprehend Mardell and his daughter single-handedly.

It was an arduous journey back to Martha's house. Cora's head was pounding from the effects of the blow, and several times she felt so dizzy she had to stop and lean against a tree. She ached from their love-making but this particular pain brought a rush of blood to her cheeks and a little smile to her lips.

She put her hand over her belly. Had Jack got her with child, she wondered? Her heart swelled with joy and longing at the thought, but then trepidation set in. Not because of what Ned would say. Her father wouldn't judge; he never did. It was the thought of bringing up a child born out of wedlock which troubled her.

Because that was how it would be. They could never be together, her and Jack. At dawn, as she'd watched his sleeping form, how untroubled he looked while at rest, she had briefly considered staying – becoming part of his family would provide enough money to keep Ned in good health. Then, with deep regret, she'd dismissed the thought. If her past were ever exposed, even Jack's good name wouldn't be enough to save her from the gallows. She had to get herself and Ned away to safety.

And Jack wouldn't leave his life for her. He had duties to consider. He was the son of earl and heir to a large estate, and his future lay there, looking after his family and his tenants. The sudden realisation that she would never see Jack again slammed into her with such force that she had to cling to the tree for support. For a moment reality gripped her chest hard and squeezed again and again; she feared all the air in her lungs would be forced out, and she would have no breath left. Tears stung her eyes, and she swiped at them angrily.

Collect yourself, Cora, she thought. *It's no use.* She couldn't ask Jack to leave his family for her.

She had no idea how long she stood there, in the clutches of despair, but finally she bullied herself into action. With grim determination she put one foot in front of the other and made her way home to Ned.

Angry shouting greeted her when she neared Martha's cottage, and caution made her proceed quietly, under the cover of the trees. Her heart thumped wildly in her chest at what she saw, and she stepped behind a tree, steadying her trembling hands against the rough bark. Four men were attempting to restrain Ned, and Cora's instinct was to run out from her hiding place and defend her father, but against four men? She only had one shot in her pistol. Helpless, she watched as they cuffed him roughly and punched him in the face, and tears of frustration welled in her eyes.

Two other men were looking on from the sidelines. One of them Cora recognised as the local magistrate, a corpulent, bellicose individual, who was shouting orders to his men in a booming voice. The other, a young cold-looking and elegant nobleman she recognised as Jack's companion on the night of the robbery – the man George had described to her.

Martha was nowhere in sight, and she hoped that the older woman had made it back safely from the hanging the day before.

Ned was buckling under the restraints; even though he wasn't a well man, he was still strong, and his captors had to use considerable force to subdue him.

'Never!' he roared in response to a question from the cold-looking man.

It was then Cora realised that the men were after her.

Oh, why had she not come home straight after seeing Uncle George? Why had she gone to the hanging? She knew why; because she had promised George, and it was the right thing to do. But she blamed herself for not warning Ned that someone was on their trail, blamed herself for dithering and getting hurt in the process. Blamed herself for having love-making on her mind when she should have been protecting her father.

If they hurt him, I'll never forgive myself. Please, God, don't let them hurt him

Chewing her lip, she debated whether to jump out from the bushes. She was wearing men's clothes – they would likely believe that she was the young highwayman. Jack's companion was bound to recognise her and would undoubtedly point the finger. She would go to the gallows, and that might well be the death of Ned. But he would definitely go to his death if he were to be accused of her crimes. She had to do something.

She was about to step out from behind the tree when she felt a light tap on her arm. It was Martha, and she was holding a finger to her lips. Taking Cora's hand, she dragged her deeper into the forest and out of earshot of the magistrate and his men; then she flung her arms around Cora, nearly unbalancing her.

'Thank God you're all right! When I saw those nasty characters setting upon you, I ran to get help, but when we got to Tyburn village, you'd disappeared and I feared the worst. I looked everywhere but couldn't find you, and I had to go home and tell your father. Worst thing I ever 'ad to do. He's been sick with worry and were just about to go looking for your when the magistrate and the constable and that other fella turned up.' She let go of Cora and ran her eyes over her clothes, tutting. 'I expect you saw what happened.'

'They arrested him.'

'Aye, your father has taken it upon himself to shoulder the blame for all them robberies that 'ave happened in the area.'

'No! They'll hang him for sure. And it's all my fault!' Cora hid her face in her hands.

Martha put her hand on Cora's arm. 'Don't fret. There's 'ope yet. The magistrate – now there's a smart cove, and no mistake – he knew he was looking for a young man, not someone Ned's age, and Ned confessed that 'e was trying to cover up for a friend, but that the lad was long gone, up north. They decided to take 'im away all the same, but I don't think they'll hang him. I heard them talking about holding him until he softens up. Their words not mine, but they'll keep him in the magistrate's cellar for the time bein'.'

'I've got to get him back,' said Cora. 'A damp cellar will be the death of him.'

Martha gripped her arm tightly. 'Aye, lass, I reckon it could be, but you've gotta think. Don't rush in there and let 'is sacrifice be for nothing. Know anyone who can speak up for him? Someone high up perhaps?'

Cora's thoughts turned to Jack, but she dismissed the idea. She didn't think he wielded enough power to intervene with the magistrate. *There must be another way,* she thought. *All I've got to do is find it.*

Martha was prattling on about something. '... and that other man, an intimidating sort o' fella, he said something about having recognised Samson, and I thought to myself, 'e's probably got designs on that beautiful beast hisself, so while they weren't looking I shooed him away lest they confiscate him.'

'The other man recognised Samson? Was that how he tracked us down to your cottage?' Cora sent her a bewildered look. 'But Samson's been stabled under your wood shelter since we left. He hasn't been anywhere. Except that night ...'

The night Jack took her to his family gallery.

Had she inadvertently led the man to Martha's cottage? Had he been watching her, biding his time, or did he know what Jack got up to and had followed him too?

The hows and the whys were bringing on another headache, and she pushed the mystery to one side. She had other things to worry about for the moment.

First she had to retrieve her horse. She knew exactly where he would be: at his favourite grazing spot in Lord Heston's wheat fields. It seemed fitting somehow that Cora's horse should eat himself fat on the grain of a man who had scared her natural mother to death.

An idea struck her – perhaps Lord Heston might intervene with the magistrate on Ned's behalf if she were to confront him with the truth of her parentage. He was of a higher rank than Jack, and although he wasn't universally liked, he was well-respected and might do so out of fear for his reputation.

Cora and Martha waited until they were sure the magistrate and his men had left, dragging Ned along with them; then they returned to the cottage. The place had been turned over, very thoroughly, as Cora had expected, but to her relief they hadn't discovered the loose brick by the chimney breast where Cora had hidden Jack's watch, as well as the miniature and the ring her father had given her. Nor had they thought to look among the dried twigs Martha used for kindling, which were stacked in an untidy pile in the lean-to beside the cottage. Here Cora had hidden her other pistol and her rapier.

Having armed herself, Cora hugged Martha, who implored her to be careful; then she set off on foot to look for Samson. She walked across the scraggy heathland with long, purposeful strides, her jaw set. She had lost George, and the pain was still fresh. She had let go of Jack because her past could be exposed if she stayed, and that would put her father in danger. She couldn't lose Ned as well. His natural time might come soon, she realised with gut-wrenching clarity, but she refused to lose him a second earlier than she had to, and not for a crime he hadn't committed.

She found Samson where she had expected to, munching his way through summer-ripe corn with a look of utter contentment. She whistled sharply, and the horse pricked up his ears, snorted appreciatively and trotted towards her.

'Good boy,' she whispered as she stroked his muzzle. 'There's no one quite like you, Samson, is there? George says hello.'

The horse headbutted her gently and nipped at the jacket she was wearing. 'These clothes are not mine, I know, but you'll have to bear with me. There's something we need to do.' She eased the bridle she'd been carrying over his head while she spoke to him in a soothing voice; then, when it was secured, she led him to a tree stump, swung herself up and urged him forward with a nudge of her knees. Riding without a saddle wasn't terribly comfortable, but Samson knew her so well that it was almost as if she could command him with her thoughts.

She set off across the field at a brisk trot, her mind focused on what she needed to do.

Rupert watched her from the cover of the woods. He couldn't quite believe his luck in coming across the highwaywoman.

Too late he had noticed that the old crone with Mardell had freed the highwaywoman's horse, and he cursed the fact that he hadn't been fast enough to stop it. It was a fine horse, and he wanted it for himself, so when the magistrate had carted the prisoner off to Hounslow, Rupert had decided to look for the animal.

Finding the highwaywoman here was doubly lucky. The question was, how to overpower her? He had no doubt she was armed. Keeping his distance, he decided to follow her and see if an opportunity to apprehend her should arise.

As she rode, Rupert had to admit that she was a very accomplished horsewoman, and he couldn't help feeling a grudging admiration for the way she commanded her horse while riding without a saddle. Her bearing was proud and regal, yet completely in accord with the horse's powerful strides. Her hair, tied back with string, was thick and lush like the horse's mane, and the strength in her legs was mirrored in the rippling of the horse's thighs.

He enjoyed a challenge, and he felt a rush of lust combined with respect, a need to possess and control her the same way a man might govern a strong-willed animal.

Rupert smiled to himself and began to steer his horse forward. Breaking her in and taming her promised to be most diverting.

Something made him stop and mutter a curse under his breath. She was wearing breeches and a navy blue coat, but it wasn't the fact she was wearing men's clothing that jarred – she had been dressed thus the first time he saw her. What caught his attention was the subtle metallic thread embroidery on the pockets and the cuffs, just catching the sunlight; those weren't just any man's clothes. He recognised them only too well.

The breeches were nondescript, a plain, light-coloured wool, but the coat … It was the same cut, colour and size as the modest navy-blue Jack favoured.

It took a moment before the implications hit him. This could only mean one of two things; the highwaywoman had either robbed Jack of his clothes just as she had stolen Rupert's waistcoat – and that still rankled – or Jack had willingly taken his clothes off and left them where she could take them. On which occasions did a man strip off both his breeches and coat? When he slept, bathed or …

Bedded a woman.

Had his cousin bedded her?

While he pondered this, the highwaywoman suddenly spurred her horse, galloped about fifty yards, then swung sideways and disappeared into the trees. Rupert cursed himself for lowering his guard and allowing her to give him the slip. He urged his horse towards the place where she had ridden in between the trees, but there was no sign of her; he uttered another oath.

Sensing movement behind him, he turned slowly, the hairs standing on the back of his neck, and found himself looking down the barrel of a pistol, cocked and ready to fire. Swallowing hard, he forced himself not to swear out loud.

'Good morning, young sir,' he said and lifted his hat. 'How fare you on this fine day?'

'Leave the small talk for the drawing room,' came the curt reply. 'How did you find my father, and what are they going to do to him?'

Rupert looked from her face to her pistol, then back again and was slightly taken aback by the look of utter contempt in her eyes. 'I see you're a man of few words,' he said. 'Except you are, in fact, a female if my eyes are not deceiving me, and you're wearing my cousin's clothes. Tell me, did he give them to you, or did you have to "work" for them?' He raised his eyebrows to show her exactly what kind of work he was referring to.

He could tell from her sudden heightened colour and the way she choked back a gasp that his remark had hit home, but he was unsure whether to derive satisfaction from this or be enraged that his plans for having this filly before his saintly cousin had been thwarted.

Her pistol hand didn't waver; instead her finger tightened on the trigger. For a moment Rupert worried whether he might have gone too far; he didn't know this woman at all, but she was likely highly strung and unpredictable.

'I suppose your questions are reasonable enough,' he said and tried to keep his tone as level as possible lest she made good the implied threat and pressed the trigger. 'The magistrate will keep him in his cellar until the accomplice comes forward. A young male friend, your father claimed, although you and I both know that no such individual exists. So does the magistrate. As for how I found you, madam, that's very simple. I followed you home the day my cousin saved you from being trampled and recognised the horse in your lean-to from the night you robbed me. And after you'd disappeared from your cottage, my enquiries led me to the old widow's place.'

The highwaywoman regarded him with narrowed eyes. 'I see,' she said, 'and I suppose I ought to congratulate you on your cleverness.'

Rupert inclined his head. 'Madam, should you choose to bestow such an honour upon me, it would be most graciously received.'

'Tch! I don't doubt it. Except I have a better idea.'

With lightning speed she surged forward and slapped his unsuspecting horse on the rump with her reins. Startled, the animal reared and bolted, and all Rupert could do was cling on to the reins until he could get it under control. When he'd finally managed to calm the beast, the woman was gone.

But not before he'd got a very good look at her.

There was a curious birthmark on her cheek, which he hadn't seen on the night of the robbery, probably because he'd been more interested in committing the details of her horse to memory. However, now that he'd seen her up close, her striking eyes intrigued him far more than her birthmark. With a jolt he realised where he'd seen such eyes before, and when the implications of that hit home, it made him see the highwaywoman in quite a different light. He swallowed back the revulsion at his earlier thoughts of bedding her, and tried to understand how what he'd learned linked to Old Man Tyrrell's story.

Was his cousin in possession of the same knowledge? he wondered. Maybe, maybe not, but why Jack hadn't handed the thief over to the authorities and cashed in his wager with Rupert made no sense.

But that wasn't important now. What mattered was how he could use this information to his advantage. If Jack had knowledge of the highwaywoman's identity and hadn't shared this with the magistrate that would make him an accomplice – it could land him in prison or lead to transportation. Which would pave the way for Rupert to inherit the earldom.

Tightening his grip on the horse's reins, he felt one step closer to the inheritance to which he'd come to feel wholly entitled.

Chapter Nineteen

Jack's parents were waiting for him in the drawing room when he returned in the carriage.

'What happened?' his father asked without preamble when Jack bent down to kiss his mother on the cheek. 'You didn't retire to the town house, I gather.'

'No, I stayed at an inn at Tyburn,' Jack admitted. His father would find out anyway, would get all the juicy details from his servants, who in turn would have got the information from the innkeeper and his wife. It was likely he already knew that Jack had spent the night in company of a woman. Usually it vexed him that his father always knew what was going on, but right now he had a more pressing matter on his mind. 'Father—' he began.

'Tyburn? You went to the hanging?' His mother had trouble concealing her surprise.

'Hah!' said the earl. 'I imagine you were anxious to see another highwayman hang for his dastardly deeds. As I recall your childhood experience had quite an impact on you.'

'Yes, it did,' Jack replied, 'but I had a purpose in being there. It wasn't for entertainment.'

The countess shuddered and turned away, and Jack cursed inwardly at the way his father could speak so bluntly about highwaymen, a subject which still caused his wife anguish whenever it was raised. It also annoyed him that his father could think he'd attended for entertainment; a hanging may be regarded as such by many, but Jack had never taken to it, a fact his father was well aware of. However, now was not the time to argue the point. 'Father, I need to speak with you urgently. It's about your cousin, Captain Blythe.'

'My cousin? I thought we had already discussed the matter.'

'There's more. I'm convin—'

His explanation was interrupted by the butler, who entered the room after the briefest of knocks. Jack threw up his hands in exasperation. 'Pardon my intrusion, m'lord, but there's trouble in the south field. A bullock has knocked down a fence, and the horses are bolting from the paddock. The grooms and the stable lads are rounding them up but they need your opinion as to the fence. The damage is quite significant, I'm given to understand.'

The earl rose immediately. To Jack he said – with relief, he thought – 'We'll have to postpone our conversation.'

After his father had left the room, the countess rose as well, and slid her arm through Jack's. 'You must understand, it causes your father some distress to talk about his cousin. But I'm familiar with the captain's story, so why don't you accompany me on my morning walk and we can talk about it?'

'Are you certain, Mother? I'm going to be very blunt on the matter.'

'Fie, Jack!' She slapped him on the arm with mock seriousness. 'Do you think us women to be such delicate creatures that we must always be coddled?'

'No, I suppose not,' he conceded. There was certainly nothing feeble about Cora.

'Good, because I didn't rear you to be such a mealy-mouth. Now come, let's walk. I've tied a posy for little Henry's grave and I'm most anxious to hear why you sent for a spare set of clothes as well as the carriage.' She winked mischievously and let him guide her through the tall glass doors and down the steps to the park.

They strode along until they reached the family mausoleum, where the countess placed a pretty posy of summer flowers in front of the plaque bearing the name of Jack's younger brother, Henry, who had died from a childhood fever. Jack stepped back to give his mother some privacy, and she stood there for a few moments in front of the plaque. Then with a sigh and a sad smile she turned around and slid her arm back through Jack's.

'Let's go to the garden. I do so enjoy sitting there.'

The formal garden was rich with summer blooms; the countess ducked under an arch covered in climbing roses, whose heady scent filled the air, and seated herself on a moss-covered stone bench. Jack followed and sat down beside her.

It was hard knowing where to start, so he decided to get straight to the heart of the matter. 'I've fallen in love, and I wish to seek Father's permission to marry.'

His mother sent him a puzzled look. 'I was under the impression you wanted to talk about Captain Blythe.'

'I'm coming to that. It's a related matter.'

'How so?' his mother said, arching her eyebrows. 'Who, may I ask, is the lucky lady, and where is she at present?'

'She ran off. But don't worry, I'll find her. I always do.'

He grimaced. Cora was determined to give him the slip, but he was equally determined to find her. He guessed that she'd left because she was afraid her identity might be discovered, and she had good reason. Jack didn't know how far Rupert had got in his investigations, but if he'd also succeeded in uncovering who the thief was, he'd have to pay him for his silence.

However, he'd deal with that problem later.

His mother sent him a startled look. 'Ran off? You're not intending to wed a lady against her will, I hope.'

'It's complicated, but she does need a little persuading. And she's no lady,' Jack added.

'Is she a merchant's daughter, perchance? Or the vicar's eldest? I do recall you were rather taken with her beauty as some point.'

'No, Mother. Cora Mardell is from a labouring family, or at least that's how she was reared.'

'The lower classes?' The countess stared at him. 'I understand that young people may wish to marry for love, but would a lady of good breeding not be more appropriate? Then your wife would belong to the same sphere as you. There's also a bride's dowry to consider; an estate is expensive to run, and an injection of cash is always welcome. One day, when your father is … gone you will have to carry the burden of that responsibility. Do not dismiss it lightly. However lovely this young woman is.'

'She has no dowry, that's true, but there's more to it than that.'

'More!' she exclaimed. 'Dear Jack, you're the next in line to an earldom, and you wish to marry a low-born girl. What could be more inappropriate?'

'I'm convinced she's not low-born at all.'

'You're *convinced*? Pray, is there some doubt about the lady's parentage?'

'I believe she is the daughter of Captain Blythe, father's cousin. The resemblance between them is too striking to ignore.'

'So, in addition to belonging to the lower classes she's also illegitimate.'

The countess's voice rose a notch, but Jack chose to ignore it. 'Not only do I believe her to be his child, I have cause to believe that she's also the daughter of Lady Heston.'

'Lady Heston? But she has only sons.'

'I'm referring to the first Lady Heston,' Jack explained. 'The one who ran away after the birth of her child.'

'But the baby died!'

Jack shook his head. 'Cora's father, the man who brought her up as his own, switched the babies that night.' Jack pushed his fingers through his hair, piqued that the discussion wasn't going quite as he had hoped. He'd never thought his mother a snob, but perhaps he'd been mistaken. 'So although Cora's not a lady by birth, she's a lady by blood.'

His mother rose abruptly, her face drained of colour. 'You cannot marry this girl.'

'I understand that you and Father might be worried about the scandal, but no one need know her true parentage. She's the daughter of a man named Ned Mardell and I would marry her under that name, so …'

'You cannot marry her,' the countess repeated. 'It is impossible!'

'Impossible? Because she's low-born? It may be unusual, but surely it's not unheard of.'

'It has nothing to do with her social class. It—' The countess brought her hand to her mouth. 'Your father and I … we … Oh, this is too much to bear!'

Puzzled and with a growing sense of unease, Jack rose too and took her hands in his. 'What is too much to bear? It cannot be that bad.'

The countess wrenched away. 'Your father and I weren't always happy.'

'I have often sensed a strained relationship between you, but how is this relevant? Are you not happy together now?' His observations had pained him, and he truly hoped their relationship had improved.

His mother looked back at him with a sad smile, the same smile he had seen at the mausoleum. 'Yes, for the most part. Ours was an arranged marriage, as I'm sure you must know, and although the choice of husband wasn't mine, I believed it imperative, as my parents did, that a woman should marry well. I put all thoughts of my preferred beau from my mind, but I believe your father was still in love with another when we married. It saddened me, but I did all I could to be a dutiful and loving wife in the hope that he would come around in time. Then, to our great joy we had you, and later little Henry.'

Jack swallowed hard. Although he had been but five years old at the time of Henry's death, the reminder of his family's loss always brought a lump to his throat.

'There was a time after little Henry died that I … Well, the thought of losing another child caused me so much anguish that I rejected my husband. I know he sought comfort in the arms of another – he had a man's needs after all – and I've always suspected he took up again with the lady whom he'd loved before our marriage.'

'Who was this lady?'

'Oh, dear Jack,' she said and reached out to caress his cheek. 'Will you not sit?'

'If it pleases you, Mother, but only if you sit with me.'

Having made sure his mother was comfortable, he sat down beside her. 'Please continue,' he said, trying to keep his voice level; his mother had alarmed him with her reaction. 'Who was my father's lover?'

'He never said, and I never pressed him. Only that she was the wife of someone in our close acquaintance. When Lady Heston took flight in the middle of the night with her newborn babe, and Geoffrey seemed so affected by her death, I ... well, I drew my own conclusions.'

A sliver of ice ran down Jack's spine as her words sank in. Cora bore a striking likeness to the captain, but there were similarities to his own father too. He had thought this merely due to the fact his father and the captain were cousins, but what his mother had just said gave it a whole new significance. His father had been unfaithful to his mother with the wife of a close acquaintance. What if ...

The blood left his face as realisation ripped into him. There could be no happy ending for him and Cora, only the shame and pain of incest, inadvertently committed, but committed all the same. Unable to speak or think, or to perceive anything but ugliness and despair, he turned on his heel and left the rose garden to wander aimlessly through the park until the shadows grew long. By the time he finally turned in for the night his limbs were heavy and leaden, as if he'd aged ten years in a single day, but still only the one thought occupied his mind.

He had made love to his own sister.

Chapter Twenty

Watching Lord Heston from afar as he oversaw the harvest, Cora waited patiently for an opportunity to catch the man on his own. He spent most of the day in the company of Master Kit, and she was just about to give up when she saw him sending the young man on his way and rode off towards the apple orchard.

Cautiously, she followed Heston, taking care to stay out of his line of sight. Seemingly unaware of her presence, he inspected the apple trees, which had already begun to drop unripened fruit. Finally, as the day was drawing to a close, Lord Heston turned his horse around and began to make his way back to his estate.

Satisfied that he was alone, that her mask was in place and her pistol in working order, Cora pushed out from the cover of a densely laden apple tree and blocked his path.

'I say, what's the meaning of this? Am I to be held up on my own land? It's an outrage!'

His words were impassioned, but his voice was cold, almost biting, and Cora felt a shiver run down her spine. She thought of her natural mother, a gentle and fever-sick lady, scared out of her wits by this man, and her resolve hardened. Pushing up her mask and with her eyes boring into his, she said, 'I wish to speak to you, Lord Heston.'

'I know you,' he said and pointed an accusing finger at her. 'You're one of my labourers. I hardly think the likes of you can have anything to say to me which will be of interest.'

'Actually, you might find that I do,' Cora replied tersely. 'The magistrate is holding a man in his cellar. My father, Ned Mardell, and he's innocent of the charges laid against him. I want you to use your influence with the magistrate to ensure his release.'

Lord Heston regarded her as if struck dumb; then his laughter, low and menacing, echoed in the dusk. Cora's pistol hand shook a little, but she willed it steady. She'd heard a thing or two about Lord Heston over the years, none of them particularly flattering, but to secure Ned's release from prison she was willing to do a deal with the Devil himself.

'Pray, why on Earth would I do such a thing?' he said. 'If your father's been apprehended by the magistrate, it must be because he's not as innocent as you suppose.'

It was as if Lord Heston could see right through her. Had she not thought so herself only recently; that Ned was not entirely innocent of wrong-doing? 'Who is completely innocent,' she countered, 'except perhaps a newborn babe?'

Lord Heston's eyes narrowed to mere slits as he studied her face, as if he wondered where she was going with this conversation.

'Ned Mardell raised me as his daughter,' Cora continued. 'He gave me these items to use as leverage, claiming that they belonged to your first wife. The ring was a gift from you, I assume: it's inscribed with a C.' She held up the miniature and the ring. For a moment Lord Heston remained deadly quiet, and if Cora hadn't made a habit of observing people, she could easily have overlooked his well-concealed agitation.

'May I see?' he said at length.

Moving closer, Cora handed him the items and then dug her pistol into his ribs.

'There's really no need for that, young lady. I have no intention of destroying your trinkets with a pistol aimed at my heart, which, by the way, is the least sensitive part of me.'

Cora retreated a little, seeing that he spoke a certain amount of sense, and allowed him to examine the miniature and the ring. Finally he handed them back to her with a shrug.

'The miniature did indeed belong to my late wife. It was originally her mother's, but upon her death it came to Sophia. The ring I've never seen before; I wasn't aware that she owned such a sentimental piece of jewellery, but that doesn't mean she didn't. My former wife had many secrets. What I would like to know is how they came to be in your possession.'

'Through the woman who called herself my mother,' said Cora. 'Sarah Duval. Your wife's maid.'

This time there was no doubt he was rattled. His nostrils flared, and he gripped his horse's reins so hard his hands shook. 'Sarah Duval,' he sneered. 'That thieving, conniving floozie …'

'Not so. She was a loving wife and mother,' Cora countered, taken aback by the vehemence of his reaction to her foster-mother, who could have been nothing but a simple maid to him.

'Tell me,' he said, his voice once again under control, 'why I should help anyone associated with that hussy? She's brought me nothing but grief.'

'Because not only am I the adopted child of Sarah Duval, I'm also the natural daughter of your first wife, Lady Sophia. These trinkets, as you call them, are proof of my identity.'

Lord Heston's face turned ashen. 'Her daughter? How? That's not possible! The child died with her.'

Cora shook her head. 'My father was … well, he was there, and he switched the babies because she implored him to.' She levelled her pistol at him. 'She feared what you might do to me when you discovered that I couldn't possibly be yours.'

'It's nothing compared to what I might do to you now,' he muttered with a curl of his lip. 'What do you want from me?'

'All I ask is that you get the man who has been my father these many years out of gaol. I've no intention of laying further claims on you or your property if that's what you're worried about.'

'And if I don't?'

'Then I shall let it be known that you drove your wife to her death and buried the wrong child in the family plot. You'll be a laughing stock.'

He glowered at her; then he shrugged. 'Who would believe you? The word of a simple country girl against that of a respected nobleman? Anything you may choose to use as proof, like these trinkets here, are stolen goods belonging to my family's estate – you'd be transported, I imagine. Or worse.'

Cora shivered but held her head high. 'But *you* believe me?'

'Yes,' he said, 'as a matter of fact, I do. I always knew Sophia must have taken a lover, although I never guessed his identity. They were far too careful for that. I can see now that you are indeed her daughter. There are … certain features, although your eyes are not from her. You'll have a hard time proving it though, and features can be – how shall I put it? – "improved" upon. You may wish to consider that,' he added with an unpleasant smile.

It took all the self-control Cora possessed not to shoot him there and then. The man was evil; she could sense it with her entire being, and the world would probably be a better place without him, but she was no murderess.

'And the ring?' she asked.

'I've already told you, I didn't give it to her. Her lover must have done, and I'm grateful to you for having provided me with his identity.'

Cora scoffed. 'I've done nothing of the sort. But since my mother – both my mothers – are in their graves you cannot harm them. I've learned that I resemble Captain Blythe, the black sheep of the Lampton family, and I have no reason to doubt my source. The captain's given name was Cecil – the C must refer to him, not you.'

'Your powers of observation are quite remarkable, wench, but in this case I fear you may be wrong. It could be a C, but the script is so detailed it's hard to tell.' A knowing grin spilled across his lips, and he shrugged. 'This looks more like a G to me.'

'G? But who—'

'Someone close to the captain, someone else with a family resemblance – his cousin, Geoffrey Blythe, perhaps. Also known as Lord Lampton.'

'What did you say?'

Cora's pistol hand started to shake again, and her finger tightened on the trigger, almost instinctively, but she willed herself to steady it. Another small smile from Lord Heston told her that her reaction hadn't passed him by. *Damn him to Hell,* she thought.

'I'm quite sure you heard every word, but I shall repeat them if you wish. I never saw Captain Blythe show any particular regard for Sophia, but Lampton was always very attentive to her. Perhaps you're the daughter of my first wife and my neighbour, and not his cousin as you supposed.'

Cora stared at the ring; then back at Lord Heston, wide-eyed, as the implications hit her. Last night she and Jack had lain together; if what Lord Heston claimed was true, then that would mean … No, it couldn't be true. She refused to believe it.

'You're lying!' Even as she denied it, she felt herself crumble inside.

Lord Heston arched his eyebrows in query. 'Why, you've gone quite pale. How can this new information possibly affect you? You should rejoice in your connections, however illegitimate. Now you can confront the earl about his shady past, and in return for your silence maybe he'll secure your father's release. And pay you handsomely too, no doubt.'

Gritting her teeth to regain her composure, she shot him a haughty look and pushed the vile thought aside. 'I have no interest in money.'

'No interest in money? Then you are but a fool. Only the dead can denounce Mammon quite so readily.'

She lowered her pistol although she kept it cocked and at the ready. 'You may go.'

'You're not going to shoot me?'

'Not today.'

He chuckled again, sending further shivers down Cora's spine, and inclined his head in a mocking, exaggerated manner. 'I thank you, madam, for sparing my life. In return I shall not inform the magistrate of your trespassing and threat to my person, but rest assured that, should our paths cross again, I will not be so indulgent next time.'

Calmly he turned his horse and rode off in the dusk without looking back. Cora couldn't help feeling a grudging admiration for his nerve; he had no way of knowing whether she would shoot him in the back or not.

She had held her nerve with him, but his words had hit home. Fearing that she might be sick from their impact, she gripped Samson's reins to steady herself.

Jack and she had made love not once but twice. He had planted his seed in her, perhaps starting a new life, and this gift of a child, even one born out of wedlock, would have been her comfort now that he was no longer part of her life. What should have been treasured as a joyful memory was now tarnished forever. If what Lord Heston claimed was true, Jack was her half-brother, and they had committed a terrible, terrible sin.

The thought left her numb, paralysed, her heart cold.

Chapter Twenty-One

Cora rode without any clear idea of where she was going, but somehow she ended up in the forest, and at the earliest opportunity she slid off Samson's back and collapsed against an old oak tree.

Her chest felt as if it was surrounded by bands of steel, squeezing hard, and the mere act of breathing was almost too much of an effort. She felt adrift on a sea of emotion with nothing to hold on to and longed desperately for Ned, who had always been a fixed point in her life.

But Ned wasn't here to banish her turmoil. Nor could she lie to herself; she wanted Jack like she wanted no other, and if she had ever, deep inside her, felt a tiny glimmer of hope before of them being together, however unrealistic, it was now completely eradicated.

Nor could there be any joy at the thought of a child.

Hugging herself against the ache in her heart, her fingers brushed against the handle of one of the pistols tucked into her belt. She pulled it out and stared at it, weighing it in her hand.

Some people chose to end their lives when they suffered heartbreak.

For a long moment Cora sat there toying with the pistol, cocking and uncocking it absent-mindedly, and contemplating what would happen if she *did* turn it on herself. Jack would marry someone of his own station and forget about her. Lord Heston would live out his days with the bitter knowledge that his wife had cuckolded him by his nearest neighbour. It would serve him right. Her father would be freed, and Martha would look after him, she had no doubt of it. Not many would bemoan the loss of a pauper turned highwaywoman; instead scores would rejoice that the road was a safer place.

The thought that she could be carrying a child stayed her

hand against this momentary madness. A child, regardless of the circumstances of its conception, was a precious gift. Even if she couldn't look after it herself, she had a duty to bring it to term and then place it with a loving foster-family, just as she herself had been. A small sob escaped her at the thought of having to give up the only thing from Jack which could truly belong to her, but she had to find a way to cope somehow.

Shaking with emotion, she fumbled to return the pistol to her belt. Just then she felt a hard nudge on her shoulder, and thus unbalanced, she accidentally pressed the trigger. The shot went into the tree behind her in a shower of dry bark and lichen, echoing in the evening air and startling a handful of nesting crows.

Shocked, she dropped the pistol. On her right Samson snorted and scraped the leaf litter; then he brought his hoof down on her shin.

'Oww!' Cora scrambled to her feet. 'Why, you miserable creature!'

Samson snorted again, a low throaty sound almost like a purr, and headbutted her gently.

'I ought to make mincemeat out of you,' Cora muttered, rubbing the place where Samson had clipped her. 'You ... you crazy animal. I could've shot you. Or myself.' She shuddered at the thought.

And why am I talking to a horse?

Taking Samson by the bridle, she rested her head against his mane, and for a fleeting moment it was as if Uncle George was with her. *Thank you,* she thought. *Thank you for making me see sense.* Life was far too precious to throw away; the way George's life had been cut short was testament to that.

Resolutely she got back on her horse and rode back to Martha's cottage.

'Cora, my dear, you look like you've seen a ghost.' Martha opened the door cautiously to Cora's gentle knocking. The cottage lay in darkness and no fire was lit. 'And where've you been all day?'

Cora slid in through the narrow gap and dumped a sack on the table. 'I've been checking Ned's traps,' she said, not meeting Martha's eyes, 'and I found Samson. Right where I thought he'd be, munching the lord's corn.'

'Aye, that one's a clever beast and no mistake,' Martha muttered. 'Helped hisself to half of me turnips without as much as a by your leave. Where've ye put him? Away from me vegetables I hope.'

'Tied to a tree about fifty yards from here,' Cora replied and sank down in Martha's only chair. 'And he certainly is clever.'

Martha bustled about the room lighting a couple of tallow candles without speaking, and Cora was thankful for that. Sighing, she covered her eyes with her hands.

'There, there, my dear, ye mustn't despair.' Martha put her arm around Cora and squeezed her shoulder. 'There's 'ope yet. It so 'appens that a young lad they've got tending to your father is friendly with one of me grandchildren. Wesley's his name, and 'e'll be here any minute.'

Just then there was a cautious knock on the door. Cora stiffened but Martha opened it, unconcerned. A boy of about fifteen slipped in through the gap and gave Martha a quick hug; he stepped back self-consciously when he noticed Cora and yanked off his hat. Cora saw fair skin, dark hair and blue eyes, although it was difficult to tell in the smoke from the candles.

Wesley gave a brief account of how he had found her father last. He described Ned as being 'comfortable', but he kept staring at his boots while he spoke, and Cora was overcome by misgivings.

As much as she loathed the idea, she had thought of following Lord Heston's advice and confronting the earl with her new-found knowledge in order to secure Ned's release, but there was no telling how *he* would react, and she might find herself in the same dungeon as Ned come morning.

If only there was some way she could get to see him tonight.

As if Martha had read her thoughts, she said, 'Wesley 'ere can get you in to see your father if you like.'

'Go to see him? Now?' Cora asked. 'Won't they wonder at the lateness of the hour?'

'They might, miss,' said Wesley, 'but earlier I left the slop bucket in the room where your father is being kept, sort of by design, if you get my meaning, and seeing as this is Sir Blencowe's wine cellar, he wouldn't want anything noxious down there for too long. Mighty proud of his collection o' bottles, is Sir Blencowe. You and I look a fair bit alike: in the dark the constable won't be able to tell one from the other.'

Wesley's face split into a grin, and Cora couldn't help smiling back, despite her inner turmoil. It might just work. Then she had another idea.

'If it's possible to get in to see my father, is it possible to get him out, do you think?'

The boy thought for a moment. 'Aye, it's possible. The magistrate's house was an inn once, and there's still a trap door there where they used to deliver casks of ale and the like, but I'm not sure it's such a good idea,' he added and exchanged a look with Mrs Wilton.

'Nonsense.' With new energy flowing through her veins, Cora stood up abruptly. 'If it's at all possible, I intend to get my father out now. By the time they discover that he's fled, we'll be long gone. And trust me: I'll make sure you don't get in trouble for this.'

Wesley shrugged. 'Oh, don't worry about me, miss. I know how to look dumb.'

Later Martha drew her tattered shawl closer around her and watched Cora prepare to leave with her grandson's friend.

'In the light from the moon, ye young'uns look like nothing so much as a pair of rascally lads off on a midnight adventure,' the old woman said. 'If only your errand was as innocent as that.' She shook her head.

They said their goodbyes, Cora for good this time. Time was of the essence, and sentimentality would serve no other purpose than to delay. Cora had packed her few belongings and some simple provisions, and saddled her horse. She'd changed into her own clothes and given Martha the too-large jacket she had been wearing.

'Good quality wool,' Martha muttered. 'Should fetch a tidy sum at the market.'

Reluctantly Cora let go of it. The jacket had been soft and warm, and the weight of it on her shoulders reminded her of Jack's arm around her, of the way he had held her close after she'd been attacked. No one other than Ned had ever held her like that before, both gently and protectively, and now she could lose them both.

If Martha noticed her reluctance to part with it, she was wise enough not to enquire further.

'The good Lord go with ye both and keep ye safe,' she said instead.

'Halt! Who goes there?'

The constable outside the magistrate's house lifted his lantern and squinted into the darkness. Wearing Wesley's hat, Cora stepped forward and into the light.

'It's Wesley, sir. I'm here to empty the prisoner's slop bucket.'

'Weren't you here earlier, lad?'

'Yes, sir, and I plain forgot,' Cora replied.

'Well, I'm sure it can wait till the morning.'

'But, sir, the magistrate will get ever so cross with me. It's his wine cellar down there, and I'm charged with looking after it for him and keeping it clean. Can't have no noxious odours mixin' with his precious bottles, that's what 'e'd say. I don't want ter lose me job, and I'm sure you wouldn't want to tell him that you wouldn't let me go down there, sir.'

Frowning, the constable considered this for a moment. 'Oh, all right then,' he grumbled and lowered the lantern, 'but be quick about it. This ain't no inn, and the prisoner ain't no gentleman with servants dancing attendance. He's a criminal, and it's high time he felt the consequences of being on the wrong side of the law.'

He motioned for Cora to follow him around to the trap door by the side of the house, just as Cora had hoped. He slid back the bolt and opened the heavy doors upwards, then handed her the lantern.

'There you go, lad. Now do what you came for and begone with ye. I ain't got all night.'

Cora slipped down the narrow staircase to the cellar and heard the bolt being driven home.

'Bang on the hatch when you've finished,' the constable shouted through the heavy wooden doors.

'Will do, sir.' Cora listened as his footsteps disappeared; then with a grin she clutched the bunch of keys she had managed to unhook from the belt of the unsuspecting man. Wesley had explained the layout of the magistrate's residence to her and told her which keys would get her from the wine cellar to the rest of the house.

That boy will go far, she thought.

Holding up the lantern, she spied a lumpy shape on the floor against the cellar's back wall.

On the floor. Against a damp wall. Had they no heart?

She rushed to her father's side, unprepared for what she saw. It was Ned, all right, but he was barely recognisable. Someone, the constable's men no doubt, had beaten his gentle face to a pulp; his eyes were swollen, his nose broken and encrusted with dried blood, and his clothing torn.

Instinctively, she cried out in anguish and rage. This was *her* fault and hers alone. This had happened because *she* had been foolish and not listened to those who knew better. Damn it all, why hadn't she heeded Ned's words?

Ned stirred. 'Is that you, Wesley, my boy?'

His words were slurred, as if he had been drinking, but

although he was kept in a wine cellar, Cora saw no evidence to support that.

'No, it's me, Father,' Cora replied, taking his hand in hers with a strange sense of *déjà vu*. Another prison, another broken man. She shook herself. Ned's life wasn't over yet, but she had to hurry. No time for bemoaning fate. They had to leave, and quickly.

'Cora?' Ned fought in vain to sit up, and she put her arm under him for support.

'I've come to get you out.'

'No!' Ned tried to pull away. 'You mustn't be here. It's too dangerous. They're still out there looking for you.'

'And I'm in here pretending to be Wesley.' Cora smiled and rattled the keys. 'With the constable's keys.'

Despite being in obvious pain Ned chuckled. 'Always the resourceful one, eh? But I have to disappoint you. I'm not sure I can walk.'

'You don't have to walk very far, Father. Wesley's waiting with Samson a couple of houses away from here. I've packed and I'm ready to go. I suggest we take the road east towards London; they'll be expecting us to go west. We can hide with a contact of Mr Isaacs until we can get passage on a ship. We could go to Spain; we still have a few coins left,' she added, ignoring his penetrating gaze. 'So you see, I've got it all worked out. We'll be so happy in Spain, I'm sure of it.'

Ned smiled indulgently; then he sighed. 'I'm not well, Cora. Surely you know that?'

'What's a few cuts and bruises? You'll soon get better, and the sun will do you good.'

'Inside, Cora. I'm not well inside. It's my lungs, and my heart. And I couldn't leave your mother. Don't ask me to.'

But Mother is dead, she wanted to say. Fear snaked up her spine at the thought that Ned's mind might be ailing as well.

Still with her arm supporting him, she said, 'Can you stand?'

'Aye, I think so.'

Helping him up, Cora expected to be weighed down by his body, but it shocked her that she was able to support his frame without problems. It was as if half of her father had melted into nothing.

No time to think about that now. She helped him to a set of stone stairs, which led up to the kitchen. Here she let him rest on the bottom step while she unlocked the door at the top, and then returned to help him up the stairs, locking the cellar door behind them. With her arm around his scrawny waist, she led him through the scullery, where pots and pans had been left upside down on the draining board to dry.

Ned stumbled and knocked against one of the pots. Supporting her father with one arm and holding the keys in the other, Cora watched in horror as the pot wobbled precariously before settling back on the draining board with a muffled thump.

Unaware that she had been holding her breath, Cora let out a sigh of relief. 'Just as well the cook and the scullery maid sleep upstairs. Wesley told me.'

'Observant lad,' Ned remarked with a tired grin.

'He certainly is.'

She unlocked the back door, and they found themselves in Sir Blencowe's overgrown garden, which offered plenty of shelter against the moonlight. Cora's heart sang with joy.

Ned was free.

They found Wesley at the agreed rendezvous. Together they helped Ned into the saddle, and Cora took Samson by the reins. She handed Wesley his hat back, and, reluctantly, the keys. 'Wouldn't it be better if you came with us?' she asked the boy.

'And leave the constable wondering why I'm taking so long asking to be let out of the cellar? How far do you think you'd get if he raises the alarm?'

Cora had to admit that Wesley's words made sense, but she was loath to send him back.

'I'll be all right. I'll sneak back into the cellar from the house, lock the door behind me and call for the constable to let me out.'

'And the keys?' Cora asked. 'How will you get them back without him noticing?'

'I'll drop them in the flower bed and pretend to find them.' Wesley shrugged, unconcerned. 'He knows I come from a good, steady sort of family. He won't suspect a thing.'

Cora was still not sure. 'But …'

'Stop fussing, girl, and let the lad get on with it,' Ned growled. 'Sounds like a decent enough plan to me.' Although he spoke emphatically, her father slumped in the saddle as if holding himself upright was too much of an effort. That settled the matter for Cora.

'All right,' she said, 'but be careful. And thank you, from the bottom of my heart. I owe you a huge debt.'

They followed the road out of town, taking care to stay close to the side and shelter if they needed it. Fruit gardens and fields soon gave way to the eerie desolation of the Heath and its Stygian darkness, which, although good for hiding, made travelling difficult. Ned didn't complain but Cora could sense that every pebble and pothole in their path caused him great discomfort.

When she spied a lonely light from a carriage coming their way, Cora led Samson away from the road. Ned groaned as the horse stumbled across the scraggy heather, and although she was worried that they hadn't made as much progress as she would have liked, Cora decided to take a break.

'Take me to your mother's grave,' Ned demanded in a voice which gave away that it was a huge effort for him to speak.

'But that means going south. We have more chance of hiding in London than on the open heath.'

'I never wanted to leave her, and you know that.'

'That's the first place they'll think to look for you,' Cora protested. It was a couple of hours before daybreak, and once the sun came up she and Ned would be completely exposed.

Ned sighed. 'I'm spent, Cora. I haven't got any strength left in me; my bones are weary, my heart is pained with longing. This is my last request. Will you deny me, daughter?'

'Father, you …'

'I'm dying, my heart. I love you, but my place is with Sarah now. You have your life ahead of you. You must …' He stopped, overcome by a sudden, hacking cough. Tears stung Cora's eyes – she knew she could do nothing to alleviate his agony. Helpless, she watched as his ravaged body shuddered with the last of his strength.

'You must live your life, Cora,' he whispered finally and wiped away a speckle of blood from his lips. 'Love a man; have children, lots of them. Remember me kindly and forgive me for stealing you away from your rightful place in society.'

Cora took his hand. It was cold and dry, and she rested her cheek against it to warm it up. 'There's nothing to forgive. You're my one, true father, and I'll remember you with more than kindness; my heart will swell with love when I think of you.' A single tear ran down her face, and she wiped it away; then resolutely she took Samson's reins again. 'Come, let's find Mother.'

When the sun rose, Ned drew his last breath.

Cora had tried to make him as comfortable as possible. He lay on the ground beside her mother's grave, his head on Cora's coat and covered by an old blanket. He had stopped shivering, and his earlier pain seemed to have left his body. When he turned his eyes on his daughter for the last time, he had the look of a man who, despite deprivations in life, had everything he could ever wish for. With a catch in her throat Cora leaned closer to hear the final word on his lips.

Sarah.

Then he was at peace.

Chapter Twenty-Two

Cora sat hugging Ned's body for what seemed like hours, but neither prayers nor tears seemed appropriate. Her father was at peace, reunited with the woman he had loved above all others. Shedding tears over his passing would be selfish.

All the same, thought Cora as she laid him down gently and rubbed the feeling back into her stiff limbs, life without Ned would be dismal, and she knew she would miss him unbearably. Who would take her to task when she did wrong? Praise her when she did right? Or fuss over her first-born with that silly expression that grandfathers were often afflicted with?

Love a man, he had said. She'd always wished for herself the kind of love her parents shared. She'd found it with Jack, and their night together was the life she wished she could have had. Her father was gone now, but another obstacle had been thrown in their way, one neither of them could overcome despite their depth of feeling. The tragedy was that she'd already discovered the kind of love her father meant, and never would again.

With a stick she began digging a grave, but it hadn't rained in days and the ground was rock hard. When the stick broke under the pressure, and she found herself on her hands and knees clawing at the dirt with her fingers, Cora realised the futility of her endeavour. Instead she went in search of a shovel. She knew that if she didn't bury him quickly, wild animals might make short work of his body and she couldn't bear that.

The tears finally came, stinging, selfish tears, both welcome and unwanted at the same time, and she threw herself on the ground and cried till there was nothing left inside her.

* * *

Rupert sipped his brandy, enjoying the peaceful Brooks's atmosphere after his encounter with the highwaywoman. His mind kept wandering back to his unsettling encounter with her. It had left him rattled – who in their right mind wouldn't be after looking down the barrel of a pistol? – but he was also puzzled by what he had seen.

Her striking eyes and her general resemblance to his own father was too obvious to ignore. She could well be one of his father's by-blows; from the little he knew of the captain he'd had a mercurial temperament, and Rupert wondered briefly how many more illegitimate children of his father's there might be. Then he shrugged. It made no difference to him – they would have no claim on Rupert's own paltry inheritance, most of which was gone now at any rate.

He swirled the brandy in his glass, frowning as he did so. There was something else which nagged him, something on the periphery of his mind and tantalisingly out of reach. Sensing that it could be significant, he tried to recall the highwaywoman's every feature. She had the same hair and build as his sister, which strengthened his belief that she was related to him, but there were other elements where she differed. The way she sat on a horse, for instance, as if she was born into superiority. Who else rode ramrod straight like that?

'Buggered if I know,' he muttered. Swigging from his brandy, he nearly choked when the answer came to him.

The highwaywoman rode exactly like his uncle, the earl.

Absently he dabbed at the tears brought to his eyes by the alcohol burning in his throat. Perhaps the highwaywomen was his uncle's by-blow and not his father's. The two cousins shared enough of a family resemblance – their black hair and blue eyes – for this not to be completely unlikely.

The thought caused him a great deal of mirth, because if he had guessed correctly and Jack had bedded the wench, that would mean his saintly cousin had committed incest. And even if it had no basis in truth, it would be fun to see Jack rattled.

He chuckled quietly just as Jack entered the club's lounge, and he quickly replaced the smirk with his most benevolent smile.

'Cousin, how fortuitous. I was just about to go in search of a game of cards to pass the time. Now you can join me.'

'Thank you, Rupert, but no.' Jack sank down in a chair opposite. 'I find I'm not in the mood tonight.'

Rupert snapped his fingers at the club's butler. 'A restorative drink for my cousin,' he said. 'And put it on my bill.' *My uncle will cough up the money,* he added to himself, then he turned back to Jack.

Jack seemed a mere ghost of his former self. Despite his expertly tied neck cloth and expensive but understated wool jacket, he looked ragged. Dark circles underscored his eyes, and lines were etched from his nose to the corners of his mouth. Rupert wondered when he had last slept. Lost in thought, Jack only reacted when the servant returned with a glass of brandy and a crystal decanter.

'Thank you, Forbes,' he said, managing a smile; then he drained his glass in one and let the man pour him another.

Watching with a bemused smile, Rupert could guess the reason for Jack's despondency.

'Trouble with the fair sex?' he asked.

Jack shot him a look. 'That obvious, is it?'

'When a man looks as long-faced as you do, it's bound to have something to do with a woman. Always does.' Rupert laughed.

'You have no idea,' said Jack.

Rupert looked around him to check that the servant was out of earshot, then he leaned closer. 'Actually, I do. This woman, she isn't just anyone, is she? She's the one who held us up. We made a bet, and you found her first. Congratulations, Jack. I owe you a hundred guineas.'

Jack sent him a startled look. 'What makes you say that?'

'I saw you in town, saving her from being trampled by horses.

Later I, eh, chanced upon her, and she wore a coat identical to your favourite one. The midnight blue with the embroidery. I seriously doubt a woman of her ilk could afford such an item.' He pointed to what his cousin was wearing. 'And I see you're not wearing it this evening. Did she steal it, or did you part with it willingly, after a tender moment perhaps?'

He paused for effect, hoping to get a reaction from his cousin, but Jack merely looked at him, expressionless. The only testament to any emotion was a muscle moving in his set jaw.

'What mischief are you up to now, Rupert?'

Rupert put his hand on his heart, feigning innocence. 'Not mischief. I was merely curious about her appearance; she's so like your dear father. In fact, I wouldn't be surprised if she's the result of the earl sowing his wild oats once upon a time.'

'That wouldn't be so unusual.'

Rupert narrowed his eyes, frustrated by Jack's apparent *sang-froid*. 'I know you have bedded her,' he sneered.

Jack paled visibly, but a sip of brandy seemed to restore him to his former equilibrium. 'And you have proof of that, cousin? Because if you don't, you ought to be careful before making such assertions. Very careful.'

Proof?

No, of course he had no proof. He only had his instincts and his powers of observation, as well as something very important nagging at the back of his mind. So why …

It came to him in a flash. His and Alethea's looks favoured their father with little of their mother's looks. His father and the earl shared certain strong family features.

But Jack looked quite different.

He regarded his cousin over the rim of his brandy glass. Jack had his mother's looks, and now that Rupert studied him more closely, he could see nothing of the earl in him. Was it simply that Jack was more his mother's son, or was there something entirely different at play here? Could it be that

Rupert's own prospects hinged on the fact that Jack had none of the earl's features?

His head swam with possibilities, but each and every one of them saw him as the head of the family and the next earl. It might come to nothing, but if there was even a chance that Jack wasn't the earl's natural son, he would explore it. In the meantime, perhaps sowing the seed of suspicion in Jack's mind would lead to a breakdown in the relationship between father and son, and the earl would appoint Rupert his heir. It was worth a try.

To hide his agitation he smiled casually. 'Perhaps all is not lost, dear cousin. Perhaps your sin is not as great as you think.'

Jack glared at him suspiciously but remained silent.

'Perhaps this … highwaywoman, or whatever she is, is not your half-sister after all.'

'For heaven's sake, Rupert, I've had enough of your conjectures. If you have something to say, spit it out. First you accuse my father of sowing his wild oats and me of committing incest, now you retract your statement. Make up your mind.'

'I have. I put it to you that you're not your father's son.'

'I beg your pardon?' Jack remained seated, but there was a hard, intense gleam in his hazel eyes, and he reminded Rupert of a large cat ready to pounce on its prey. Nevertheless, Rupert had his attention now.

Emboldened, he continued. 'Alethea and I look like our father; my father and yours share a family resemblance. But you? I don't see any resemblance between you and your father. That woman of yours looks more a part of this family than you do. Do you not wonder how that can be?'

'This is absurd!' Jack protested, his shock visible.

'Is it? As you said, sowing wild oats is not unusual.' Rupert had trouble concealing a smirk and noted with satisfaction how Jack clenched his fists. No doubt he was longing to sock Rupert in the jaw, but was too well brought up to do that here at the club.

He rose slowly. 'What are you insinuating?'

'I'm insinuating nothing, merely making an observation.'

'Well, if you value your life, you'll keep your observations to yourself. Another word from you on the subject, and it'll be pistols at dawn, cousin or not.'

With that he turned on his heel and left.

Unconcerned, Rupert ordered another brandy. He enjoyed riling his cousin, but he doubted very much that the chaste Lady Lampton had done what he had suggested. She was devoted to her husband and had been for as long as Rupert could remember. The only way he could even hope to inherit would be if he somehow managed to push Jack and his father apart.

'Had a falling out again, the pair of you?'

Rupert looked around to see his godfather, Lord Feltham. He disliked the old curmudgeon, who was as fat as a barrel, with ill-fitting clothes, and in the habit of breaking wind. But Lord Feltham had been his mother's choice of godparent. Rupert tried to stay on his good side, for the sake of her memory if nothing else. He rose politely and indicated the chair Jack had just vacated.

'Uncle James, would you care to join me?'

Lord Feltham eyed him through narrowed, piggy eyes. 'Aye, don't mind if I do, although I should like to know how you brought about such a fit of pique in your cousin that he can't even spare a moment to greet an old man.'

'A minor disagreement,' said Rupert smoothly. 'I must apologise on his behalf. Brandy?'

'Thank you kindly.'

Forbes brought the drink, and the two men soon settled down to discussing various gentlemanly pursuits as Lord Feltham had a keen appetite for certain sports, in particular boxing, which Rupert shared.

'In my day we had proper fighting, between real men, not all these namby-pamby rules.' Lord Feltham growled and waved a hand dismissively. 'Why, only the other day I lost ten guineas because my man wasn't allowed up again after the count of thirty. I was most put out.'

Rupert smiled in what he hoped was an affable manner, but he gritted his teeth and wondered how soon he could make his excuses without appearing rude.

The old man accepted his offer of a second drink, then a third and didn't seem to be in any hurry to move on, to Rupert's frustration. In the end, Rupert decided that the only way to escape was to make up a lie.

'If you'll excuse me, I think I'd better go after Jack. I don't like being on bad terms with him, and it was such a silly argument in any case.'

'What washit about?' Lord Feltham was slurring his words, but seemed alert enough to expect an answer, so Rupert shrugged and explained.

'I merely commented that I thought it curious that he looks so unlike his father, in a family where all the males seem to resemble each other a lot. He flew into quite a rage over it.'

Lord Feltham chuckled. 'I should think so. Although ...'

He paused suddenly as if he had said too much; Rupert's interest was piqued.

'Although?'

Lord Feltham cleared his throat. 'Your aunt could have had any man she liked, you know. She was the belle of the season, but I do recall her having a particular regard for the youngest son of the Marquess of Dereham. I'm quite surprised she married my esteemed friend in the end, but I suppose it must have been agreed between the families. There were rumours, though.'

Pretending not to be the least bit interested in such gossip, Rupert inspected his fingernails. 'How so?'

'Some say she walked to the altar an unwilling bride,' said Lord Feltham with a hiccup. 'That would have been no surprise, hardly anyone marries for love after all. A fêted beauty like Lady Alice, as she was back then, would always fall prey to the ballroom gossips, especially when she had *beaux* such as the son of a marquess and an earl dancing attendance. Those spiteful old tabbies,' he added and belched for emphasis.

'The youngest son of the Marquess of Dereham ...' Rupert mused. 'What became of him?'

'Oh, he's the current marquess now. As bad luck would have it, or perhaps as *luck* would have it, depending on your perspective'—he attempted to fix Rupert with a sharp look but his eyes were slightly out of focus—'his oldest brother died in a riding accident, and the second brother was killed fighting the Scots in '45, leaving him to inherit everything on his father's death.'

'By which time his sweetheart was already a wife and mother,' Rupert commented drily, pretending to have no inkling where this was going. However, he wanted to keep his godfather talking and feigned innocence. 'How can this possibly have a bearing on why my cousin takes after his mother and not his father?'

Lord Feltham glanced around the room; then leaned forward and whispered conspiratorially, 'There was some talk.'

'About my aunt and the marquess?' Rupert raised a haughty eyebrow, but he had trouble concealing his excitement as he imagined his inheritance getting closer and closer.

'Mm-hm.' His godfather sat back in his chair with a self-important smirk. But his grin faded as if he realised only now who he was talking to, and he added briskly, 'But that was nothing but idle nonsense. Your aunt is a lady. It's inconceivable.'

'Indeed it is,' Rupert said and blithely ordered another round of drinks. His mind was in turmoil. Could it be that Jack was the son of the marquess and not Lord Lampton? If it was true, he would have to find a way of confronting his aunt under circumstances where she couldn't deny it.

The question was how.

He stayed at the club for a while longer, until he could extricate himself without rousing the old man's suspicion. It wouldn't do to underestimate Lord Feltham, even in his inebriated state.

As he left the club, asking for his hat and cane, a thought occurred to him.

'My cousin, Lord Halliford,' he asked the doorman, 'is he still here?'

'No, sir, he left about an hour ago.'

'For my uncle's town house at Devonshire Place, I presume,' Rupert said loftily.

The doorman shook his head. 'I believe it was his lordship's intention to return to the family estate at once.'

'At this hour?' Rupert hovered by the door uncertainly. 'Are you sure?'

'Quite sure, sir.' As if sensing Rupert's indecision, he added, 'How may I be of service? Do you require a conveyance yourself, a hackney coach perhaps?'

A *hackney* coach.

How Rupert hated that word, hated not having his own private carriage. How they must laugh at him behind his back, he thought, as resentment gnawed away at him, but he controlled himself. If his conjectures were right, it wouldn't be for long, and then who would have the last laugh?

Was it possible Jack had decided to confront the countess with what Rupert had insinuated? If so, Rupert wanted to be there when the scandal broke. His aunt and uncle may have brought him up as their own, but now it was time for him to take his place as their heir.

Chapter Twenty-Three

As he was jostled from side to side in his normally comfortable carriage, it seemed to Jack that Benning found every pothole and stone in the road on purpose.

But the physical discomfort was as nothing compared to the agitation he felt, a curious mix of trepidation and hope. Concern for his parents' happiness and his own future if what Rupert had suggested turned out to be true, and hope that if it were, there would be nothing preventing him from marrying Cora. What the future would bring for himself and Cora, and for his parents, he dared not think of just yet.

Another pothole nearly flung him onto the floor, and he muttered an oath, though in all fairness to Benning he had commanded the man to spring the horses. The experience brought him to his senses. There was no real need for haste because how could he possibly confront his mother with such accusations? He needed to think of the right way to approach Lady Lampton on the subject, but so far he had come up with nothing. He knocked on the ceiling of the carriage and asked Benning to slow down.

Devil take it, why did love have to be so complicated?

When the carriage pulled up outside his family home, he was still no nearer to a solution. He left Benning to see to the horses and took the servants' stairs up to the gallery – the way he had brought Cora. It seemed a long time ago. Lighting a candle, he held it up to study his father's portrait closely. An exquisite painting by a well-known artist, it was a great likeness to the living person.

And none of his father's striking features were present in his own looks.

A desperate, sinking feeling in the pit of his stomach told him that perhaps Rupert had spoken the truth, and he realised that he was hopelessly trapped. He couldn't marry Cora without shaming his mother, and that he could not contemplate. He had to speak to her.

He left the gallery and climbed the staircase to the bedrooms. It wasn't too late, and he hoped his mother would still be in her boudoir, where she often retired in the evenings before she went to bed.

His knock was answered by a curt, 'Enter.' Not from the countess, but from the earl. His father rarely entered his wife's domain, preferring instead to spend his evenings in the library, and this unusual occurrence made Jack suspect that they were debating the conversation Jack had had with his mother the day before.

Graceful rosewood furniture and a scattering of Chinese rugs against the backdrop of floral wallpaper made the countess's private salon as refined and understated as the woman herself. His father was already seated, in a chair more suited to showing off a lady's elegant bearing and modish dress than offering comfort to a robust gentleman, and he looked about as confined as he must have felt.

'Mother.' Jack gave a terse nod; he still hadn't forgiven her for stealing away his hope of happiness, and had it not been for Rupert's wild assertions, he would have chosen to stay in London for the foreseeable future, thus putting some distance between himself and his parents.

'Jack.' The countess greeted him with a gentle smile, but her eyes were dark from sadness, and Jack's heart softened a little. The earl's greeting was more measured, and he appeared out of sorts, which for some absurd reason filled Jack with a sliver of hope.

'May I speak with you, Mother?' he said.

The tension in the room was palpable, so much so that the sound of a pin dropping would have been magnified to the roar of cannon fire. Jack's gaze rested on his mother, who had taken up a place by the marble fireplace, where a fire burned low. He took in her regal bearing and the pallor in her cheeks, and thought it odd that the earl should remain seated while his wife was standing, but he reminded himself that he was in his mother's rooms now, so perhaps this role reversal was to be expected.

'Of course,' said the countess. 'I thought you would have more questions for me following our earlier conversation. I have spoken to your father, and it—'

'Mother,' Jack interrupted, 'before you go any further there is one question I need to ask of you.' Jack glanced at his father, who frowned but said nothing. 'It's … of a delicate nature.'

The earl spoke for the first time. 'Fear not, my son. Your mother and I have had a frank discussion; one we should've had years ago. There are no secrets between us now.'

Jack hesitated. His father might say they had no secrets between them, but in his own experience people never bared all. 'Very well,' he said. 'It was something Rupert suggested.'

'Rupert?' Jack's parents exchanged a look, so brief Jack almost missed it, and the earl got up from the chair and began pacing the room. 'What can *he* possibly have to say on this matter?'

'It's about Mother.'

'Well, go on, son, spit it out!'

Jack took a steadying breath. 'He claims that I may not be my father's son, and as much as I have tried to ignore it, I can see with my own eyes that there is very little likeness between us.'

The countess gasped as the colour left her face completely, and the earl stopped pacing and stared, white-faced, at Jack; then in two strides he was by his wife's side. 'Come now, my dear. You mustn't take any notice of what my nephew says. No doubt he'd had one drink too many.' He led his wife to the chair he had just vacated, and the countess took a seat without protest. Then he turned to Jack.

'Where is Rupert now? I wish to speak with him.'

'He was still at Brooks's when I left him,' said Jack.

'He has some nerve. I know for a fact that your mother has never broken her wedding vows, and that she readily gave up on any attachments she may have formed elsewhere when she became my wife. You favour her in looks because it sometimes happens that a child favours one parent more than the other. That is all.'

'So there's no truth in it at all?' Jack experienced a mixture of emotions; relief that he was the true child of both his parents, something he'd never had any reason to doubt before, coupled with renewed horror that he and Cora had committed a mortal sin by making love. He hadn't really believed Rupert, yet his cousin's accusations had kindled a hope in him which had now been extinguished for the second time.

'No,' said the countess. 'And I'm afraid my views about something else have been mistaken all these years too. It grieves me that I shared this mistake with you before making absolutely certain. In the past pride prevented me, but when I observed your distress … a mother cannot escape pain when her only child is faced with such anguish … well, I set my own feelings aside and decided to clear up the matter once and for all.'

'Which mistake?' Jack looked from one parent to another, his heart suddenly pounding.

'There is no question about your parentage,' said his father. 'There are, however, some questions about Rupert's.'

'*Rupert's?*'

The earl took his wife's hand in his. 'Many years ago my cousin, the captain, fell in love with a young lady of our close acquaintance – Sophia, later Lady Heston. Her father wouldn't consent to the match as he had already chosen a husband for her, and Cecil, as you know, later married Elizabeth, Rupert and Alethea's mother.'

Jack nodded.

'They were both desperately unhappy in their marriage, and Cecil rarely frequented the marriage bed. In her loneliness and despair Elizabeth turned to me in the hope that I – as his

246

cousin and friend – could persuade him to do right by her. Your mother and I were experiencing our own difficulties after little Henry's death, and Elizabeth had such great need of me … well, I'm afraid I succumbed. I was indeed unfaithful to your mother, but not with Lady Heston.'

The countess looked aggrieved at this, but she didn't pull her hand away.

'Later Elizabeth confessed to me that our liaison had resulted in a child. Rupert is *my* son by blood, not the captain's, and your half-brother. It seemed natural for me to take Rupert under my wing when he was orphaned, and Alethea too, although she is the captain's own child.'

'And you had no relations with Lady Heston?' he asked, shocked by these complicated revelations but elated too that perhaps there may now be a future for him and Cora.

'None whatsoever. Your mother made an erroneous assumption. My sorrow for Lady Heston came at a time when we were both still grieving over losing Henry, and the manner of her death just added to our strained circumstances. It was a terrible time.'

'So the woman I mentioned is the captain's child?' Jack asked.

'Yes,' said the earl. 'I knew my cousin well, and I always suspected he'd taken up with Sophia later when their paths crossed again. With this woman's likeness to him it's clear to me that he must have done so.'

Jack was overwhelmed with relief that Cora was not in fact his sister, but their future together was still far from certain. The inescapable fact was she'd perpetrated a string of crimes, and now that Rupert knew who she was, for Jack to pursue her would only endanger her and her father.

He sighed. 'There is another matter which is now preying on my mind.'

'Yes?' The earl stilled, and a wary look crept into his mother's eyes.

'Rupert,' he said. 'I suspect he has sometimes wished he was your heir. That is, of course, impossible as long as I live, and if I have heirs of my own. But perhaps if he were to have more agreeable prospects it might curb his spendthrift ways and reckless nature.'

'What are you suggesting, Jack?' The earl shook his head. 'Even if I acknowledged him as my son, he's illegitimate and could never inherit.'

Jack regarded his father with a mixture of respect and disappointment. For so long he had felt annoyed, and hurt, by the way his father favoured Rupert. Now his father's actions clearly showed that Jack was in favour, and perhaps always had been. Jack's affection for his father was tinged with exasperation.

'I merely meant that perhaps you need to find a different way to help Rupert.'

'Are you suggesting I've acted dishonourably? This is absurd!' The earl's voice rose, and, letting go of his wife's hand, he drew himself up to his full height.

Jack met his father's challenge without backing down. 'No, sir, only that you have been too preoccupied with estate matters to give this proper thought, and it has caused great resentment in my cousin.'

His father gave an indignant snort. 'But you clearly have. Pray, what would you suggest I do to make up for this supposed neglect?'

'Give him something worthwhile to do: help him go into a profession. Perhaps he could have a small fortune of his own, some land even. He has nothing aside from an allowance, and as his uncle – and his father in truth – you need to provide him with the means to live independently, not just ensure his comforts.'

'Hmm.' The earl began pacing the room again, and then stopped by the fireplace and slapped his hand down on the marble mantelpiece so hard the countess jumped. 'By Jove, you're right, Jack! I could never acknowledge Rupert as my son, so I spoiled him and ignored his reckless spending. Perhaps I have acted dishonourably – but it seems to me that there is sometimes a very fine line between honour and dishonour. I shall listen to your advice for it seems you know Rupert better than I do.'

'Thank you, Father. I think you'll see Rupert's nature improve greatly.' *I certainly hope so*, he thought, and remembered the way they had parted at Brooks's. He'd seen a glimpse of how deep a grudge his cousin bore against him, even if it had been well hidden by his attempt at riling him.

The countess had been quiet for a while but now she spoke again. 'What about the young lady you wish to marry?' she asked. 'Miss Mardell I think you said. When we last spoke, I expressed my misgivings about her background, and your father shares those. And now we have received news from Blencowe of a man named Ned Mardell being held by the magistrate for highway robbery. Is he a relation of hers?'

'Mardell's her father,' Jack replied. 'He's in prison?'

'No longer, I'm afraid,' said the earl. 'He escaped from the magistrate's cellar last night. The lad who collected the slop bucket late in the evening swore Mardell was there, asleep on some blankets, when he left, and the constable didn't think the man would've had the strength to leave anyway. The lad's been questioned, but he's a disingenuous sort with no connections to Mardell, and there's no reason to suspect he's involved.'

A lad, Jack thought, smelling a rat, but he said nothing.

'There's more,' the earl continued. 'They found a newly dug grave in the forest about a mile south of town. When they inspected it, they found it to be Mardell's. They've left him there, next to his wife's last resting place, God bless his soul.'

Cora. Her father's escape had all the hallmarks of her handiwork. Jack would have laughed if he hadn't known how desperately sad she must be at his death, and he vowed that even if he never saw her again, he would arrange for her father to have a proper headstone. 'I'm sorry to hear he's dead,' he said quietly.

'Even though her father is gone now, it would cause quite a stir for you to marry her,' said the earl.

'I'm aware of that, but it's irrelevant,' Jack replied. 'I fear the lady will no longer have me, so there will be no scandal.'

'She would refuse the son of earl? How extraordinary.' His father raised his eyebrows, and despite his incredulity Jack thought he detected an element of relief. In his mother too.

If only that were all there was to it, he thought. If they knew the rest, they would be even more relieved. Mardell had died with the secret that the highwayman was his daughter, but Jack still knew, and so did Rupert. They couldn't risk Rupert exposing Cora to the authorities. Maybe one day, when he was no longer so resentful of Jack, they could be together. But until then, they would have to remain apart.

The earl turned to his wife and knelt in front of her. 'As for scandal and speculations I'm glad we've cleared up this matter between us. It's been too long for either of us to harbour ill feeling. Can you forgive me for all the wrongs I have done you?'

A tear ran down the countess's cheeks, and, laughing, she reached up and cupped his face between her hands. 'Oh, Geoffrey, you silly man! I forgave you a long time ago.'

Helping her up, the earl took her in his arms, and she dropped her head to his shoulder with a sigh. Jack suddenly felt surplus to requirements.

Casting a glance over his shoulder and rejoicing in their obvious affection for each other, he left his parents. Picking up a candle, he retired to his room.

As he undressed, he stared out into the night, mulling over the conversation with his parents and the revelations about his cousin. Rupert had always felt more like a brother to him than a cousin, but with what he knew now, maybe that wasn't so strange.

Back in his mother's boudoir he'd had a momentary, crazy thought that if he were to give up his inheritance in favour of Rupert, he might forget about the humiliating robbery and let him and Cora be together. But he'd quelled the thought as soon as it had entered his head; he'd spent his whole life learning how to manage the estate, preparing for this job for as long as he could remember. He was more than qualified to do it, whereas Rupert didn't have the knowledge, inclination or experience to run a large estate successfully. Out of duty to his family, to their tenants and everyone else who depended on the estate for their livelihood he had no other option than to forget Cora. He only hoped she was safe wherever she was.

'But I can promise you this, Cora,' he muttered to the reflection in the dark window glass, 'I'll care for your father's remains. I know how much he meant to you.'

Hiding in the shadows outside his aunt's private salon, Rupert had heard enough. His head spinning, he staggered along the corridor to his bedroom and yanked open the window. The shock of the cool evening air on his face made him gasp, but the chill was welcome. Clenching his fists, he stared out into the night as he entertained murderous thoughts.

So, he was not his father's son. Everything he had taken for granted about his life, had known about himself, about his past, present and future, tumbled down like a house of cards. A thousand thoughts and feelings flew through his mind at the same time, so fast he could capture only a few of them.

Confusion and pain. Anger at the deceit they were planning.

He twisted his cane in rage. There was nothing he could do about it – even if he could produce enough evidence for a court of law. Who would believe him, and not his uncle, a respected nobleman whom everyone held in high esteem? No one, was the answer.

What did the future hold for him now? The question injured him like the sting from a wasp, venom coursing in his veins.

Bringing his hand up, he banged it several times against the window frame so hard the glass panes rattled.

Then came the relief that whatever he chose to do from now on, he could do without a guilty conscience, because he owed them nothing. His next move would be to secure the earldom, and he had no compunction about the means required to obtain it.

Chapter Twenty-Four

Despite the lateness of the hour, the Black Dog Inn was crowded when Rupert entered. Pausing in the doorway, he took a moment or two to allow his eyes to adjust to the blanket of smoke. His other senses were insulted by the rancid smell of tallow, unwashed bodied and stale beer, the clamour of voices and the raucous laughter from the tavern doxies.

As he made his way across the dirty floor to a secluded corner at the back, he was jostled by beefy serving wenches bearing tankards of ale and platters of food. A group of unshaven, sweaty men were clustered around a table where a game of dice was under way, and it sounded as if the stakes were high. In front of the large fireplace at one end of the room sat a lone figure, huddled in a mud-splattered cloak with two pistols tucked into his belt. He coughed repeatedly, either because of the smoke from the fire or an ague of the chest. Rupert gave him a wide berth and sat down at a table.

'What'll it be, sir?' A serving girl appeared almost immediately and leaned forward to display her ample bosom to its advantage. She smiled what she might have imagined to be a winsome smile, but it was nothing but a grimace of blackened and missing teeth. That, combined with the dark circles of sweat under her armpits and several unidentifiable stains on the front of her dress, made Rupert draw back in distaste.

'A tankard of ale,' he said hastily, trying not to breathe in her body odour, 'and a word with the landlord, if you please.'

'Right you are,' she replied. She sent him another smile, and Rupert grimaced back while he suppressed a shudder. He may have bedded wenches like this one in the past; now he saw himself as Jack must have done. A wastrel bringing the family's name in disrepute because he had nothing better to do. That it was Jack who had been his self-appointed spokesperson with his uncle and aunt rankled even more.

After a while the landlord appeared. 'You requested my presence, sir. How may I be of assistance?'

'Discretion,' said Rupert, placing a guinea on the table.

'Is my middle name,' countered the landlord.

Rupert sized him up. A thin, tired-looking man, the landlord wore a leather apron, and the sleeves of his shirt were rolled up to the elbow to display wiry arms, which seemed at odds with his scrawny frame, but his eyes were shrewd and intelligent. Rupert decided he would do.

'All right,' he said, lowering his voice. 'I need two men who are prepared to do a job for me, no questions asked. High risk, but well paid.'

'Within the law or outside it?' the landlord asked. A smug smile pulled at the corners of his thin mouth.

'I said no questions. But trust me, it's not for the squeamish.'

Nodding, the landlord closed his hand over the coin. 'I know the men you want. Meet me at the back in half an hour. They'll be waiting.'

Half an hour later, behind the Black Dog, three shadowy figures met and conducted their business in secrecy. A heavy purse changed hands while Rupert outlined his plan and gave a description of the targets.

'The viscount usually goes riding in the mornings.' He went on to explain the route Jack would normally take and what he wanted the two men to do when they had overpowered him.

'Will he be alone?' asked one of them, a burly man with beefy overarms and a neckerchief encrusted with dirt around his neck.

'He often accompanies the earl in the mornings, and if that's the case, you'll have to wait until another day,' said Rupert.

'Right you are, sir.'

'Bind him and bring him to the clearing we talked about.

If he resists, show him who's boss, but remember, I want him coherent. Do I make myself clear?'

'Aye, crystal clear,' growled the other man, who seemed a little cleaner and a little more intelligent.

Satisfied, Rupert nodded curtly. 'Now I must bid you goodnight, gentlemen, but remember, there's more where that comes from, provided you do my bidding and follow my instructions to the letter. He must not be allowed to escape.'

The next morning Jack informed Benning of his plans to re-bury the body of a man in the forest, and instructed him to ready the necessary equipment.

'Re-bury a body, m'lord? Would that be the highwayman everyone's talking about?' The groom eyed him curiously.

'That's no concern of yours,' Jack snapped, and Benning was wise enough not to ask further. Instead he went about his preparations, muttering to himself, as was his habit.

Jack ignored him. Cora had been on his mind all night and he hoped that she wouldn't leave the area until she'd ensured a proper burial for her father. From their whispered conversation during their night of passion he had ascertained that Cora and her father planned on going to Spain, but he suspected that her plans had changed now.

And if he managed to inter Mardell's remains in the churchyard, he was certain Cora would wish to visit her father's new grave, at least once. Perhaps then he could see her one last time. He had to tell her he understood now that it was too dangerous for them to be together, but the thought of uttering those words left him almost breathless from pain.

Alethea found him as he and Benning were preparing for a lengthy sojourn in the forest.

'Where are you going?' she asked when she noticed their equipment and Jack's scruffy attire.

'Nowhere.'

'Something's going on: I know it. It's about that girl you

like, isn't it? I knew it, Jack! Oh, I just knew it!' She flung her arms around him.

'Slow down,' he said and extricated himself gently. 'What do you know?'

'That you are to be married, you ninny. I heard my aunt and uncle discuss it yesterday afternoon. I was playing the pianoforte, and they didn't think I was listening, but I was. Oh, you'll be so happy, I'm sure of it! You lucky, lucky thing!' Excited, Alethea bounced up and down.

'Alethea ...' Jack began, but then stopped. He had never kept any secrets from her. Guilt stole over him. Although Alethea knew Cora looked a lot like her father, he didn't know how she would react to the knowledge that Cora was her half-sister. And what about Rupert? Should he tell her they were only half-siblings? On the other hand, Alethea was one of the most sensible and sharp-minded people he had ever known, despite her youth. He owed it to her. 'I'll tell you all, but later. It's not that simple.'

'Tell me now!' she cried.

With a sigh, Jack agreed. Mardell was dead and his body wasn't going anywhere. What difference did half an hour make? 'All right, but not here. It's a complex matter, and I don't want to be overheard.' He inclined his head in the direction of the groom, and, getting his meaning, Alethea nodded imperceptibly.

Riding side by side down a secluded lane towards the Heath, Jack trusted his instincts and told his cousin everything that had happened.

When he finished, Alethea's pretty face was sad but determined. Reining in her horse, she stopped and put a slender hand on his arm. 'I'm honoured that you trusted me enough to share this with me, and it makes no difference to me that your intended is illegitimate, because I stand to gain a sister in more ways than one. However, it saddens me that my parents were so unhappy. Obviously I don't remember them, with my father dying before I was born, and my mother when she had me, but I'm sure they didn't deserve such wretchedness.'

She smiled briefly, but then turned serious again, and her eyes were concerned when she continued. 'As for Rupert, I love my brother – despite his penchant for getting into trouble, but I mistrust him intensely. He wants to be the next earl, and if he should get wind of this, it would be ruinous for us all.'

'Even if he does, he could never hope to inherit. Father cannot acknowledge him openly. He may have been indulgent when it comes to Rupert, but he'd never do anything which would lead to my mother being humiliated. Rupert would gain nothing other than being cut off without a penny.'

'And if he resorts to other, baser, means?'

'I'll be on my guard.'

As they continued on their ride, Jack said nothing further, and Alethea appeared deep in thought. He wondered where Cora was and prayed that she stayed away from Rupert.

They had reached the part of the lane where the woods were densest before they petered out into Hounslow Heath. Alethea turned to Jack with a smile, and he opened his mouth to say something, but didn't get a chance. Two men leapt out from the bushes on either side of the path. One caught the bridle of Jack's horse and pointed a pistol at him; the other pulled Alethea from her mount, muffling her startled scream with a dirty hand.

Instinctively Jack reached for his rapier, but the man shook his head. 'I wouldn't do that if I were you, mister. It'd be a mighty shame if my associate 'ere had to snap the lady's delicate neck, now, wouldn't it? Such a pretty neck 'n' all.'

Meeting Alethea's frightened eyes, Jack stopped.

'Now, if you'll be so kind as to give me that sword and get down from your 'orse, I'd be much obliged.'

Glaring at him, Jack handed him the rapier and got down. 'There's a purse in my pocket,' he said. 'Take what you came for and release my cousin.'

The man prodded him in the back with the pistol. 'A tempting offer, but it ain't your purse I'm after.'

'Well, state what you want, and I'll give it to you. Only let the lady go.'

'Sorry, can't do that. The two of you will fetch a pretty penny. 'Ere, Toby, toss us that rope.'

The other man complied, taking his eyes off Jack for a moment. While his attention was elsewhere, Jack elbowed the first ruffian in the stomach. Winded, the man clutched his middle, and Jack wrested the pistol from his grip.

Then his head exploded with pain, and he remembered nothing more.

Cora looked back one last time at Mr Isaacs. It was early, and she left by the back door, away from prying eyes. Last night she'd come to pass on the sad news that Ned had died, and, seeing her distress, Mr Isaacs had insisted that she stayed for a meal. At first she'd hesitated, fearing that her presence would endanger Mr Isaacs, but afterwards she'd been grateful for his offer. When he offered her a bed to lie down on for a while, she accepted that too. She hadn't realised just how tired she was.

Her old friend had lit a seven-armed candle holder and said a prayer in his own language. Although Cora didn't understand the words, it had given her comfort. Afterwards she had slept like a baby.

Knowing that the magistrate might be looking for her in his hunt for the escaped prisoner, she had maintained her disguise as a young man. Tucking her black hair under her hat, she was able to ride out of town unchallenged.

At the nine-mile stone she hesitated. Going straight on would take her to London, turning left would take her towards Lampton Hall.

And Jack.

She still had his watch in her pocket. Jack had hinted that it had sentimental value because his cousin had given it to him – returning it would be the decent thing to do, would it not?

How do you propose to do that, my girl?

She could almost hear Ned's voice in her head. No, indeed, how would she go about it? She could hardly ride up to the front door and announce her intention to return an item of stolen property. With his cousin on her trail, she might end up on the gallows – and Jack too perhaps, as an accomplice. She couldn't let that happen. Perhaps if she hid among the trees in the park, she might chance upon Alethea and could ask her to give the watch to Jack.

You're fooling yourself, she thought. The watch was merely an excuse for seeing Jack one last time, even if from a distance.

Resolutely she nudged Samson forward and took the left road. It might be dangerous, but Jack had said he would like the watch back, and if there was a way of getting it to him, she would find it.

She heard the smothered scream when she was about half a mile from the estate and reined in her horse sharply. Someone was in danger, a woman by the pitch of the scream. The wise thing to do would be turn around and get away from here, but instinct kicked in. Someone needed her help.

What if it was Alethea?

The sound came from dead ahead on the narrow lane. Trees and bushes lined both sides of it, and – conscious stealth might be best – she slipped down from Samson's back and led him in among the bushes. Quietening him with a hand on his soft muzzle, she made her way to where the sound had come from, under cover of the dense shrubbery, and peered out through the leaves.

The scene that greeted her sent her heart racing: Jack was held at pistol point by a scruffy-looking individual, and another man had his hand clamped over Alethea's mouth.

She ducked back behind the leaves and lay flat on the ground, lest the men should spot her. Reaching for her pistol, she wondered how best to overcome the attackers, but there were two of them, both with pistols, and although Cora was fast, she doubted she'd be able to get off another shot from her second pistol before one of them fired on her.

Just then there was a sickening crack, and Cora clapped her hand over her mouth to stifle a gasp. One of the men had hit Jack over the head with the butt of his pistol, and Jack crumpled to the ground. Helpless, she watched as the men bound his wrists and tossed him over the back of his horse. Then they bound Alethea's hands to the pommel of her saddle and led their captives further into the forest.

Bile rose in her throat, and on shaking legs Cora followed them at a safe distance, her pistol cocked and ready.

Chapter Twenty-Five

When Jack came to, he was lying face down on the forest floor with his hands tied behind his back. Groaning with pain, he rolled on to his side and tried to sit up, then craned his neck to look for Alethea. A sharp kick in the ribs sent him sprawling, but not until he had ascertained his cousin's whereabouts.

Alethea was sitting a few feet away from him with her back against a tree and her wrists tied in front of her. She had a defiant, mulish expression on her face but appeared to be unharmed, and Jack took heart.

I know that look, he thought with pride.

But rebellious or not, they were in a dangerous predicament. Whatever these men wanted, it wasn't money, at least not the few guineas Jack carried in his purse. He had no notion what they truly wanted, but it didn't bode well.

Suddenly, he was pulled up and his head was yanked back by the hair. 'Well, well, well, look who's awake.' The man planted his fist right on Jack's cheekbone; then kicked him in the stomach. Dark spots appeared before Jack's eyes, and he feared he might pass out again, but the other man stepped in.

'There's to be no damage. We just keep them till the other gen'leman gets 'ere.'

'What about the girl?' said the one called Toby. 'Are we allowed a bit o' sport? The gen'leman didn't specify nuffink about no girl.'

'No, I'm specifyin' it,' said the more well-spoken of the two men.

'That ain't no fun, Pete.'

'Mebbe it ain't, but you're getting well paid, so keep your gob shut and your hands to yourself.'

Toby glared at Pete; then, muttering profanities, he moved

away and sat down on a tree stump, from where he continued to scowl at Jack.

Jack studied the two men surreptitiously. They had mentioned a third man, a gentleman, and he wondered who that could be. What could he want from him and Alethea? Were they being kidnapped for a ransom perhaps? To be sure, Lord Lampton would pay whatever sum they demanded to have his son and niece safely returned, but somehow it didn't fit. While highway robbery was rife in these parts, abductions were rare, and they usually involved children or ladies, not grown men.

Alethea's words came back to him. *I mistrust Rupert intensely.*

Could Rupert have a hand in this? He hoped not. However, thinking about who and why would do him and Alethea no good. He had to think of a way to overpower the two men before whatever reinforcements they were waiting for turned up.

And he would have to think fast because when the others arrived, Jack had a horrible feeling that it would be the end of him.

He noticed his rapier lying on the ground a few feet away, where the ruffians must have thrown it when they entered the clearing. Slowly he shuffled sideways on his backside and over a sharp stone on the ground he had spied when Toby punched him. Then he began to work at the ropes binding his wrists, ignoring the pain as the stone cut into his skin.

He had almost finished sawing through the rope when there was a rustle in the bushes, and a man appeared.

Rupert.

The betrayal was like a bodily blow. He hadn't wanted to believe it, still couldn't quite conceive of it, but it was clear now that Rupert must have born him ill-will all the time they grew up together. Jack wasn't sure which was worse: knowing that Rupert had hired these men, or that he had harboured malicious thoughts for so long.

How could I be so blind, he thought? How could Alethea, eight years his junior, see what he hadn't?

And now Rupert would be his downfall. Alethea's too, for she was a witness to whatever happened to Jack. He had to try and reach Rupert somehow, to get him to see that whatever grievance he had with Jack, harming his own sister, an innocent bystander, would be forever on his conscience.

But even if he could be persuaded not to harm Alethea, Jack couldn't believe that Rupert could be convinced to give up his search for Cora.

'Rupert,' he said. 'What's the meaning of this? Who are these men, and what do they want with us?'

'It isn't they who want something from you, but I,' Rupert replied. Ignoring Jack's protests, he turned to Pete, who appeared to be the one in charge. 'Good work, men. Now I must ask you to leave me alone with my ... this man and the lady.'

'Wot about our money?' Toby grumbled.

Rupert took a purse out of his pocket and tossed it to Pete, who opened it and began to count. 'As I promised: you're well rewarded. You'll find it's all there, and more besides, as a token of my appreciation that you can keep quiet about my affairs.'

The last was spoken with the utmost civility, but there was no mistaking the undertone. Jack saw that the two men had understood perfectly.

'Our lips are sealed,' said Pete. 'Toby, it's 'igh time we was on our way.'

With one last look of loathing in Jack's direction, Toby followed his associate, and the men were gone as stealthily as they had arrived.

Rupert turned to Jack.

'Alone at last.' He grinned.

'Rupert, I demand to know what this is about.' Hoping to buy time, Jack feigned ignorance. It was only a matter of moments before he would have sawn through the rope. If only he could stall Rupert.

Rupert tutted. 'I never took you for a fool, Jack. It's very simple: I'm the son of an earl and I intend to inherit my father's title. Yes,' he added as realisation dawned on Jack, 'I listened in on your little tête-à-tête with your loving parents. Did you really think you could hide the truth from me?'

'We can come to some sort of arrangement,' said Jack. 'You don't have to do this.'

'What, pray, could we arrange? I find it very hard to believe that you would give up your birth right. You must die. You can see that, can't you?'

Rupert sounded almost reasonable, as if he were merely debating the pros and cons of planting wheat, but his eyes glittered with the dangerous sheen of a madman.

'And Alethea?' asked Jack. 'Must she die too?'

Rupert glanced at his sister. Alethea stared back, her eyes huge, but not with fear or pleading – never pleading, not Alethea – but with defiance. With her head held high, her chin out, and her eyes promising Armageddon, she was like the Queen of the Nile, beautiful, regal and deadlier than the asp that killed her.

With shock, Jack realised that she reminded him exactly of Cora. Whatever Rupert planned to do with her, like Cora she wouldn't go willingly to her death. The thought filled him with pride for his young cousin.

Rupert must have seen it too for he took a step back in alarm. 'Alethea wasn't meant to be here, but now that she is, what else can I do but to get rid of her too?'

Jack tried a different tactic. 'Rupert, we were friends once. Remember when we raided Sir Christopher's fruit garden? The look on that old miser's face ... Or when we stuffed the housekeeper's mattress with holly? I never saw such a shade of puce!'

For a moment Rupert smiled with a faraway look in his eyes. 'I remember you getting me into trouble for that,' he said.

Jack recalled it quite differently: Rupert coming up with the ideas, and himself being caned. 'We had fun, though. Doesn't that count for something?'

Rupert regarded him steadily, and Jack was convinced he was coming around. But Rupert's wistful expression was quickly replaced by a hard stare.

'That's by the by,' he said coolly. 'It's time to end this. But I'm not an ogre; I'll give you a choice of who gets to die first. Does my sister get to see you die, or vice versa? And if you're wondering how I plan to get away with this, it's quite simple; you were attacked by a highwaywoman, and I came to your rescue. That'll put your lady friend nicely in the frame, don't you think?'

'She'll never be caught,' said Jack. The mention of her made his heart jolt, and he hoped Rupert couldn't tell that his words were pure bravado.

'No? Well, I beg to differ. I'm sure she'll want to visit her father's grave one last time. Surely she'll have heard his body was discovered by the magistrate, or if not, she soon will. All I have to do is lie in wait for her.'

Jack's hands were nearly free, and when they were, he was certain that he could overpower Rupert. Then he would make sure his half-brother received all the help available to those suffering a sickness of the mind. He just needed to buy a little more time.

'My father has always seen you right, hasn't he?' he continued. 'You never wanted for anything, and no demands were made of you. A title and an estate comes with the heavy burden of responsibility. Wouldn't you rather be without it?'

'You don't think I'm up to the job?' Rupert sneered.

'Frankly, I don't think a title is worth committing murder for.' Jack's right hand was almost free. 'It'll weigh too heavily on your conscience, my friend.'

'I disagree. Since you will not play the game and tell me who dies first, I've decided that it'll be you, if only to silence you.' Rupert pulled out his pistol and pointed it at Jack.

Finally he was free. Before Rupert had time to cock his weapon, Jack jumped up and grabbed the rapier. But the feeling hadn't returned to his hands after they had been bound so tightly, and his grip was clumsy. Deftly, Rupert sidestepped the weapon, socked Jack in the jaw with his elbow, and wrenched the blade out of his hand. With his boot he sent Jack sprawling on the ground again, and he pulled Alethea up by the hair.

Alethea shrieked with shock and tried to strike him with her bound hands, but Rupert took her hard by the arm and held her away from him.

'You've made a difficult choice for me. I had thought to spare you watching my high-and-mighty sister die, but now it'll give me the greatest pleasure to see the pain in your eyes,' Rupert shouted at Jack.

He put the pistol to Alethea's temple and cocked it.

'Rupert, for pity's sake!' Jack scrambled to his feet. 'Think of what you're d—'

The shot echoed in the forest, and Alethea fell sideways. Inside, Jack broke into a thousand pieces.

'Oh, God! Please God, not Alethea!'

He dropped to his knees, wanting nothing more than to die himself if only to end the unbearable pain in his chest. Slowly, averting his eyes, he crawled towards her body, preparing himself for a most horrific sight. He knew he was going to do die, but it didn't matter anymore. All he wanted to do was cradle his innocent cousin in his arms before his own life ended. If only he could hold Cora one last time too.

But on reaching Alethea, he found her staring back at him, very much alive. He blinked, unable to believe his own eyes. Sitting up, Alethea shook her head.

'I … I'm unhurt,' she said in a daze, as if she couldn't quite believe it either.

Jack's eyes travelled to Rupert, who returned his look with a dull expression and a curious half-smile. His hand dropped to his side, and the pistol slipped from his grasp. Blood bubbled from Rupert's lips, and he tumbled to the ground like a felled tree.

'Rupert!' Jack rushed to his side.

'Never was ... much good with ... pistols.'

'Don't talk. We'll get a physician. You'll be all right. You'll see.'

Rupert grabbed Jack by the lapel, and Jack leaned closer to hear what he was saying. 'Alethea ... wasn't supposed to ... be here. Didn't want ... to harm her. Promise you'll look after her. She ... trouble.' He let go of Jack's coat as if it was too much effort to hold on. Then his eyes lost their focus, and his head fell sideways.

He was dead.

Solemnly Jack closed Rupert's unseeing eyes; then looked up when he sensed movement behind him

Cora was standing a few feet away, by the tree where Alethea had sat only a moment ago. Smoke still rose from the barrel of her pistol, and the hand which held it trembled uncontrollably. Her eyes were huge with terror and revulsion.

'Cora ...'

With a shriek she dropped the pistol and fled into the trees. Before Jack could get up, he heard the sound of thundering hooves disappearing in the thicket.

'No! Come back!'

It was too late: she was gone.

Again.

He turned to Alethea, unsure what to do. No matter what Rupert had intended to do, the loss of his cousin was still raw, and he feared the two men might return. He had to see Alethea to safety, but if he did, Cora might disappear out of his life forever. Thus torn, he looked between Alethea and where Cora had vanished. Alethea made his mind up for him.

'Go after her.'

'I need to see you home first.' Though it wrenched his heart to acknowledge it. 'What if the men return?' Helping her up, he quickly cut her bonds.

'I doubt they will. After all, they've been paid.' She snorted contemptuously. 'We're not that far from home. Someone is bound to have heard the shot. Help will be on its way.'

Jack glanced at Rupert's dead body. 'How do we explain this?'

'We follow Rupert's plan; to be just, it was well thought out. I'll say we were attacked by highway robbers, and that Rupert came to our aid but was killed. I can give a very good description of the two men. If they know what's good for them, they'll disappear.'

'But will you be believed?'

Alethea smiled. 'Oh, I'll swoon and do a very good impression of a damsel in distress. Blencowe will be hanging on my every word. Just go, Jack. Don't miss this opportunity for true happiness.'

'If you're sure …?' Jack hovered, his hand on the horse's bridle.

'I'm sure. Now go. I will stay with Rupert's body. Say my goodbyes.' Tears welled up in Alethea's eyes. 'Oh, Jack! Rupert was misguided, but he was my brother. I shall feel the loss keenly.'

'We all will,' Jack said and meant it. He swung himself into the saddle and spurred the horse forward in a gallop.

He found Cora exactly where he'd known she would be. She stood with her head bowed in front of the graves in the forest clearing. When Jack came closer he could see that the larger of the two boards – the one bearing Sarah Duval's inscription – had been knocked aside roughly and scrawled with foul words.

Lord Heston, he thought, and rage welled up in him. Who else would desecrate the grave of Cora's mother?

Startled, Cora swung around with the second of her two pistols raised, but she lowered it and returned it to her waistband when she saw who it was.

'Who would do such a thing?' she asked him with stifled sob.

His heart clenched at the sight of her distress, and, taking her hands, he drew them to his chest, caressing her fingers as he did so. He was relieved when she didn't pull away, and it touched him how his nearness seemed to comfort her. He intended to comfort her the rest of his life if she'd let him, and now that Rupert was gone, her secret was safe. Their secret.

'Lord Heston, I should think,' he replied. 'He always had a bone to pick with your mother. But don't worry, the man will get his comeuppance one day. Right now we need to talk. And just so you know – I've chased your horse away.'

'Why?'

'So you can't run away from me again.'

With a wan smile she shrugged. 'I'm finding it hard to run away altogether. I love this place. I was happy here.'

'And I love you.'

He drew her closer to kiss her, but she pulled back, shaking her head.

'No, Jack, we mustn't. I beg you, don't tempt me. I fear I might be your sister. We committed a terrible sin when we … when we made love.' she added in a whisper.

'And what has made you draw this conclusion?' he asked, surprised.

'Lord Heston.' Cora shuddered visibly. 'I showed him my mother's ring as proof of my identity because I needed his help to free Ned. He told me it was likely given to her by your father – Geoffrey. His initial was on the ring.'

Jack shook his head. 'He was wrong. Please let me explain, Cora. You're not my sister.'

'How can you know? If the earl is my father, how can we not be siblings?'

'He's not. Your father was the captain, as I always suspected.'

Cora stared at him, incredulous. 'But why would Lord Heston claim this?'

'Who knows? I've never liked the man and wouldn't put it past him to try and cause mischief. Or perhaps he truly believes it to be the case. Either way, he is wrong.' Jack held out his hand, and slowly, tentatively, she took it. 'Come, let's sit,' he said and pulled her towards a large tree stump.

When he was certain Cora wasn't about to leap up and disappear, Jack began his tale.

When he had finished, Cora stared at him dubiously. 'But how can we be together if Lord Heston knows I'm his first wife's child?' she said.

Jack shrugged. 'It's unfortunate, but I don't believe he'll divulge our secret. He gains nothing by revealing he was cuckolded, or by attempting to discredit our family, especially as he's hoping for his son to marry Alethea.'

'But think of the gossip, if he does. The damage to your reputation, and your family's. Society will shun you.'

'Society is fickle. There would be gossip, yes, but it'd die down as soon as another scandal broke.'

Cora sighed. 'But you must be aware that – regardless of my blood – I was reared differently to you. I'll always be seen as a labourer's daughter.'

'I know, and we'll announce it proudly while we hold our heads up high.' Jack brought her hands to his lips and kissed each palm in turn.

Desire shot through Cora, and she felt her objections melting away. 'And he was a highwayman too, in the past,' she said fiercely, in a final attempt to get Jack to see sense. 'If that comes out …'

'Then that is whom I shall marry: the highwayman's daughter.'

Sighing again, Cora leaned into him and put her head on his shoulder. 'It won't be easy. There'll be those who think they can take liberties with me because of my background.'

'Then they'll taste steel.'

She looked up and met his eyes, which glinted dangerously. Smiling, she said, 'You can't duel with every man who insults me.'

'I've no intention of doing so. I should imagine my reputation with a rapier precedes me and I'd only have to duel one or two.'

'And their wives?'

'What do you care for women's gossip? You're not a timorous schoolgirl.'

'Our children might,' she whispered.

'Our children will have everything they could ever dream of,' said Jack forcefully.

'They'll be rich, to be sure.'

Holding her closer, Jack smoothed back a lock of her hair. 'That's not what I meant. They'll have parents who're devoted to them, and to each other. It'll make them strong.'

Shaking her head, Cora withdrew from his embrace. 'It'll never work. I'm a murderess.'

'Devil take it, woman!' Jack laughed. 'I love you and wish to spend the rest of my life with you. I'll protect you as you protected me. You saved my life, and my cousin's. Rupert had lost his mind and would have … well, let's not talk about that now. Tell me how you found us.'

'But, Jack —'

'Just tell me,' he insisted.

Cora pulled his fob watch out of her pocket and handed it to him. 'I came to give you this.'

'Is that all?' His hand closed over the watch, still in Cora's hand. Cora met his eyes and saw that it wasn't true. 'I recollect you stole something else from me that night,' he continued.

'Yes, your hair.' Cora swallowed hard.

'Oh I wasn't referring to my queue: I was referring to my heart.' He caressed her hand with his thumb. 'The moment I saw you I was lost. Only I didn't know it then. Say you will marry me? Whatever troubles we face, it can be nothing compared to a life without you.'

She met his eyes. Jack was right; they could brave whatever transpired, and they would do it together. His scent and the protection of his strong arms were so familiar that when she leaned back into his embrace it was as if she had finally come home. 'Your heart?' she teased. 'Do I get to keep it?'

'Of course.' Holding her close, he kissed the top of her head. 'But you're obliged to take care of it and not sell it to some middleman.'

The clearing echoed with his laughter as Cora thumped him on the shoulder.

Epilogue

Edward John Blythe was born exactly seven months after the marriage between Miss Cora Mardell and Viscount Halliford, causing a flurry of gossip.

As she held her baby in her arms for the first time, however, Cora's happiness was complete and she knew words couldn't hurt her. There would always be wagging tongues wherever she went: she was a labourer, and her father had stood accused of highway robbery – although the magistrate never found any evidence to support Ned's confession. All she could do was hold her head high, but the sense of completeness and belonging with Jack helped her weather the gossip. As Jack had said, the busybodies would eventually tire of the game.

Little Ned had his mother's wild, black curls, his father's eyes, and his cousin Alethea's temperament. No one could be in any doubt about his lineage.

'He's so small,' said Jack, who had come to sit on the bed as soon as the midwife would allow it. 'Will he live?'

Cradling Ned with one arm, Cora reached up and stroked her husband's worried face. It was never far from their minds that they had both lost siblings still in their infancy.

'That's not up to us, but we'll protect him as best we can,' she said. 'Besides, look how heartily he suckles. I think he's a fighter, this one.'

He met her eyes, and she saw humour behind the concern. 'I suppose with you as his mother that was inevitable. I believe you can do anything, Cora. Let's hope our son is the same.'

'So can you, Jack, and I for one, hope he takes after you.'

When she was sufficiently recovered from the birth, Jack took her for a walk in the vast gardens of the estate. With Little

Ned held safely drowsing against his shoulder, he held his arm around Cora as if he never intended to let go.

It was a fine spring evening, with a sky the colour of apricot and a light breeze. The majestic oak trees rustled their leaves as if greeting the young family. Sighing into her husband's embrace, Cora thought it impossible to be any happier than she was at this very moment.

When Jack steered her in the direction of the family mausoleum, she sent him a questioning glance. 'A strange place to take your wife for an evening stroll, don't you think?'

Then she understood why. Among the ancient earls and countesses, a new plaque had been erected. Kneeling down with a lump in her throat, Cora ran her fingers over the carved relief of a masked man on horseback; then traced the names of the three people who had meant the world to her once: Ned Mardell, Sarah Duval Mardell, and her baby brother, Tom.

'I've been meaning to do this for a while,' Jack said, 'and Father and Mother agreed, but I wanted it to be a surprise. The highwayman was my idea. I hope I did right.'

Eyes brimming with happy tears, Cora rose and hugged her husband and son close. Little Ned snuffled in his sleep but didn't wake.

'I thought you'd want to keep quiet about my lowly connections,' she said.

Jack shook his head. 'I owe your father a debt of gratitude. If he hadn't taken you in and brought you up as his own, I would never have met you. I love you, my heart. Whatever you are, I'll never be ashamed of it. I look forward to the rest of our lives together.'

'And I love you,' she whispered against his chest.

About the Author

Henriette lives in London but grew up in Northern Denmark and moved to England after she graduated from the University of Copenhagen. She wrote her first book when she was ten, a tale of two orphan sisters running away to Egypt fortunately to be adopted by a perfect family they meet on the Orient Express.

Between that first literary exploit and now, she has worked in the Danish civil service, for a travel agent, a consultancy company, in banking, hospital administration, and for a county court before setting herself up as a freelance translator and linguist.

Expecting her first child and feeling bored, she picked up the pen again, and when a writer friend encouraged her to join the Romantic Novelists' Association, she began to pursue her writing in earnest. Her debut *Up Close* won the New Talent Award in 2011 from the Festival of Romance and a Commended from the Yeovil Literary Prize. Her second novel, *The Elephant Girl*, was published in 2013 and her e-novella, *Blueprint for Love*, was also published that year. *The Highwayman's Daughter* is Henriette's third novel with Choc Lit.

www.twitter.com/henrigyland
www.henriettegyland.wordpress.com

More Choc Lit

From Henriette Gyland

Up Close

Too close for comfort ...

When Dr Lia Thompson's grandmother dies unexpectedly, Lia is horrified to have to leave her life in America and return to a cold and creaky house in Norfolk. But as events unfold, she can't help feeling that there is more to her grandmother's death than meets the eye.

Aidan Morrell is surprised to see Lia, his teenage crush, back in town. But Aidan's accident when serving in the navy has scarred him in more ways than one, and he has other secrets which must stay hidden at all costs, even from Lia.

As Lia comes closer to uncovering the truth, she is forced to question everything she thought she knew. In a world of increasing danger, is Aidan someone she can trust?

Visit www.choc-lit.com for more details including the first two chapters and reviews, or simply scan barcode using your mobile phone QR reader.

The Elephant Girl

Peek-a-boo I see you …

When five-year-old Helen Stephens witnesses her mother's murder, her whole world comes crumbling down. Rejected by her extended family, Helen is handed over to child services and learns to trust no-one but herself. Twenty years later, her mother's killer is let out of jail, and Helen swears vengeance.

Jason Moody runs a halfway house, desperate to distance himself from his father's gangster dealings. But when Helen shows up on his doorstep, he decides to dig into her past, and risks upsetting some very dangerous people.

As Helen begins to question what really happened to her mother, Jason is determined to protect her. But Helen is getting too close to someone who'll stop at nothing to keep the truth hidden …

Visit www.choc-lit.com for more details including the first two chapters and reviews, or simply scan barcode using your mobile phone QR reader.

More from Choc Lit

If you enjoyed Henriette's story, you'll enjoy
the rest of our selection. Here's a sample:

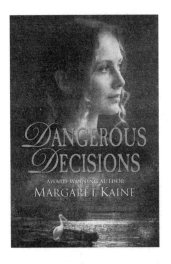

Dangerous Decisions
Margaret Kaine

**Have you ever ignored
a sense of unease?**

Helena Standish knows that a
good marriage would enhance
her father's social status but
she's wise enough not to
accept any handsome fool.
The wealthy and enigmatic
Oliver Faraday is considered
an ideal match, so why does
Helena have faint misgivings?

Nicholas Carstairs has little patience with frivolous pleasure-
seekers or an upper class that closes ranks against outsiders.
Why then is he entranced by the lovely 'girl in the window' –
a debutante who would appear to be both of those things?

A champagne celebration at Broadway Manor marks the
start of a happy future for Helena, but no one can predict
the perilous consequences of her decision or the appalling
danger it will bring.

Can George help Susie to overcome the sense of desolation she
feels as the result of her past-life regression or will history's habit
of repeating itself ruin all chances of her finding happiness?

Visit www.choc-lit.com for more details
including the first two chapters and
reviews, or simply scan barcode using
your mobile phone QR reader.

Highland Storms
Christina Courtenay

 Winner of the 2012 Best Historical Romantic Novel of the year

Who can you trust?

Betrayed by his brother and his childhood love, Brice Kinross needs a fresh start. So he welcomes the opportunity to leave Sweden for the Scottish Highlands to take over the family estate.

But there's trouble afoot at Rosyth in 1754 and Brice finds himself unwelcome. The estate's in ruin and money is disappearing. He discovers an ally in Marsaili Buchanan, the beautiful redheaded housekeeper, but can he trust her?

Marsaili is determined to build a good life. She works hard at being a housekeeper and harder still at avoiding men who want to take advantage of her. But she's irresistibly drawn to the new clan chief, even though he's made it plain he doesn't want to be shackled to anyone.

And the young laird has more than romance on his mind. His investigations are stirring up an enemy. Someone who will stop at nothing to get what he wants – including Marsaili – even if that means destroying Brice's life forever …

Sequel to Trade Winds.

Visit www.choc-lit.com for more details including the first two chapters and reviews, or simply scan barcode using your mobile phone QR reader.

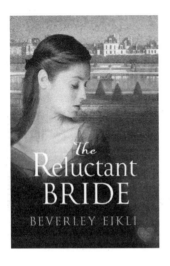

The Reluctant Bride
Beverley Eikli

Can honour and action banish the shadows of old sins?

Emily Micklen has no option after the death of her loving fiancé, Jack, but to marry the scarred, taciturn, soldier who represents her only escape from destitution.

Major Angus McCartney is tormented by the reproachful slate-grey eyes of two strikingly similar women: Jessamine, his dead mistress, and Emily, the unobtainable beauty who is now his reluctant bride.

Emily's loyalty to Jack's memory is matched only by Angus's determination to atone for the past and win his wife with honour and action. As Napoleon cuts a swathe across Europe, Angus is sent to France on a mission of national security, forcing Emily to confront both her allegiance to Jack and her traitorous half-French family.

Angus and Emily may find love, but will the secrets they uncover divide them forever?

Visit www.choc-lit.com for more details including the first two chapters and reviews, or simply scan barcode using your mobile phone QR reader.

CLAIM YOUR FREE EBOOK

of

The Highwayman's Daughter

You may wish to have a choice of how you read *The Highwayman's Daughter*. Perhaps you'd like a digital version for when you're out and about, so that you can read it on your ereader, iPad or even a Smartphone. For a limited period, we're including a **FREE** ebook version along with this paperback.

To claim, simply visit ebooks.choc-lit.com
or scan the QR Code.

You'll need to enter the following code:

Q201402

Introducing Choc Lit

We're an independent publisher creating
a delicious selection of fiction.
Where heroes are like chocolate – irresistible!
Quality stories with a romance at the heart.

Choc Lit novels are selected by genuine readers like yourself.
We only publish stories our Choc Lit Tasting Panel want to
see in print. Our reviews and awards speak for themselves.

We'd love to hear how you enjoyed *The Highwayman's
Daughter*. Just visit www.choc-lit.com and give your
feedback. Describe Jack in terms of chocolate
and you could win a Choc Lit novel in our
Flavour of the Month competition.

Available in paperback and as ebooks from most stores.

Visit: www.choc-lit.com for more details.

Keep in touch:
Sign up for our monthly newsletter Choc Lit Spread for
all the latest news and offers: www.spread.choc-lit.com.
Follow us on Twitter: @ChocLituk and Facebook: Choc Lit.

Or simply scan barcode using your mobile phone QR reader:

Choc Lit   *Twitter*   *Facebook*
Spread